She was beautiful; so white, so golden. Her eyes—golden. They were pure luminosity.

The Vardian trembled with his need. He took the edge of her dress in his fingers, and pulled the garment from her. She stood before him naked. Her exquisite high breasts were capped with gilt. In her navel a drop of yellow resin spat.

"Don't be afraid of me," he muttered.

"It is you who fear."

The words had been inside his skull. The mind speech was unlike any other. He shuddered. Her eyes seemed to eclipse the world.

Then he fell to his knees. On his knees, only then, he knew.

Cast from her light, a shadow rose behind the girl on the hot red wall. It was the shadow of a being much taller than the girl, though also long-haired and high-breasted, its many arms outstretched, and swaying upright upon the coiled tail that formed its lower body.

"Ashkar," said the Vardian. He bowed his head as wave after wave of ecstatic and wondrous terror burst through him, until eventually he fainted.

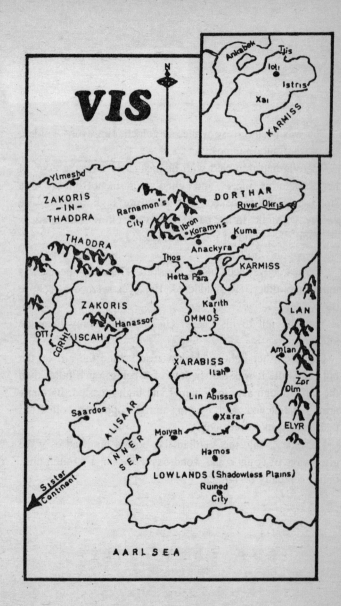

ANACKIRE

Tanith Lee

DAW BOOKS, INC.
DONALD A. WOLLHEIM, PUBLISHER

1633 Broadway, New York, NY 10019

FIRST PRINTING, OCTOBER 1983

1 2 3 4 5 6 7 8 9

DAW TRADEMARK REGISTERED
U.S. PAT. OPF. MARCA
REGISTRADA, HECHO EN U.S.A.

PRINTED IN U.S.A.

DEDICATION

To Oliver Cotton

FOREWORD

From the beginning, as the beginning was remembered, the dark races had mastered the major continent of the planet and given it their name: Vis.

North, west and east, the Vis lands ran, ruled by men with copper skins and black skins, lands cruel and often glamorous, and a people glamorous and often cruel, possessed of many and various gods. A people who responded to the curious erotic stimulus of the red star, Zastis, which appeared for several months of each year in their night-time skies. A people proudly at peace after a long history of war, and mythologically united under an ultimate titular king—the Storm Lord, ruler of Dorthar and the dragon city of Koramvis, whose very name (Heart of Vis) demonstrated its eminence. Koramvis indeed, of all the spectacular cities of Vis, was reckoned generally the most powerful, and the most beautiful. High-towered white wonderful Koramvis, the heart-brain of Dorthar, beneath a dragon-comb of mountains. In less than half an hour Koramvis fell and was shaken to pieces, left thereafter in wreckage, like a broken glass.

Ultimately south of the continent there spread a region of land, mostly infertile, Plains called Shadowless for their overall sparsity of vegetation, which ended in a brief maze of jungle against the World's Edge. There the water opened that was called the Sea of Aarl—the sea of hell. Between the World's Edge and the kingdoms of the Vis, in the barren flat country of these Plains, lay the places of the Lowlanders. Once, the Lowlanders had had some greatness. There was evidence of that at least in one dark, ancient ruined city, far to the south. But the Lowlanders had come to be very little in the regard of the Vis. A white-skinned blond race, and yellow-eyed, they were xenophobically disliked, occasionally feared for their rumored telepathy, despised always for their lack of temporal strength. They had no kings, no leaders. They lived in scattered villages, or in the sprawling ruin. They were immune to the Red Star, sexually reticent, passive, inimical, alien. Monotheistic, they worshipped only one deity, the snake goddess Anackire, eight-armed and serpent-tailed—nor did they worship her in any recognizable Vis manner, offering her no sacrifices of blood, not even the burning of incense. Their proverb explained: "Anackire asks nothing because She needs nothing, being everything." To such values the Vis paid no heed. Gods are like their people. The gods of Vis were demanding.

For several centuries the contemptuous antipathy of the Vis for the Lowlands had obtained, at a level, neither lessening nor growing worse. Then there came to be a Storm Lord, Amrek son of Rehdon, who supposed himself under the special bane of Anackire the goddess of the Plains, for from his birth, his left hand was scaled to the wrist—a serpent curse. This High King took it on himself to gouge the last trace of the pale people from his world.*

By then, however, there had come to be at last a king among the Lowlanders. He too was the son of the former Storm Lord, Rehdon of Dorthar. For his mother he had had a priestess of a Lowland temple, Ashne'e, a woman whose face resembled the face of Anackire. This man, Raldnor, whose destiny had at one time led him even to live disguised among the Vis themselves, a commander of Amrek's own armies, flying Amrek's emnity, had taken ship for Zakoris. And so placed himself in the hand of a fate which thrust the vessel from her course, through storm and fire, into the unknown surrounding ocean reckoned to be the sea of hell. And here he had found the second, lesser continent of the planet, the lands of a race physically kindred to the Lowlands, but temperamentally dissimilar—passionate and warlike. They were soon eager to follow the magnetic Raldnor to the rescue of his people, for justice and, let it be said, for spoil.

So war engulfed Vis after the long peace. Raldnor, as it seemed, touched by Anackire Herself, woke the Plains from their apathy. While his army marched toward Dorthar, the ships of the Sister Continent fell upon the adjacent lands. Swords rang, catapults discharged fire. Zakoris and Alisaar were besieged, starved, burned. Karmiss was taken, and Ommos, ringed by enemies, gave in. Lands friendly to the Lowlands were spared— Xarabiss, Lan and Elyr. They were infiltrated only in the way of the alliance, occupied only in the way of commerce, but that thoroughly. Wild barbarous Thaddra beyond her mountains missed the war entirely, save for an influx of refugees, and a later military strike from defeated Zakoris.

* See the novel, *The Storm Lord*.

The last battle of the Lowland War was fought on the plain beneath the hills of Koramvis. The Lowland army, betrayed and cut off finally from the aid of the men of the Sister Continent, outnumbered by the legions of Dorthar, seemed set for destruction. But Raldnor had unleashed in his kind the terrifying mental powers known in their legend as the Sleeping Serpent. By will alone, or so the stories ever after claimed, the Lowlanders caused the colossal earthquake which shook down and destroyed Koramvis the Beautiful, before the horrified eyes of her soldiers and lords. While from the mountains' feet above the toppling city, Anackire Herself rose like a golden moon in the black sky.

Koramvis fell, and the might of Dorthar fell, and the mastership of Vis was altered.

Having won the last battle then, Raldnor, son of a Storm Lord and a priestess, chosen Elect of the goddess, went away. A woman he had loved, and believed dead, had cried out to him with her mind—or rather with the mind-spark of their unborn child, still living in physical stasis in her womb. He abandoned kingship, power, his people and his god, and went to find them, his lover and his child, and the world lost him. Nor was he ever seen again—save in legend, or vision. He became one of that small host of heroes, like the Vis King of old, Rarnamon, who would appear like a bright ghost in the center of conflict, rallying warriors to victory. He remained, too, in the many who were called for him, the myriad "Raldnors" born at that season, and for seasons after.

Twenty Vis years passed, marred by a minor skirmish here or there, mostly years of surface quietude.

On the plain below the wreck of Koramvis, the new city had been built, shining white as Koramvis, perhaps more lovely even than Koramvis, though Koramvis now, of course, having become a myth, was nonpareil. Anackyra, the city's name. It boasted ten temples to Anackire, chief god of the Vis pantheon. They had made her their own. White bulls died on Her altars. The sexual temple lore of the Lowlands had been augmented and moulded to Vis forms. The Daughters of Anackire would lie with any man whose financial gift was offered to the goddess; such acts were holy.

In Anackyra too, the young King had been crowned, and the old titles retained. For the first occasion in known history, Dorthar's sanctified Storm Lord was pale-haired—hair white as salt. Raldanash, Raldnor's son by his marriage to the white-haired Sulvian of Vathcri, kingdom of the Sister Continent. Yet, blond heads beneath the diadems of the Vis were common now.

In Karmiss, the golden hair under the helm-crown was that of a Shansarian reaver-prince. He had taken a Karmian name with the Karmian crown, that of one of the island-kingdom's long-ago valorous lords—Suthamun. It was Ashara-Ashkar, the Shansarian (or Vardian) Anackire they worshipped currently, in the capital of Istris.

But between the coasts of Dorthar and Karmiss the small anchored boat of land known formerly as Obek, was now Ankabek. Ironically, it had become the site of the most orthodox Anackism in Visian Vis. The tiny island was dedicated solely to Her temple, a building of black stone, as in the Lowlands. While all about stood groves of the warped little red trees of the Shadowless Plains, which now grew to great heights and lushness in the rich soil of the north.

BOOK ONE—*The Salamander*

ONE

Dawn came to Istris over a silver sea. The slim-towered capital, which was also the mistress-port of Karmiss, released a shower of birds on the sky, a shoal of slender fishing skimmers on the water. The dawn bell rang from a cupola high on the Ashara Temple—a custom of Shansar-over-the-ocean.

Kesarh Am Xai, standing at his casement, looked into the sunrise and cursed it.

Hearing him speak, the girl still lying in the great bed murmured, "My lord?"

Kesarh did not glance at her.

"Get up. Get out."

He stood where he was, naked, his back to her as she obeyed him.

The mixture of his blood showed clearly, the tawny lightness of his skin, the black hair, dark eyes. His looks were arresting, the young face vivid with intelligence and power. Tall, sparely and strongly built, his body also was possessed of a natural and powerful physical grace, elegant even unclothed. In the flesh, his lineage had served him well. In all other ways it had failed him. He was, among the minor princes of Karmiss, one of the least. A stray Shansarian had got him, the more forward of twins, on a lesser princess of the old Karmian royal house, in the frenetic year following the Lowland War. The other twin was a girl. They were not alike, Kesarh and his sister, though they had shared the womb in closest company. Val Nardia was an exquisite white-skinned doll, with light eyes almost the shade of honey. And her hair, as sometimes happened with mixed blood, was the same fabulous scarlet the rising sun now dashed on the bay of Istris.

So, he cursed the dawn, and his sister.

The slut he had taken to bed the previous night was gone.

11

Kesarh turned and began to dress himself, drinking the last cupful of wine from the jug as he did so.

Going outside, he paused, looking at the guard on duty there. Since adolescence Kesarh had thought it wise to have his apartments guarded. This man, however, was leaning on the wall, asleep—even despite the fluttering past of the girl. Kesarh drew his dagger. Catching him suddenly about the throat, the Prince pressed the honed blade into the sentry's skin. Blood welled and the man came to himself with a startled oath.

"So the assassin would have caught you, and thereafter caught myself."

"My lord—I'd have woken—"

"Yes. Like this. But the blade through your windpipe."

Kesarh let him go, and watched the fellow straighten in his unblazoned mail, a hand to his bleeding neck.

"You can choose, soldier," Kesarh said. "Seek my sergeant and ask him for ten lashes. When you have recovered from them, return to my service. Or else surrender your issue-weapons and the clothes I put on your back and lose yourself in the alleys, or whatever other hole you were dug up from."

"Yes, my lord."

The soldier, mouth twisted, bowed. He was Karmian, dark hair and copper skin. There was a lightness to his eyes, but that might be only a Vis heritage. He would choose the lashes, probably.

Kesarh walked on along the corridor, his black mood enhanced yet ornamented by the soldier's respectful hate striking between his shoulderblades.

His sister's modest apartments were already busy and vocal. In the antechamber the chests stood piled and ready. The female fussings irritated him and he walked straight through the scurrying and swirling of skirts, the stares of big painted eyes, into her bedchamber.

Val Nardis was standing, as he had stood, before a long window, but facing into the room. The moment she saw him, she froze all over her stillness. He too had stopped dead. From childhood he had been used to seeing her in such silks and velvets as their station allowed, her hair plaited with jewelry, and at her throat invariably their dead mother's golden torc with its three black Karmian pearls. Now she was dressed for the coming heat of the day in a gown of unbleached linen. Her skin was without cosmetics or gems, and her hair hung loose about her, one long combed flame.

Something checked him, he was not sure what it was.

He indicated, not looking at them, the two women who were in the bedchamber.

"Send them away."

Val Nardia drew in one deep breath. But she did not have to say anything to the women, they were already in retreat. The door curtain rustled and the door was closed. Beyond, the antechamber had turned very quiet.

"Have you come to bid me farewell?" Val Nardia said. Her eyes had fallen and she was pale, a pallor easily discernible through such fair skin. She looked even younger than her youth.

"If you like. Farewell, dearest sister."

"Don't," she said. She swallowed; he saw the movement of her throat. "Don't upbraid me, Kesarh. This should be a happy day for me, and you should be happy for me."

"Happy to see you go, to waste your life. Be happy then, you witless mare."

The lash of anger seemed to release them both. She looked up at him in fear as he came toward her. He stood less than a foot from her, and reached out and grasped her suddenly by the arms. Her eyes filled at once with moisture, perhaps not tears. She looked at him, shaking her head.

"All this for Ashara-Anackire. All this to be buried in Ankabek."

"I shall be a priestess of the goddess," she cried out. "Is there something better for me here?"

"*I* am here."

"You—" she whispered. Tears or not, the drops ran out of her eyes.

"And it's because of me that you're leaving the court."

"No, Kesarh."

"Yes, Kesarh. You're afraid to the roots of your spirit of me, and of yourself when with me. Aren't you, my little sister?"

They regarded each other. "Let me go," she said eventually.

"Why? In Lan it's thought quite proper."

"Kesarh—"

"Father and daughter, brother and sister. To lie together, to wed, even." He grinned at her. She watched him it seemed in a horrible fascination. "Let's fly to Lan and be married, and live in the hills and spill a horde of brats."

She struggled between his hands, then ceased to struggle. She lowered now not merely her eyes but her head.

"It isn't that you want me," she said, "but only that you must have me. Everything you desire you must possess."

"I've little enough. A title that means nothing. A cupboard euphemistically called a room in the lower palace. A strip of land at Xai that yields nothing but rotten gourds and diseases. But if you'd stay, I might wrest something from the rubbish. For both of us."

"I only want peace."

"Which is to be had away from me?"

She looked up again and into his eyes.

"Yes."

"And in a few nights, Zastis will be burning in the sky. What then? You're not white enough or yellow enough, my half-breed sister, to ignore the Red Moon."

"There are disciplines practiced in Ankabek, learned from Lowland temple lore—"

"And none of them so effective as a man against you in the sheets. You've had Zastis lovers, Val Nardia, if never the one you truly wanted."

She wrenched away from him at last, and he laughed softly, his face now full of contemptuous dislike.

"No," she said, "you've never been able to commit that wrong, at least."

"But you think finally I shall force you? Is that why you're running away?"

"Yes, then, if you must have it. Running from you. Oh, not simply your lusts, your demands. From everything you are. Your corrupt dreams, your plans, your clever brain fermenting into a sewer—"

He caught her by the hair this time and pulled her sharply against him. Her slanders were cut short as he brought his mouth down on hers.

At first she grit her teeth to keep him out, but he had also cut off her breath. Soon her lips parted to gain air. The tingle of Zastis was already apparent to those susceptible. He felt her trembling tension alter, and suddenly her hands were locked across his back. For a lengthy swiftness of moments he swam strongly in the fragrant coolness of her mouth, in the pleasure of her own strength answering his, the narrow hands fierce on him. Then her struggles abruptly began again. She pushed at him, clawed at him, and he stepped away, drunk on her and dazzled.

To his bemused, amused, furious surprise she had snatched up a little fruit knife from a table.

"Get out," she said. Her voice was no more than a cough, but the tiny blade glinted.

Kesarh turned. He retraced his steps to the door, paused, and glanced back at her. At once she raised the knife, poising it to be thrown.

"Farewell, *gentle* sister," he said. "Remember me in the hot crimson nights, alone on your religious mattress."

Only when the door had closed on him did Val Nardia carefully replace the knife beside the fruit. It required care, since she could see nothing now for her tears.

In the stony under-palace, Kesarh's guard sergeant surveyed a covered court, and the long post at its center, thumbs hooked in his belt.

"Yes, that's his way, our Lord Kesarh. To send you on your own authority. You're not the first by any means, soldier. Nor won't be the last. Too much beer, was it? Or too much of the other thing?"

The Karmian guardsman—he had given his name a year ago as Rem—said nothing. The sergeant did not expect him to. With ten lashes in the offing from the prescribed whip, known among the men as Biter, few saw anything to joke or intellectualize over.

Kesarh had ten private guard, the permitted number for a prince of his lowly lights, a by-blow, with the royalty and the elite yellow-man's blood in different parents. The bastards of the conqueror Shansar king and his brothers did much better. Kesarh's ten men, however, mysteriously and schizophrenically fluctuated. Number Seven, for example, could be stocky and scarred one day, stocky and smooth the next, tall and smooth the next. Secretly listed under every single number there were now ten soldiers, which added up to a hundred, ninety of them unofficially in Kesarh's private army. The practice was not uncommon, but Kesarh was more subtle, and more accumulative, than most. He also had a distinct and conceivably unfair advantage. Charisma was either natural to or absent in a leader. The Prince Am Xai had a goodly share, a peculiar dark and pitiless human magic that kept his men enthralled even though they frequently had some grievance against him, for his brand of justice was often bizarre, and occasionally actually unjust.

And this one, now, was going to get Kesarh's malevolent unjust justice all nicely cut into his back.

"And who do we send you to to be looked after," the sergeant said conversationally, "when we take you down?"

The sick and the punished did not lie up here. The whole force, save those ten on duty, were billeted about the city.

Sometimes they deserted, but there were always more to be found. This one, this Rem, had been a thief, had he not?

"There isn't anyone," said the soldier flatly.

"What, no friendly doxy you keep in a burrow somewhere?"

"Not just now."

"Kin?"

The soldier glanced at him.

"I don't ask idly," said the sergeant. "If there is someone, you'll need them."

The soldier who called himself Rem looked out at the whipping-post, the iron cuffs hanging ready from it.

"Yes."

"Well, then?"

"A woman," Rem said. "The red house on Slope Street, near the harbor." He smiled in an unsmiling way. "She may refuse. She's the mistress of a dealer in rope and cord. He's out of the city at the moment."

"As well for you. All right, soldier. Strip to your drawers, you know the formula. It'll come fast and hard, you'll feel it less that way. And no worse after. Call me any names you like while I'm doing it. I was a whip-master in Zakoris twenty years ago, and good enough then."

They walked out together to the post and Rem put up his hands into the cuffs, letting them snap closed. The two guards, the picked witnesses, grunted their commiserations. The sergeant gave him a drink of raw spirit that tasted itself like the edge of a lash.

Then the whip named Biter came down on his back.

Rem, as they suspected, was not his name. But the name she had pinned on him, his crazy mother, he would hardly use that. Even the abbreviated form it had come to have was too suggestive to a keen ear. Growing up in the middle environs of the city, and now and then its slums, through the white dusts of the hot months, the gray snows of the cold, every tenth or eleventh male child around him named for Raldnor of Sar, the Lowland hero, Rem's name had brought nothing but trouble. His childhood had been spent fighting, and when he went home, he was battered and beaten there, too. His mother's protectors did not care for him. His mother did not like him either.

Latterly, he had come to think some of those blows rained on his immature head responsible for what had now happened five times in the past five years. What had been happening, in fact, when Kesarh Am Xai had walked out of his apartments and found him.

Coming back to himself with the prince's dagger eating at his throat, it had been wiser to pretend. The prince had obviously assumed Rem was dozing on duty, the slumber of a fool. To be a palace soldier to one of Kesarh's unspoken ambition and arrogant strengths might lead somewhere. Rem sensed about Kesarh some special vitality, some gift for earthly power. The work beside brought regular money, and privileges. Rem did not want to sink back into his former trade of robbery with violence. The job of a soldier was similar enough, but it was lawful. The best fee for what you did the best—that was a logical goal.

If Kesarh knew what had happened to Rem by his door, there would have been no choice. It would have been dismissal. The streets again, the old ways, going nowhere.

Rem had glimpsed the girl come out of the room, shivering, one round shoulder uncovered through a tangle of dark hair. Then the pain shot through Rem's skull like a lance. He knew what was coming, but there was nothing he could do. The girl did not notice. The palace corridor misted and went out and the picture flashed in behind his eyes like a flame. What he saw was absolutely clear, as these visions were always clear. A woman stood there, in his mind. He could not make out her garments but he caught the glimmer of violet jewels. Her hair was red, that blood-red color once rare, now less so, from the mixing of the blond and dark races. But not only did he see all this, he saw into her body, into her womb. A creature coiled there, in its silver bubble, sexless and sleeping. There was a shimmering about it, the pulse of an aura. He felt its inherent life, smelled it, like air before a storm. Such feelings, when he was his normal coherent self, he would have ridiculed. The mind-pictures that had come to him since late adolescence he would also mock and reject as soon as they were done. He would accuse himself neither of empathy nor prescience. The things he saw were like symbols and, so far as he had ever known, had had no relevance to his own existence. Otherwise, it was a kind of madness he had confessed to no one, and until today he had never been caught out.

That Kesarh himself should be the one to catch him was the worst of all bad luck.

But the lie had held. And Rem was used to beatings.

When they took him down he was conscious, and had not expected to be otherwise.

It somewhat surprised him, therefore, after he had been got

into the wagon—en route to the harbor and paid to make a detour through Slope Street—to fall into a whirling nothingness. He came out of it to find his companion, the man detailed to play nurse until they reached the house, and a leather wine bottle. Rem drank, and nearly brought the vinegar back. There seemed no pain in his body until he moved even slightly. Then it shifted in shreds off his bones.

"We're here, Rem. The house you said."

Rem agreed with a ghastly chuckle, and somehow he and the other soldier got him out.

The gates in the russet brickwork were shut, but hammering brought a porter. It was the same sullen old man Rem recalled from a year ago, the last time he had been here. The house itself looked much the same, a narrow dwelling with no windows facing the street. The vines were a little thicker on the walls.

The porter was difficult. Master was away. Mistress would have to be told. They persuaded him to go tell her. Rem began to laugh. The other soldier was bored and ill-tempered and the wagon gone.

"You can leave me here," Rem said, leaning on the gate.

"Yes. She's sure to take you in. Only a bitch'd turn away a man in your state."

"Then she may turn me away. For she's the bloodiest of all bitches."

The soldier shrugged. He went off to find a wineshop, his duty accomplished.

Rem hung on the gate. The heat of midday began to drum down on him and he was starting to faint again when the porter came back and let him in.

He walked across the court and into the house and into the room the old man had specified. The edges of his sight were vague, and so the shabby gaudy chamber made no impression. In the center of his eyes, however, the woman seemed brightly in focus, absurdly just like the bright clarity of the visions. The long youth of the Vis was starting to desert her, but it was her disappointment, her bitterness that had drawn her face into such hard dry lines. She had always been telling him of that bitterness and that disappointment, seldom any details, but a generalized medley of wrongs. How royalty had once loved her in Dorthar. How she had been ill-treated and used by the processes of intrigue, the foul treacheries of the court at Koramvis in the last days of its power. And how his father had deserted her. She had always hated Rem for his father's sake. She had informed Rem that, even in the cradle, she had known her son would fail to love her.

He felt rather sorry for her. Her dark hair was elaborately dressed by the maid she beat with a rod when the girl displeased her, some old style, of that lost Koramvin court no doubt. The pins were gold-plated, and from her ears swung heavy black pearls, the untrue kind caused by injecting ink with the cultured grit.

She looked at him, the lines deep-cut between her brows, her wizened mouth turned down.

"For more than a year I see nothing of you. Then you come here like this and in disgrace. Am I supposed to care for you? How should I? What will he say when he comes home?"

"Your friend the merchant will say nothing, if he's sensible. He will, besides, get some money from the coffers of the prince I serve."

"Yes, he might like that," she said spitefully.

"Or he can take one of his bits of cord and hang himself."

Through the shirt they had thrown on him he felt his own blood soaking, scalding. The chamber trembled, and before he could stop himself he fell to his knees and vomited on the floor at her feet.

She jumped away in revulsion, calling him a string of gutter names. At the end of them she employed his given name, with all the searing scorn she could summon.

He spat, and said, "Even kings are capable of vomiting, mother."

"*Rarmon!*" she screamed. "*Rarnammon—*" in a perfect seizure of malice.

He stood up and the pain filled him with despair. Business had fallen off, for the rope merchant, his mother's recent protector, and two of the three servants had been sent packing. The damp storeroom they had occupied would be empty and Rem could lie up there. Of Kesarh's bounty, they would feed him and perhaps make sure he stayed alive.

He waited therefore until her railing ran out, knowing it was useless to ask her for compassion. Only as a child had he once or twice uselessly done that, as Lyki slapped his head over and over back against some wall or other, or the day when she had caught him stealing from her and plunged his hands in boiling water.

She had been very pretty once, but how ugly she was now. He was close to vomiting again, but somehow controlled himself, knowing she would take it as one further insult, and all this would then go on much longer.

*   *   *

By mid-afternoon, the traveling-chariot was well advanced on the white road that led from Istris to Ioli, a journey of two days. Thereafter half a day's riding should see them at the brink of the narrow straits where floated the isle of Ankabek. The nights between the days would be spent at discreet inns warned beforehand. The road was excellent, and in the hot season there was not likely to be anything to delay the party, which was a small one, although their speed was not great. The fine bred racing chariot-animals usual on the Vis mainland were less common in Karmiss, while the horses of Shansar-over-the-ocean did badly during long voyages and were less common still. Therefore thoroughbred zeebas drew the vehicle, capable of galloping, but only in bursts.

The Princess sat reading among her cushions, or else she merely gazed over the chariot rail, into the sun-washed haze. The girl who accompanied her had begun a flirtation with one of the two outriders. With good fortune, the little entourage would get back to the capital before Zastis bloomed in the sky.

The gilded day flushed into fire and a lion-like dusk. They had reached the hilly country that tomorrow would pour down to Ioli, and so to the northern strip of sea. The towered inn appeared with the first stars showing over its roofs.

Val Nardia veiled herself before they entered the courtyard. Her mantle, the escort and maid, were sufficient to command respect, and to avoid excitement. A minor princess, she journeyed simply as a lady. The inn received her as such.

In the private room high in the second tower, she ate some of the meal they had brought her. The wine was yellow—a Lowland vintage. The vines of Karmiss, burned twenty years ago when the ships fell on her coasts, had not yet come back to their fullness. Beer had come to be the drink of this land, and a fierce white spirit crushed from berries.

Beyond the opened shutters, the night possessed the sky.

Val Nardia sent the girl away and was alone.

As she sat in the chair, her book spread before her, her mind vacant and afraid, she heard a wild sweet melody rise from the inn below. A song was being sung, and irresistibly she must listen, trying to follow the words. Only one or two were audible through the floors, out of the open windows beneath. But suddenly she heard a name: *Astaris*. It was a song of Raldnor, then, the vanished hero of mixed blood, and of the Karmian princess, his lover, red-haired Astaris, said to have been the most beautiful of all women in the world.

Involuntarily, Val Nardia found she had touched her own rich hair.

When the song ended, she went to bed, and lay on the pillows, her eyes wide.

Long after the inn was quiet, Val Nardia watched the night in her window, whispering now and then the ritualistic prayers she had learned. The prayers to Anackire, the Lady of Snakes, who alone stood between Val Nardia and her dreams of terror and lust. But at last she did sleep, and saw her brother standing on a high hill against the flat flawed mirror of the sea, and knew she had called to him and that he would come toward her and she would be lost. And so, in the dream, it was.

They had been hunting, a successful hunt. Coming back at nightfall through the streets in a rumbling of wheels and clack of hooves, the King was easy enough to single out, golden on the amber horse, and laughing. There were cheers, and women, appearing on their balconies, cast down flowers. Suthamun Am Shansar had liked to keep here the informal boisterous roughness of his former court among the marshes and rocks of his homeland. They said that in his youth, for years after he had appropriated the crown of Karmiss, he would go in disguise about her cities, now a beggar, now a potter, now a dealer in livestock, just as gods had been used to do, playing with humanity. Those who were good to him in his pretended role he would afterwards reward—caskets of jewels for accommodating ladies, a stallion horse for some struggling groom who had given the poor beggar a coin. And those who treated him ill in his acting he would summon later to the palace, and there turn their bowels to water with the truth. They would have deserved it, for any who had not recognized their king by his hair or skin should have known him from his heavy accent and difficulty with the Vis tongue.

But he had been mellower in the past decade, more concerned to be known for what he was, aristocrat and master. The old title of "Pirate-King," which had made him merry years back, could now cause him to scowl and shout. He had married only with his own kind, and his few Vis mistresses bleached their hair and painted pale their flesh.

Entering the palace, they took their noise in with them. Feet tramped and weapons clanked; there was the barking of dogs and hissing of hunting kalinxes, and over all the uproar of men intent on enjoying themselves. Suthamun liked noise of almost any type. In the long and glittering hall, minstrels came running and strings and drums struck up.

Suthaman, in the midst of a bellowed laugh, broke off. His blond brows drew together.

Into the hall had walked Kesarh Am Xai, one of his guard at his back, a pair of matched black kalinxes stalking on leash before him.

Kesarh, cursed by the Vis blackness of his hair, had arrogantly seemed to make a feature of that black. His guard, of whom everyone knew there were far more than ten, wore dark mail on ceremonial occasions. He himself, as today, was most often seen in black clothing, relieved only by the fine pectoral on his breast showing in gold and scarlet the fire-lizard Am Xai had taken as his personal blazon. Amrek, the damned tyrant and genocide of Dorthar, had worn black, as if to flaunt his preference for his own race. And Kesarh—even the kalinxes were black. Also, of course, splendid. Where had the cash come from to purchase or breed such beasts? The mother had had little to leave him and the Shansarian father had not bothered.

Suthamun studied the kalinxes, their cold blue eyes spitting malice, but the hand on the leash ruling them utterly. They had run with the rest, and taken the first kill, working together, and separately from the pack, a thing one rarely saw. Suthamun had instantly wanted them, but to demand anything from this lesser prince would be uncouth, ungenerous. Somehow, Kesarh would make him sweat.

The King was very aware of Kesarh, and did not like him. For one so lowly to attract so much attention was in itself an indictment.

Kesarh had reached the end of the hall where his lord was standing among his brothers and favorites. A little attentive quietness had come with the prince, and it was all at once possible to hear the tune the musicians were playing. Resarh looked full at the King, a leisurely, blank, immovable look, and then followed it with a short graceful bow.

The two kalinxes, stopped like stone on their plaited leash, laid flat their tufted ears. The vicious things had responded to the vicious mood of the king, and were now showing it off to everyone.

Suthamun laughed.

"The hunting was timely. Did you have pleasant sport, Kesarh?"

"Yes, my lord." Kesarh smiled. They both spoke the tongue of Suthamun's home, the current language of the Karmian court.

"Your cats there, they won you that."

"True, my lord. Dortharian kalinxes are often the best."

Suthamun stared at them greedily. By Ashara's Amber Nipples, why should this nothing own such animals?

"Dortharian, eh? They must have strained your purse."

Another smile.

"Somewhat, my lord. But they weren't bought as an indulgence of myself. I wished to try them today, to see if they merited their praises. Since they do, I'd rejoice if I might present them to your majesty, as a gift."

The crowd in the hall rustled, gave off a bird-flurry of little laughs, and then clapped.

It would have been ungenerous to demand. It would now be ungenerous to refuse.

Suthamun himself now smiled. He snapped his fingers and a groom ran to take the double leash from Kesarh. Trained to perfection, the cats made no demur, even their ears rose. They were led magnificently away. Suthamun steeled himself, went over to Kesarh and embraced him.

The court clapped again.

Vathcrian wine came, and Kesarh drank with the King and his brothers. Uhl leaned to Suthamun's ear. The King nodded.

"I hadn't forgotten. A day's sport, an evening's work. Gentlemen, follow me upstairs. You also, Am Xai. You can leave your guard here."

Up the stair, they passed into one of the council rooms. Lamps were already alight. On a wall, in exquisite mosaic, was a map of the world, including the outlines of the second continent. The place names of all the mighty areas had been put in with gold, Shansar most prominently. Mosaic fish frisked in the seas between, and marine volcanoes bled cinnabar.

Suthamun strode directly to the map, and stood gazing at it. When he turned back his face was self-consciously kingly and portentous. He glanced quickly about at them all, as if to be sure they would not mock him. But none of them was such a fool. Even the arrogant Kesarh maintained that polite blankness which would alternate in such company with his polite smile or his polite solicitous frown of attention.

"Your sister rode for Ankabek today," said the King.

"Yes, my lord."

"We were pleased to grant her desire to devote her life to Ashara, the one true goddess."

Kesarh bowed.

"Val Nardia was agleam with her gratitude, Sire."

Suthamun checked, but the young man's demeanor was faultless.

"And you," said Suthamun, "what shall we do with you?"

"My King knows I am his own to order to anything."

Suthamun flung one arm back toward the map.

"Zakoris," said the King. "We remember, do we not, how my brother of Vardath took black Zakoris, and how Zakoris collapsed? And then, how the defeated lords of Zakoris made inroads on Thaddra. And there they roost around the north sea edges of Thaddra, and from there they make reavers-war on Dorthar. My brother of Dorthar, the King Raldanash son of Raldnor, has sent to warn me how his northern coasts are harried by these pirates. The guardians of the northeastern towns of Karmiss have also sent me word that so-called 'Free Zakorian' raiders have been sighted, and smoke on the beaches of Dorthar."

Suthamun, Pirate-King, paid homage to his past neither with word nor gesture. Fifteen years ago, he himself might have found this funny.

"For the safety of Karmiss," he now said weightily, "and to demonstrate my concern for the Storm Lord's lands, I've been thinking to dispatch a force of men and ships to rout the pirates. I myself was in the sea battle at Karith when the Vis put light to the water and the waves rattled with the bones of yellow-haired men."

It seemed his brothers recalled this, too. Their faces were set. The few Vis councillors who were in the chamber lowered their eyes.

Only Kesarh in his black did not look away, and so the King's eyes met his at once.

"The captaincy of this force I mean to give into the hands of a man with youth and vigor on his side, a man not yet famous in Karmiss, but that through no failing on his part." If this was sarcasm, the King did not stress it. "A Prince of the old royal house, with the blood of the goddess' own people—Kesarh Am Xai, I offer this command to you. Do you take it?"

Kesarh showed nothing. He simply continued to meet the King's eyes.

"You honor me, Sire."

And the King shook his hand, while the haphazard council congratulated him heartily.

The stinging bees of Free Zakoris sailed in small swarms, but it was sure Suthamun would send an equally small portion of the Karmian fleet against them. It was, besides, a fleet soft from easy times, and mostly Visian, for mainly those Shansars who had wanted to remain under sail had gone home. Add to that unpreparedness and lack of size, indolent ship lords, then place in charge a prince without kudos and with no more experience of a sea-fight than the fire animal of his blazon, the salamander.

It could be phrased to look like an opportunity. It could also be an invitation to disgrace and death.

The long northern sunset was almost finished as the barge came from the pink water and ground on the stony beach of Ankabek. There had been a delay after all, a zeeba casting a shoe, some hours spent in shining loli. But the barge had waited, of course, and the crossing was only a matter of hours, the sea all calm, and the mysterious island growing before them from the shadows and the light, so it almost seemed enchanted, blessed. As it was, indeed, must be.

Val Nardia stared toward it with a curious yearning, touched by the beauty of the portents, and the last aching sunglow on its heights.

Above the landing, a village spread along the slope. Men came toward the beach with torches, and with them a woman walking like a ghost as the twilight closed the world.

The court escort was already back in the barge, only the girl stayed fidgeting with the Princess' belongings, suddenly bursting into tears and kissing Val Nardia's hand. Val Nardia spoke quietly to her, a reassurance, but her awareness was fixed on the woman walking among the torches. Then she was near, and the servant girl dropped to her knees.

The woman was a Lowlander. There was no mistaking it. Her hair beneath a smoky veil was lighter than a morning sky. Out of her ice-white face her eyes shone, the gold of the torch flames.

She looked at Val Nardia with these eyes, and seemed to pierce her through with them. The Princess did not resist the gaze. She opened herself, eyes, brain and soul, to it, and so felt no fear, only a great astonishment. Did the Lowland priestess read her mind? It was well. Let all the sin and sadness be known, and then there might come healing.

But the woman merely said, in a low, still voice, "We have expected you, lady."

The sentence had all the courtesy of one who, being the child of the goddess, could afford to be gracious.

"And I," said Val Nardia softly, "have longed to arrive."

The priestess glanced at the torchbearers who now took up Val Nardia's slight possessions. They walked back, past the village and up the slope.

The priestess went after them without another word, and Val Nardia followed her.

Behind them, the barge dwindled at the edge of the water.

Ahead the dark path darkened further among tall trees. Where the torchlight lit them, their leaves showed red: These were the sacred trees of the Lowland temple groves. Presently, too, the evening breeze began to wake a tinsel sound from among them where discs of thin whitish metal were hung from the boughs. It was an hour's walk.

The temple of Ashara who was Ashkar who was Anackire stood at the island's summit. Black stone on the black of night, its windows revealed no lamp, it had no ornament. Only in its size did it differ from the temples of the Plains. The upright slot of the door was very high. No one called to be let in, yet the black doors swung inwards. Beyond, a dull sheen of light was the only hint of the temple's life.

The men with torches placed their burdens neatly just within the doors, then turned and filed away. They were Vis, or mixed-blood, Karmian with Shansar and Vathcrian, but they had been trained, or had grown, to other ways. They seemed barely human.

The priestess stood within the doorway now.

"You enter here," she said, "the Sanctuary of the goddess. For all that seek Her, She waits. As, for those who do not seek Her, She is not."

A note seemed to chime in Val Nardia's heart; the music of the discs on the trees sounded all at once.

She went swiftly into the Sanctuary, and the doors, without apparent agency, swung shut behind her.

TWO

The ceremony was conducted on the wide raised terrace before the temple. The building had formerly housed the Karmian love goddess, Yasmais, but she had been cast down and chased away to the little shrines of the Pleasure City. Now the temple was Ashara's, the watery Anackire. Her smaller image had been brought out and she balanced on her golden fish tail, her eight white arms outspread like rays.

The magician-priest of the King slit the throat of a white bull-calf. In Shansar they had always offered Her blood before a battle.

Above, the sky was clear and innocent, but the Star had

already manifested there and at night blazed behind the moon. At this season, all things came to have a sexual underlay, even magic and religion, certainly the acts of war. And it was a bad time to fight, who did not know that? The fair men of the second continent claimed immunity from Zastis, but one noticed they did not seem quite indifferent and had grown less so, those that lived long in Vis. Only the pale people, the Lowlanders, the Amanackire, took no heat from the months of the Red Moon.

Rem shifted in his mail. Other men shifted, the crowd surged and whispered.

The priest cried out his prophecy of victory, and the Karmian cymbals clashed, and the crowd found release in a shout.

So much ceremonial, and so few ships. Three, to be exact. Three ships, undermanned, rowers on double-pay in their unwillingness, and half that in arrears until Kesarh himself had somehow found their wages. They were old ships, also, the cream of the Karmian fleet of thirty years ago, patched up and pretty and liable to take water. The captains were here, and would presently swagger to the harbor and embark. They would make sail around the coast toward the mouth of the straits. The Prince Am Xai and his twenty guard—he had admitted to keeping, shockingly, twice the number permitted him—would ride ahead and await this speck of fleet at Tjis, the town which had sent the latest report of Zakorian activity.

It was a farce, and this religious frill only made it worse.

Rem shifted again, and his new scars gave him a dry little pang, and he thought of Doriyos.

Rem, once called Rarmon, had been six days lying up after his lashing. The physician he had managed to bribe the merchant's man to fetch, had tended him thoroughly, and he had healed very well and very fast. But sprawled hours long on his belly in the damp heat of the cellar storeroom, listening to the throb of the sea against the wall, he had been filled with a vague hatred for all things. Lyki came to visit him once or twice. She had not been friendly, but she had had the man bring him soup and beer and bread. Thankfully, the beer and the physician's draughts sent him to sleep more and more often as the pain died down.

On the sixth day, Zastis was visible just before sunrise, a wicked blush. Rem had left the storeroom, used the functional bathing facilities of the merchant's house, and looked for his mother. She was still in bed. The merchant would be home tomorrow, perhaps. Rem left two silver Karmian ankars for Lyki, lying amid the cheap jewels by her mirror. She would know what that meant.

On the street by the very gate, Rem met one of his fellow soldiers.

"I was sent to fetch you. Our Prince has been selected to murder Free Zakorians at Tjis. I, and you, are picked to die with him."

They had laughed, and spat on the notion, and Rem had agreed to find himself at the palace by nightfall. It had given him an odd feeling, nevertheless, that Kesarh, having sent him to his whip-master, should next call him back to such specific service. Probably it meant nothing, Am Xai had simply stipulated a number, which in Rem's case was nine, and the other nine Nines were for some reason unsuitable or elsewhere.

To go toward the Pleasure City was inevitable in any case, it was not merely the warrior's death qualm pushing him toward the life-urge. By day, the area was less glamorous but, naturally, busy. A glorious tawdry glitter of sun and sequins shot from everywhere. Turning through a fancy little arch into the Ommos Quarter, he soon reached the House of Three Cries, deplored its name as ever, and knocked on the door.

The elderly Ommos, whom Rem always had the wish to throttle, let him in at once, having first peered round the door like a tortoise from its shell.

"Enter, enter, dear master. He is free. He has kept himself for you since the Star opened its eye, such is his love for you—"

Rem thrust a coin on the old villain and went up the endless twisting unclean stair. The contrast when, having knocked again, he opened the topmost door and stepped into the room, was very great. This airy chamber at the top of the house was clean and calm, and scented with the flowering shrubs Doriyos grew in two ceramic urns beneath the window. Doriyos himself was seated between them at work on mending one of the countless broken musical instruments he would collect, repair, play sweet-noted, and thereafter sell, or more often give away.

Seeing his guest, however, he grinned, put down the stringed oval and crossed the room. Reaching up, he kissed Rem lightly on the lips.

"I was told you keep yourself for me," said Rem good-humoredly, "yet you allow anyone into the room."

"I recognize your tread on the stair, hand upon the door."

Doriyos was beautiful, pure Karmian, a skin like honey and eyes like black onyx, and with a bronze-copper tinting to enhance the fine dark hair. He dressed simply and ornamented sparely. The gold chain around his neck had come from Rem, in the not-so-distant days when Rem was yet a thief. But the gold drop in his ear was another's gift.

Used to the healing pain, and in his physical eagerness, Rem forgot. Stripping, he heard the exclamation and wondered what had caused it.

"Your *back*. Who—"

"Oh. I fell foul of the Lord Kesarh. It's nothing, almost better."

"*Nothing?*"

"I should have thought, and warned you."

"You should have told me. Who tended you?"

"A physician."

"Whose?"

"I went to Lyki's house. Probably a mistake. But she so enjoys being disgusted with me."

"You should," said Doriyos, so softly Rem stared at him, "have come to me."

"You have. . . . You might have been busy."

Doriyos smiled. "What the old man downstairs says to you when you come here, when he tells you I love you, it isn't a lie. I would have looked after you, and no one else would have come in."

"No other client."

Doriyos shrugged. "I've been a whore since my eleventh birthday, I was sold to it. But I'm not a slave anymore. I do this because I know how to do it—"

"Yes, that's very true," said Rem, and so the conversation had been curtailed.

The Star made the first union partly frantic, swiftly bringing a shrill choking ecstasy, and, after the briefest interval, kindling up again into a slower and more profound pleasure.

The shadows were the color of Lowland amber on the walls when Rem came back to the bed and put the ring into Doriyos' palm. The stone in the ring matched the shadows.

"You," said Doriyos. "You don't have to pay me."

"A gift."

"I know the worth of amber." There was a pause, and then Doriyos said, "You're going to fight, aren't you? This Zakoris idiocy—I heard talk in the market. Your Prince Kesarh, who has you flayed."

"It seems so."

Rem had not mentioned the summons. But, as the Shansarians boasted they were with lovers or kin, he and Doriyos were sometimes sympathetic enough to share a mild telepathy.

"I can't say be careful, you'll have no choice. I can't say again even that I love you, because I see you rather uncare for it."

Rem shrugged. His eyes were full of a peculiar hurt he had not shown for the wounds on his back. The black hair that thickly curled along his head and neck fell in spiraled locks over the broad low forehead. For a moment he was vividly handsome, as sometimes he could be.

In that moment, sounds came from a room below, grunts and screeches and the *splat* of a soft whip as unlike the Biter as could be imagined.

"Bless the goddess, Gheal is busy once more," said Doriyos piously. And the two young men burst out laughing.

So the farewell was merry if not gladsome.

The crowd's alertness recalled Rem. Something else was going to happen.

Kesarh stood in his jet-black mail before the altar. All this trumpery of sacrifice and prayer had given him public attention. He seemed poised, yet electrified, and cut a strong figure, impressive and elegant.

A great bowl of beaten silver had been brought, in which a knot of serpents writhed and hissed.

A momentous hush fell over the crowd. One of the favorite sorcerous tricks of the Shansarians was about to be perpetrated. The magician-priest thrust his arm into the bowl and raised it, a mighty snake, more than half the length of a man, gripped in his fist. The snake twisted, its scales like metal or mirror, then suddenly flattened out, grew straight and rigid, quivering to immobility in the hand of the magician.

The crowd gasped.

The snake had become a sword, as expected.

The King, Suthamun, came over the terrace. It had been noticeable, his brothers and legal heirs were not present. He took the sword which had been a snake, and placed it in the hands of Kesarh Am Xai.

"You go to do our will. Go then, with our favor, and with Her's."

Kesarh held the sword, faultless showman, up for the crowd to see. When he spoke, his voice, heard for the first time, was startling: cool and dark, and carrying with the ease of an actor's.

"For the honor of my King, and for the glory of the goddess." He waited, and then, just before they could cheer these sentiments, he called out to them with an abrupt and vocal passion: "And for Karmiss, the Lily on the Sea!"

The crowd responded instantly and with fervor. It was a garland aimed for the hearts of the Vis.

Rem thought wryly, *Well managed, my lord.* And then, with a wholesome lifting of his spirit, *Perhaps he doesn't mean us to die at Tjis, after all.*

It was an eight days' ride along the rambling coastal roads, two men of the twenty detailed each day to ride ahead or drop behind and keep the three Karmian galleys in sight. Rem, part of this detail on the first day, noticed another piece of business had been managed. In order to avoid an open act of war against Zakoris-In-Thaddra, the ships were not flying the Lily of Karmiss or the fish-woman of Shansar. Their blank sails had been powdered each with a scarlet salamander.

After a couple of days, the party of riders was ahead. Those that rode in from ship-watching, when relieved by others sent back, gave their ordinary reports. The three ships were still afloat, sails hopefully out, the oars looking lazy. The weather was hot and almost windless. They joked to each other about whether it was better to bounce all day on a zeeba, or groan all day over an oar. They knew they must reach Tjis first, and so they did, but making bivouac on the hills the night before they were due to sight the town, a pair of riders came at them out of the dusk and from the wrong direction—that of Tjis itself.

"What is it?" Kesarh asked these two messengers. His own charioteer, he had only just left the vehicle, and stood stripping off his gloves while he listened.

"My lord—the King sent us no word—are there only these few men?"

Kesarh said, "There are ships coming, a day or so behind us."

"Thank the gods—the goddess—if they can be hurried—"

"Probably. I deduce you now expect the pirates of Free Zakoris to pay a personal visit?"

"Yes, my lord. Last night they touched Karmiss west of here, we saw villages burning. Poor villages, sir. It was done from spite. The guardian feared for Ankabek—"

Kesarh's extraordinary presence seemed to intensify. His men knew why. Prince Kesarh's lady sister had only just gone to Ankabek, had she not?

"But there are beacons the island would light," the messenger hastened on, sensing something, "and none showed. Besides, the Zakorians're superstitious about holy places."

"Not the holy places of a woman-god," said Kesarh. His face was forbidding.

The messenger said quickly, "But they came on in this direction, air. Eastward, away from the sacred island. The watchtower below Tjis put up red smoke at noon. A man rode in just before sunset, who's seen them himself, at anchor a handful of miles off."

"How many ships?"

The messenger was an optimist who had not been told the strength Istris had sent. He said confidently, almost casually, "Seven, my lord."

Only one of Kesarh's soldiers swore.

Kesarh waited, then he said to the messenger: "I take it you've good reasons for thinking they may not come on at you immediately."

"Zastis, sir. Zakorian ships always carry women. And the villages they plundered were great beer-makers—they'll be celebrating. Unless we're unlucky."

"Actually," said Kesarh, "you may be."

Kesarh dispatched a single rider back toward the Karmian ships. They all heard the order. The galleys were to come on at battle speed, with relays of sailors at the oars when the rowers flagged. It would not be unheard of, nor would it be popular. He expected the vessels in the bay southeast of Tjis by dawn tomorrow. One could visualize the reactions. That accomplished, he took his guard sergeant aside, said something, and remounted the chariot. Their pace had been steady but not punishing, the tough zeebas could manage a few more hours through the warm red night.

"You. Nine, and the two Fours, your animals look the freshest. Follow."

The three ran to remount. Rem with a curse of sheer interest, surprising himself. One more minute and they were charging down the bad road in the wake of the chariot, as fast as the zeebas would gallop.

Kesarh reached the town of Tjis two hours before midnight, his team bleeding and foaming at the bits, his three men at his back on mounts practically dying. The pace had been remorseless.

The gates flew open, and the doors of the modest mansion likewise. The Vis guardian himself led the Prince Am Xai to a decorated hall, and quite a decent supper was brought in, with sweet and fragrant Vardish wine.

"Our gratitude to the King," said the guardian, "is inexpressible."

"So it should be," said Kesarh, cutting himself some of the roast. "He's sent three mildewed hulks, manned by fellows who'll be too tired to fight when they get here. And even so much was an afterthought. If your town survives this adventure, your gratitude will be to me."

The guardian stared, and collected himself.

"Do you understand?" said Kesarh.

The guardian, rather pale, said that he did, and took some wine.

Kesarh watched the shaking hands ringed with rather unvaluable stones, and the wine slopping over them.

"How much wine," said Kesarh, idly, "does Tjis possess?"

"My—lord?" The guardian gaped. "What do you—"

"This will go quicker," said Kesarh, with an awful smile, "if you answer my questions rather than asking your own. How many barrels, skins and jars of wine would you estimate are in Tjis tonight?"

The guardian gulped, made an intelligent guess, and offered it.

"Excellent," said Kesarh. "I noted you've prevented a panic evacuation. Keep things as they are. Get your guard out and use them, and anyone with arms and legs, to cart the wine. The square before this house here will do for a collection point."

The guardian sat amazed.

Kesarh pushed the wine flagon sloshing toward him.

"You can set a noble example with this."

Very slowly, the guardian rose with the flagon in his hands, and wandered out.

Initially on being roused, the town thought the Free Zakorians upon them, and chaos reigned. It was Kesarh himself, riding about the short narrow streets on one of the guardian's zeebas, flanked by the guardian's guard, who introduced an element of ruthless and compelling order.

In time, his strange demand was obeyed. The wine came out, off tables and shelves, up from cellars, and was dumped in the square.

Rem, a haulier with the others, saw a kind of good humor take the town. In the face of terror, any action, even if insane, was better than passive wretchedness. There was some cause for humor too, grannies rolling barrels, the wealthy squabbling for compensation, and here and there a guard taking a few minutes off to have a willing girl against a wall. It was Zastis, after all, and the death-fear qualm was surely driving toward the life-urge here.

Tjis was mostly Visian, not a light skin or a fair head had he seen—though there must be a few of them. That Kesarh was black-haired might well be a reassurance. His three soldiers were Karmian, too.

Rem was as uninformed as any man of Tjis. Until the other things began to be brought. Then he knew, and reveled in the outrage of it, sure it must fail. And not so sure. The Zakorians were drunk already, and full of pride, and scorn. It was, besides, the only chance Kesarh really had, save to turn tail and run.

They stood up black on the sunrise, a group of three at the mouth of the little cove, and four others a short distance farther in. The water was deep enough there to support them, for they were large ships, large but swift, biremes, their double rows of oar-mouths now vacant, their black sails folded. Opened, each would show the full and crescent Moon sigil of Old Zakoris, slit over by her snarling dragon. Red eyes were painted either side the beaked prows. Fast and powerful and low, they lay now heavy-bellied on the sea. There had been plunder along Dorthar's southern coast, and sport among the villages of Karmiss, screaming women and bright frothing beer.

Despite the orgy, however, there was a watch set at every prow, men with the cruel uneven profiles of Zakoris, black-skinned or dark brass. Their land had hated the yellow races even before Amrek, even before the allies of Raldnor, the Bastard of Sar—a man nearly dark as they—had brought their city of Hanassor to its knees. Karmiss now was fair game to these pirates, and any place that accepted or affianced the rule of yellow-haired men—which was to say, everywhere. Zakoris was in Thaddra now, and now able yet to make war upon the world. But the day of the Black Leopard would come back. For Zarduk willed it, and Rorn, and all the male gods of Free Zakoris.

After the dawn had come kissing across the lips of the cove, a big silent ship swung by them like a dream.

At sunrise, the tide swelled into the straits between Dorthar and Karmiss. Such a swell alone might be carrying the ship, for only the dawn wind filled her sail, on which a scarlet lizard flamed. Her oar-ports were hatched closed.

The nearest watch-horn hallooed. Others responded.

Not long after, two of the black biremes—only two, for they were disdainful—put out after the phantom ship.

The slaves shackled to the oars were fairly fit, for they had been allowed only a ration of beer, and no women. The torrent of Zastis had for centuries been reckoned a handy extra scourge against these men. At such times, mercilessly chained and prevented from relieving their sexual frenzy save in the crudest and most haphazard way, the Star might send some of them mad. Yet the unexpanded, unfulfilled energy lent power to the oars.

Losing their slack sleeping look, the biremes shot out on to the straits in the wake of their prey, like two lean black dogs.

They caught her inside a mile and offered no violence, for they could see she was apparently deserted and adrift.

Such a thing was not uncanny. Pirates, they had frequently come on vessels in a similar state. Fat merchants and their crews took to the boats, or swam for land at hint of a superior force of reavers. It had happened often enough, and there was, often enough, easy spoil as a result, items too bulky to have been rescued.

Presently they grappled her and swarmed aboard, taking care that none lay concealed below, but all was empty as a scoured jar.

The jars, on the other hand, were full.

She was nothing more or less than a wine-shop, her holds crammed with cibba-wood casks, leather skins, stone and clay jugs. They held the perfumed heady wines of Vathcri and Vardath, and Tarabann, the only good to come from that accursed continent beyond Aarl-hell.

They knew Tjis waited not many miles off up the coast, but they could let her wait, her ecstasy of fear only the more climactic for being prolonged by foreplay. There was even a jest the town might have sent the wine to placate them, and it raised much laughter.

It was the league of their patriotic and lawless brotherhood that made them assume the ship's cargo and return to share it with the other five biremes. The salamander galley they fired and left, a new sunrise on the water behind them.

There was not, of course, quite enough of the wine to go round. In the traditions of their land, they fought each other for it. Several men were knocked unconscious, or maimed, and a couple killed. The joyous riot of drinking was general enough and lavish enough and headlong enough so that by the time they knew they had been tricked, which was quite soon, it was too late.

When the first casualties began to display their symptoms, they were mocked as weak stomachs. Drunks who collapsed senseless, or rolled moaning and throwing up, were compatible phenomena. Yet presently the men of every ship became affected. Tearing gripes ravaged their intestines or their throats, their vision fragmented, they lost the powers of speech and movement. Men spewed blood, and the last disbelievers were enlightened. There had been some virulent poison in the wine. They did not know if they would die of this agent—in some cases it seemed likely, in others it was accomplished. Their terror and impotent anger were to no avail. Even the captains and officers had drunk the wine, they more than any. Bedlam and horror ruled, and in the midst of it, two Karmian galleys rounded the headland beyond Tjis and stole into the cove.

The small percentage who had not drunk, or who had not taken much, ran or crawled to their stations. Knowing their drill, this scatter of men attempted to operate the flame-throwing devices with which two of the Free Zakorian vessels were equipped. But the fires were out and all human fire out with them. Only one missile was released, fell short, and perished in the sea, drizzling. The pirates, those who could stand, could do little else. Some of the purged staggered to the rails, their knives and swords in readiness. And here and there an archer loosed a shaft, or a spear was flung. But their aim was mostly out, and their heart was gone.

The first Karmian, unlike the Free Zakorians, had come prepared. She had mounted on her deck, of Suthamun's bounty, one of the great spoon-catapults the Shansarians had perfected for naval use. Kesarh Am Xai, positioned at the prow, now gave the crew of the ballista leave to fire. Instantly the catapult thundered and spat. The large globule of flame soared out, roaring and whining as it parted the air, and splashed down on the foremost of the black ships. Primed now, again and again the spoon thudded against its buffer and the volcanic charge flew forth.

The Free Zakorians were burning, and those that could leapt in the sea, where the Karmians quickly picked them off with spears and lances, as if piking fish. The sick and the crazed even began to call for help to the ships with the salamander on their sails. While out of the thickening smog of smoke and between the towers of fire there came the crunch and crack of parting timbers and a fleece of sparks as the tall masts crashed. Beyond these noises, even as they stood away, the Karmian vessels heard the screams of the rowers trapped beneath their enemies' blazing decks.

The captain of the first Karmian turned to the Prince Am Xai. The captain was of mixed blood also, but in the modish celebrated fashion of the hero Raldnor, his skin very dark against golden hair.

"My lord, it's a well known Zakorian pirates employ only slaves at their oars."

Kesarh looked at him, unhelpful and remote.

"My lord, the men burning to death down there will be Alisaarians, Iscaians, Thaddrians, men of lands we have no quarrel with."

Kesarh smiled with such magnetic charm the captain smiled in return before he could prevent himself.

After a pause, Kesarh stopped smiling.

"If it concerns you, captain, you have my leave to go and get them out. Provided, that is, you go alone."

In flat truth, not many had compassion for the chained slaves and their agonies. The odds had been too vast against the Karmians, and now were nothing. They had already begun to shout, over and over, *Am Xai! Am Xai!* A din that gradually almost drowned the other, of dying ships and men.

By midmorning, only skeins of charcoal and metal bits and a heaven-touching smolder marked where the Zakorian pirates had gone down.

Those who had got ashore, less than thirty men, were pursued by Kesarh's own mounted guard and a pack of yowling sailors eager with blood-lust. It was butchery, not killing, on the uplands.

Some few others may have escaped by swimming under the ships and then on toward Dorthar, but the chances were against that. If the fire and the spears did not finish them, the sea and the poison maybe did.

For a long while after, Tjis drank peculiar toasts with her wine. The town chronicler made haste to note in his history what had gone into the wine of that night. Anything that was bane—rank herbs, opiates, lamp oil, emetics, purgatives, and liniments for zeebas—all these, providing they had slight taste and lesser odor, or at least so long as they smelled and tasted sweet. Even perfumes had been poured into the vats and jars. To Free Zakoris, the wines of the southern continent were scented and honied beyond any they knew. They took the thickness, and the unexpected first reply of nostril, palate and belly merely for the unusual at work. And drank deeper to grow accustomed. It might not have killed them, but it gave them to be killed.

Kesarh returned into Tjis, and the golden afternoon dulled on his darkened sword. It was not the sword the magician had made from a serpent, but his own blade, forged a year ago when no battle at all had been in the offing. Nor were the Zakorians he had ridden down on the hill the first men the Prince had slain.

Rem, who had also killed men, had been the swing and cut of that sword, and glimpsed the white fixed grin that involved only lips and teeth, the eyes hard and cold, deadly as hell, above it.

They said, Rem had heard it often, that Kesarh at fifteen or sixteen had now and then had himself shut in with armed felons, and so learned to polish his fighting, to the death. Princes sometimes trained themselves in this way in northern Vis, if not at the imperial academies of arms, but always a guard stood ready to aid beyond the door.

. They had lost only five men, none of them Kesarh's own.

The Tjisine women were eagerly offering themselves, and the Karmian crews, their ships anchored, careered about the town, instigating potentially as much damage as the Free Zakorians might have done. The guardian feasted, if without wine, the Prince and his captains.

Four girls came to dance to shell-harps and drums, Vis girls, their long black hair dripping beads on the floor as they arched their brown backs.

"My daughter," said the guardian, pointing out the prettiest arching back.

When she was tactfully offered to him for his night, Kesarh modestly accepted her.

The guest room was small, the draperies motheaten.

Rem found he had been posted at the door for the last half of the night. That was, he supposed, a jest.

The girl did not want to leave him, either through opportunism or lust, or a mixture of both. He had her again, now with scant courtesy, and then pushed her out. Affronted, she donned her flimsy clothing and went.

Kesarh lay on the bed, looking up at the domed ceiling of the chamber.

Noises of carouse and sometimes glints of feverish light came in through the window, from the town, although it would be dawn in less than two hours. He pondered how much mess the ships' soldiery would have made by sunup. It would be obvious, of course, that his own personal guard was not responsible. Tjis in any event was a flea-bite on the earth.

They had intended to send word of victory at once to Istris. He had made them wait.

A sudden lantern or torch caught the straight and naked length of the ceremonial sword leaning against the wall.

Kesarh took note of it. It was a little more than half the height of a tall man, himself, and heavy, meant only for show. Tonight he had let it be carried into the provincial feast, along with his banner of the Salamander. That was the only value of such weaponry. That and to be masked by illusion and gimcrack jugglers' play as a snake.

Sleep was beginning to come, now he was sated, sleep deadening the dull rage, the dull searching after some lost thing that kept his mind restless though his limbs were lax. And Val Nardia, how did she fare tonight, Zastis the rose of desire scorching her flesh under the sheet—

The light of the stray torch flickered on the sword blade.

He could remember seeing no women after all on the sinking pirate biremes. Dressed as men, perhaps, disguised by that and smoke, or dead or stupefied below, their hypothetical screeches mingled with the shrieks of the men.

He dismissed the idle thought. His mind was quieting now.

The sword went on flickering the light. Through his half-closed lids, Kesarh seemed to see the metal growing fluid, rippling, running like a river down the wall. . . . He turned on his belly and slept.

What woke him was the gentle touch of a hand about his ankle. He was alert, totally and at once, and as totally his self-discipline kept him utterly still, quiescent, as if yet unaware.

Had the girl come back? No. The touch was not the girl's—some assassin, then. How? The window was barred by a lattice. Number Nine, the man at the door—Rem—just possibly disloyal, or careless and dead despite the whip—

The gentle touch uncoiled from Kesarh's ankle. It began to flow upward along the muscle of his calf, the back of his thigh.

Suddenly he knew what it was. An assassin maybe, but not human. The sweat broke out over every inch of him, that he could not control, and the weighty treacly length of the creature paused again, perhaps tasting his sweat, his fear. For he was afraid of this. He had the intuitive Vis aversion to such beasts, nor was it irrational. From the size, neither small nor large, of what he felt so sensitively upon him, the snake was most likely venomous.

It had reached his lower back now, shifting smooth as milk across one buttock, the cleft at the base of the spine.

Kesarh clenched his teeth across his tongue, holding his body down to the bed with an appalling strength that must not even be felt in the shiver of a sinew.

It lay against his spine, rising and falling with his breath,

quickened a little, but not much. At any instant it might strike at
him. Even if he were motionless, some abrupt noise from the
town—

It moved again.

Now it had found his hair, wandered briefly, slipped to his left
shoulder.

The closer a bite to the throat or skull the more deadly. The
snake seemed to consider. His face was turned to the other
shoulder, away from it. It touched his arm, almost a caress. Then
swam down the arm, the rope of its body against his side.

The snake had reached his hand. He was so conscious of it
now he realized when it lifted its head, and he was already
involuntarily and unavoidably tensed for the spring that would
take him from the bed if the fangs shut in his flesh. A knife to
the wound, then fire to cauterize—And then the snake laid its
head across his hand and ceased to stir.

He waited. Waited. The snake did not change its position. He
felt the stasis in it, as if it might lie there for ever, or rather until
disturbed.

Kesarh pushed fear from his mind. He measured the attitude
of the snake, explored without eyes, by sense alone, the angle
of the flat head against his fingers, the upturned sleeper's
palm, open to it, cradling it now. There would be one second
only—

In a single convulsive movement, Kesarh squeezed closed his
fist, an iron vise about the skull of the snake.

The tail spurted into immediate spasms, lashing and thrashing
against his side, his chest and loins as he threw himself from the
bed. But the clamp of his strong fighter's palm kept the deadly
jaws bound shut. He could see it now, the seizure of prismatic
scales faded by darkness.

Kesarh raised his arm and flung the thing from him hard
against the wall, the whole length of it, the head coming free and
next moment meeting the plaster. Then as it fell back stunned on
the flagged floor he had his sword from beside the bed and
brought the metal edge down across the snake's middle.

The weapon was blunt from killing Zakorians, but it carved
through most of the snake. It lay dead, spasming still but harmless,
at his feet.

The door crashed open and the soldier called Rem, his own
sword drawn, sprang into the chamber, framed by the light of
candles in the corridor.

Kesarh recalled he had cried out, one loud hoarse cry, as he
severed the snake.

"My lord—"

Kesarh picked the snake up across his sword, bloody and broken and contorting, and showed it to Rem.

"One dancer too many," said Kesarh. "Bring in one of those candles and light these. Shut the door when you get in, or Am Tjis will come prancing to see what's wrong."

Rem did as he was told, came back with a candle and shut the door.

By the glow of the newly lighted wax, he could see the ceremonial sword had gone from its place against the wall. Kesarh had slung the dead snake down where the sword had been.

"Witchcraft," said Kesarh. His tone was light and clever. "If I'm to credit such things. Can it be Ashara-Anackire practices against me, leading me to think all this while her serpent was a blade? Never trust a woman." Kesarh sat on the bed. "But then you wouldn't, would you, Number Nine." Rem looked at him. Kesarh shrugged. "You went to a female person who is your mother after you were lashed. If you haven't an affectionate woman for your bed at this season you're either diseased, deformed, a Lowlander, or prefer boys."

"Or my woman dislikes nursing."

Kesarh said nothing. He reached for the wine jug and drank directly from it. It had beer in it tonight. A reaction was setting in all over him, his finely controlled body now rigidly trembling. That was like the cry. He ignored it.

"You ran in here like a kalinx to defend me, Number Nine. Suppose you'd found me in the grip of four well-armed men? Or did you merely think I was in a Zastis dream?"

Rem said nothing.

"I think I can trust you," said Kesarh. "Of course, I'll have you killed if I find I can't. And I would find out, my Rem."

"I'm sure you would, my lord."

"However this happened, this gambit with the snake, someone was at the root of it. Someone—maybe Suthamun himself."

"Or an heir, jealous of your sudden fame. His brothers. Prince Jornil."

"That's astute. But then, I should have died in battle with the pirates, shouldn't I? This was a provision if I did not."

"You sent no victory messenger to Istris," Rem said.

"Quite. I may send one now. News of my victory, and my . . . nearness to death from snake-bite. I mean to take refuge from any further hopeful assassins. A very safe refuge, but a place where I'll be allowed one companion only, and where besides I'll need :. .ne sincerity—Ever milked snake-poison, Rem?"

"No, my lord."

"You are about to. That thing over there is indeed venomous, but dead. Safe, unless your hands are open anywhere."

"No, sir."

"Then I'll direct you. Use your knife." As Rem went by him, the Prince lounged back on the bed. He indicated the beer-wine jug. "Drink, if you want."

Rem drank.

"A beaten child," said Kesarh, his eyes shut, "continually tries to placate and to earn the favor and affection of its harsh parent. Is that what you would do?"

"I'm older than you, my lord. Almost two years, I think." Rem bent over the snake and forced wide the jaws as directed. "And where is your lordship's refuge to be?" Rem inquired.

The dark voice was barely audible from the bed.

"Ankabek of the goddess."

The departure was circumspect. Only after they were gone was Tjis to discover what had occurred. No doubt unsavory rumor would take up the tale. A prince, Vis in appearance, all at once a hero, all at once in danger of his life. The idea of treachery would be but too apparent.

The guardian, privy to calamity, had already muttered a phrase or two most unguardedly indicative of such suspicions.

The ship was a lightweight skimmer with a discreet sail, perfumed strongly by fish. Four Tjisine rowers had been taken on. The guard sergeant of the Prince Am Xai's men, and one soldier, had gone aboard with him. It had been done at first light. The Prince could not walk and had had to be carried to the ship. It alarmed the guardian to see Am Xai so sick. Having seen the corpse of the snake, the guardian was fairly certain his recent savior would not live, despite the healing skills of Anack's priests.

The ship put off around the headland, and disappeared.

She ran well, taking all the early breeze, the rowers fierce at their oars. They had been given gold, and besides owed him something, the man now a tossing shadow under the sketch of awning.

The morning went by with strips of heat-wavering coast to port and flashes of sun on the oar-smashed water. Later, as they turned more northerly, hints of Dorthar's edges grew visible, far off and blue as sapphire, more pastel than the sea. A current drove in across the straits hereabouts, sucked toward the smaller island. They chased it and bore on.

The Tjisine ship beached at the landing place of holy Ankabek not long before sunset, at the same spot, and almost the same hour, that the temple barge had brought Val Nardia.

They, however, were not looked for.

As the rowers hung exhausted over their oars, a group of men came from the stony village on the slope. There was a short discussion, and one man boarded to look down on the lord under the awning.

Then the men went away, and Kesarh cursed them in two or three vicious phrases. Nevertheless, before the sun quite met the sea, they were back with a stretcher of matting between poles. The temple would receive the invalid. The rest might sojourn on the beach till morning. They must then return to Karmiss.

Kesarh, his light-skinned face the color of the bone beneath, eyes bruised, skin polished by sweat, his hair and garments drenched with it, began to rave and cry out: His life was threatened—he must keep someone by him.

Seeing the state he was in, not wishing to tax him further, the porters accepted that Rem should also go with them.

There was not much to be seen in the afterglow, red sky, red leaves on the tall trees. Then night fell. Finally the coal-black temple stood up on the coppery air above. Turning aside, the men with the stretcher took a subsidiary path that ended among a group of buildings. Lights were burning in this area, while the temple loomed lightless and soulless at the head of the incline, removed in every way.

The stretcher was carried into a cell with cream-washed walls. Kesarh, lifted from the matting to the pallet-bed, seemed to be unconscious.

"Someone will come to you."

The men filed out and vanished again into the descending groves of trees.

Rem looked over at the bed and Kesarh grinned at him. The cell was lit by a wick floating in oil. This, and the illness, far milder than it seemed, lent to the Prince's feverish face a glaze of pure evil.

A minute or so after, a priest came across the clearing between the buildings, and passed into the cell.

Rem had heard of the priests and priestesses of Ankabek.

They modeled themselves, apparently, upon the Lowland religious of the Shadowless Plains. If to be a black ghost was the intention, then they had done well.

The hooded figure bent over Kesarh.

"Who are you?" said Kesarh, clearly. "Are you my death?"

"Your death is not here," said the priest.

Rem's spine crawled.

The priest asked no questions, but touched Kesarh gently at the forehead, throat and groin. Kesarh thrust the hands away. They were pale hands, paler than his own.

"The poison of the snake has almost left you," said the priest. "I shall have medicines prepared. Rest. You will be well."

"No," said Kesarh, with a desperate breathless rage, "I'm dying. Don't you think I know?"

"Life is sacred. You will be tended."

"Too late."

The priest drew back.

Kesarh said in a loud distinct whispering, "My sister is here. The only kindred I have. My sister, the Princess Val Nardia, from the court at Istris."

"Yes," said the priest.

"I must see her," said Kesarh. "Talk with her, before I die."

The skin twitched once more across Rem's shoulderblades. Discomforted, he moved nearer to the doorway, farther from Kesarh.

The priest had not answered.

Kesarh cried out: "Will you deny me? Tell her I'm here, and why. Dying. Tell her, do you hear?" The ache of the poison in his veins seemed to turn to knives and awls. He fell back, clawing the mattress, his eyes blind.

On his left forearm the puncture wounds of the serpent's fangs, discolored and open, showed violently in the yellow light.

When almost every drop of venom had been forced from the sacs of the snake, Kesarh had dragged it off the floor and slammed the points of the teeth through into his flesh. There was enough slaverous filth on them by then to do the work he wanted. No longer enough to do more than that. He had needed, as he said, some sincerity, to earn the protection of the sacred island. The pain at least was doubtless real, as the fever was. A small sacrifice for his plan. But now there seemed to be also some second plan, tangled with the first.

Rem leaned in the doorway. The scene beyond the cell was impartial and nothing to do with them. The night was very fragrant from the trees. White stars were netted among the boughs. The red Star smoked.

Somewhere a contralto pipe began to play, melodious and wandering. He thought of Doriyos.

Behind Rem, Kesarh was panting, thrashing on the bed, damning the priest to Aarl, a spot neither, presumably, believed in.

Rem stepped aside to let the priest go by, out again into the impartial clearing, the ethereal surety of night.

THREE

Val Nardia stood motionless, surrounded by the dark, while before her the slender candle of the shrine fluttered in its vein of glass.

Aside from the candle, the shrine was empty.

It was for the novitiate to conjure there the relevant image of meditation or fantasy; if desired, the visitation of the goddess Herself.

Val Nardia had existed now on Ankabek twenty days. At first, she had been tensely strung, wishing to rush forward into the security of this religion so mysterious and so profound, and there be lost. Afraid also that the arms of the goddess would not hold her tightly enough, and she would slip away, her thoughts and her dreams coming on her like ravening tirr. But almost instantly tranquility had replaced her nervous seeking, and her doubts. Some luminous unseen air, indiginous to the great temple, enfolded her. With no effort, everything that was spiritual within her rose like unbidden music.

Even the persuasions of Zastis might be channelled, used in other ways, a flame that would burn in alternate vessels. She commenced to know the wonderful freedom of the human heart discovering, suddenly and in surprise, that through itself alone may be evolved communion with the Infinite.

Yet the knowledge and the state were primal to her. She had not had time to understand entirely that either condition, the world *or* the spirit, was valid; that the soul was capable of as mighty adventuring as the flesh, conceivably more.

She was not ready therefore, and poorly defended. A priestess

had come, a Vis woman, yet with that ambiance of the temple.
The priestess had given her the news.

And now, the only image Val Nardia could conjure beyond
the candle-flame was that of her brother. Of Kesarh, drifting on
the shores of death, less than half a mile from this room.

Most of the lamps about the clearing had been doused. The
piece of midnight which moved did not resolve itself until it
entered the dim seepage of light from the cell. A woman's
shape, slender, folded in a cloak.

Rem stood up, waiting.

There was no need of a guard. Not here. No assassin surely,
even of the King, would dare pollute this sanctuary. Yet Kesarh
had not trusted, required some guard. The trustless would seldom completely trust, of course. Rem had recalled once or twice
the screaming, burning sea beyond Tjis, and dismissed the memory.
Rem had done deeds enough himself to haunt himself, if he
wished so to be haunted.

He thought the woman a priestess, and was prepared to offer
her some courteous cautious challenge, when the oil lamp in the
cell started a glint of red under her hood.

"My lady."

The Princess Val Nardia looked at him, her eyes wide, as if to
ask a question, then the question became apparently superfluous.
She went by him, and into the cell.

Rem glanced after her, and saw Kesarh. The medicines had
not greatly quieted him. Either real or exaggerated, the fever still
pushed him in a slow dance from side to side of the pallet.
Banked up by the rough pillows, his head was now tilted back.
He looked ghastly, dead but reflexively animate. It must terrify
her.

Rem was about to speak. But Kesarh's voice came out of the
slowly tossing corpse, and told him in three words to walk off.
Then it told Val Nardia to draw the curtain over the door.

The footfalls of the soldier went away. There began to be a
long soundlessness.

"Kesarh," Val Nardia murmured.

"Come closer. Snake venom isn't contagious." She did not
stir. "Did they tell you what I said they should tell you?"

"That you might die," she said. "They told me that."

The smudgy eyes glared at her out of the livid face.

"Did you believe them?"

She had not discarded her hood and it obscured her; her head
was bowed.

"I woke before dawn. I thought it was a dream—some vast and deadly stillness surrounding me—Tonight, they told me you were here, and why."

"You'd heard I was to fight Zakorian pirates in the straits."

"I knew nothing of that. We're out of the world, on Ankabek."

"*We?* My glorious victory means nothing to you, then. Or my death at Suthamun's order."

"The King—" Her head was raised. The swift movement after all dislodged the cloth from her shining hair. She saw him stare at her, and fell silent.

"The King," he said slowly, "guesses what I might become, in despite of him. He's realized, maybe, I won't be content with a strip of mud at Xai and ten soldiers at my back." Kesarh let go the tension that had seemed to hold him. His body sank down into the pallet, his eyes shut. "But all that's ceased to matter. If I die, I'll trouble Suthamun no longer."

Not seeing her, he heard the rustle of her cloak. Then the fragrance of her, either some perfume or her very skin, hair, soul, flowed into his brain. He did not raise his lids. For some reason on the black behind them he saw the empty space where the sword had stood in the chamber at Tjis, the sword which had reverted to a serpent—or been filched by some clever method through the bars of the window lattice, just before the snake was fed in there. Then Val Nardia's fingers came down like weightless birds on his forehead. He sighed at their coolness, their gentleness.

"Don't speak of dying," she said. "Believe in your recovery, and you will recover. They would never have left you alone here if they thought you close to death."

"Why not?" he muttered. "There's my soldier to watch me. And they sent you."

"I wasn't sent. They only told me you'd asked for me."

"And in compassion and pity you overcame your aversion, and forced yourself to my bedside."

Her hand drifted from his face and he reached out and caught her hand in one of his. He opened his eyes and looked at her, into the radiant light of her beauty where all the illumination of the tiny room seemed concentrated. She was white, afraid for him and so, for now, no longer of him.

"Since we were children," he said, "whom did we have to trust save each other?"

Her eyes faltered. They were bright with tears.

"Kesarh—"

"If you want me to live, I'll live for you. Poison, disease, the wound of any battle—nothing. I'll run through flood and fire and thunderbolt, unscathed. You can make me invulnerable.''

She wept then, briefly. She did not, even weeping, take her hand from his.

Later, the fever going out, he slept. In the sleep, once, he spoke to her, calling her, as in their childhood together, *Ulis*. It was the name of a rare scarlet summer flower, indigenous now only to the cultured gardens of Karmiss.

He returned once, and stopped ten paces from the curtained door. Having been dismissed, Rem's purpose on the island was nullified. And there was no menace in the darkness under the foliage; nothing.

The sense of oppression emanated from the cell itself. Its source was presumably the Prince Kesarh Am Xai. Rem had no urge to meddle, and had gone away gladly, not even curious. He did not understand the feeling; it was hypothetical yet threatening, like unknown footsteps heard by the blind.

Having checked the clearing this second time, Rem once more moved off, on this occasion toward the low summit where the temple stood.

Ankabek was now immeasurably quiet. To one used to nights in Istris, or in some camp of men, the quiet was unfamiliar, partly disturbing. It seemed trembling always on the brink of an insidious whisper.

Near the temple, the trees fell back, and the inflamed eye of Zastis sheered through filiments of cloud. The darkness reddened.

Rem halted, considering the temple, its great doors closed, walls windowless.

Why had he come up here, to look at this?

Yet strange, he would not be the first to think it: The pale people of the Lowlands who built their cities and temples of black stone, the dark Vis who built in crystal and stone whiter than salt.

Rem moved forward again. He had a peculiar urge to touch those immutable-looking doors, maybe crash his fists against them. They would not let him in. He was neither worshipper nor acolyte. Ashara, Ashkar, Anackire—his mother had reverenced other gods, Yasmais, chiefly.

When he was not far off, the big immutable, impenetrable doors swung inward. There was only the mildest noise. Some mechanism, then, must be automatically in operation under the threshold. Any might enter, who had the wit to approach. Of course, that was what they said of the goddess. Seek Her, you will find Her. Seek Her not, She is not.

A vague glimmer, hardly even to be called light, hung inside the temple. He could walk into it, or away.

Rem, once called Rarnamoon, walked into the temple. When, after a few steps, the doors swung shut behind him, he hesitated, looking back. But they would open again when he returned. This was no trap. He went on.

The passage was lofty but unornamented, somber stone, that gave none of the magnification to his movements he had expected, no echo. The fount of the infinitesimal light seemed to be ahead of him. Gradually he discerned that what lay ahead was a blank and featureless wall. But he proceeded, and beheld that on either side this wall the end of the passage branched into a new corridor. In each of these the light was a little more definite, and they curved away, out from the heart of the building. Randomly, he entered the left-hand corridor and followed the curve of it. The light was decidedly more vivid, but again there were no decorations, no painting or carving of any kind. The wealth of Shansar-conquered Karmiss had been diverted to create this place, and gifts had come from Dorthar, and tribute from Xarabiss, Alissar and Lan. It could have been one of the richest wonders of the continent, a-drip with jewels, its temple guard stationed like statuary—but Ankabek had no guard. Only mysteries.

The curve turned out, then inward, circling. But the light unencouragingly dwindled. Then the wall ended ahead and Rem, passing beyond its angle, found himself, just as he had been some minutes before, beside blank stone at the juncture of three passages, his one of them, the largest leading off to a pair of tall shut doors. It was a replica of the entry in every respect.

Rem strode down toward the new exit, but here the doors did not respond. He retraced his way therefore, and took the new left-hand curving corridor. This, leading back, became the right-hand corridor of the entry, as he had suspected.

In the original passage, Rem cursed softly. There would be a secret kept at the center of all this, inside the black drum of stone that the passages endlessly led to and encircled. The means of getting to it, however, were well-concealed. There was no mark on the stone to indicate anything at all.

All at once, the windowless, pointless O filled him with doubts. The light which had, it seemed, no source, began to make him uneasy. He took another long stride back toward the first pair of doors—

And the pain shot through Rem's skull like a lance.

He fell against the wall, shocked and powerless—it was too soon for this thing to happen again. Then the world went and the pictures came.

There was a mask, half of it cast from black marble and half from white. Then a second mask replacing the first, half gold, half silver. And then a third, half fire, half snow—

A man dashed from behind the mask. He was a Zakorian, howling and in agony. He had been poisoned by wine—no, not wine, by fruit, yellow fruit rolling under his feet, while behind him a bonfire flapped its skirt at the sky. The fire was that of burning ships, reflecting in black water. In the air also, where Zastis blazed. Then the flames sank. There were three women. One had hair like ice, and one hair like ebony, and one hair like blood. He saw into the womb of each of them, and in each case it was filled. The woman with ebony hair raised her fist and her face grew ugly. It was his mother, Lyki. She darted toward him with the rod gripped to strike and he flung up one arm to shield his head.

"No!" The voice that came out of him appalled him, it was not the voice of a child, but of an adult man.

He stared at the woman. Nor was she Lyki, but a stranger, Vis, dressed for the temple, and her hands relaxed at her sides. Behind her, two shadow-shapes: male priests.

This was almost amusing, to be caught twice. Next time, when? Next year? Tomorrow? Perhaps in a fight or battle, killed because the vision came and he could not control it. No, not the vision. The madness.

"Forgive me," Rem said to the Vis priestess of Anackire. "I was trying to find the inner sanctum. I'm very tired. Dizziness—"

Her dark eyes looked back into his paler ones. He knew, as if she had told him so, that she did not believe what he said. That she knew, and the men behind her knew, he had been possessed. Lowland telepathy learnt by the Vis. . . . Had she peered inside his skull?

"You wished," she said, "to find the Sanctuary of the goddess?"

"It's well-hidden."

"I will show you."

Rem balked. He was nauseated, superstition crowding him, and the undertow of fear.

"No."

"Come," she said, and his eyes followed her though he did not.

She went to the blank wall between the three passages and

knelt, and leaned to it as if to kiss. After a moment, the stone quivered and a portion of it fell slowly backward. A glow of light poured out. It was a mechanism like the doors, then, if not so amenable. Probably the marks on the wall were clear enough to those trained to recognize them.

He did not want to enter their temple anymore. It had become saturated by what had happened to him. Yet, in those instants, there seemed nowhere else to go.

Rem walked after the priestess, and the two priests, like guards, came after him. Perhaps, despite this show, he was trespassing and they meant to punish him. It occurred to him that he expected punishment in every avenue of life, expected and no longer resented punishment, and that this might be a fatal flaw.

The piece of wall which had fallen in had formed a tilted bridge on to a flight of ascending steps. At the top of these an opened arch let out the light.

The priestess glided ahead of him. In the arch she became a silhouette, stepped to one side and vanished from sight. Rem reached the arch.

The core of the stone, as the windings had suggested, was round. There were no colonnades, and still no carvings. All about the perimeter of the floor jets of fire spurted from openings, volcanic in appearance and certainly unnatural. They lit the high vault of the great black chamber, and sent waves of brilliance across and across the floor itself, which was one whole extraordinary mosaic. Gems flashed there and skeins of color. Myriad legends seemed depicted, legends or dreams—figures of men and beasts, winged things, chariots and ships and hurtling golden stars—his eyes abandoned it giddily. And there was something else to gaze on.

Across the wide room, four black pillars stood up against a curtain of gold. Closing off the crescent of the chamber's end, the curtain was perhaps sixty feet in length, in height much more. Its folds hung thickly, and as the light burst on the faces of these, the curtain seemed made of laval rain. Scales of pure metal composed it. Thousands of them. The gold curtain alone showed where the rich offerings of Vis might have gone.

One of the priests said to him, "In this manner, the Lowland temples were made."

"And so finely dressed?" Rem blurted in marveling anger.

"Yes," the woman answered, "centuries ago. So finely, and more finely."

"And beyond the curtain," Rem said. "What's there?"

"She is there."

He shrugged to stop himself shivering. "Your goddess."

"Anackire."

The outer temple, the passages—they were a trick, a safeguard. Uninvited, none might enter here. Yet they had brought him here, because they sensed some supernatural element at work on him. He should resist, or he would lose himself. He winced at his thoughts. They were out of all proportion—Yet the sensation did not abate. He was turning to go when one of the men behind him, the other who had not spoken before, said quietly, "Cross the mosaic. When your feet touch the sky-borne dragons, the curtain will open."

"More technology to astound the credulous."

The man's head was lifted in its hood. The eyes which looked into his were the color of the scaled curtain.

"Only logic," the Lowlander said. "To approach so close to Her expresses a wish that you might see Her. And yet, to see Her at once, and always: How then are we to remember what She is, that an effort must be made to attain Her? Men grow too easy with familiar things."

Rem turned again and observed the curtain. Its very wealth seemed to draw him, that and the thunder of flame across its fire.

He did not look for the dragons, but he must have trodden on them twenty paces or so from the curtain. Like a bright wing it soared away. Framed between the central pillars the statue rose, and stopped him like a blow.

She was only a small goddess, three times his own height, maybe a fraction more. The beauty of Her, the perfection of Her lines, led one to forget She had been fashioned. And yet She was bizarre, unhuman and terrible. That men and women, creatures of the world, could turn to this as to a mother—He smiled wryly, recalling the mother he himself had been given to.

Beneath the statue, a foible of the second continent he had been used to think, the bronze trough was filling with serpents as if with water. They came freely into or vacated the trough through holes that led away into their warrens under the floor. Their gold scales glittered like the huge scales on the looped curtain, and like the coiled tail of the goddess, for She too was a snake from the belly down. Her eight arms were upheld or outstretched in the traditional modes. He did not know their meanings, but some appeared benign, others cruel. Her eyes seemed to meet his own. Lowland eyes.

He, too, might have some Lowland blood, but then, Lyki would surely have flaunted it. It did not matter.

He had glimpsed representations of this goddess in the Ashara temples of Istris and Ioli, but they were not like the statue before him now, even when Ashara's fishtail had been transformed to that of a water snake. Nor was the Vathcrian or Vardish Ashkar quite like this. And yet, Anackire Am Ankabek, modeled on the Lady of Snakes, the arcane deity of the Shadowless Plains— some part of Rem told him he had already seen Her, long ago, far away. Before he was even born.

Above the clearing, but west of the temple, the red trees gave way to oaks, and it was possible to look out between them to the dark blue sea of the long afternoon. Among the grasses stood a small stone Anackire, rough layman's work. No offerings had been set before Her, for this was Ankabek, and She needed nothing.

Since the fever had left him, Kesarh had mostly slept. The priests of the place had come and gone. Day and night had come and gone. Rem had been at the door, or within call, except when sent away. Val Nardia had remained. Last night, waking, Kesarh had found her sitting on the low stool, exhausted from watching and asleep, her head beside his on the pillow. They had been together only what their blood had made them, brother and sister. And now, brother and sister still, they had come up here to gaze at the innocent sea. There was time enough for a prolonged convalescence. His last order had kept the two ships and their men at Tjis, where they were happy to stay, feted and adored, though the town would probably never recover. Meanwhile, the messengers must have space to reach Istris; the messenger dispatched to the King, and that other messenger Kesarh had dispatched for other purposes, the morning after the snake.

Val Nardia, paler now than Kesarh, sat close beside him. Her eyes on the ocean, she reminded him in swift sentences of their childhood at Istris, the old tower in the lower gardens from which they had watched the distant harbor, excursions into the hills. Or the summer Festival of Masks five years ago, when they had found each other in the crowds and known each other instantly. He drank the wine and water in the flagon and ate the fruits she pressed him to eat. He basked in her love, letting her see the weakness which had almost left him, nothing more. And she, he recognized, was his accomplice in the deception.

Speaking of Istris, however, brought her abruptly, like a slip of the tongue, to mention his departure. Her pallor deepened.

"When," she said, "will it be safe for you to return? Must you go in fear of your life in Karmiss always?"

"I always have gone in fear. That's how I escaped worse than a snake. But I had plans for this, the Zakorian sea-fight, the murder attempt. You see, Ulis, such things, or others like them, had to come. To be ready was everything.''

"Then—"

"Then my own men will alert the paid gossips of the capital. They'll soon be active. My heroism will be paramount, that and the treachery offered me. By the hour of my return there'll be flowers on the street for my chariot to crush, and he won't dare try for me again.''

"I shall pray to Her it shall be so. And to keep you in her protection.''

"The goddess was his weapon against me in Tjis. Her sword, Her serpent.''

Val Nardia turned from him, bewildered, at a loss.

"His corruption, not the goddess' will—But you're certain it was the King?''

"Who else?''

"Some other enemy.''

"You think I have a variety and may choose?''

"Your ambition,'' she said softly, ''but more than this—this thing in you which frightens me. This has made you enemies. Is your way unalterable?''

He saw the dangerous path now, and avoided it. He lay down on the grass and told her his head ached.

Later, as he drowsed against her, he said, ''I'm glad you came here. You'll be out of the reach of any harm. Otherwise they might use you as a lever against me. Elsewhere I'm armored.''

"You would sacrifice me with all the rest,'' she said remotely, without resentment or distress.

"Ah, no,'' he said. ''Not you.''

Not you.

Kesarh had been on the island of Ankabek ten days when the boat came from the Karmian mainland. It was full dark and the Red Moon had risen with the Star. Men ran from the village, and the arrival stood on the beach glaring at them.

"I am sent to the Prince Kesarh Am Xai, by Suthamun, the King.''

By dint of this lie, the man won through at last to the temple hostelry, and the poor cell where Kesarh now stood, healed and ominous in the sullen light.

"Good evening, Number Three.''

The man, one of the ten Threes of Kesarh's guard, saluted him. ''My lord, I have this message for you.''

The soldier recited. Seldom did Kesarh or his guard sergeant commit such things to paper. When the recitation stopped, Kesarh's expression had not changed at all. He had, of course, no reason for surprise. Matters had run to plan. The riders, pausing for nothing and appropriating new mounts as they had to, had halved the journey time, and the work was well-advanced. Visian Istris seethed on his behalf. To go back now was as wise as it had been formerly to stay away.

"And the ships at Tjis?"

"Have received an order to return, their captains and a few picked men to accept the bounty of the guardian in chariots and zeebas, and to proceed overland to the southeasternmost village on the Istris-Ioli road. Here to await yourself."

"And thereafter to ride into Istris at my back," said Kesarh. He grinned.

The ships would be slow. He had had no intention to allow his triumphal re-entry into the city to be marred or delayed. The caviling blond-haired half-blood sops who had jittered on their vessels, scared to fight, then mewling about the rights of slaves—they should run behind him through the streets, his kalinx pack, his dogs, for all Vis-Karmiss to see or to hear of.

"We'll take the boat across again at first light. Where are the rowers sleeping?"

"On the beach, my lord."

"You can have this cell. Share it with Number Nine, I'm sure he won't object."

The soldier stepped aside as Kesarh strode through the doorway and on up the slope toward the temple. Puzzled, the Number Three wondered if his Prince were going to give thanks to Ashara.

The little metal discs on the trees fluttered, making an eerie irritation of sound that seemed to burn in his veins.

He by-passed the great doors of the temple and continued along the black running wall. Quite simply, during their many conversations, his sister had mentioned where the novitiates were housed. Quite simply too, as his health improved, she had been less and less with him.

Presently an arch broke the wall. He went through into a courtyard. A single torch in a vase of thin pinkish stone trembled above a doormouth. The wind was rising on the sea. It could be a rough crossing tomorrow.

Kesarh knocked on the door. A grill was raised and a dark face showed in the glow of the torch-lamp.

"Who's there?"

"I am the Prince Kesarh Am Xai. I'm here to bid my sister farewell. Let me in."

"You may not enter."

"Either you let me by or I break in the door."

"This is a sacred place."

"Then keep it sacred. Don't risk unholy violence."

There was a whispering, and the face went from the grill. Kesarh waited. The strength which flowed in him, which would brook no denial, seemed also aware that denial would not, ultimately, be tendered. After a minute, he heard a bar retracted on the inside of the door, which then opened to let him through.

He advanced into the gloomy passage and a weightless hand fell on his wrist. He looked, and saw a Lowland woman was by him, pure Lowland from the look of her, her narrow hand now shielding a candleflame from the snarl of wind at the door.

"You see Val Nardia. She is here. Follow, I'll guide you to her."

Something in this astonished him. He nearly laughed. They were naïve, then, or more wily than he had thought them.

Kesarh went after the woman and the flame, both blonde, ghostly on the unlit passages. There seemed a mile of these, serpentinely twisting, sloping up or down, and all lightless. Now and then the candle touched a side-turning, or the recess of a door. He suspected the obscurity was a device to confuse intruders, or profane visitors like himself.

Abruptly the woman halted. They were at another door-recess. She moved about and faced him.

"This is Val Nardia's chamber. She is in the shrine just beyond. You should not disturb her there. Her meditation will shortly be ended. She'll return, and find you."

For a moment, he wondered if that were some trick, but then the Lowland woman said to him: "There are high slots in these walls, open to the sky. In the dusk before dawn you should be able to see quite well. The Princess herself can direct you."

Kesarh lifted his eyebrows at her impassiveness.

"You imagine I'll be here all night."

She merely looked at him. Her face was unreadable. Only the yellow eyes gave any color to it, and the violet jewel depending on her forehead—the Serpent's Eye, gem of the goddess.

"Well," he said, "I intend to be off the island by sunrise."

"Then she will light a lamp for you."

Kesarh suddenly laughed.

"How much do you want for this? Or is it to be a gift to the temple?"

"My lord," the Lowland priestess said, "the only gift which is required will be given."

"A riddle. I said, how much?"

"My lord," the priestess said. That was all. He glimpsed her leaning toward the candle and heard the snake-hiss as her breath blew it out. In the sheer blackness he did not see her go, nor hear it. No glimmer came from the slots above, if slots there were, this place was turned away from the moon and the Star.

Kesarh fumbled with the door and felt it give. The room beyond was lamplit, and he went into it, slamming the door shut on the black outside. The encounter had angered him. He glanced about, and perceived instantly the other curtained doorway. Ripping the curtain aside he gazed into a fresh lightless passage, which presumably led to the shrine the woman had mentioned. With an oath, he pulled the curtain to again and gave his attention to the empty room.

It was spare and small and, to Kesarh, unbeautiful. At junctures, Val Nardia's own possessions stood or lay, the chests he had seen piled up at Istris for her departure, a box of Elyrian enamel, the plain mantle she wore here. The bed was low and slender. Lying on the pillow was a dying flower that he had tucked yesterday into her hair. He picked it up. A little of its scent still lingered, but mostly now it was perfumed with Val Nardia, and he crushed it in his hand.

Then he heard the noise of the curtain behind him, and next the long indrawn gasp.

He turned. She was barefoot, and had carried no light through the dark. Now she seemed half-blinded, by the lamps, or by him.

"How did you come here?" she said.

"Your priestesses let me in. I came to say good-bye. I leave tomorrow."

"But," she said. Unlike the face of the Lowlander, Val Nardia's gorgeous face was utterly readable. She had flown here for sanctuary, but the sanctuary had abetted him. She was betrayed.

"There are no windows in this room," he said. "You can't see the sky. Or the stars. Not even Zastis."

She took a step toward him. "You must go. Go now."

"When you believed I might die, you were full of grief and fear. Now you pack me off, maybe to my death, like a doll you tired of. Is that how you considered me, all those years we were

children together? A toy. Useful, comfortable. Made of wood or
rags.''

''No,'' she said, ''that's how you think of me.'' Her honey
eyes widened. ''Something for your use. Your admiring slave. A
game you played. For your *use*.''

''Let me use you then,'' he said. ''And you, Val Nardia, use
me.''

She opened her mouth, and this time he knew it was to
scream. Before she could make a sound, he had closed the gap
between them. He grasped her against him. The gauzy robe she
wore, the shift under it, made no barrier. He seemed to feel her
body and its detail as if both of them were already naked. The
hand he had clamped across her mouth he drew away, closing
her mouth instead with his own. She struggled, as she had
struggled before, but more frenziedly now. Even, she tried to
bite him, his lips, his tongue, as they invaded her. But the bites
were ineffectual, she could not bring herself to hurt him, even in
this. He knew a blazing stab of pity for her, pity which was also
love, and could have wept himself as he drew his head away.
She was too breathless now to scream. Besides, who would hear
her?

Her hands went on beating at him, clawing at him. She tugged
at his hair, scratched his throat—but again, strengthlessly. And
all the while she muttered her one word of entreaty and
objection—*No*, sometimes his name mingled in it—and he muttered her name, or the pet name, Ulis. It became a litany
between them, a song, meaningless.

Soon he lifted her and carried her over to the mean bed and
put her on it, and lay down over her.

He could feel the tensions of her flesh, all the agony of Zastis.
The fastenings of the robe came undone with ease, and the rough
lace beneath. He found her breasts, moulded them, tasted their
sweetness. She struggled still against him, her clutching hands
now like those of one who drowned. But he thrust her back
under the water and drowned with her. The room seemed scarlet
from her hair, the hair of her head, and the ulis-petalled hair of
her loins.

At the final invasion, her eyes were open, meeting his,
her hands fierce on his shoulders, her mouth hungry for
his, forgetting at last all words. Almost instantly she became
a whirlpool, a whirlpool which clasped him, dissolving him.
Her cries came, louder, higher, endless. She seemed to be
dying against him, but somewhere in her death there surged

his own. He lost her, but not the essence of her, never that.

In the defended stillness of death which followed, he smiled, lying on her hair, her flesh, thinking this too a victory, quite conclusive.

FOUR

The first of Suthamun's heirs, his eldest legal son, waked in his love-bed and kicked the nearer girl into communication.

"What's that din?"

The girl did not know. Nor did the other, when he kicked her.

Prince Jornil rose from the bed, petulantly furious. He was clear Shansar from both parents, but birth and growth in Karmiss the Lily on the Ocean had caused him to be a twining plant rather than a tree. He had never had a moment's doubt of himself or his future. Only his father's wrath could make him blink.

He stood, goldenly handsome in the window, listening incredulous to the uproar out in the streets. He knew nothing about it. It was not for him or his.

When a servitor informed Jornil the hubbub sprang from a crowd, gathering to watch the return of the Prince Am Xai into Istris, Jornil laughed aloud.

Paid word-mongers had prepared the way. Then genuine rumor and real truth had augmented everything. Making camp in the eastern hills above the city, the returning heroes had paused, sending some ahead to collect and bring them out their finery for a processional entry. Somehow Prince Kesarh had persuaded them that Suthamun would countenance acclaim for the victory. Even the single lost ship would be forgiven. Because he had been clever, the three captains and their ship-lords thought themselves clever, too, and were not difficult to convince.

In fact, Suthamun Am Shansar had had no intention of drawing the public gaze to their achievement. Having received the official messenger Kesarh had sent, the King had had prepared a slight speech of commendation to be delivered in council, by the Warden. The King himself would, after an interval, extend a fairly private audience to the Prince Am Xai, thank him, give him some small gift; upbraid him gently and with magnanimous brevity for the loss the galley. As for an entry into Istris, Kesarh and his twenty men might come in at any time. The ships might also make free of the harbor as they wished.

The going-out had been stagy, to display Suthamun's excessive care for clean shores. He had himself reckoned the Free Zakorian menace less than it was, or he would have sent his own captains in Shansar-built ships, and under the command of his brother, Uhl.

Suthamun, though, had reckoned without Visian Istris. Men in Shansar had a weakness for show, but it was show of a different sort, magic or mystic often, generally significant. Little events were seldom blown up to gales with hot air. When the crowds came out to cheer him home from a hunt, the King had failed to see it was the pleasure of event they rejoiced in, not his royal self.

There had, additionally, been the touch of organization. Men who, at sun-up, had stationed themselves about, stating which streets should be kept clear, therefore encouraging the crowd to pile up on either side. The women who had gathered or purchased flowers, declaiming on the lord they would cast them to, garlands for his greatness. And there were the others, who had spoken from the beginning—At last, a dark man who would safeguard their honor and their security.

By midday there was expectancy, press of people and loud sound throughout all the wind and stretch of streets and avenues from Istris' White Gate to the palace. Banners had been hauled from chests and hung out of windows. Hawkers sold colored streamers, bells and squeaky trumpets, with the wine and sweets. Only the Ashara Temple, last bastion on the route before the palace was reached, gave evidence of extreme uninterest.

A few minutes after noon, the word of an approach began to fly.

On the heels of this faultless rabble-rousing forerunner, the Prince Am Xai came through the White Gate from the Ioli road, in the midst of his cavalcade.

Drummers marched in first, six of them, in black burnished mail, setting a brisk solid tempo. Directly after these came bronze horns and rattles, and then the Lily banner of Karmiss borne high on the music. After the Lily banner prowled two nubile girls, dressed in ribbons and little else, with lilies in their hair. They led by ropes of flowers two black gelded bulls, docile and obliging. The crowd was quick to see the analogous joke, or perhaps they were helped. *"Free Zakoris!"* the cry went up.

Free *gelded* Zakoris, led by the dulcet Lily. The girls flirted and blushed. They were wenches from the hills, earning money beyond their dreams. The bulls, too, were from the hill farms.

Ten soldiers rode by, and two soldiers walked in their trotting wake, carrying between them the outspread banner of Kesarh's blazon, the Salamander in gold on a scarlet ground. The overall approving noise winged into cheering. The crowd started to call his name, as men had on the ships at Tjis: *Am Xai! Am Xai!*

They could already see him, standing in the brazen chariot. He wore red today, the color of the wine with which he had made dupes and corpses of the pirates. His team of zeebas was black, black as his hair. Despite the uproar, he held the team in perfect check with one hand. The other rested almost idly on the chariot rail, loosely holding in its grasp a gold-handled whip. The symbols were exact. Not many missed them, though most would not have given them a name. The stance of facile strength and grace, the warlike masculine beauty which seemed to encompass Kesarh, surrounded by his men in their dark mail, in control of all things, so it seemed. The image of a king. A Vis king.

They were bawling now, and the flowers were coming down like rain.

He turned now and then, acknowledging them. None of Suthamun's riotousness, or the heirs' simpering or smiling contempt. Kesarh was different. His courtesy and his arrogance enthralled them. They felt they had been noticed, as was their right, by a god.

Such was Kesarh's presence, which he understood, and used so plainly and so well, having waited so patiently for a chance to use it.

Behind Kesarh rode twenty more of his men, all the Twos and all the Fives of his one hundred. Altogether, almost forty of his personal guard were on view through the procession.

The heroes of the ships, who rode after, were more gaudy, and the crowd made a fuss of them, naturally. But they tasted the vinegar on the honey. Even the blond, dark-skinned captain named—along with many others—for his looks: Raldnor, even he on his costly horse knew he was not that day's darling.

By the time the Prince reached the Ashara Temple, the crowd was thunderous and the incense of broken flowers hid the fact that no sacred incense rose from the holy terrace.

People burst across the square as Am Xai reined in. His guard held them back good-humoredly, for they were good-humored themselves, wanting only to come closer to their focal point.

The black bulls were led by their floral chains across to the temple and up the steps, the Prince and his guard following, and the crowd spilling after.

The priests, who had been watching from eyelets, were doubtless perturbed. None came forth.

Kesarh stood, with unflawed poise, calmly waiting, demonstrating that the fault was not his, but he would overlook it. The crowd, however, began to shout and yell at the temple. Eventually a solitary flustered priest scurried from the porch to be greeted by abusive applause. He was a Shansarian, or at least enough of one to fulfill the rigid strictures of the Ashara Temple.

He hurried to Kesarh, but before the priest could speak, as if he had been asked, Kesarh said, in his carrying actor's voice: "I'm here to sacrifice to the goddess, in the sight of the people, for my victory at Tjis."

The priest looked about him, decided, and ran away.

The crowd cat-called, protested. Then fell quiet, anxious to see what Kesarh would do.

What he did was to hesitate an instant, as if in thought, then walk directly up to the marble altar on the terrace.

He said nothing further, but a motion of his hand brought the pair of bulls to him, a man now at either side, the girls melted away.

Kesarh drew his knife. The edge was honed to a razor—he had been expecting this.

With a swiftness that was astonishing, and an atrocious accuracy, he swept his arm across the black taurian necks, slicing both throats before the stroke was ended.

Blood spouted, gushed. The great heads flopped, the bodies spasmed and sank, almost as one. Drowned in gore, the flowers unwove and streaked the steps with brackish red. But he had been so agile, there was not a splash on his fine clothes; even his hands were unmarked.

Long ago, in the past of the past, kings had sacrificed in such a way.

The priest, who had only gone for reinforcements, rushed out with his fellow officiates upon the terrace. Unneeded.

The King was stripped naked, save for the cloth about his loins. He had been at exercise with stave and bow, was en route to his bath, and that it was in this way and this state that he took the audience was significant. The insult was a blatant one. That the young man in the wine-red garments knew himself insulted, what rank he had totally ignored, must be certain.

"Well," Suthamun said to him, letting the slave place a mantle at last across his shoulders. "Your explanation?"

Kesarh Am Xai looked at his King with enormous blankness.

"My explanation of what, my lord?"

"Your dance measure through my streets. Of that."

"You gave us free entry, my lord. Your people chose to honor us, in your name."

"*My* name? You flounced back into Istris as if you'd re-taken Zakoris herself, instead of a brace of boats."

"Seven ships, my lord."

Suthamun, wrapped in the robe, sat down and drank wine. None was offered elsewhere. There were a number of others in the room, watching with interest. The oldest son, Prince Jornil, ate figs and stared at Kesarh's clothing. As the father had coveted kalinxes nearly a month ago, the son now coveted this elegant costume. It irked Jornil that Kesarh, who had, and deserved to have, no revenues, could procure such tailors and such dyes.

"Seven ships," said the King. "Or were you seeing more than double the number?"

There was a long pause. The offensive question apparently required an answer.

"Seven, my lord," said Kesarh. "If you fear my reckoning is out, you might ask the captains you yourself appointed, Lios, or Raldnor Am Ioli."

"I'll ask them nothing. They're disgraced. With you."

Another long silence. Kesarh kept his eyes down, knowing what Suthamun might behold in them, should they be raised.

"You must excuse me, my King. I thought, when you sent me to Tjis, I went with your blessing to gain some renown for myself."

"Did you? Then you should have waited for me to tell you so. You were sent, you Visian dog, to burn refuse on the sea. No more."

There was a vague murmuring about the room. Suthamun ran his eye over it, daring it to grow louder, and it died.

The talk had reached the palace, the talk of the streets. Kesarh had been set on in the coastal town by agents of some enemy, some high enemy, who was envious. Only the skills of Ankabek had saved him.

That the King did not mention the sojourn at Ankabek was also evidential.

Kesarh waited. He waited for Suthamun to see that regal

unfavor toward him now could reek of villainy. But Suthamun did not, or would not, see this.

"You came in," said Suthamun Am Shansar, "like a young leopard. You can creep out again like a mouse. You will go at once to your estates at Xai." Kesarh's head came up and his eyes flashed like drawn knives. And Suthamun smiled. "Yes, my Salamander. The fire's out."

The ragged man bowed low, the third time he had done so.

"They're selling locks of black male hair, saying it's yours, sir. And the poet made a fine job of the paean; he's singing it over in the eastern city by now. And the women—women we never funded—mooning over you, refusing their lovers—"

"All right," the shadow said from the chair. And then, to another, and to the ragged man's great relief, "Pay him what I told you."

When the paid man had gone out, Kesarh rose and filled a glass goblet with water. This indeed was no hour for wine.

The mistake had been in not realizing fully he played this game against a dolt. Suthamun, too much an idiot to make the correct move, the move which would have laid brick on brick—

Kesarh drank the bitter water.

"What else?"

His guard sergeant handed him a package. It had been opened, tested for its motive.

Kesarh examined the contents.

"Raldnor Am Ioli's third best ring. A love-token?"

The sergeant showed his teeth.

"Better than writing it, my lord."

"True. He doesn't like Suthamun's response. Rather than blame me, he blames the King. Another fool. This one more convenient, perhaps, if he keeps his promises. Are those men ready to ride?"

"Yes, my lord. One fifth, as you ordered. The lads we've had longest, and most often seem about you."

"They won't like Xai. But then, neither shall I. There's another man. One of the Nines, Rem. A Karmian with light eyes and friends in the Ommos quarter."

"I know him. We put Biter to him not long ago."

"Find him and send him there. The King gave me just until sunset to get out of Istris."

There was a sound beyond the apartment door, the man on guard there striking the floor with his spear. Next second the door was flung wide.

A servant stood fluting in Shansarian: "Through the will of Ashara, the First Heir, Prince Jornil of Istris," while Jornil brushed by him and walked into the chamber.

Kesarh looked at him. Jornil beautifully returned the look. The light of late afternoon tumbled against him like a loving woman. The door was shut at his back.

"An honor," Kesarh said shortly. "You're here to wave me off."

"I'm here to tell you to leave those clothes behind you when you go."

Kesarh stared at him, then all at once he laughed, only one harsh note of it.

He pulled another flagon over and gestured to the sergeant. As the door closed a third time, Kesarh presented Prince Jornil with a drink of wine.

Jornil put the smoky glass down untasted.

"Come now," said Kesarh. "Did you think I put something in it?"

Jornil beamed. They spoke in the Vis tongue. Despite the announcing servant, Jornil had some difficulty with the language of his fathers.

"No. But I don't like your wine."

"Karmian grapes."

"Quite. The clothes. . . ."

"Of course, my Prince," said Kesarh. He put his hand to the fastening of the tunic. "Now?"

"Oh, you can simply discard them here. I'll send someone for them."

"And do have them well-laundered. I rode at least three miles in them."

Jornil picked up the wine, regarded it, put it down again.

"Is it true what they're saying? I mean, that my father attempted to have you killed?"

Kesarh considered.

"It isn't true. But I wonder why you should think someone is saying it."

"It's common gossip on the street. A poisonous snake at Tjis—"

Kesarh now burst out laughing. Jornil, not intending to, laughed with him.

"A minor wound in battle. No snake. Nor is there any reason on the earth," said Kesarh, "for Suthamun to have need to kill me. He can send me to Xai, a living death. Much worse."

Jornil, who did not like Kesarh, but who was yet vastly drawn

to him, and who had been intermittently yet fascinatedly jealous
of him since their childhood, snorted with amusement.

"I may come and visit you there."

"Don't, for the goddess' sake. A royal progress to Xai would
finish it. No. Remember me here. Wear these clothes for me.
This dye, they tell me, was mixed with the blood of thirteen
virgin girls, to get the color so exact."

Jornil, between belief and scorn for Zastis quickening, lifted
the cup of sour young wine and drained it.

Xai was situated on the plains of southwestern Karmiss, many
miles from the capital. It was a journey of fifteen to seventeen
days, mostly due to the poverty or nonexistence of the roads.
The inns were also poor, or nonexistent. The land was flat at
Xai. Wild zeeba herds galloped across it, as if themselves unwilling to linger. Two small villages crouched on the estate. The
villa itself was ramshackle. Patchy jungle-forest, adrift in a
swampy lake, gave the house its characteristic aura and odor.

Kesarh had spent enough of his childhood in this place to
know how much he detested it.

Like a sick lion, he fretted in his confinement. At night, or at
odd times during the blazing days, Zastis drove him to couple
with the wretched women who were his possessions. He rode,
exercised, and tried to hunt the sterile country. The men he had
taken with him got drunk on the vile local beer and spewed it up
again, cursing Suthamun, or Kesarh, or their gods.

He had been there a full month before he had any unsolicited
word. Then it was from the source he partly anticipated: the
half-blood captain, Raldnor of Ioli.

Twelve days later the man arrived, with an escort only of
three. Which boded rather well.

They sat on the roof terrace under awning. As the sun began
to set over the forest in the lake, birds rose and fell in screaming
clouds.

"I've come to see more and more distinctly," Raldnor Am
Ioli declared with soft persistence, "how we were used. I, my
fellow captains, yourself, lord Prince. All to be sacrificed. Then
Suthamun to send some favorite and clear the seas, getting glory
over our backs. We were the taster at the feast. Meant to die to
prove the strength of the bane."

Kesarh smiled slightly. At his signal the girl refilled the
Iolian's cup.

"And so naturally," Am Ioli said, "instead of reward—

punishment. My captaincy retracted. And fined—*fined*, by Ashkar—for making unsanctioned public spectacle." He drank. His pale blood was not from Shansar, but out of Vardath, hence his Vardish name for the goddess. That too was useful, in the matter of basic loyalties. "Is Suthamun insane?"

Kesarh shrugged.

"The King believes in the supremacy of his own yellow race. Men of mixed blood—even of such favorable coloring as yourself, sir—are a blot on the purity of his people. I didn't properly understand this, I confess, until Tjis. Now, Raldnor, I wonder how long I shall understand anything."

"You're in fear of your life, still."

"If I died at Xai, it would go unremarked."

"No. The capital's alive with your praises, even now."

"Till the mob forget, then. After that—another snake, maybe."

"He could reach out to all of us."

"So he could."

They drank. Raldnor Am loli banged down his empty cup.

"Other than fly Karmiss like felons, what solution?"

Kesarh said, "I could hardly get off the island, having been regally detained here. He'd like me to attempt it, possibly, then invent treason out of it. A lawful execution would follow."

"This *is* Suthamun's madness."

"His obsession. But what hope does any man of dark blood have since the Lowland War?"

Ruffled, Raldnor intuitively smoothed his feathers. Until recently, the accident of coloring which had earned him his illustrious name, had worked as an aid rather than a drawback. The godlike Storm Lord Raldnor himself had been a mix.

The sun was in the lake, drowning and burning like one of the Free Zakorian ships. The wine, too, was nearly gone.

"Berinda," Kesarh spoke peremptorily to the girl. She looked at him with the soft, wounded eyes of the born-broken slave, then slipped away to refill the jug. "In any case," Kesarh murmured, "I'm surprised you think me worth your concern, sir. After our discussion at sea."

"Those galley-slaves you left to roast?" Raldnor met his eyes coolly. "It was an act I loathed, my lord. But your ruthlessness, while I abhorred it, do abhor it, led me to expect—how shall I put it?—great things of you. A shining future. You'd destroy anything that stood in your way."

"And you," said Kesarh, "would rather risk yourself beside me, than find yourself in my way."

Raldnor, with a certain humorousness, nodded.

He was an audaciously clever and perceptive man. These very qualities would occasionally cause him to behave foolishly and blindly.

"You asked if there might be a solution to the King's malice," Kesarh said. "There may be. Something that will show his hand to the people so openly he won't dare to try again. Something stamped with such ironic justice that Istris will never forget it. It'll hurt, too, if you like your revenge with salt on it."

Raldnor shifted. He now knew himself in the presence of what he had already sensed he was in the presence of, aboard the Karmian galley. But, opportunist that he was, his eyes were open and his hands steady as he said, "Please enlighten me, my lord."

In a couple of sentences, Kesarh obliged.

"By all the bloody gods," said Raldnor, whose Vis mother had been a successful whore in Ioli's Pleasure City.

Across the roof, against a sky which had lulled to bronze, the girl Berinda was coming back with more wine. She had heard nothing of what was said, nor would it have interested her. Her mind was fixed and held by fundamental things. As she leaned to fill Kesarh's cup, she remembered how he had lain with her, and she inhaled the male scent of him like some drug.

He paid her no heed.

The priestess Eraz became aware that another had noiselessly entered the Sanctum, beyond the curtain of golden scales. Eraz looked, with her inner eye, out into the unseen space. The persona was immediately recognizable, not only for itself, but for the infinitesimal secondary element which was now in the midst of it, fainter than the warmth of a dead coal.

It was presently the time when the luminary fires of the temple burned low, and when the curtain before the goddess did not rise merely at a footfall on the sky-borne dragons of the mosaic. These were, too, the hours between midnight and morning known in the ancient mythos of the Shadowless Plains as the Wolf-Watch. The hours of the insomniac, of doubt and self-dislike, and, sometimes, of death.

The Lowland priestess moved from behind the curtain and into the body of the Sanctum. She crossed to the spot where the Princess Val Nardia stood, her head bowed, alone and in silence.

"Do you seek the goddess?"

Val Nardia faltered.

"I seek. She isn't to be found."

"Yes. Always."

Val Nardia turned her face not simply downward, but away.

"I've sinned. She's not for me."

"If you'd thought Her not for you, you would not have come to Her, Val Nardia of Istris."

"I've sinned—sinned—let me confess it, and give me a penance."

"That is the way of your mother's people. Anackire awards no penance, no suffering. The symbol-stretching of Her arms which are retribution, destruction, torment, the inexorable curse—these are metaphysical. We inflict our own torture upon ourselves. We chastise ourselves."

"My sin—"

"Your sin is only sin because you will have it so."

"*No*. Help me!" Val Nardia cried, looking up, catching at the woman's robe.

Eraz said, "The help is in you. You must help yourself. What we have done is the past. We reiterate the deed, or we dismiss the deed."

Val Nardia gasped. "You hate me," she said abruptly. "Your kind hate all of us who have the blood of Vis. I shouldn't be here. *Your* goddess, not mine."

Eraz did not glance at her, her eyes were lamps. She seemed not to be human.

"Yours, if you will accept Her. You don't need my comfort, Princess. This is what we try to teach you. You need only Her, and to know the power within yourself."

"You disdain to listen. My crime—"

The golden eyes returned to her.

"Search firstly within yourself. Then, if you fail yourself, you may come to me."

Val Nardia flung away. She ran across the mosaic and, reaching one of the obscured exits, ran down it into the ground.

Eraz paused. She became in her mind two persons, as she had trained herself to become. The first said to her, This girl has no fortitude to bear these things. She understands nothing. Eraz answered, Each of us has the fortitude to bear all things. For centuries, my people believed they were the victims of this earth, ordained to suffer and to perish, finally to be expunged. But at last they were shown another way. They believed then they would be world-lords, as in the depths of the past. This now is the path they would tread. Val Nardia is in the hand of the goddess. She must come to know this. But I think, too, her destiny forbids it.

And far off, she was aware of Val Nardia, hastening through

the under-temple, wrapped in her black pall of shame, and the tiny new-lit candle at the core of her, blacker to her than all things else.

Storms tore through Istris, dry storms without rain. There began to be some fears of drought. Then water speared from the swollen cumulus and the bright summer hail that flamed where it struck stone or metal.

In the last quarter of Zastis, came a Karmian feast day, the Festival of Masks. The marble walks were still running with rain at sunfall, but the skies had been polished of cloud, from the apex sheer to a magenta sea.

The city began to resound like a beaten drum, flaring into mobile lights that ran frenetically everyway. Vanes of colored glass hoisted on the street torches turned the boulevards mulberry, amber, indigo, the shades of Aarl, till they were smashed. In wild costumes the richer rabble and the more adventurous well-to-do paraded themselves, concealed by the represented faces of sun and moon and Red Star, beasts, demons and banaliks.

The palace itself, seldom demure after dusk, had blazed up like a bonfire, cacophonous with music and buffoonery.

There were rumors the King might go abroad in the city later, suitably hidden in a mask of gold, that old escapading streak getting the better of him, as the tales told it had so often done before. What beggars would win horses tonight? What thirteen-year-old virgins boast, ten months from now, that Suthamun Am Shansar was responsible for the wailing thing bouncing on its springy womb-chain?

There was another rumor too. It had started somewhere around the harbor. Kesarh Am Xai had come back, without the permission of his King. Even before the rain stopped and the sky hollowed, this theme was current everywhere. The King himself had heard it reported, and furiously laughed it to scorn.

"Who is Kesarh Am Xai?" Suthamun had demanded. "Am I familiar with the name?"

As night climbed, the drink poured like the rain and lovers coupled in the fever of the Star in doorways, on roofs, on bell-hung carts, kissing through masked lips, starting up or down into faces of sunbursts and orynx. Drunks had visions. Some spoke of having seen the Prince Am Xai here or there. Of having shared a beer jar with him in Lamp Alley, or discussed pirates in the lower city. Or he had gone by with a swirl of his cloak and two or three of his soldiers, on not so secret secret business somewhere, but masked like all the rest. This was a new apparition.

Generally, Istris saw ghosts at the Festival of Masks. Numerous times the hero Raldnor Am Anackire himself had driven his chariot along its roads, red-haired Karmian Astaris at his side, and men had fallen on their knees and tipsily fainted. Of course, it was quite likely someone had been dressed to fool the populace, some dark-skinned man donning white hair and a fair imitation of the old Dortharian scale-plate dragon mail. And there were many red-haired women now, from the mixing of bloods.

Jornil, the Oldest Son, First Heir to the King, did not recall from whence the idea had initially sprung. He thought it his own entirely, and it appealed to him at all his various levels, of vanity, of mischievous caprice, of envy and of idiocy.

In the beginning, the elegant clothes of the marvelously san-guine red dye had required some alteration. Kesarh was leaner at waist and pelvis than Jornil, and longer-legged besides. When the necessary amendments had been carried out—somewhat un-der the pretext that the discrepancy was in the shoulders, which would need widening—the notion was introduced that Suthamun might not wish to see his heir in the apparel of one disgraced.

Jornil was careful of his father. The other heirs were children; it was not so much a chance of being cast off, or even of a loss of privileges. It was more some incoherent thing that had to do with the stronger personality of his sire, which had cowed Jornil from the cradle, and helped, with the obverse cushioning of Karmiss, to make him what he was.

So, he did not put on the prized clothing. And thus began to look for some opportunity to get away with putting it on. Then, as the festival approached, the second notion was introduced.

In fact, one of the re-fitting tailors had supplied the first caution against wearing the clothes. The suggestion of assuming them on the night of the masks came from a girl, cunning not only in bed. Both had been paid to do this service for the Prince Jornil. The paymaster was a fellow with loosely curling black hair, Vis, but lighter-eyed than most. Only the girl recognized him as a man who had previously attended the Prince Am Xai, and she had the wisdom to forget it.

The rumors that Kesarh had been spotted in Istris amused Jornil greatly. When he left the rowdy feast in the palace hall, and went to change into Kesarh's red clothes, he needed his sun-ray mask to hide his excitement.

Since manhood, he had been sensitive to Kesarh. Kesarh had seen to it, in some off-hand, under-played fashion, that he should be. Now, to *become* Kesarh for a night was awesome, a challenge. On top of that, to carry on his father's legendary tradition, haunting the city in disguise, added its own sauce to the jaunt.

Suthamun would go mad, if he ever learned the truth. But Jornil, along with nervousness, had gained a total lack of respect for his father's ability to reason.

When he had on the clothes, he pulled off the sun-ray mask. The mask he replaced it with was quite unremarkable, save that one half was black, the other half white. Pouring back from the crown of it, the wig of thick black hair covered up his blondness.

Jornil strutted for himself in front of a mirror. Then went out, his legs moving in Kesarh's long stride, by lesser passageways, into an inside court. There he mounted a black zeeba, and his escort of five guards, their mail washed dark, unfurled a small banner, signaled with a fire-lizard.

They pelted out into the city.

It was nearly midnight, and the carnival was in some places escalating, in others getting sluggish.

When the first cries went up—*Am Xai—It's the Prince Am Xai*— Jornil grinned hugely and unseen.

He went on grinning a long while, till his jaws ached. He never for an instant questioned why he, who ostensibly had everything Kesarh had not, should be impelled to this, and gain such enjoyment from it.

Inevitably the enjoyment and excitement started to take fire from Zastis. He began to want a girl, and to look about for one he fancied.

Both he and his escort were by now fairly drunk. Coming into a square where the celebration was still exuberant, he thought to dismount and make his way on foot. His guard enabled him to push through. A procession was winding over the square, singing and shrieking, with jugglers throwing fire-brands. He had turned to look at it, when a girl came out of the crowd and fell against him.

Her face was covered by a kalinx mask, but her perfumed hair streamed from it over her shoulders and her breasts, which were almost bare. She was dark, a Vis girl, and she clung to him.

"My Lord Kesarh," she said hoarsely, "Zakorian pirates killed my brothers. You avenged me, and countless others like me. And I've loved you ever since. Yasmais answered my prayers and brought you here, risking the wrath of the King. I've followed you for miles, daring myself to speak to you. Don't send me away."

Jornil breathed fast. He reached out and thrust aside her mask, as he felt Kesarh would have done. She was pretty. She even closely resembled a girl Kesarh had once kept in the palace.

He whispered something in her ear. She pressed herself to him, exquisitely making contact with every part of him, through Kesarh's clothing.

The girl led Jornil across the square, his five guard meandering after. They turned into a side street, and then into the courtyard of an unlit delapidated house.

Already unlacing, Jornil hastened into the dark beyond the door, his breathing like a bellows, and leaned the girl against a wall.

The guard loitered just outside, a vestige of security, mostly persuaded they too might get a turn with the girl.

His head tipped back to drink from the passing wine-skin, the fifth guard choked. The sky was falling on him off the top of the wall, and holding a knife that suddenly replaced the wine in his throat.

The cart with its streamers and bells raced clattering and ringing through the streets, dragged by three terrified zeebas. When the congestion of people ultimately slowed its rush, and men had climbed up on it to try its cargo, they found only one item.

The body of the Prince Kesarh Am Xai, dressed in red, which red nevertheless did not obscure the multiple wounds. It had been stabbed and slashed, pierced, hacked, practically butchered, until only the masked face remained uncut. Which masked face, when it was uncovered, revealed itself as that of the princely heir, Jornil.

The night was turning toward morning, but in the windowless room she could not see it, could not see moon or stars, or the Red Star itself. As he had said. Her brother, Kesarh.

And she had only to think this to feel once more his hands and mouth upon her, his body upon her, within her, and the anguished frenzy they had created not once but many times through the brief hours they shared together. Each coupling had exhausted her, wrung her to emptiness. She had not been able to think, to fight anymore, either physically or with her spirit. She had lain beneath him, beside him, curved into the angles of him, pinned fast to the mattress, wrapped in his arms, a comforted prisoner. And no sooner did awareness reclaim her than her stirring flesh sought his as he sought her. Again, no space for denial. It had been no rape. As he had told her, he had used her, and she him. They had tried to extinguish themselves, breaking like waves on the shores of each other's lust and life. Or so it had seemed to her.

Then he left her, to return to Istris—not as he had gone away, better than that. He had been sure. His sureness and his strength had shone with a fierce dark light in the little dark room and she had not wanted him to go. She had been afraid, for when he was gone, she would be alone. She would have at last the space to know what they had done.

He had kissed her, put her aside, gently now.

"I'll come back. I'll take you from this stone box. When I can, when it's safe for you. Till then, be here for me."

And he had kissed her once more with a lover's kiss, so letting her drop back among the covers. He had walked out of the room and away, and she had become for him an accomplishment, set on one side, no longer a priority. Oh, she knew that much.

While for herself—

He was now a colossus, closing her horizons. She had escaped him, but he had pursued her. The goddess of Ankabek had given him the means, and so the goddess had died like a light. Kesarh dominated now. His black intention. His power. Shadow on shadow.

Could it be that, twins, each embodied an opposing principle, as each had been formed to an opposing sex? Val Nardia, timidity, a shrinking from the world. And he, a hunter, a devouring.

Kesarh was evil. She knew it. Had known it since their childhood passed behind them. Cruel, pitiless, some essential atom missing from his soul.

She had struggled so long with this. No remedy had suggested itself. Yet, there was a remedy. She had realized as soon as the other, inexorable realization came to her.

She had attempted to pretend at first that it was not so. But her body, her body which had betrayed her to him, her body mocked her, content with what it had done, and had sealed her to its purpose, and his. For her body was with child. The child of her brother.

Val Nardia considered she had been stupid to approach the Lowland priestess. The people of the Plains were not like the Vis, not even like the races of the Sister Continent, Vathcri, Shansar, but unique to themselves. And pitiless as Kesarh, in their passionless way.

She stood up. Shrinking from the world, she had now come to that crossroads of both the cowardly and the brave, and chosen her direction.

She stepped onto the stool indifferently. She had gone sleepless many nights and was very tired. Using only one hand, she brought the looped end of the scarlet cord dangling from the rafter quite matter-of-factly over her head.

She felt only the slightest apprehension at what would happen. Her neck was very slight. Just so her own mother had ended her life. And as Val Nardia herself, a child of eight or nine, had come into a room and found her, so some other would come into this room and find Val Nardia.

Sighing a little, and with a strange grace, she slipped her feet from the stool.

Kesarh had sat very late over his wine, then taken the wine and a girl to his bedchamber.

The faint stench of the swamp-lake disturbed him, that and the activities of the night which he had no means as yet of knowing. The Festival of Masks had provided him with a drawn dagger, Raldnor Am Ioli had helped place the blade, and the King's Heir, if Jornil remained true to himself, had thrown himself on it.

The moment Jornil had ordered Kesarh to gift his processional clothes to him, the plan had begun to quicken in Kesarh's brain.

Raldnor's men had started the rumors of Kesarh's return— false, naturally. Rem, who had seen to the tailor and the girl, had also suggested a deserted house. He himself had once employed such buildings, and knew of several about the city, from the days of his brigandage.

Am Ioli's men had performed the murder. If they had done it. If everything had gone to plan. *If.* That was the exacerbation of this. Kesarh must wait here in ignorance, must be known to wait here in ignorance. That was everything.

In the end the wine and the girl relaxed him. He fell asleep, a sleep deeper than the center of the land he lay over.

Then, in sleep, a hurricane rent the darkness in his skull.

He woke, crying out, and the girl caught his shoulder.

"A dream—a dream, my lord," she muttered, trying to soothe him.

He shook her off, reeling up from the bed.

"Not a dream."

She reached out and he struck her away.

She sank back, whimpering, and he went out and up the stair to the roof terrace. Here he stood in the star-reddened night, the pulses of it beating on him, staring away toward the forest.

There was a kind of nothingness inside him. As if some vital organ had perished, and yet he lived.

He did not know what it was, and gradually, forcefully, he thrust it from him. And away. And away.

When he went back, the girl was folded on the floor.

"Come here," he said. "You were right. It was only a dream."

She crawled back to him and caressed him until he wanted her and took her. He fell asleep again, and as he slept, Berinda curled against his spine, smiling like a forgiven child.

FIVE

Against a blue dusk no longer tinged by Zastis, the magician's hands flickered and a rain of light fell from them. In the shallow bowl beneath, the bones of a recently dead animal, clean and white, glimmered. There was a prolonged hiatus. Beyond the window, stars hung in streams above the bay. A star smoked also on the highest palace roof, a morbid beacon to all Istris: the funeral watch-fire of a King's dead, custom of Shansar, burning now for more than a month.

"Well?" Suthamun eventually rasped. "What do you see?"

Suthamun's magician raised his head, and the mysterious light among the bones went out.

"You were wise, King, to call him back from Xai."

"Was I? That was the advice of my council. Black men and yellow. He's made himself popular, a little hero. My Vis didn't care for his exile. This tale I tried to kill him—twice—at Tjis, now here in the capital, my assassins falling on my own heir in error—*By Ashara!* It was the rabble here did that—black and brown scum—drunken—killing my boy, knowing him even in those damnable filched clothes. Or else Free Zakoris. Infiltrators revenging themselves on Kesarh—mistaken—" Suthamun broke off. His grief was real but oblique. His eyes were dry, yet he had wept in rage when they brought him the corpse. Jornil had been, if nothing else, a symbol of the continuance of Shansarian rule in Karmiss, that dynasty of reavers. Now Suthamun's oldest legal heir was seven years old. The rest were mixed-blood bastards, or daughters. Useless.

"King," said Suthamun's magician, "even the High Lord must sometimes listen to the desire of his people. You could have done no other thing than return the Prince Am Xai to your court."

"And now I must pet him, make love to him, to please them, keep them quiet. When he was the cause of my son's death. And I never raised my hand against the dog. *Never*. The story about Tjis—it's a lie."

"You believe Prince Kesarh might also be implicated in the Heir's murder?"

"I don't know. Free Zakorians, the mob, Kesarh—yes, why not? In Shansar I'd have put him to the test, the Three Ordeals, fire, water, steel. But I daren't, not here in this liars' land."

"You do well to humor him, King. The constellations that companion his birth are arresting. And the goddess has spoken here, a low soft voice, indecipherable, but evident."

Suthamun, impatient and afraid, reined his pacing.

"What do you mean?"

"The Aura of the goddess has passed across the fate of the Prince Kesarh. It would, King, be pointless now to oppose him."

Suthamun grunted. He longed for wine and noise; the ten-night-long Shansarian death-feast, loud lament and toasts to the shades, that had eased him. But they were done. And tonight Kesarh would also sit at the table. He had been welcomed back discreetly, at noon today, having passed through the city incognito as a thief. As one of his own assassins, perhaps?

There had been nothing to link Kesarh with the death of Jornil—save the clothes in which Jornil had died. But despite the Aura of the goddess, diplomacy, magic, what-have-you, one would be slow not to, yet he saw the event from an oddly angled perspective, from the dramatic epic view of what he had been, a tribal lord in a land of omens and sagas. For Kesarh to think Suthamun strove to murder him, and so to have Suthamun's son dispatched while playing Kesarh—Suthamun to carry the blame—these were Shansarian vengeance-moves of the highest order. The King, if he credited them as such, gave them also that much respect.

He did not prophesy from them a particular threat to himself. It would have been absurd to do so. Kesarh was nothing, save transiently to the Vis rabble. And even with the foremost heir missing, Suthamun and his five brothers yet stood between all men and the Karmian throne.

*   *   *

The fire on the palace roof was doused. It smoldered out as Zastis had done, conflagrations of love, life, death, showing no great difference from each other.

The summer too began to flame and die. The flames of leaves rotted on the trees. The reeds beside the pools turned sallow, then black, and the sunsets thickened.

Rem, having found himself intimately involved with his master's schemes at Tjis and Ankabek, thereafter waited, at a loose end. That afternoon before he left for Xai, Kesarh had spoken to Rem. It was the first time Rem had been inside the modest royal apartment, as opposed to on guard outside it. His former trade was apparently to be put to some use. Talents Rem had been glad not to use for more than a year were again called on. With the correct blend of implicit coercion and silken payment, he had seen to it the required persons were suborned to Kesarh's will. As a result, Jorníl was now ashes, and Kesarh back at Istris, installed in new, more lavish rooms, a party to most of the King's social calendar.

The situation astounded Rem. To live off a man's enforced bounty, the cold blade of his hate, though sheathed, always waiting at your back—Kesarh seemed quite unmoved. Only the intense stillness of his eyes sometimes belied it. He was aware, he was vigilant. His brain worked on, even as he drank Suthamun's wine, or as the girls ran to kiss him on the streets. Before too long, appeased by Suthamun's ironic punishment and the victim's glory, Visian Istris would forget Kesarh's wit and bravura. It was only a matter of time. And then, if only then, some accident might be arranged. Kesarh would know all this. Know it more competently than did the King.

But Rem himself was weighed down, uneasy. He considered again and again quitting the Prince's service. It would mean a fat fee gone. While, knowing what he now did, Rem might find his own life in danger. In flight without wages was a state that did not appeal. There was, too, some abstraction that kept him loyal. To carry out such tasks for a man bound you to him, more than fear or prudence.

Another thing troubled him besides.

What had happened at Ankabek, the sudden second subjection of his reason to those mind-pictures, too close upon the first—so he had awaited other such subjections in constant nervousness for days and nights after. Even now. And the night of the temple, the statue of the serpent woman, so irrationally familiar.

Weeping storms visited the city. The nights grew cool, then chill. Kesarh had awarded presents to the council, and the Warden, but he must conjure some other insurance before the cold months came, for already the mood of the city was changing. Part of the roof of the Ashara Temple had been found to be unseated. During this stormy weather tiles had crashed in the street. Shansar and Vis alike were dismayed at the augury, which could be adapted to almost anything bad.

Kesarh went modestly but openly in his black, with only two guards, to offer to Ashara for the joy of Jornil's soul. Istris, suitably alerted to the happening, watched in somber approval.

A doleful letter from Lyki somehow found Rem at the lodgings he was then frequenting. The rope merchant was sick and crotchety. Lyki herself was unwell. It seemed she needed a physician and her protector, miserly after his losses, would not send for one. The thinly disguised cry for alms was adorned by veiled references to her own former generosity to an unloving son. Hating her, but unable to do otherwise, Rem sent her money.

An hour after this charitable deed, he was summoned to the under-palace.

The rain fell like arrows on the streets, and in the open court. Kesarh came striding at him out of the downpour, and began to speak to him while they drowned, and lightning curled in a wedge of purple light over their heads.

"He's done something almost clever," Kesarh said, and Rem knew he meant the King. "He's thinking of recalling my sister to court. I value her. She could therefore be used against me."

Rem nodded. Kesarh handed him a sealed packet.

"Take her this letter. Only to her, do you understand? Breakneck speed. Your mount's over there, with cash to buy a new one if it drops dead under you."

"Ankabek," said Rem.

He did not want to return to Ankabek.

Kesarh looked at him, and Rem knew there was no choice. Again, it was not exactly fear. He had been trusted, trusted by something that could, with just as much facility, kill him minus a second thought.

The ride was wet all the way. The tall skies of the hill country roared, and the Ioli road was slick as sweetmeat.

On the coast the sea collided with the shore in quake. At first they would not put out for him. When he had bribed them enough, they rowed him cursing, but the waves had looked worse than they were.

After the usual preliminaries of landing, he was conducted on the long uphill walk to the temple, through a rain now red from sacred leaves.

He waited three hours in a stony building, trying to coax the fire to dry him, trying intermittently to find someone to whom to reiterate his urgent duty as messenger to the Princess Val Nardia.

Finally he gave up on both and fell asleep, and then they came and he had to follow them out again into the rain.

They led him to the temple, and in one of the two curving corridors performed their door-opening sorcery. His reluctance, when he thought he would have to re-enter the body of the temple, startled him. But in fact the way went down, this time, under the temple's core, presumably. He ended up in an insignificant room, which was suddenly lit by the coming in of an apparition. He guessed at once he was for some reason meant to be affected, impressed. That did not diminish anything.

She was a priestess, a white-skinned Lowland priestess, with the Serpent's Eye on her forehead. All the rest was gold, gold hair, gold robes of scales—like the curtain he recollected—gold eyes. Her eyelids and lips were golden, too, and her sails. She entered unannounced and merely stood before him, looking at him, and he felt something of his self-will give way at once.

"You were sent by the Prince Kesarh?"

"I was," she said tightly. Her voice did not sound human. There was a resonance somewhere, not striking against him, but somehow . . . *inside* him.

"You have brought a letter for the Princess."

All at once, he knew.

"What's happened?" he said, "what is it?"

"Raldnor," she said. Just that, no other thing.

It appalled him, for there was no sense on earth for why she should know his given name. He was afraid, and would not question her. He said, "I'll ask you again. What's happened?"

"You will follow me," she said, "and you shall see what has happened. Then you'll return to her brother, and tell him what you have seen, and all you have been told."

They walked through a long corridor, barely lit by slotted windows high above. Then through an iron door, as if to a dungeon. Steps went down, and below another door was opened for them by two of the hooded priests.

As before, Rem knew himself led, helpless and unwilling, toward some profundity. His head began to ring, he felt again something of the weird disorientation he had experienced in the boat, the world shifting; chaos.

There was smoke now, incense, unlike the incense of Ashara,

more subtle, darker, permeating everything. (He had heard they did not use incense here.) A gauze curtain drifted aside. Another. The smoke, the curtains, sight, all misted together. The center of his body seemed empty, as if he were hollow. Chanting came from somewhere, all around it seemed, one word over and over, or did he imagine it—

Astaris. Astaris. Astaris.

Then the sound stopped. The mists cleared. They were going into quite an ordinary chamber, though lamplit and without windows. In the midst of the room was a bed or couch, with draperies drawn close.

The golden priestess, glittering from the lamps, clasped a tasseled cord, and the curtains slid away.

There on the bed lay the young woman Rem had sometimes glimpsed at Istris, even more frequently here, the Princess Val Nardia. She was asleep, her hair spilling around, saturating the pillows with its color. He noticed something else. Her belly lifted high under the black gown, the firm rounded lift of early pregnancy.

"Yes," the priestess said, as if he had remarked on this. "Now go closer, touching nothing."

Not wanting to, he did. So he beheld the terrible marks on the neck. Somehow, these people had remolded the face, disguising the bulge of the eyes, resettling the tongue within the mouth.

"Who did this?" Rem said. But he had no image of the King's men somehow here and at the work.

"Val Nardia took her own life. She despaired. She had learned nothing."

Rem started round on the woman, a gutter expression nearly on his lips. But he saw it was not lack of pity, but pity itself which had prompted the callous-sounding phrase.

Instead he asked, "When did she do this to herself—yesterday? today?"

"Some months past," said the priestess quietly.

He began automatically to say that was not possible, and fell silent. At last he only said, "How have you preserved her like this?"

"Certain medicines, certain drugs. And yes, also methods the Vis would term magic. Things known to the ancient temples. But we don't abuse her, Rarmon. Her body is empty, the spirit free. We retain her bodily life only that the child shall also live. When the child is ready, it will be brought forth. All of her will have death's freedom then."

He had flinched at her use of his abreviated name almost more than at her use of the longer, older name. Sweat had broken out on him, though the room was cold.

"The child's important. Important to you."

"Important, certainly."

"Why? How do you know?"

She smiled. He was surprised, for they did not often smile, the pure-bred of her race. They had suffered so in the past, for centuries, maybe that was why. This smile said gently, scornfully: *You know our means.* But she said to him, spreading her hands in a gracious mimicry of Vis theater: "Anackire."

He glanced at the dead girl again, then away. Something was whispering in his brain, a memory he did not want, the brain-vision of three women, white-haired, dark-haired, scarlet, and of their wombs, which he had seen were filled.

"And the father," he said matter-of-factly.

"Return to him and tell him," she said, "what you've been shown, what I've spoken of."

"You know the father's her brother, then."

"As you, also, Rarmon, know it."

"Don't call me that."

"It is your name."

He felt sick. He needed to be away from the room and went to the doorway.

"Not anymore."

There were women in the outer chamber, he had not noted them before. Though nauseous, he was steadied now, as if by a blow, or icy water.

When they reached the upper passage, he said to her, for want of something else whereby to behave as if all this were normal, "I'll take his letter back to him then."

"As," she said, "the other message was also taken back."

Rem checked.

"From Suthamun?"

"From the King."

"Before me?"

"And left yesterday. A secret well-kept. But then, ours also. The King's messenger does not know all I have told you. Nevertheless, the King will have news of her death before the Prince hears of it."

Though he walked the rest of the distance through the under-temple, Rem was already running. He ran physically across the island and between the stripes of the rain. On the beach he fought a man, throwing him over and mashing his lips against his teeth, to get the boat back in the water.

Regaining land, he almost killed the first zeeba, and the second that he stole when purchase was refused him.

He had thought often, as he rode to Ankabek, of using this opportunity to be gone from Kesarh's service. There were other ports around the coast. He might have risked some leaky merchantman to Dorthar over the straits. But not now. Rem, between the attacking madness of visions, and the strangeness of the temple, had still seen them together, in the cell, on the hill, Kesarh and his sister. An exile from the landscape of heterosexual love, Rem had found himself now and then fascinated by the ethics of it, as by some rite he could comprehend yet never know, and never wish to know. It had the bizarre glamour of most alien things. The close relationship did not enter his calculations at all, save as a permissible theory for Val Nardia's suicide.

And Kesarh had looked at her, in his illness and in health, as Rem never saw him look at any other thing.

And the King would have news of her death before Kesarh.

Rem glimpsed now Suthamun might use it.

The mason was a muddy color, almost the shade of his light hair, which he' wore so proudly and fashionably long. Two soldiers had come on him at home, and brought him here, surreptitiously, by back ways, jollying him to dumbness, promising rewards while the edges of swords gleamed in the torchlight. The man in the chair was Kesarh Am Xai. The mason had never seen him, but had heard him described often enough. It seemed Kesarh had found out something about him, too. A couple of things, neither of which would be beneficial to the mason should others also learn of them.

"Am I to—to—believe I've been spied on, my lord?"

"If I were you, I'd believe it."

"But why—what possible interest could your lordship have—"

"The Ashara Temple," said Kesarh Am Xai. The mason gaped. "You're in charge of the restoration around the Eastern Cupola."

The mason nodded. He had been pleased to get this portion of the job, which carried kudos, and excellent fees if well done. The roof was being tended in several places since the storms had laid bare its weakness. But the Eastern Cupola was the trickiest spot; so much weight, so much ornament to be preserved.

"Someone," said Kesarh, "suggested that, if unattended, this area of the roof might have given way entirely. During snow, perhaps."

"Indeed—indeed, yes, lord Prince. Quite likely. The heavi-

ness and cold of the snow making brittle, overbalancing a structure already out of kilter. Very hazardous. Some of the ceiling
might have fallen into the temple itself.''

"When?" said Kesarh.

"When, my lord?"

"If unrepaired, when would this happen?"

"Already the repairs—''

"Indulge me.''

"Rest assured, Prince Kesarh. Even unrepaired, not for several more years.''

The mason did not want to meet Kesarh's dark Visian eyes,
but found he had to. Caught and held, he heard Kesarh say,

"You will see to it, sir, that not only the ceiling, but the
Eastern Cupola too, fall into the temple before the first month of
the siege snow is ended.''

The mason almost fainted. He had realized something was
coming. Not this.

"But, my lord—''

"The occasion," Kesarh went on smoothly, "will be some
religious observance, when the whole court is present. And the
King, and the King's brothers, naturally.''

The mason sank to his knees. His legs had given way, his
bowels and bladder almost. To be informed of all this would
mean he would be watched hereafter, under sentence of swift
death by Kesarh's men if he revealed or attempted to reveal any
of it. Nothing could have been more explicit. The eastern end of
the temple was the King's place, directly before the figure of the
goddess. If the Cupola fell, it would crush anything and everything beneath to powder—and pulp.

"I see you're pondering my ingenuous transparency, and what
it must entail.''

"But you'll kill me anyway," gasped the mason. "Even if I
could do it, how could I expect to live?''

"The baker who poisons his dough soon has no customers.
Let me amaze you: I deal honestly where I'm able. Those who
serve me are recompensed. Only those who displease or inconve-
nience me get their wage in pain. Your choice is simple. Agree
and benefit. Refuse, and have your sins revealed to all and
sundry. Thereby you'll lose your position, and perhaps end up in
the harbor, if I feel particularly insecure.''

The mason kneeled on the floor. He began to sob. Kesarh
watched him.

"How could it be done—timed to fall so exactly—''

"You'll have some help with that. Tomorrow someone will

come to your house to discuss the details. There can be no mistakes. Now get out. Your tears and urine about to spill on the floor won't enhance it.''

When the man was gone—there were several useful by-ways out of the new rooms—Kesarh walked through into the bedchamber.

The girl he had brought from Xai was staring at one of the gilded books left lying open. Of course, she could not read.

She looked up at his step, adoring him. She was not unattractive, wholesome, and had improved on the nourishing diet he had seen to it she now received. She was also a half-wit. The combination suited him. At this time he needed no one about him, even a slut in his bed, that he could not rely on.

He thought of Val Nardia. She would have the sense to do as he had written, feign some illness, not allow herself to be pried from the sanctuary.

Whenever he thought of her now, he felt a curious nothingness, as if some wounded nerve were deadened. He had drunk fire with her at Ankabek. It had exemplified all Zastis, that one night. And yet now, whenever she came to mind, only this lack of feeling came with her. Why? Was he sated there, as with all the others? No, it was not that.

He abandoned the reverie, and moved toward his safe little wine girl. There would be time, before the etiquette of dinner—

There was not time.

The spears clashed on the marble outside and there came rapping against the doors.

Suthamun had summoned him.

Kesarh had no more apprehension than at any other hour. He lived in a constant state of attentive self-guard, a sensitivity to peril, as an animal did. He found this neither pleasant nor unpleasant. He was used to it. It was, to him, synonymous with the nature of living. Other men who did not grasp this truth were sluggards, or imbeciles.

The kernel of Suthamun's blond court was gathered in one of the frescoed side chambers off the banquet hall.

It was the general scene, servitors padding about, hangers-on conniving or preening or sulking. By the fountain two of the council were discussing something as frivolous as Iolian chariot races. Kesarh nodded to them, and they bowed. The King stood with his brother Uhl and the scarred half-brother who was also a favorite. There was something unique. Kesarh took heed of it instantly. The usual loud music the Shansarian court so much enjoyed was absent.

Abruptly, Suthamun shouted clear across the room. "Kesarh!

Here to me." The tone was well-meaning, as it had been since
the recall from Xai. Those words of going, *Visian dog,* might
never have been uttered. Yet there was another element now. A
modulated depth, not unlike the timbre a priest assumed in some
holy declaration.

Kesarh began to walk forward. He looked unaltered, but his
wariness had now increased.

He was thirty paces away when Suthamun called out again in
the peculiar tone.

"Kesarh, I received ill news today. Ill news."

It flashed through Kesarh's brain that his own messenger and
the secret rider of the King had passed each other on the road;
that Val Nardia had already denied the invitation back to court
and here the denial was, about to be thrust at him, an accusation
dressed as a regret, maybe a request that he persuade her otherwise.

Suthamun now came toward him in turn. His face was
puckering, swollen with consternation. The crowd about the room
was noiseless, all eyes and ears. "Ill news," Suthamun repeated,
yet again.

Kesarh stopped and waited.

"I'm grieved to learn it, Sire."

"Alas. Your grief, your grief for sure. Word came to us not
two hours ago, from Ankabek. Your sister—" the voice rang,
hesitated.

Kesarh went on waiting.

"Your sister, the Princess Val Nardia, is dead."

Those closest to Kesarh saw his color go, like light blown out
in a lamp. That was all. He said nothing, and then the King
reached him, took his hand, in commiseration.

The murmur went round, and round again, and ended.

The King said loudly, "It offends me to add to your burden,
but there it is. Val Nardia hanged herself. She was with child—
She slew both herself and it. The goddess alone knows what
possessed her."

They had been speaking in Shansarian, of course.

It seemed to Kesarh as if he had never learned that tongue,
and now sentences were delivered to him without meaning. Yet
the room had faded to smoke, the floor disintegrated, gone. This
then was why, the nothingness, the death of the nerve, the
nightmare at Xai—

As if he had no control of his mind, a chain of creatures stole
across it. A little child, laughing, a young girl singing, blushing,
combing her hair, a young woman with her mouth yearning
toward his, her arms locked about him.

It should be possible to leave this place. But it was not possible. The deceptive smoke was treacherously full of people. An enemy gripped his hand, exalting. Now one must show decorous, suitable anguish. Nothing more.

She had hanged herself. Val Nardia. And a child, their—his child—

Probably his hands were cold, cold as the hands of certain men before they must kill another. Suthamun would feel the coldness in the hand he had taken. But the hand was also still. It did not tremble.

Kesarh returned the pressure of the King's palm.

"My lord," he said. His voice was eloquent, subdued, as ever excellently pitched. He had not, after all, forgotten the Shansarian language. "You show me too much care of me, taking it on yourself to bring me these tidings. I don't deserve your kindness. For my sister, I knew nothing of a child, nor do I know why she should do this to herself. The goddess has her now. Val Nardia is with Her, in Her all-cognizant forgiving arms. My sorrow will last my lifetime. I can scarcely express, my lord, how your solace, extended toward me at such a moment, moves me."

They whispered all about him in the smoke. He could have smiled. Suthamun let him go. Kesarh knew his eyes had not left the eyes of the King. Kesarh knew that his eyes shouted louder than the King's histrionics. Let Suthamun read what he liked there. Soon it could no longer matter.

She passed like music through the air, her pale gown reflecting in a polished floor, her blood-red hair.

She passed with flowers, ten years old, her little breasts already blooming through her dress, a doll trailing from her hand. *"Kesarh, where are you? I couldn't find you."*

Val Nardia.

He drank wine with them, and went to eat with them. He ate. He discussed other topics, rationally. They gave him margins for his seemly grave distress. They condoled, they praised her beauty, and he thanked them with great courtesy.

He wanted to tear them apart, scraps of skin, bits of bone.

It would be seemly also to beg the King's leave to retire early, but not too early. She was a woman, not even his wife or mother, less than a comrade, father, brother, son—Though perhaps he had lost a son, too, did they but know it.

At exactly the correct time, he begged leave, got it, and left.

In the second black hour of morning, Rem came to the doors of the new apartments. He showed the soldiers, two of the

Sevens, Kesarh's authorization, and got himself let in. Rem had gone too long in a saddle and too long without sleep. He had become sure he was also too late, yet the impetus of the attempt not to be, failed to let up until he knew.

Arriving in the first chamber, he found out. Lamps still burned on their stand, describing the shards of a smashed wine jar. Against the wall a girl huddled, the Xaian girl, Berinda, her cow-calf eyes all unquestioning misery. She said nothing. Rem moved to the inner door and knocked. There was no sound. Rem opened the door and walked through, and presently into the bedchamber.

There were no lights here, only the moon coming in through the window. Against that, the straight male outline of Kesarh was immediately to be seen.

"It's Rem, my lord."

"I know it's Rem. You wouldn't have got in past the guard if you were anyone else. They don't fall asleep. None of you do, after ten lashes."

The voice was the same, constant. "My lord, I tried to reach you before the King—"

"I'm sure you did." There was a pause. Kesarh said, "Where did they bury her?"

Rem could be sure of nothing. He was too tired to be able to assess. It had to be told.

"My lord, did anyone mention there was a pregnancy?"

"Yes. They mentioned that."

"The priests there, they think they can bring it to term."

Kesarh was silent, immobile.

"Somehow," said Rem, "they've preserved the body. They claim they can preserve her till the baby's grown, then birth it. It's some kind of drug-witchery. Probably lies. It looked real enough, as if it might happen as the woman said."

"All right," Kesarh replied, as if everything that had just been related were feasible. But then, "I'll go there. He'll expect me to, be pleased, think I'm no holiday in grief, idle—I'll see to it. You did what you could. Get out now."

"My lord. Did you understand—"

"No. It's gibberish like everything else. Get out."

"My lord—"

"By the nonexistent stinking pits of Aarl get out. Go straddle your whore-boy or eviscerate your shrew of a mother. Anything. Away from me." Kesarh had hardly lifted his voice, but he had turned. There was a piece of the smashed jar in his hand and he was working his fingers around and around it, fluid showing dark, wine or blood. The moon gave just enough illumination. He was crying. Not couthly, detached as his stance and his diction had been, but messily and completely as a child.

Rem backed a step, recollected, and turned round to walk out of the door.

As he shut it, he heard Kesarh briefly laugh, despising him.

In the end, no one investigated Ankabek. The King, it seemed, wished to keep Kesarh near him, to comfort and sustain the Prince. Suthamun gave no sign if Kesarh's resilience annoyed him. The King had learned the game, or thought he had, and played it now with all the interest of an intriguing hobby.

Kesarh did not speak of Val Nardia in public, in private did not ask again for her burial place, or query the tale of Lowland witchcraft, the hypothesis of a child growing in the stasis of a live-dead womb. The King's own messenger had been given some notion of a modest stone marking her ashes, near the temple precinct. To the worshippers of the goddess suicide was neither a sinful nor an honorable recourse. No stigma had added itself. For a minor female aristocrat sufficient had been done.

Kesarh appeared to accept both the King's patronage and the blank wall of death. He was thought, by many not directly initiate, to be the current royal favorite. His displayed but disciplined bereavement was admired.

Several days after the headlong ride back from Ankabek, walking through the lower city, Rem met Doriyos, guarded by the elderly tortoise from the House of Three Cries. Doriyos came up to him and stood slim and well-mannered before him, and said, "I never see you anymore."

Rem smiled, mostly at Doriyos' beauty, which shone like a lamp in the sallow day.

"I'm sorry for that."

"Sorry for me, or for yourself?"

Rem smiled.

Doriyos said simply, "You're in love with him, then."

Rem stopped smiling.

Doriyos said, "I mean, with your lord. Your Prince."

"Wake up," said Rem. "Stop talking like some coy girl. That was what I had you to avoid."

Doriyos cast down his eyes. "And you learn, too, the speech of the beloved."

Rem walked on and left him standing there, his light slowly dimming, like the last summer sky.

*   *   *

The skies turned to slate and bore great winds. Then to grayness and to stillness. The skies became low ceilings of gentle ivory from which there parasoled the pitiless fore-taste of the snow.

Raldnor Am Ioli propped with practiced ease a column of the covered walk, inwardly admiring himself, in his furs, the bright pallor of his hair, against the backdrop of a snowy garden.

When the first flecks drifted into Istris, he had found himself once more at the outer fringes of high society. With the first thaw, on the fringes of the court itself. Now the second snow, the three-month-siege snow, was down, the city Lowland-white, and ice creaking in the harbor. And Raldnor had strolled through the royal gardens in chat with a significant official. Pausing here among the columns, he had already seen the Warden of the council slowly patrolling on his own constitutional. When the man came level, they would exchange a few polite words.

Raldnor was pleased with himself. He had aided Kesarh, taken indeed a mighty risk for him, but it had turned out well advised. Kesarh had that mark on him, that devastating escutcheon of natural advantage. His ruthlessness, his magnetic personal power, exercised at will, effortlessly, were sure symptoms of greatness.

King-Maker. That was a title for Raldnor to toy with.

He had added his own revenues to help buy the council. They were all amenable now, predisposed. Kesarh's own gold, so marvelous to those who had reckoned him in poverty, had sprung it seemed from a careful use of reliable bankers, and trade ventures that had brought in consistent though concealed profits. The business had been initiated by Kesarh at the age of thirteen. That was impressive enough. Impressive too he had, even as a boy, not squandered anything, lived as if poor in truth, letting the monies grow, never showing he had wealth until it would be opportune.

The Warden was nearly level now. A half-blood Vardish Vis, as Raldnor himself, but dark in looks: Suthamun's sop to the people.

"Good day, lord Warden."

"Good morning. A cold one."

"All we'll get now, my lord, until the spring."

The Warden had paused, his clerk at his back, his guard farther off. Others patrolling the walk would note whom the Warden of Istris stopped beside.

"I must thank you for the wine, Raldnor. A very welcome

vintage in this weather." Raldnor bowed. The two unmentioned jars in which the wine had gone were banded with precious metals and gems. "And tomorrow we give thanks for a new heir," said the Warden. "The blessing of Ashkar, to replace lamentation for the loss of a son so quickly with hymns of joy at the birth of another."

"Yes, indeed."

They stood solemnly, considering the blessing of Ashkar.

The boy-child had been born on the first day of the siege snow, to one of Suthamun's lofty Shansarian wives. In antique Dortharian belief, that would be the soul of Jornil returning. Tomorrow, the whole court must roll their chariots through the whiteness to the Ashara Temple, where the repairs upon the roof had been just now suspended until spring. Skeletons of scaffolding reared from the heights, like an extraordinary forest. Levers and cantilevers held all supported and secure.

"I shall drink a cup of your good wine before setting out," said the Warden. "The temple, I think, won't be warm."

He passed on, leaving Raldnor Am Ioli satisfied. Raldnor himself would not be at the temple ceremony. There was no particular reason for this absence. For the King-Maker had, in this respect, been told nothing at all.

The wind was blowing in across the bay, and smoking snow flared along the streets. The royal household struggled through it. Shansarian horses trapped in gold slid on carpets of ice.

Inside, the temple was unwarm, as predicted, its lamps tilting to the wind. But Ashara, balanced on her burnished fish-tail at the temple's eastern end, and clothed only in carven hair, did not feel the cold.

For a child, no blood was shed, but perfumes. A soaring window of thickly colored glass threw down its lights into the pillars of incense, through which the new heir was now brought, quieted by soporifics, to be shown to the goddess.

Suthamun stood in the shadow of her four right hands, Uhl and the younger brothers beside him, and near them their sons, the chosen nobles. The Prince Kesarh had by many been expected to stand there with them, close to the King. But Kesarh had effected the same mistake twice. Until now decorous and modest, all at once he had made it plain, as when he had come back from Tjis, that he anticipated favor. Some remark had casually been let slip concerning his placement in the temple. Suthamun, softly this time as velvet, had seen to it the Prince Kesarh was requested to stand farther off.

The ceremony, which in Shansar would have been conducted on open rock or in some hut before the totem, having gathered clutter, dragged.

Amid the chants, a dull crack of sound far above went unheard by several. Of the royal party, only Prince Uhl glanced upward, instinctively; those who watched saw Suthamun smile, shaking his head. He, like most others, took the noise for a solitary blotting of the wind against some loose strut of scaffolding. The state of the roof had earlier been viewed by palace officials, and it was safe. Among the scatter of other heads raised, the Prince Kesarh's did not number. Though he had heard the sound, he knew perfectly well what it was.

Perhaps five minutes later, another sound began, however, which caused the chanting of the priests to stumble. At first almost inaudible but gradually burgeoning, it was a strange rushing, like that of water. A stream of powder sprinkled down out of the air and across the altar.

Very few now did not look up. Unblemished, the pale dome above the goddess' head showed signs only of permanence. Then came a colossal bang. Women wailed. Shouts rang out. And from the square beyond the doors cries arose. A hill of snow had poured down the surface of the temple roof, crashing to the ground. Almost immediately the concourse of people recognized the frightful blow for what it was, although such shifts did not normally occur until the spring thaw. A wave of reaction flowed through the gathering. Suthamun was seen to smile again, as he leaned forward under the goddess' hands.

And then another woman shrieked.

There was just the space for that, and for a sudden veining to appear like a web in the dome. Then the dome cracked like eggshell. In white thunder, the eastern roof dropped into the temple.

Tons of masonry fell, descending like a driven bolt, and, striking earth, splashed out again in all directions. Missiles hit stone and flesh. The great colored window was riven.

The cacophony of screams, terror and agony, mingled with a muffled continuous after-rumble. The powder dust stood, a wavering column from floor to sky. Very little could be seen through it, only the blundering of figures, the isolated lick of fire from smashed lamps, and above them a horrible impious thing— the goddess Ashara with half her head torn away, in silhouette against the cold open void now skewered in the broken window.

It was the Prince Kesarh, his forehead bleeding from a shallow gash, who called his own men into instantaneous action.

Suthamun's slight had set Kesarh well outside the major zone of impact. Now he seemed shocked to life while others about him could only gaze or crawl or invoke their gods, some of whom were not Ashara.

Kesarh led the twenty of his guard who were in the temple straight into the smothering flour-like dust. Presently, from the corners of the precinct, men ran to help them. Nobles hauled at the smashed enormous debris, bloody, coughing, dusty, with the common soldiers. Kesarh himself worked like one possessed, in an icy fever. Some of the blocks were not to be lifted by men alone, they would require zeebas. Slaves erupted from the temple. A dreadful generalized outcry came from everywhere.

All they could find at first were dead. Uhl lay on the altar, his skull squashed like a fruit, and the officiating priest next to him. The child, the new heir, had been hammered beneath them.

Suthamun, when Kesarh's men lifted away the broken beams which had obscured his face, was still alive.

Kesarh went quickly to him and knelt down. An incredible weight lay on the King's chest. Black blood ran thinly from his mouth. His eyes turned sluggishly toward the Prince.

"Have courage, my lord. They're fetching a team of zeebas to raise the stone."

The column of powder was lessening now. Through the swirl of it, those uninjured or only slightly harmed were creeping near. The dreadful outcry was sinking to a dreadful anguished murmur without words.

Kesarh maintained his vigil by the King until teams of beasts were led along the aisles, profaning the sanctuary. Then he rose and assisted in the work of haulage.

As suspected, no other who had been at the central point under the eastern dome had survived. The four younger brothers of the King were barely recognizable. The scarred half-brother had been struck down by a falling hand of the goddess Herself. Suthamun was uncovered, and seeing his wounds, it was apparent he too could not continue for long. It was actually unapparent how he might still persist.

They rested his head tenderly on cushions so he might lie and look up at the jagged vault of sky. A sick priest came, and whispered prayers. Kesarh knelt again. The crowd watched, and the window mouthed the snowy wind.

After a while, Suthamun died.

If he had guessed anything at all, he had not been enabled to voice it. And Kesarh, annointed with his own blood, kneeling with such grace and such steadfast strength by the man he had killed—not one who saw him forgot how he was, the galvanic rescue attempt, the nobleness inherent in each line of his compassion.

But beyond everything, the omen loomed.

It seemed Ashara herself had flung her malediction against Suthamun and his house. It could hardly have been more clear.

Only the engineers themselves knew the truth. The cavity which had been made beneath the upper roofing, hidden from the eyes of searchers, and the small fire which had been left smoldering with the pot of oil a supported and mathematically devised distance above. It had all been mathematically coordinated, with the skill of men familiar with the values and forms of architecture, and of men knowledgeable in methods of carnage. When the oil exploded, a fire took out the carefully balanced underpinning of the Cupola. The way it had been nurtured, it had needed only that to hold it firm, only the destruction of that to fall. It seemed merely negligence was responsible, and weather, or fate. Or Ashara.

An interview was, despite superstition, sought with the mason and those men who had worked on the eastern roof. None of them were to be found. It was assumed they had fled, quite sensibly, out of the way of justice.

The council was seated in the map-chamber, under the mosaic.

Outside, across the city, the funeral bells still clanged, and on the height of the palace the funeral beacon, barely put out it seemed, once more gouged the twilight with its reddened eye. Suthamun's second wife, the mother of the baby which had died with him, had mortally stabbed herself an hour later. They were brave, the women of Shansar, if impetuous. She had been laid beside her husband on the pyre, the infant in her arms. The brothers were consumed a score of feet away. It was a family affair.

Now Istris waited, and all Karmiss beyond her walls, to hear who should take up the reins of power. The potential King, of course, was known. It was to be the most mature heir, the seven-year-old Prince Emel. But seeing he was a child, there must be a regent, and all the legal guardians, Uhl and his brothers, and the oldest legal sons of these brothers, had been killed with Suthamun. It was truly a catastrophe of epic proportions. Now the choice stood between a bevy of bastards or lesser sons, men very young in years themselves, and popularly unknown. Men who had never looked for anything and who had made no mark in any sector of the city's political life.

There had been argument, some of it heated. It was mooted that the lord Warden himself might take the traditional step to the regency his position had allowed others in the past. There were instant raucous jeers from the edges of the room, where those men who had bought a place at the council, supporters of this or that faction, objected. But for the most part, these bystanders were partisan noise-mongers and little else. The Warden silenced them, and declared he had no aptitude for a regency, and no appetite either.

At this point, a figure pushed through the press, signaling he wished to speak.

Shansarian customs of tribal council had altered the format of the Karmian institution. In Vis times such free-lancing would have been unacceptable. But the Warden beckoned.

"We grant you the floor, Raldnor Am Ioli."

Raldnor stepped out on to it, and looked round. He was used to commanding a ship, when granted one; this doghouse did not bother him in the least.

"My lord Warden. Gentlemen. At the commencement of Zastis, seven Zakorian pirate galleys were ravaging the Karmian and Dortharian coasts. King Suthamun, a wise and canny master, sent a man he trusted to rid the seas of them. Not aware of the Free Zakorian strength, he gave him for the work three ships, nor of the best. I know. I captained one. When we learned what we were up against, I was for sailing home. But my commander, Kesarh Am Xai, held us where we were, and with ingenuity and valor, the sacrifice of one listing ship, and the loss of five men—*five*, gentlemen—won us the day." There was a noise of approval now, scarcely any of it paid for, especially from the Vis in the chamber. "Forgive my enthusiasm," said Raldnor. "I was impressed. Remain so. The Prince Kesarh is a mature leader, known to Istris by elite report, and by sight. He is, moreover, of royal blood. His father was a Shansarian officer. His mother was a princess of the Karmian royal house, whose roots go back to the time of Visian Rarnammon—"

Raldnor broke off as a shout went up all around the chamber. It was the old cry—*Am Xai*. Raldnor mused, standing in the thick of it, hearing dimly behind the racket the screeches of roasting slaves chained to their oars. It was a point to remember. Once you were of no use to him, he would leave you to burn.

The council was bustling, conferring. They had undoubtedly known, simply been waiting for the proper cue. Three at least had been frankly bought.

Presently they withdrew to the privacy of another chamber to deliberate.

Raldnor went on musing, perambulating the corridors without, as others were doing. Even musicians had been called to play in one of the rooms, a deferential lament harmonizing with the bells, still music.

The stroke of ill-luck which had brought the end to Suthamun's current dynasty was peculiar. Ashkar's doing?

Raldnor, who believed in chance, did not however believe in *this* chance. That he had been excluded from the astonishing plot annoyed him and left him with a feeling of relief. He had sense enough, he thought, to demonstrate neither emotion.

The bells had stopped and it was nearly midnight when a train of messengers raced through the halls.

The loiterers, alerted, crowded back toward the map-chamber. The council filed in. The lord Warden nodded to them all.

"The Prince-King Emel has been summoned. It's late for the child, but by the laws of our Sister Continent, his fatherland, he must be present." There was a pause. "We have also," said the Warden, "sent for the Prince Am Xai."

Not long after, a sleepy blond child, bemused but well-schooled, was led to the doors by his nurses, and from there into the chamber by two of his guard. The Prince-King Emel sat where he was asked to sit, and graciously accepted a sweetmeat from the Warden.

It was an hour later that Kesarh arrived.

He walked into the council, the crowd giving way for him, like a creature of silent thunder, his black clothes, his black hair blown from riding, his face distraught. He had remained behind at the site of the King's pyre with those other mourners who would stand vigil there all night.

"Your pardon, Prince Kesarh, that we called you from the death-watch."

"I can go back," Kesarh said.

There was a little whispering. Raldnor of Ioli listened, awe-struck despite himself. The man's theater was incomparable. His entrance, his looks, his voice, had carried them all.

"Yes, my lord. You can go back. First I must ask you, in the Name of the goddess and by the will of this council of Istris, if you will act regent for Emel son of Suthamun, until he shall be of sufficient years to assume the throne of Karmiss?"

There was no answer. The stillness went on and on, Kesarh at the center of it like a sword.

The interval in sound awoke the child, who had fallen asleep on a stool. He raised his lids, and saw across from him a tall man like a shadow. Then the shadow moved. It came toward Prince Emel. At the final instant it kneeled at his feet. Emel recollected, and he got up.

As the words of assent buzzed in the air, Emel waited to go back to bed, drowsily looking at the shining black mane of the man who would be his death.

SIX

A marble world.

As the months of the long snow continued, the landscape was sculpted to them, seeming incapable of change. Windless, white, the silver lace of ice in all her bays, Karmiss lay as if asleep.

The new lodgings Rem had taken, however, though spacious, were kept warm. There were even nocturnal companions, comely and skillful, who might be hired from a nearby wine-shop, if one felt the need. Rem found himself prey to an intermittent nostalgia for Doriyos. Now and then, Rem visualized returning to the House of Three Cries, but knew he would never do so.

There had been an alternation of Rem's status in the Prince Am Xai's personal guard. In the wake of the Festival of Masks, his pay was splendidly augmented. Then, five days after the wild ride back from Ankabek, too late to be of service, there had come a metamorphosis of position. Rem ceased to be a number. There were thirteen Nines, at this juncture, and he was no longer one of them. He was all at once in charge of fifty men who would, in the name of the Prince, answer solely to Rem. The advancement was welded to, yet apart from, the hierarchy of the guard, the membership of which had currently escalated to over two hundred. The guard sergeant who had lashed Rem now greeted him with respectful equality.

Rem, acknowledging these novel conditions, was far from complacent. Mostly, he had been required to organize escorts.

At regular intervals, autonomously, he exercised in the under-palace, sword and shield, body combat, or those coordinating arms it could be fatal to mislay. A couple of times he would find the Prince himself also at exercise. On the first day of the siege snow, Kesarh had called Rem into the court instead of one of the paid masters. Stripped to the minimum, they fought for thirty minutes. The sexual element, forever intrinsic yet forever irrelevant to such contests, angered Rem. In the end the anger won him the bout. He sent Kesarh sprawling, half stunned.

Kesarh seemed amused. Rem knew the Prince had merely permitted his concentration to flag. Rem had seen how Kesarh could fight even in sham. The victory was a mean one. Almost an insult.

When the eastern roof of the Ashara Temple crushed Suthamun and his peers, Rem was not in the building, not even on duty in the square outside. He had realized something was prepared, had known there must *be* something. But the magnitude of it shook him.

He was ordered to captain a detachment of Kesarh's guard during the funeral procession and the ghastly Shansarian death-watch. Slow-striding after the purple-draped chariot through the snow, he had felt the same sort of affront as at the insulting victory in the exercise court. Somehow, it had all been too easy. And when the messengers came floundering over the torch-lit ice to summon Kesarh to the council, Rem stood expressionless, wanting to laugh or curse, something, anything, to acclaim the grandiose and sinister triteness of it all.

But Am Xai was regent now. His secret guard were official, every one of them. His apartments had once more improved, transmuted to the upper palace, with all that implied.

In a stretch of months, he had traveled a vast distance. Answerable at last only to the predisposed council, and to a seven-year-old child who, if the stories were accurate, worshipped him.

He would kill the child. That much was obvious.

How long would he let it exist? A year? Two years? How much of life would the Prince-King Emel be allowed to know, before some unforeseen mishap rendered all valueless?

Any idea of sentiment for infancy or kindred would be a nonsense, now.

Since the night he came back from Ankabek, Rem had detected no trace of grief or unease about his master. The public lament for Val Nardia had been perfect and quite false. Yet the anguish Rem had interrupted must still be there, somewhere, surely? The gnawing worm known only to Kesarh's most private privacy.

And the weird sorcery at Ankabek—had Kesarh dismissed that, as he had seemed to, as Rem could not?

For despite all reasoning and explanation, he believed still what the golden woman had told him. That across miles of snow and frigid water, under the frozen ground, in the cold womb of one dead, the first fruit of their incest, Kesarh's, Val Nardia's, their incest and their obsessive love, mindlessly swelled toward awakening.

Waiting in the antechamber of the Prince's apartments, Rem knew he was here because of Ankabek. He felt a kind of urgency, sifted with oppression, heavy on the air.

Yet Kesarh did not come in for some while.

In the interim a physician passed through the room, on his way from the women's suite. The girl Kesarh had brought from Xai, Berinda, had conceived during Zastis. Rem had seen her about, walking with a proud, bewildered big-belliedness. Yesterday she had begun labor pains long before her time. Gossip said she would lose the baby. It would be stillborn. She was simple, not fit to bear. All this was like some perverse omen, distorted echo—of that other thing, on the island.

Through a long window, Rem could look into the colonnade across the wide court below. Presently he saw Kesarh pass with the Prince-King. Emel was excited, giggling, his pale skin rosy.

Rem turned from the window with a grimace.

A few minutes later Kesarh entered, his darkness softened by the purple of Karmian mourning, worn for Suthamun as never for Val Nardia.

They went into an inner room.

As the doors closed, Kesarh altered. Rem recognized he was seeing the Prince's private face, or some of it.

"Ankabek," said Kesarh. "Do you remember, months ago?"

"Yes, my lord."

"Tell me again what you told me that night."

"You didn't credit it, my lord."

"No. Tell me again."

So Rem told him, more fully than before, of the priestess, what she had said to him, and what he had been shown.

Kesarh let him go all through it, watching him. The private face was still, and dangerous. Afraid?

Rem concluded. There was a gap. Then Kesarh walked to a chest, unlocked it, took a paper. Turning, he held out the paper to Rem.

"Read it."

Rem did so.

"They sent—"

"A man. Anonymous. He came to my sergeant and left this with him. It seems he knew the proper channels. How?"

"Not from me, my lord."

"No. I didn't think it was from you."

"It says—"

"It says my child will be born at sunrise, on the day of the Lion-Feast, Shansarian calendar."

"Nine mornings from today."

"It would take at least seven days to get there. If anyone was fool enough to travel such a distance in the snow."

"Which gives a day or so in hand for your lordship to make suitable excuses."

"Doesn't it. Judged to within a hair's breadth. They obviously expect me to go."

Rem kept silent.

Kesarh poured himself wine, then drained the goblet straight down to the dregs. He had drunk from the jug rather in that way at Tjis, after the serpent. His back was to Rem now. He said, "I want you here. Awake and alert for anything. Raldnor can play with Istris awhile. I hope for his sake he doesn't get a taste for it. The Warden will cover my place. You'll set your men where and how you have to, to see everything is done in fair order. And to take note of anything I might not care for. Is this clear?"

"Yes, sir."

"How fortunate you were once the strategist-leader of a promising little band of cutthroats." Kesarh turned again, smiling at him with great charm. "And how fortunate, too, you deserted them for me."

Rem stood like a stone. The interview appalled him, for reasons he failed quite to grasp. Certainly Kesarh's private face was gone now, simply the grayness left in it, which might only be reaction to the weather. Shansarian blood disliked the bitter temperatures of this clime. One recalled occasionally, he was part Shansar.

"I'll be taking ten or twelve men. Enough to manage a boat. I'd rather have you with me. But in my absence, I need you here."

Once again, the unerring stab of casual and deadly trust.

Gratuitously, Rem responded to its blazon.

Just then, an awful screaming broke out somewhere inside the walls. His hand went to his dagger but Kesarh pushed the hand free.

"It's only that poor little bitch from Xai. They must have told her her child's dead." Kesarh hesitated. Something moved behind his eyes, and then was gone.

To make a journey to his sister's grave was eccentric for the season, but pardonable, estimable, perhaps. It showed a certain naïveté.

He would never have done it, risked leaving his prize even in the lacuna of the snow, save something drove him. An absurdity. Though he knew she was dead, he had never known it. She lived on for him, somewhere, unextinguished. Ankabek was at odds with both these feelings—the certainty of her death, the intuitive rejection of her death.

Whatever grisly witchcraft they worked on her, he would end that. Or was she, somehow, impossibly alive again, as she had never been anything else? It rode with him, on his back like a devil, as the horse his regency had brought him thrust its way, often breast-high in whiteness, toward the coast.

By killing herself she had won his contempt, his horror and his hatred. Their telepathy, haphazardly conveyed from the Shansarian side, had remained undeveloped, yet it was there; from birth, a part of them. He did not recognize it, had never considered it. Even when he woke at Xai crying out, or after, when he recalled that wakening. Nevertheless, Val Nardia had forced him, through the fact of that telepathy, to participate in her death.

The guilt for her death was another matter. That he accepted, shrugging it behind him, branded by it.

For the rest of his days he would carry that, the mirror of her terrified flight whereby to see himself, what she had fled from.

They led him into an unimportant room under the temple.

"Well," he said.

A Lowland woman stood before him. She seemed to be the one from Rem's narrative, but she was not dressed as she had dressed for Rem. Her garments were plain, only the violet gem on her brow to indicate anything.

"My lord Prince," she said, "you're here in good time."

"Tomorrow's sunrise, according to your instructions. And if I'd been delayed?"

"It did not seem," she said, "you would be."

There was nowhere to sit. He leaned on the wall and the melting snow slid from the shoulders of his cloak. The trees had cast it down on him as he walked over the island, though the air was becalmed like the sea.

"I'd like to know your name," he said conversationally.

"Eraz, my lord."

"Ah. The name of the hero Raldnor's foster mother."

"I was born in Hamos."

"The hero's foster village. Now a large town, I gather."

"A room has been prepared for you, in the precinct of the novitiate."

Suddenly he remembered her himself. This was the bitch who had led him to his sister, like a veritable madam, that last night—*"How much do you want for this? Or is it to be a gift to the temple?" "The only gift which is required will be given."* He would have remembered sooner, but his eyes were dazzled from eight days' snowscapes, aching from that and lack of sleep, his whole body dull with weariness.

"First," he said, "I'd like to see my sister, the Princess Val Nardia." He paused and said, without any expression, "Why did you tell Suthamun she was dead? To protect her?"

"She is dead, my lord."

"Oh no. Dead women don't bear."

"I'm sorry to prolong your distress, my lord Prince—"

"Don't worry about my distress. Worry about whether or not I decide to put your bloody temple to the torch."

"No," she said softly, "you won't do that. You have built your reputation high in Karmiss. Such an unpopular deed would destroy all you had worked for."

"All right. Just you, then. An official burning. Premature Lowland burial rites. When your unholy sorcery is exposed."

"The Lord Kesarh doesn't believe in sorcery."

"That's true. But you could try to convince me."

"Then follow."

So he let himself be led again. Yet when they got there, a curtain of figured gauze stretched midway across the room.

"No farther, my lord."

"What's to stop me, aside from the drapery?"

"Little. But you would kill your child."

"Assuming I accept there is a child."

"Assuming you accept there may be a child."

It was possible to see through the gauze to a shadowed bed. What lay there was hidden. Incense braziers burned about the bed, as they had burned in the chambers outside. Priests had let them in, priestesses passed quietly up and down between the smokes and the flimsy screens of veiling. It had been exotic but insignificant. None of Rem's deep-seated, passionless awe had communicated.

"On a concealed bed," said Kesarh, "there could be anything. A peasant girl, perhaps, near term, brought on by your drugs."

Eraz raised her left hand, and the heavy drapes about the bed started suddenly to furl upwards. A showy bit of conjuring, obviously, some lever in the floor, or unseen accomplices.

The curtaining, then its shadow, left the bed.

Kesarh said nothing. For a long time he merely stood, gazing at the figure of his sister as she lay in her black robe, her scarlet hair. Her belly rose, great with its prisoner, her hands like white flowers spilled either side, and, at the robe's black edge, the upturned stars of her feet.

Eraz had laid her fingers lightly on his arm. He became aware he had moved abruptly forward. "Not yet, my lord."

"What are you doing?" he said. The words, unpremeditated, unclever, hung in the nothingness.

"Magic, if you wish. The will of the goddess."

"Damn your goddess. She's dead—you say she's dead?"

"She is dead. It is the child which lives, and with the turn of the tide, the breaking of the dawn, the child will be brought forth."

"Why?"

"Because Anackire wills it."

"Why Val Nardia's child? Mine?" He heard his own voice. It made no sense. He asked questions which did not matter to him. There were other things, but he did not know them to ask.

"Children of one womb and one birth," she said. "A double being reunited, creating a third. A gateway. In spirit, it is not actually your child, lord Prince. It is another child, older. But still a child of a double being, two who are one. One that is two. I can't convince you, my lord. Let someone take you to the prepared room. Rest there."

"Here," he said. "I'll stay here. Have them bring a couch, some food. Here. I shan't leave this place until you work your magic."

"You're tired. It shall be done as you want."

He caught her wrist. The grip must have hurt her, it was meant to. Through the mist of the temporary snow-blindness, her eyes shone like distant flames.

"Whatever you owe your goddess, try to recall who *I* am."

But she did not reply, and somehow she slipped from him and was gone. She had vanished before, the blown-out candle—How ridiculous it was. All of it unreal. Even alone, seeing Val Nardia before him, he could not now break through the flimsy gauze.

They brought seating, food and drink. He had left his men at the village. He required the priests to taste the food for him, and the wine. It was a pedantic insurance, he did not really suppose it necessary.

He took the refreshment sparingly, not meaning to fall asleep. And gradually his trained body, like an obedient dog, responded to his demands. Wide awake, he sat and watched Val Nardia through the blurring of his sight and the curtain.

At midnight, so he judged it, hooded black-robes began to file into the chamber. There they perched against the walls, motionless, like comatose birds of prey. Then the women came. They passed across the curtain and hid everything from him.

Kesarh rose, but they made way for him at once. He went back and stood by the gauze.

The priestesses entered, and between them another woman not of the temple, presumably from the village near the landing, or some other habitation on the island. She was a Vis, sheer Vis from the look of her. At the curtain she halted, to leave her shoes lying on the ground, and to throw off her dress before them all. Under it she was naked, a matron in her late middle years, of no attractions, but strongly made. The curtain parted. He could not quite distinguish the seam, but the woman stepped through. No others. Only she. And only her flesh, no other thing, to pollute or disrupt the vacuum of the spell.

Chanting started now, all round him. It irritated Kesarh. Its insistence on some word or group of words, over and over.

The light was going down. Everything was murky.

The woman had approached his sister. It occurred to him what she must be: a midwife for the dead.

He stood at the curtain and watched as nothing at all happened.

After maybe an hour of watching this, he went to the table and took more wine, to keep himself on his feet. When the monstrous lightning flash happened he wanted to witness it. To know when the trap-door allowed them to send through the alien child, soon to be presented to him, from between his sister's dead legs, as his own miraculous offspring.

The prelude to the light woke one of Kesarh's twelve men, and vacating the chilly village bivouac, he went to urinate.

Beyond a walled yard, the slope ran into space. Below, the sea smoldered on the beach of stones. The soldier, eased, but cursing with the cold, was yet arrested by some quality either of strangeness or unrecognized beauty in the dawn.

He walked to the low wall, and looked out along the straits into the east.

Clouds hung like a puff of icy breath at the horizon, just turning the shade of milky amber. Through this amber a slip of palest gold now pushed its way.

Emanations of the cloud had muted the disc of the sun. The man could look directly at it as it rose, round and luminous and curious, like some new planet born from the world. Indeed, this was what the sunrise resembled, the birth of a child, the round head emerging from a womb of cloud.

The man did not know why they had been dragged to Ankabek. Some duty, they had heard, to the Prince's sister's tomb—that surely could have waited till the thaw.

Yet the dawn held him there, in the snow-locked silence, feeling himself the sole human thing awake on the earth that saw the coming of the sun.

The chanting had stopped. Something had happened, but he was not sure. Had he slept after all on his feet, and missed it?

Then he saw the village woman bending forward. The room seemed to shake with a kind of noiseless thunder he did not know was Power.

The unlovely hands were thrusting, inside Val Nardia's immobile body—The midwife bent to her task, rough, capable and indifferent.

There was a welter of blood. Kesarh's own breathing seemed to choke him. He expected the girl to shriek or spasm, but she was still, as if . . . she felt nothing.

The child came out in the woman's hands. He saw it. Amid the scald of blood, the dancing cord joining it yet to the recesses of his sister's body. There was the glint of a knife. The cord, severed, fell down like the dying snake at Tjis.

The midwife did something to the child, then turned and held it out toward all those behind the gauze.

There was no sound.

The arms of the child were moving slowly, and the head. It lived, though it did not cry. It was very white, as if luminous. Kesarh's eyes seemed to have cleared. He could perceive the fruit of his seed and of Val Nardia's dead womb was female. A daughter.

In the door, the priestess Eraz stood momentarily in his way.

"Yes," he said. "I saw it happen. I'm the witness to your sorcery."

"One will take you to the room now, where you can rest."

He could hardly keep his balance, though he saw her with sharp clarity. "And when I wake up," he said, "I may wring your neck."

In the village above the beach, Kesarh's well-disciplined soldiers kicked their heels, and attempted to pay for the food they were brought, as instructed. But the payment was left lying. Nor did they offer any violence to the women of the area, though there was nothing else to do.

As the day began to go, they regretted they would have to spend a second night in the wretched dump.

Kesarh had other plans for them.

He was awake, dressed for traveling and drinking the wine left him, when the priest entered his room.

"Good," said Kesarh. "Go find Eraz, and send her here."

The priest, a dark man, looked at him. He had learned the way of looking that the Lowlanders had.

Kesarh observed it, then said, "Either you do it, or I do it. I think you'd all prefer the former."

"Generally," said the man, then, "the priestess Eraz is not summoned like a common serving-wench."

"And generally I'm not kept hanging about."

"My lord," said the priest, "in this religion, a priest is the equal of a king. Or the greater."

Kesarh crossed the room. He struck the priest a blow that sent him staggering. The hood slipped away. For a moment, only a cowering Vis lurched in the corner.

"But you see," said Kesarh, "I don't value your religion. Now get out and do as I told you. And while you're at it, have them fetch me some decent wine."

Eraz brought the wine herself, a curious almost playful addendum to the comparision with a serving-wench. It was Vardian liquor, some of the kind that had undone the Free Zakorians.

"The wine of the Shadowless Plains is not to your liking," she said.

"No. I like nothing from there."

He was restored, or seemed so. There was no mark of exhaustion on him, no hint of pain or unease.

"And you'll be leaving us shortly."

"As soon as you've prepared my sister's body for the journey."

Eraz met his eyes. She was, predictably, without readable expression.

"You will not trust her death rites to the temple."

"You'd burn her, wouldn't you? Cremation, the way of your Plains."

"And of Shansar, which blood is in your veins, and hers. But the ashes should lie in the earth, unscattered, the spot to be indicated by stone."

"She'll have a tomb in Istris, in the old way."

"Very well, my lord. I'll see to it. There's no need to fear corruption. Our drugs will keep her beauty pristine until you reach the capital, and for longer than that."

"I begin to think your drugs may have killed her in the first place."

"You don't think that, my lord. You know the truth. Should you remove the golden torc from her throat, you would see—"

"Yes," he said. "Then you must accept my bemused wonder at your genius, musn't you?"

Eraz said softly, "And the child?"

"One more to swell your sacred ranks," he said. He drank the Vardian wine and refilled the cup and drank again.

"Not so, my lord. She is not ours."

"It's nothing to me," he said.

"Your daughter," Eraz said.

"A little white slug. Keep it."

"No, my lord," she said, her softness now impassive. "The child must go with you."

"Because it's mine? The result of incest? In Lan across the water that's nothing at all."

"Then send her to Lan, my lord. But she shall not linger here."

"Because of the incest, then."

"Anackire," she said.

"Oh, more of your stenchful snake-woman. She wants my child dead, presumably. One day old, out in the snow. And I don't think any of my men are capable of nourishing it at the breast. Why don't you merely kill the thing yourself? Smother it, starve it, freeze it to death here? Why did you force it to live at all?"

"Our medicines, which so offend you, will also preserve the child. She will sleep until Istris, nor will she hunger. She may lie warm, enclosed with her mother."

"Impossible."

"As impossible as the event you witnessed at sunrise, my lord."

* * *

The men who brought the wooden box to the shore helped break the ice there, so the boat could put out again.

Kesarh's guard did not complain, though the sun was down on the ocean, and all the west, sky and water, an empty savage crimson.

They rowed across the sunset and the icy sea. A little wind was stirring for the mainland and they raised the sail to take it. There was no sound save the mutter of the canvas, the touch of the waves, the pull of the oars. The island of Ankabek drew away, the last light describing it oddly, a floating skull.

Beyond the sail, Kesarh sat in the bow, with the long box. It was fastened shut, holding her close, the living child, too, asleep as if still coiled in flesh. Holes had been affected in the planking of the box to admit air. It lay at his feet and he did not look at it.

The afterglow went out and blackness came. There were no stars, only the faint luminescence of the cold, and the low far pallor, like a thread of platinum, that was the snowy mainland shore of Karmiss.

Somewhere in the black as they rode, an hour off yet from landfall, Kesarh's soldiers heard the planking of the coffin wrenched apart, and the lid come up with a precise ripping out of nails. They said nothing. They continued to row. They had learned early on in his service what was the Prince's concern, not theirs.

Behind the sail, Kesarh looked down into Val Nardia's face.

Their mother's torc with the black pearls concealed her throat. Otherwise, it was true, her beauty was unmarred, her dreadful pointless beauty. It seemed to him it would have been the same with them, if she had been ugly.

Presently, he lifted her free of the box. He left the unconscious child, a bundle of wrappings, to tumble among the rugs with which the box was lined. He did not care what happened to the child.

He held her in his arms, his sister, her head against his shoulder, the flood of her hair shawling over both of them, dark now in the darkness as his own.

And so they passed like a ship of ghosts across the soundless glimmering sea, to Karmiss.

Rem opened the door of his lodgings and two of the visitors walked in. Two others took up casual sentry posts in the passage, and the door was shut.

Outside, the watery gusty snow of incipient thaw rippled down the benighted building, rattling the shutters. The man's cloak was beaded with it. He threw it off and across a chair.

"I trust the money and the documents arrived previously," Kesarh said.

"Yes, my lord."

"And you and your men are ready."

"Yes."

"Baffled by it all, my Rem?"

"As baffled as you require, my lord."

"My requirements are those I stipulated. The ship you're to take is the *Lily*, Dhol's vessel. When you reach the port of Amlan, you'll accompany Dhol's man to my commercial agent in the capital. She doesn't understand," Kesarh added, for Rem had glanced at the girl. "Nothing, in fact. She thinks the child's her own, the dead one, come back to life."

"Nor has anyone disillusioned her." Kesarh looked at him, only waiting. Berinda stood in her dripping cloak, rocking the swathed thing that was the baby, smiling down on it. She looked more aware than Rem had ever before seen her. Rem said, "and I'm to give the agent in Amlan your letter, and the child. What then?"

"Come back over the water. He'll find it a home, an obscure home, and get me word. Somewhere Ankabek can't suss, even by magic. One day the female may be of use to me. If not, she'll be no use either to my enemies."

Rem hesitated. Then he said, "The child of your sister."

"No. The child she refused to bear. They made her body bear, that's all."

"And the sorcery meant nothing to you."

Kesarh smiled; his eyes were cold. Rem held his gaze, not wishing to.

"I'm not here to discuss my emotions. I'm here to leave you the brat and its wet-nurse. I considered exposing it on the shores of Karmiss, when I got it there. Your work is to remove it from my unloving grasp to Lan. You see?"

"Yes, my lord."

"Yes, my lord. You've always gone about like a prince rather than a bandit, my Rem. You look more like one, too. One of my girls once told me you have a likeness to the old statues of Rarn Am Mon."

Rem schooled himself. His heart disproportionately clamored, but he showed nothing. Kesarh had turned away, taken up his cloak.

"On the ship," he said, "you're just another minor noble, voyaging with your guard and your mistress and your favorite bastard baby. The vessel sails with the morning tide."

When he was gone, the two escort clanking behind him down the stairs, Rem stayed where he was. He stayed there until the hoofs of zeebas rang through the alley.

He looked at Berinda again, wondering how she would react to the departure of her god. But in fact the baby was now her god. She believed in her muddled way it was hers, the life expelled in agony from her womb, cold clay, carried out as she screamed, but brought back warm and breathing. Something of her very own, at last.

Rem sat her in a chair and brought her the mulled wine Kesarh Am Xai had not bothered with. Berinda laughed down at the baby as she sipped the drink. Rem beheld only a crescent of tiny skull above the blanket. It was a white-skinned child, the pale hair like gossamer on its head, all Shansarian, it seemed, unless the eyes were dark.

It was when he told Berinda they were leaving now, as she got up obediently, lifting her bundle of slight possessions from the floor, that the blanket slipped from the child's face.

Rem's heart rushed again, again for no proper reason, save that the eyes of the child were not dark at all. They were like smoky golden suns.

The crossing was a matter of nine or ten days, something less, maybe, with seasonal winds rising. Once the Lannic coast came in sight on the left hand, it would be a passage of sixteen to eighteen days to reach the port of Amlan.

The *Lily* was a merchant-trader, a heavy ship winged by great sails. Her ship lord, Dhol, had served the Prince's agents on business ventures in the past, and thought no more of this, housing Rem in his own unluxurious cabin. Rem's three soldiers slept under awning on deck, used as he was himself to rainy makeshifts. In the cabin, Rem allocated the bed to the girl and baby. He himself stretched out on the floor, something Dhol might have been interested by, had he come in to see.

The time of year was not the best for traveling. Dhol, a money-grabber, always got out before the other trading vessels of Istris. On the whole, the weather was kind to them, raining and blowing consistently, but without serious threat. The push of the wind was actually fortuitous. By noon of the ninth day, the shadow of Lan hardened behind the rain.

"The food to your liking?" inquired Dhol, eating in the cabin with them tonight, to celebrate the sight of Lan.

Rem complimented Dhol on the food.

Seated on the bed, the girl played with the baby, talking to it. As Dhol launched into their first dialogue, some inventory of sea weather, Rem's mind drifted from him and settled by the child.

She was certainly not quite normal. He had begun to wonder if the incestuous union had brought about some flaw. Nothing so simple as, say, deafness, for sure. She heard things. Or blindness— she saw them, too, in a baby's way of seeing. And she could make noises though he had never heard her cry. Somehow he sensed she had not cried at birth. But what was it then, this strange haunting otherness? Perhaps imagination. He had been around fewer babies than most men, having never got a woman with child.

"And by the gods, and Ashara, the king-mast cracked like a—"

Dhol was interrupted by something outside. Sudden shouting, that had nothing to do with the activities of the ship. Dhol looked at the door.

"What is it?" Rem asked. The girl paid no attention.

"I'll see. Sighted a big fish, perhaps. They try to spear them, spear and line—can pull a craft to bits—" Dhol got to his feet. "Continue with your food, sir."

A wave of dizziness, hollowness, went through Rem's head. There was no warning pain, it was not really like the other times. But suddenly there was another man standing where Dhol stood, and one of the iron candle-wheels, obviously deprived of its marine balance by some malign hand, flung sideways with enormous force and struck him on the temple—Rem came to his feet and the scene cleared. Dhol was thrusting out of the door, and had not noticed.

Almost involuntarily, Rem followed him.

The deck was loud with noise, and its cause was almost instantly apparent. From the northeast a great dark shape was shouldering out of the rainy dusk, a red smear at her prow. Already she was close enough that their own port-side lights picked out two flaming eyes glaring from the murk, and, high above, the Double Moon and Dragon device of Old Zakoris.

"*Pirates!*"

Dhol was panting with fear.

"Can you outrun her?"

"Never. Never had to. Never seen one come this far to the south—"

Rem stared, as men hurtled everywhere about him, yelling. The black ship was like a phantom, an undead come back from Tjis to take vengeance.

His three soldiers forced a way to him.

"What orders, sir?"

"The ship lord says he can't outrun her, and that seems likely. The Free Zakorian biremes are cut for racers. This thing wallows at the best. But no doubt he'll try."

"You can already feel it."

This was so. The rowers' stations had been alerted below. The wooden husk swarmed to a new internal rhythm. They were rowing for their lives, now.

"If that fails, as it probably will—" Rem looked through the rain at the phantom. Over the din the *Lily* was making, he could distinguish a thin murmur, a glad shouting from the Free Zakorian as she gained. "Since we haven't," he said, "sufficient wine to poison them on this occasion," the three men grinned, "there's a ship's boat forward. Cut it loose and jump for it. Your priorities are the child and the girl."

"Yes, sir."

One minute later the Zakorian rammed them.

The shudder that took the merchantman and the howling of pleasure and fear, obscured the crash the boat made, hitting the water. One of Rem's men swung over after it on the piece of a rope, dropping neatly, despite the turbulent rollers, amidships. Rem already had the girl at the side but, clutching the baby, she recoiled. "No!"

The Free Zakorians were boarding them like a tidal sea, pouring down the deck. Already the shrieks of dying men slit the tumult.

"Take the child from her and throw it in the boat," Rem said to the other two soldiers. The third man in the boat was poised, ready to catch. "Don't make a mistake. You know whose child it's supposed to be."

The second soldier nodded, reached out and gripped the baby. Berinda started to scream.

The other man spun, brought up his sword and sliced with it, and pirate blood rained through the rain. Rem turned in time to stop a knife going through his back. He hit the Zakorian between the eyes and as he reeled drove his own knife into the man's armpit, where his tattered mail left him bare. Even as he went down, four others sprang over him, trampling on him as he died, to come at Rem. The second soldier twisted his blade from a mass of hair and sinews. Rem halfnoted the girl had stopped screaming. "The Kidling's safe in the boat," the second soldier murmured, almost confidentially, ripping a man's palm open. "And the girl, too." He finished speaking as one of the Free

Zakorian knives slammed through his throat. As he fell, the other Karmian fell on top of him, a pirate crouching on them both to retrieve his dagger.

Two Zakorians hammered at Rem; the other would rejoin them in a moment. Hideous and boring, the fight had only one predictable outcome.

Rem drew his sword and slashed off a man's ear. Throwing away his knife into someone's wrist, he seized the knife-hand of the nearest Zakorian and keeping that pinned, pulled the man against him. Grappled, his Zakorian shield cursed him, rather entertained by the move, flexing to free his armed hand, the other punching again and again across Rem's spine. Rem threw himself back against the ship's side, the Free Zakorian going with him, loosening a little all over at the impact. Rem managed to crack the man's knife from his hand and broke their grip. Now Rem struggled upward, but found after all the Zakorian was tenacious, had him again. He would have to take the man with him. Rem felt the rail, kicked desperately, and then the air gulped beneath him. The Free Zakorian, still scrabbling, lay on him in the air, then rolled away.

The sea, when Rem struck it, was itself like a blow, the coldness seeming to suck all the strength from him in one huge gasp. As he came up, he heard the Zakorian splash down not far off.

Rem fought to reach the tossing thing ahead which must be the boat.

His hands closed on the wood at the same instant the swimming Zakorian's hands closed on him again. Then one hand lifted. Rem knew it was the backswing of another knife. He tried to kick once more, but in the freezing water he could not seem to make it happen. Then his third soldier leaned over him and ran the pirate through.

The soldier hauled Rem into the boat.

"You should have got away," Rem said. His teeth were chattering from the cold and he could barely enunciate. "Thank the gods you didn't."

But the third man, his sword still slimed from the pirate in the sea, was already leaning again to the water. It parted to accept him. There was a black arrow-shaft where his eye had been.

Rem pushed himself up and over on top of the moaning girl, the silent child. "It's all right," he said to them. "Keep still. It's all right." And nearly laughed.

More arrows flickered about the boat, but hit nothing. The

ocean was more choppy now; it was getting rough and they were drifting, away from the ships.

Eventually he raised himself. No one else had come after them. Only a little convention of corpses, drifting too, bobbed on the sea. The ships, locked like fighting kalinxes, were half a mile away. The *Lily* was already burning.

Rem unshipped the oars and began to row for the memory of land to the east.

The boat took water, but somehow failed to sink. Rem rowed, rowed, and time ceased. He lost track of everything but the grinding tear of his muscles, the squealing of the boat, the vicious teeth of the cold. He rowed in a dream, or a nightmare, and did not wake up until they ground on a beach of silken ice. The rain had stopped.

He herded the girl inland with him, having sketchily hidden the boat in case the Free Zakorians decided to pursue them after all. In the scoop of a low hill he made a fire. Day was beginning to melt the darkness, and show him Berinda's face. Her eyes were full of a fear that seemed unable to go away. She watched him, afraid of him, clearly, as of all things. She held the child pressed close, and in the end exposed her breast to the searing cold in order to feed it. Despite the temperature, this act appeared to calm the girl. Rem was glad.

He lapsed back on the hard ground, and looked toward distant hills, a dark soft blue still chalked by snow, and beyond these higher forms yet, mountains found by the light of dawn, then fading away into it. They would have to move soon. Northern Lan was unpopulous. They were miles from anywhere that might give aid. The land smelled empty as a clean blue bowl.

Above the globe of the woman's breast, the eyes of the child had fixed on him. They seemed to see him distinctly. Between sleep and reality, he felt again the strangeness of the child. *What is it?* he thought. As if now, of all moments, that was relevant. And yet, it almost seemed he came to understand . . . She called him. Somehow she spoke to him. There were no words. Gradually he became aware of some profound thing, some purely spiritual hugeness, trapped there in the small and helpless soft shell.

The soul was in the eyes. And though it was the frame of a baby, it was not the soul of a baby at all.

And then sleep washed over him. His consciousness went away.

When it came back, the girl and the child were gone.

* * *

Berinda crooned to her infant as she walked. She told it stories. Her own discomfort was nothing to her now. She felt more hopeful. The disasters of the night had been an error. She had left them behind with the dead fire and the sleeping man. Now she would seek her lord, her dark and beautiful lord who cared for her, who was the father of her child, and he would make them safe again.

She sensed no echo. No shadow of another Vis woman, walking with a fair-haired child, fell across Berinda's confused fancy. She had never been told of Lomandra, who carried the child Raldnor from the malevolence of Koramvis, in her arms . . . Or, if she had been told, Berinda had forgotten.

The sun was high and she had gone quite a way, when something moved on the rock above her.

It was a white wolf, looking bigger than the sky, and three others of its kind were behind it.

Berinda screamed. But she had come too far to be heard.

BOOK TWO—*The Dawn Child*

SEVEN

After the rains, the young summer rose and walked on the hills.

In the shining evening the hunter strode out of the wood, his kill over his shoulder, and stopped to take in the sweep of the land, the valley tucked below into the slopes, and the village that was his home. There were five dwellings, no more, but each alive with people. The nearest town lay seven days' ride away. The village had only two zeebas. Many had never seen that town.

The hunter was ignorant, but at peace. The warm shadows running on the hills, the bright ending of the day, enchanted him without words or knowledge. Besides, his household would eat well tonight, and there would be enough to share with the neighbors.

Something then, a wisp of brightness out of the sky and down on the hillside, caused him to turn and look.

The hunter drew his breath hard. His hand reached for the knife in his belt. He made no other move.

Three things were picking a way along the hill just below him, one was a shadow, two were lights. A pair of wolves, a black one, and a white, both spectacular in their coloring and their size. And between them, something else. It was a child, a maiden child, he could see as much from here, for the little breasts had blossomed on her. A child also of the Plains People, for she was whiter than the albino wolf, and the hair that sprayed behind her, so fine it fluttered out even at her steps, was pale yet golden as a sunrise.

The hunter stared. He had heard of such things, children of the wild whose kin were beasts. It was not so much wonder as ordinary fear that stayed him. The huge wolves might attack him, if they should scent the kill he carried. The child would then attack him too, sister to them, no longer to his kind.

The black wolf halted. Its head swung about, and he saw the jetty nostrils widen. At once the white wolf hesitated, turned, looked at him. The girl-child looked last of all.

As soon as she did so, the hunter's fear increased—and diminished—both at once. It became rather another fear. Though naked, there was a diadem of flowers on her head. He squinted at these, because her gaze filled him with some peculiar sensation he seemed never to have felt before.

The dying light trembled. One further new feeling slid through his mind, easy as water over a stone. And his fear went out. Confronted by the great wolves, the fey, unhuman child, he stood unafraid. He watched them until they turned again and went across the hill, into the mantle of the dusk.

His wife was at her loom when he came in, but started up with a glad cry. He prepared the meat and she cooked it, and later took some in a covered dish to the nearby cot where the husband, laid up for a while, had not been able to fend for them.

Later still, under the lamp hanging from the beam, the hunter played a board game with his wife, using pieces of bone he himself had carved to intricate and beautiful shapes. His wife won, as she often did, and they laughed.

And even later still, as they lay on their bed in the warm darkness, he said, "I saw a wolf child on the hill."

"I thought there was something," said the hunter's wife. "All evening, I thought so."

"Why didn't you ask?"

"You'd tell me in your own good time."

So he told her.

They slept till sunrise, when the little red sheep they kept in the yard began to bleat, wanting the pasture.

The hunter's wife rose and dressed. She kissed her husband.

"You sleep. I'll see to Babbya."

Smiling, he turned on his side, and smiling the girl sought the door, combing her black hair as she went. She loved her man well, though he was some twelve years older than she. But then she had cause. He was a fine man, and besides, her father.

Outside, the sun stood on a hill. The red sheep frolicked. Between the two, the wolf child waited on the slope, her face to the hunter's door.

The hunter's wife took in her breath, as the hunter had done. In her case, it was purely awe. The figure on the slope, perhaps ten years old, looked like one of the exquisite bone figures from the board game.

There was no sign of the wolves, only the wolf child, with flowers in her sunrise hair.

The hunter's wife slipped back into the house. She put a bread cake and some fruit into a dish, wine from the village vine-stocks into another. She re-emerged, bowed, then carried the offerings out beyond the yard, beyond the village, but not far up the slope, and left them there. The child watched her. The hunter's wife came down again, went through the gate in the stockade and into the yard, and kissed the red sheep on its nose. "You must stay here. Or her brothers may come and eat you."

The child could not possibly hear what the woman said, but the child suddenly curved her mouth—a smile. She stepped down the slope to the dishes. She did not comport herself like a wolf child, and she seemed to know what a dish was for. Gracefully, she took a berry from one and put it in her mouth. Then she raised and took a sip of wine from the second dish. She left the dishes neatly, turned, and ran away like a ghost of the wind.

The hunter's wife laughed with joy at the beauty of her movements.

When her husband woke again she said to him, "Not a wolf child. A banaz." Which in the mythos of Lan was a rural deity.

"A Lowland banaz, then."

"Why not? Since their king made them lords, they walk all Vis where they will, and their sprites would do likewise."

About noon there was an outcry. The sons of the fourth and fifth houses had seen a wolf sitting on the slope looking at the village. Men ran on to the street made only by footfalls.

The hunter went out, too, and beheld it was the black wolf, its tongue lolling like a ribbon.

"Fetch your spears!"

"No, no. It's the familiar of a banaz."

"Rubbish. It's a wolf and we must kill it before it comes for the livestock, or for us."

One of the younger sons unwisely hurled a broken pot at the wolf. It missed. The wolf panted in the heat. Or laughed.

Just then the hunter's wife went up the slope toward the wolf, carrying a dish of meat from yesterday's kill. The men shouted, but the hunter said, "Wait. My daughter-wife is clever in these things." Nevertheless he put his hand to his knife, as he had in the evening on the hill.

A few feet away, the woman bowed to the wolf and set down

the dish. The wolf came to the dish and began to eat. The woman walked down the hill again.

When the black wolf had finished, it rolled on its back in the early dust and rose up a gray wolf, and ran away.

The village muttered.

For a month, almost until Zastis, this kind of thing went on. A wolf would be seen on the periphery of the village, or the wolf child herself. None of the village animals were harmed, or the young infants or girls. Offerings came to be made, not only by the hunter's wife, and were either partaken of or spurned. Women working among the vines became accustomed to the wolves, as to a couple of large dogs. The men would leave them portions of a kill, and began to say such phrases as: "The white wolf didn't come today. I missed the shape of him on the slope."

They were more innocent and more knowing in the hills. They could accept such things.

To the child they put up a small altar, and left there items which might please, flowers, honey, beads. These were not touched.

Then, one morning, the hunter's wife opened her door and the wolf child was the other side of it. She did not speak, and maybe was unable to, having spent her formative years with wild beasts. Yet she smiled, and her smile was lovely. The girl stood back, and the wolf child came into the cot.

The hunter's wife made no opposition, but she was unsure now of what to do. She watched the wolf child, who was a banaz, pause by the curtain of the sleeping-place, turn away, put one finger, so white it seemed luminous, on the rim of an iron cauldron.

"Let me learn from you," said the wolf child.

The girl started. She was deeply shocked that the child had spoken to her. Then the shock lessened. She realized with a sweet delight the banaz had not spoken in words at all, but by impression only, in the way of the Lowland People, from inside her skull.

She stayed with them in the house only a few days and nights. She learned swiftly how to be human. It was as if she had always known, merely wished to be reminded.

She clothed herself in garments for the first time, clothes of a girl-child from the sixth house, whose daughters were still young enough to provide them. And she might always have been clothed. She observed the flow of the loom, the bubbling of pots, the gamboling of Babbya, all with equal intensity. She braided her hair and unbraided it. She washed herself in the stream, but, as the hunter's wife had noted, true banaz that she was, the wolf child had always smelled clean, and of a strange natural perfume, like a flower.

She knew the Vis language, either that or she had no need to know it, taking information with tactful delicacy from their minds. Although no one but the hunter's wife had direct communication with her, and that seldom.

By night, the wolves slept at the door.

The village left the altar standing.

The hunter's wife began to love the child, even in these few days, love her as the daughter-sister the gods had not yet granted her. But the child in her village clothes, her hair like sunbeams, seemed older than a child. She seemed a woman.

And on the fifth day the hunter's wife wept, and the wolf child stroked her hair, her hands a caress, her eyes that were like suns eclipsed by a remote gentleness.

"You must get the loan of a zeeba," said the hunter's wife to her husband. "You must go south."

He frowned, at his wife's sorrow, the child's silence.

"Why?"

"She's told me, in the way she tells me things. She wants you to take her to the town. And—to sell her there, as a slave."

"There are laws," he said, "against the sale of Lowlanders."

"She gathered herbs on the hills today, to stain her skin and hair."

The hunter stared, as at the first. And afterwards he stared almost in a renewal of fear as he saw the child standing under the lamp, her hair brown as wood, and her skin swarthy, which before had not even tanned.

The wolves dashed, black and white, over the brim of the blue hills, and ran with the cart and zeeba for several miles.

The child regarded them, but did not make a sound. That she spoke to the wolves within her head was likely.

When the wolves dropped back and did not reappear, the hunter said: "You'll have taken away the luck of my village."

But he knew that was unfair and untrue, and after-seasons proved as much.

The town of Olm lay in that nebulous region of borderland where Lan married with Elyr. Mountains towered over the town, the backbone of the landscape. Somewhere up amid their spines was to be found the ancient kingdom of the Zor, leaderless now, save that it gave its fealty to the king at Amlan. The Zor had, centuries ago, held to itself a religion currently commonplace: The worship of a woman god, to whom the serpent was sacred.

The carts that came jumbling into the marketplace of Olm had all manner of goods to sell. Even slaves were sometimes sold there, Though Lanelyr, like her parent lands either side, dealt sparingly if at all in slavery. Indeed, to some extent it was the blond man of Shansar and Vardath who had revitalized a flagging trade. In the second continent there were now countless Vis slaves at work for fair-skinned masters. And in the marketplace at Olm, a small group of blond Vardians, merchants of flesh of all kinds, stood with wine, watching a woman on a dais. She was a snake dancer from the Zor, a contortionist limber as the giant snake through whose silver coils she wheeled her brazen body.

Such sights, inserted between the drapes of her litter, brought only exasperation to Safca, the daughter of Olm's Lannic guardian. But then, the world exasperated her; the world, her youth, and her lack of opportunity. She still fantasized occasionally that some lord, riding through Lanelyr, would see and be seduced by her, sweeping her away to worthier things. But she knew herself too homely to have such an effect.

"Go on," she said to her bearers impatiently.

Her outrider leaned to the litter, and explained the obvious: The Vardians were in their path and might well refuse to move until the dancer was finished. Such a scene would look poorly.

"If I must wait here, then," said Safca, "I'll visit the stalls."

She got out of the litter, enamel beads in her hair, her spirit crumpled, and started to walk across the market. The outrider dismounted, and walked now at her back, hand ceremonially to sword-hilt.

She was recognized on most sides, and offered politenesses, of course. Only the Vardians quite ignored her.

Perversely, Safca Am Olm idled to inspect the cages of multi-colored birds directly beside them. Through bars and feathers, she covertly watched, disliking the invaders' paleness and their language, wondering through all her antipathy if one might turn and find her interesting merely because she was a contrast.

But they did not turn.

The dancer on the dais fulfilled her ritual—once, such dancing had been nothing less—and went away, roped by the snake. Presently, it became apparent the rostrum was to be used for a slave auction.

The guardian's daughter stood in the burning sunlight, pretending now she watched the stage.

The Vardians drew her. One in particular. She considered if it would be possible to enjoy a foreigner. Zastis was not so far off. Could this man be enticed as a lover? They said the men of the Other World were immune to Zastis, but how could that be?

The first owners showed off their wares. As they were bid for and sold, the Vardians did nothing at all. Next came a chain of slaves from the backlands, handled by the public auctioneer. They were unexceptional, three men and a couple of slovens, no doubt brought to this by debts.

One of the Vardians, the one Safca had become fascinated by, pointed out the sloven at the end of the line.

But no, it was not the sloven. Another stood just beyond her, a child, eleven or twelve, a girl with a wave of hair, too light to be all Vis, too dark to be legally one of the yellow people.

"Twenty copper parings," the Vardian called out, "for the child."

"Twenty, master? That's not—"

"Vardish copper. Not the impure muck of Lan."

Safca lost her temper with this man who spoke with an accent, reviled her country, and would not look at her.

"Ten parings of silver," she cried, much clearer than a bell. "Good silver from the guardian's store. Nothing imported."

Here and there, some of the Lannic crowd laughed.

The Vardian turned at last. His look was frank, unenthralled and touched by menace. She held it, alarmed, sweat starting on her forehead. Involuntarily her fingers closed over the lucky bracelet she wore on her left wrist and never took off. Slowly, he turned back. "Fifteen parings of Vardish silver, by Raldnor."

She lost her head. "By Raldnor!" she shouted, "and by Yannul the Lan, one of his captains—" there was more crowd noise "—twenty silver parings."

The Vardian turned again. She withered in his gaze. Without another accented word, leaving their wine, he and his companions walked off across the market.

She felt silly, degraded almost. She should have left well alone.

Lan, neutral throughout the Lowland War, had given many of her sons to fight for the hero Raldnor against Dortharian oppression, not least Yannul, the wandering acrobat, who learned the trade of soldiering beside Raldnor in Xarabiss, then used the knowledge fighting side by side with him and with his army, across the length of Vis. It had been Yannul, too, who made the perilous voyage with Raldnor that ended at the forest-shores of the Sister Continent. Some said Yannul had remained in Dorthar, at Anackyra, with the Vathcrian King who was Raldnor's son. Others said Yannul was in Lan. A pity he was not here. It seemed the yellow men who swaggered across Lan, her commercial conquerors if not otherwise, needed some token of the past to stay their arrogance.

But it seemed, too, Safca had bought a slave.

The child walked by her litter back to the guardian's stone house with its single tower. A bill for the money had been left with the auctioneer, who in turn Safca saw paying another. This fellow had long hair down to his shoulderblades, a mark of the hills, for in the towns and cities now men wore their hair only the length of the neck—a fashion of Vathcri and Vardath. Probably, the hillman was the child's father.

Unnerved, Safca had barely glanced at her purchase. In the courtyard, she sent the child to be properly bathed and fed and clad. It was to be presented to her in her chamber before the evening meal.

But the shadows were still short beside the brass fountain when two of Safca's girls ran out to her in uproar. It seemed the swarthy child, dipped in the tub, had come out like a star.

"White skin—yellow hair—Oh, lady, a Lowlander for sure—"

"And she's dumb, lady" the other added. "Can't speak a word."

Safca went to see.

The maiden child sat where she had been left in the water, appearing quite composed. She was definitely a Lowlander, not even second continent blood could account for quite such crystalline pallor. It was dreadful, Safca knew. The penalty for sale of a Lowlander was fining and flogging, and for buying one it was any and every penalty the prosecutor thought suitable. What must she do?

"Little girl," said Safca, "can you hear me?"

The child, whose face was most unusual and entirely grave, looked at her, then nodded.

"You were taken in error," said Safca, firmly. "I'll manumit you as soon as the clerk comes and I can bribe him. Do you have somewhere you want to go back to? The Plains?" Safca said, wildly now, "Must I send you there? The expense—I'm not able to!"

The child shook her head.

It was odd, since she had not spoken aloud, that Safca knew
the shaking of the head did not mean exactly "No." Merely *Not
yet.*

Zastis bloodied the night sky.

Safca took as her lover one of her litter-bearers. No better
prospect offered, and the arrangement was at least discreet, the
man flattered, hale, and willing. Yet Safca resented her submis-
sion to the Red Moon, she who was not beautiful. While she
made do, and, sated, must put the man from her bed, her
brothers lay all night with their wives and concubines, her
prettier, more important sister with a chosen noble. Since Safca
could not choose the manner of her pleasure, it seemed to her
she would more gladly have done without it. And so, for a night,
she admitted no one to her bed, and burned in it.

At midnight, sleepless and in a rage, she stole down through
the house to walk in the cool courtyard of the fountain. In the
brief colonnade, she halted.

The brass of the fountain was ruddy, the water playing like
strings of glass beads, and everything else dark. Almost everything else. For the white Lowland child was standing by the
basin, and something was with her—

Safca's heart turned over. At first she did not believe. Wrapped
about and about the child's slight body was a huge snake, the
very kind with which the Zorish girl had danced in the marketplace.
Which was well for a girl of the Zor, birth-trained to mastery of
such a reptile. Though not venomous, the great snakes could
crush small animals, even the chest of a man should they desire
it enough to obtain sufficient grip on him. A slender child would
be nothing.

How the creature had got in, slinking through some kitchen
hole and pouring over the wall, was now unimportant. Safca's
hand was already at her throat where a tiny dagger hung sheathed
in Elyrian enamelwork. Such a minor blade—she must aim for
one of the eyes, hoping the reflexive mindless tightening of the
coils would not persist too long, after death.

If only the Lowlander had not been dumb, she might have
shrieked for aid.

Why then did Safca not cry out herself?

At the instant this thought occurred to her, Safca became
conscious of a sound, a low, musical murmur, which was emanating from the dumb child. In that instant, too, the child lifted
her head and looked into Safca's eyes.

They gazed at each other, and the guardian's daughter slowly raised her dagger and dropped it back in its sheath.

Safca's waiting women had mentioned to her how the child seemed able to call birds from the air, and how the two shy pet monkeys from Corhl would play with her. But this—

The power the Zorish girl exercised over her snake was nothing to this. The child had no need to fear. She was in command, or rather in communication with the great serpent. Its coils were loose, separating the starlight like the fountain. Its flat head moved in her hair.

Nor was the child dumb. The sound she made over the snake, a hypnotic speechlessness of vibration, was yet articulate. Equipped with vocal apparatus and a thorough knowledge of the Vis tongue, the child did not employ them only because, in some uncontemptuous way, she found language superfluous. All this Safca grasped at once, and accepted at once. She made no objection, only stood blinking before the eyes of her Lowland servant. They had never named the child. They had called her for her supposed birthplace, and that charily. She was not displayed. The guardian had never glimpsed her.

And now the Lowlander moved a fraction, the snake slipping forward, resting its head across her palms. Both their eyes, the eyes of the child and of the serpent, were a pale clear gold, and both sets of eyes seemed glowing.

Safca realized the Lowlander was offering her the snake, offering it like a garland, all the winding terrible power of it. There was a certain rightness in that, maybe. Safca touched her lucky bracelet, and stepped back, and the spray of the fountain kissed her shoulder.

"There is no harm," said the child.

Safca opened her mouth to scream and did not scream. Her pulses thundering, she reached out and let the snake spill from the child's arms to her own.

It was heavy, both liquid and dry, an extraordinary sensation. Every hair of her body seemed upraised, no longer with fear, with some more primeval reaction. She shivered continuously, yet a strange elation possessed her. The snake entwined her bones. For she felt the glory of its strength, that did not hurt her, clear through to her skeleton, in the protective ambiance of the child.

How can I fear this thing? she thought. *Something so beautiful.*

It lasted only moments. Then the snake flowed away, rope on rope of sensation gliding off, leaving Safca trembling and then stilled. It vanished before she looked to see it go.

She wanted to speak to the child, to ask her many things, but the child would be silent now, silent in all ways. How old was she? Older than the eleven years she looked. Younger, also.

Where do you come from? Safca asked the child, over and over, in her brain, aware the child could hear if she wished, aware the child would know she did not mean a land or a people, but some other thing, less actual, more decided.

But the child, as Safca had guessed, did not answer.

EIGHT

The ambush on the Amlan road was not altogether a surprise. There had been a purchased warning at the inn the night before, somewhat unspecific, but enough. The spot itself, though he had never had trouble there before, was also a likely one, the hills leaning to the road and thick with coarse high grass. Men burst out like demons, whooping to inspire alarm and to get rid of their own tension, as they plummeted down on the riders and the five rumbling wagons.

But the wagons were full of eager unsheathed swords. Blood sprang and anointed the wine casks and the bales of silk he had had the forethought to roll in protective owar-hide.

Rem extricated his sword from a tangle of guts and kicked the corpse away in time to throw another bandit forward, off his back and over his head, and under the prancing hoofs of the zeeba in front, which finished him.

The rest of the fight was already over. Dead brigands lay strewn along the road, and a couple hung undecoratively from the wagons. Three or four more had made off alive, scrambling through the thick fur of the summer hills, the last of them dragging some of the worthy merchant's goods along with him.

"That one," Rem called. "Bring him down."

The man with the best eye for it flung a spear, and the bandit fell dead in the grass. His associates did not bother to look back, and were soon from sight.

In the old days, even two years ago, this road was clear enough of such adventures. But since piratical Free Zakoris had come to crowd the sea-lanes between Dorthar, Ommos and Lan, few ships risked the harbor of Amlan, preferring land-trips to and from the ports of Elyr in the south. Thus, the trade road to the capital had ceased to be the well-patrolled and lawful stretch it had been. Every rare cargo that ran the Zakorian gauntlet, stood a fair risk from the hungry robbers of Lan.

Having himself been a bandit, once, Rem was not ill-educated in their ways and means. Hiring out as an escort for such dainties as now remained safe and unspoiled in the wagons, he had built some sort of financial security for himself. Twenty men were in his pay, courageous and intelligent. He could have taken on more if he had needed them. Not so many, maybe, as the fifty who would have followed him in Karmiss, under the Lord Kesarh's banner of the Salamander. But, as things had stood, it would have been stupid to go back. Kesarh had had no need of him, in any case. Six years ago there had been a breath of plague in Istris, and the Prince-King Emel, though mightily protected, had evinced plague symptoms and shortly died. Less than three months later Kesarh Am Xai was crowned as King. He took two queens with him to the throne, one a Shansarian princess of Suthamun's house, and one a Vis woman.

But all that was another world. The news came late here, and the emotions the news engendered were low-voiced as distant harps.

Eight years in all had gone by, eight years, and these months of the heat and of Zastis. The child, if she lived, would be less than nine years old. But he had no reason to suppose she lived. Although he had hunted her, and the girl, Berinda, intermittently up and down this land, for all the eight years and the months after, from the north to Lanelyr and back, he had found no trace.

And even though he continued at the savage trade he had chosen in the beginning just because it would take him all over Lan and so enable him to hunt for them, now he no longer understood why he did so. Habit only, probably. For she was dead, of course. Somewhere the winds swilled through her little baby's bones, and her supernatural adult soul was exiled, riding them.

There had been none of the mind-visions, either, during these eight years. One blessing.

Sometimes he wondered about Lyki, and if she lived on with the rope merchant, or had taken up with some other. Even Doriyos sometimes moved across Rem's thoughts like a blown leaf.

He did not let himself think very often of Kesarh.

"Rem, this pig has gold buckles. Do you want them?"

"No. Split anything like that between yourselves."

They did so, rifling the cadavers before heaping them at the roadside. You left such markers in Lan. Someone went and got the haul the running bandit had taken, or tried to take, up the hill.

Then they rattled off along the road again, adhering to discipline and saving their boasting and drinking until they reached the city.

The King and Queen lived in Amlan, in a painted palace of five tiered towers. Every few months they would come out on the steps, each carried in an ivory chair as if incapable of walking, and under parasols, in a welter of guards and nobles, to dispense justice to any who asked for it. This custom, which was also prevalent it seemed in Vathcri, Vardath and Tarabann, amused Rem. While liking it, his soldier's intellect saw all the dangers inherent. One could foresee a murder on that stair, below those red and blue pillars. And it would be a pity for them to be cut down. Brother and sister, in the tradition of Lan, they were young and handsome, both of them, to a fault.

The inn was a good one, just two streets away from the Palace Square. When he walked in there were yellow lights whirling through the air, a troupe of jugglers spinning flames and bells, and somersaulting between.

Rem settled in the dark corner the inn had left for him, drinking Lannic wine, and waiting for his meal to come. The merchant's agent was to meet him here. The wagons had been sent to the warehouses, and already the tale would be abroad in the dusk, the ambush and the wily bravery of Rem of Karmiss. There should be a bonus in all that. He was glad enough for the men to share it. For himself—he looked into the somber wine and pondered, as he only occasionally allowed himself to ponder, why he built as he did, why he wasted as he did, the worthlessness, and the lack of roads to any other thing. But there was nothing in him, he knew, to merit special attention either from the nonexistent gods, or from himself.

When he looked up, two men were coming in at the door. They paused to admire the jugglers, and suddenly a kind of rippling went over the inn's inhabitants, the sort that denoted someone of importance.

Mildly curious, Rem looked more intently. He did not know the older man. He was Lannic Vis, and well into his middle years, but strong, a fighter at one time it would appear, and exceptionally well-coordinated, something that could show even standing still. He was, too, smartly if not at all extravagantly dressed, yet, unlike most of Amlan's male population, he wore his hair very long, in the old way. Rem had been in and out of Amlan many times, and had come to recognize most of the court by sight. They were frequently about, and the city was not over-large. This man, however, struck no memory, filled no niche.

One of the jugglers at that moment cartwheeled out of the melee and landed in a sweeping bow before the newcomer. Who laughed, and brushed him aside with a generous coin. The man began to walk into the room, glancing round. Here and there a cup was raised, and he acknowledged it quietly. The other walked with him, grinning, proud and poised and self-conscious.

This one was only a boy, not yet nineteen, if so close. Rem started to look at him and did not look away. He was mixed-blood, his skin tanned but not Vis, his hair crow-black. The eyes were light, bronze going toward topaz. Beautiful, like the rest.

All at once the two of them were at Rem's table. The older man spoke.

"Good evening. Should we disturb your dinner if we sat down?"

Rem in the shadow, the light behind him beyond his pillar, stared hard. He was about to say some noncommittal thing when the inn tore down the middle like a fruit peel.

There was the man, still, but almost thirty years younger. The boy was gone. All around was dust and broiling daylight.

"I beg your pardon," Rem said stiffly, "you seem to know me, but I—"

"Yannul the Lan. We served together, you and I."

The inn was there again. Rem swallowed. It had been fast.

"What's the matter?" the man said to him. He looked slightly concerned, as with a stranger.

"Your name is—" Rem cleared his throat, "Yannul."

"I'd like to deny it, but I see you know me."

"Yannul of Lan, one of the hero Raldnor's captains."

Yannul, taking this as an invitation, sat. The boy sat, too.

"Once," said Yannul.

"You're said to be in Dorthar."

"Also, once. Now I'm here. This is my son, born here. And you're Rem Am Karmiss, escort maker for caravans, and yourself once a soldier in the employ of King Kesarh."

"And how did you hear that?"

"I asked someone. The way you fight your bandits is evidence enough of the skills of an academy of arms somewhere. And this afternoon you left a few more, I gather, for the goddesses to make bone hairpins.''

The servor came.

"A jug of your best. I'm paying," said Yannul the Lan.

"Sir—the inn will pay, if you'll do us the honor—"

"If I'd done you the honor everytime you offered it, you'd be on the street by now. Take this. For the gentleman's meal as well."

The server went off.

"What do you want?" said Rem.

"My son," said Yannul.

Rem looked at Yannul's son, who smiled. Rem looked back at Yannul.

"Well?"

"You know the way it is with Free Zakoris," said Yannul. "In a year or so there'll be bloody war. There has to be."

"If you say so. You should know."

"Yes. I should. Lur Raldnor here has a wish to go to the High King's court at Anackyra, and take arms with him at the proper time against his enemies."

"The Storm Lord will doubtless be happy to have his support."

It was Yannul now who looked narrowly. His eyes scanned over Rem, as if searching something out, and suddenly the boy said, in a golden voice, "My father thinks I should arrive with at least a modicum of martial training. It's sensible. He's taught me a lot, but I need more. We were about to ask if you—"

"Would leave a profitable business to tutor you in the latest techniques for slaughtering men."

The boy—called for the hero-comrade, of course—Lur Raldnor, met Rem's eyes.

"I'm aware killing isn't a game. My father taught me that, as well. But Yl Am Zakoris has his new kingdom in Thaddra as a base, and the world knows—"

"No," said Rem. "I'm sorry. No."

The wine came then. When the servor left, Yannul lifted the jug and Rem put his hand over his cup.

"Drink it," said Yannul. "We're still talking."

Rem let the wine pour in his cup.

"I thought we'd finished. You can soon buy another arms-master for your son."

"Here? There isn't even an army here."

"Shansarians."

"They're berserkers in battle. That kind of fighting—unless you're born to the way of it, you get killed."

"He doesn't want me to go," said Lur Raldnor. "I've only just persuaded him. If you refuse, I'm done for."

"Lan's a pleasant enough place," said Rem.

"Not if Free Zakoris comes and takes it in the night."

Yannul swore.

Rem perceived the father saw himself in the son, the same spirit which had followed Raldnor Am Anackire against all the hating might of Vis. Something strange stirred in Rem. He would never have a son, he would never know this feeling, for good or ill. And for the first time in fifteen years, he wished he had known his father, or at least his father's name.

Across the room, Rem abruptly beheld the merchant's agent, standing with his mouth open at Yannul.

Yannul intercepted the look. He rose, and the young man rose, no longer protesting, only very still.

"If you change your mind, the innkeeper here knows my farm, and how to get there. Four miles from Amlan, and the grapes are potent. Think about it."

The wolves were busy on the slope above the ice, tearing something in shreds between them. Rem knew what it was. The child.

Kesarh stood at his elbow, watching the wolves.

"It's nothing to me," Kesarh said.

The wolves lay down, growling, chewing. Blood made smoking ribbons along the ice.

Kesarh had gone. Yannul's son stood where Kesarh had been, and he said softly, "It's all right. It's just a dream."

Rem woke, sea-salt-wet as from the ocean off Lan, and almost as cold in the hot close night.

He had not had that dream for years. It had happened a great deal in the beginning. Ever since that morning, new in Lan, he had woken to find the girl and the child were gone, and, stumbling across the hills he met the men from that little village, out on their wolf-hunt. They had taken him in, cared for him. But they had seen no woman, no baby. The wolves had preyed on them terribly through the snow. The deduction was blatantly there for him to make, if never spoken.

Eaten alive, that fully cognizant, fully helpless being. . . .

Rem got up. He went to the window and looked out on Amlan, the late-burning lamps, the five tops of the palace.

Yannul's son arriving in the dream, that at least was different.

Yannul's son.

At the boy's age, Rem had been breaking necks to steal purses. Lur Raldnor wanted to break necks to save the world.

The vision madness coming back tonight, when he thought himself free of it forever, had shaken Rem. Odd that, at last, the picture had brought with it some information. Who had he been at that moment in the boiling square, black jungle behind him, the man who had served with Yannul, somewhere? The obvious idea was bizarrely ridiculous. The obvious idea was that he had been Raldnor son of Rehdon and Ashne'e, Raldnor Am Anackire, the Lowland messiah.

Days went by, and no work offered itself. No merchandise was going to the port of Amlan, and the only caravans faring south had their escorts fixed. Five of Rem's men asked leave and went off in the same direction, having families in Lanelyr. On the other business, the continuous, pointless search, a man came to the inn and stood in the courtyard with Rem.

"I heard you were trying to trace a woman and a child, sir."

"That's so."

"I've come out of my way here."

"I'm sure you have."

After an unfruitful silence, disgruntled, the man said, "There's a woman in the far north, a Karmian."

"Yes?"

"She's got the child, about seven years old, a mix child, very fair."

Rem never moved. He had been brought similar facts, or lies, before. Sometimes he followed them up, and never found what he looked for.

"And the child's male," he said.

"No, a girl."

"Did you speak to the woman?"

"Yes. But I didn't tell her you were looking."

"How did she seem to you?"

"A bit simple," the man said. "Slow. But good-natured enough. And the child was bright."

Rem felt his belly tighten.

"And the limp," he said.

The man frowned.

"The child?"

"Or," said Rem, "the woman."

The man licked his lips, decided.

"Yes, sir."

Rem laughed. He did not realize the devastating darkness in

his face, something he had learned, perhaps, from Kesarh. The man, who had found out some of what Rem wanted but not quite enough, blustered, scowled, and soon hurried away, without reimbursement.

Rem walked the streets, through the market. He looked at the palace, like a sightseer. Yannul, Raldnor's captain, had once ridden all the way through the long snow to persuade his King and Queen, then children, to ally Lan with the Plains.

Yannul had married a Lowland woman, they said. And between them they had formed the glorious son who wanted to go to Dorthar.

Dorthar. Dragon land. Land of the goddess, now.

A man passed on the street. He was like Yannul's son, but only for an instant. Lur Raldnor, do what Rem would, was very much in Rem's mind. And no other thing, even by night, had come to divert the image. Rem was wary. The boy was young enough still to be at an age when sexuality was fluid, therefore corruptible, therefore to be avoided. In all his life, despite several contrary opportunities, Rem had never sought the company of any save those he could take for pay. But then he had also, in that way, grown accustomed to proximity without culmination.

Nevertheless, it was another midnight, another day, before he got his directions to the farm and rode out of Amlan toward it.

It was hardly just a farm, more a villa, built, he supposed, on Dortharian lines. The blue hills held it, as they seemed to hold everything of note in Lan, and mountains gleamed far behind in the ultimate hour of the sun. Orchards and vineyards clustered near the house. An orynx herd trundled grunting and splashing in a valley with a stream, zeebas peered from pens, and gray bis fled squawking and flapping across the outer yard, long ringed necks outstretched.

"Splendid," said Yannul when they met in the coolness of the house. "We eat early here. You're just in time."

They settled the questions of routine and pay over the dinner table. Yannul's Lowland wife, soft-spoken but shining in a dress the color of her hair, helped the two servants serve the meal, then sat down with the family. Lur Raldnor was away, on a hunt, after the wildcat that had been raiding the orynx herds of the area. A much younger son, all gold for his mother's side save for his black eyes, listened and took part in the conversation without precocity. He had the exact sound blend of couthness and dash apparent in the older boy.

Yannul and Rem ended playing a Lannic board game on the terrace in the afterglow. When the light was almost all gone, Yannul joined his servants haphazardly in kindling the lamps. Up in the sky, the Red Star was also kindled.

As Rem won the first leg of the game, Yannul said, "And I take it your mother often struck you."

Rem started.

"Excuse me," said Yannul, "if that's too raw. But I noticed you flinch when Medaci tapped the boy's hand on its fourth trip to the fruit bowl. A joke, a love-blow, no more."

Rem was discouraged at himself to have let slip so much. He said nothing now, and Yannul went on, "it's a cruel time for her. She loves them both, but Raldnor's her first-born. We never thought she'd bear, after the life she had in the old city, the Lowland ruin. For a long while she didn't. And she and he, they're like lovers, the pair of them. Not in the Lannic way, just love, you understand. If he goes to Anackyra, she'll pine. Yet at the same moment, she wants him to go, to fight, to stop the creeping dark. And she's afraid, too. We remember, you see, what it was like before."

"And what was it like?"

"Oh, you want all the military history in a nutshell, do you?"

"You must be used to that."

"Why else," said Yannul, "am I hiding here? I had a year of war, and then a handful of years playing politician in Dorthar. That was enough for me. To return and be Lan's heroic monument wasn't my design, either." A moth had come to die in their lamp and with great gentleness and the excellent coordination of the acrobat and juggler he had been, Yannul caught it and threw it lightly free, unscathed by flesh or fire, back into the night. "Raldnor had the best idea. He disappeared."

"Why?"

"Why not? He'd done all that was asked. Lost his humanity for it. He was a god. Gods either transcend or decay. Or vanish. And he'd left a son behind him. Raldenash of Vathcri, now Storm Lord. There was another boy, too; the Dortharians played a trick with that one, or tried to. The mother was a fool and a bitch. It's in my mind the baby died."

Something cold passed through Rem. He pictured the wolves, tearing—

"And the last battle under Koramvis," he said. "Witchcraft, earthquake, the goddess manifesting. Is any of that true?"

"Truth and untruth, woven as one. I'll tell you something, about the Lowlanders. One can believe they're not creatures of

this earth. Not all come in that mould. Medaci doesn't, and
when we took the ruin back from Amrek's dragon soldiery, I
think she was all that stood between me and a kind of madness.
I'd gone there out of pity, hope of justice, quite capable of
killing in hot blood, and well-trained to do it. Then I found out
the core of the Lowlanders.'' Yannul's eyes were sightless now,
looking only back. "I remember passing them on the streets in
the snow, after the massacre of Amrek's garrison, these men,
those women I'd come to save from tyranny. They were like
silent wolves, eyes gleaming like ice—they looked unhuman.
And I was sick to my soul. I'd never seen that in them before,
but I saw it after. The second continent men, they're not in that
mould either. They're blond Vis. But the Amanackire are only
themselves. They're in Xarabiss, Dorthar. You can see some of
them, now, physically almost all whiteness—skin, hair, even the
yellow eyes get pale—ice in fire and the fire going out.'' Yannul
smiled. "That last battle, under Koramvis. Through Raldnor,
they'd come to know themselves, the Woken Serpent. And at
Koramvis, Vis came to know them too. They caused the earthquake by power of will. Or maybe that's false. It didn't seem so
then. They had to win, and the odds had become impossible.
That army out of Koramvis—we should have been obliterated.
So, if the victory must come and it couldn't come from strength
of arms or numbers, it had to be strength of another kind. They
willed to live. We all did. It was like a prayer, the air so still for
miles you could sense it thrumming like a dumb string plucked
over and over. The only chance was a miracle. And the miracle
happened. Koramvis fell. As for the goddess—yes, that happened,
too, but there was a sane explanation for that.''

Along the ridge of the nearest hill there came a drifting whoop
and sudden splinters of torchlight.

The hunters were coming home.

"Please finish," said Rem.

"A statue," Yannul said, "a colossus from a hidden temple in
the uplands above Koramvis. The quake threw her in the air and
she was big enough and bright enough to see even from that
distance, through the smoke and murk. She sank into a lake
below. Another deity wisely gone to ground.''

Half an hour later, Lur Raldnor came out on to the terrace
with two wildcat tails, the frisks of the murderers who had been
viciously killing but not eating the herds.

Standing with the lamp full on him he looked at Rem with
unfeigned pleasure, and said, "I never thought you would agree.''

So glad to get this chance at Dorthar, Rem thought. But he returned the grin.

The fighter's training was one of the easiest parts of it all. Rem had so trained most of the escort-riders in his employ, and himself kept up the exercise a soldier stuck to, if he was thorough, working out with his men where he could, or alone. And Lur Raldnor, hardy and strong, used to hunting and riding, and taught by Yannul from his childhood any number of acrobatic tricks, took to the work with ability, interest and sense. It was true, Yannul had been trained in Xarabiss, whose Academy of Arms, along with those of Alisaar and Karmiss and Dorthar, was universally respected. His tutor, moreover, had been a Zakorian sadist whose relentless lessons were of the best, when viewed in the long-term. Yannul modestly reckoned himself now past the best age for imparting acumen. But his son came to Rem far from a novice, needing burnish rather than welding.

The rest was easy enough. Too easy. The household accepted Rem like a limpid pool, closing over his head with scarcely a ring formed to mark his entry.

He found himself continuously at home in Yannul's house, and strove to keep some part of himself aloof from home comforts and home intimacies. But he even liked Medaci. She was demure and unassuming, with a sweet smile. Coming out once on to the terrace, he found her with Yannul, the two of them standing hand in hand, his head bowed so their foreheads touched, like adolescent lovers. Nor, seeing him, did they break away ashamed, but separated gently, amused and friendly toward themselves, the discovered, toward Rem, the discoverer.

For Zastis, there were countless graceful means. The short ride into Amlan was no bother, and her Pleasure City was lively if the Ommos Quarter was slight. It had been simple courteously to put aside Yannul's offer of the three young servant girls at the villa, all of whom were willing and had eyed Rem since his arrival, with the tidings he had a particular liaison in the city.

Despite that, Rem suspected Yannul knew the pivot of his guest's suberfuge. That the man did him the extreme politeness of reckoning Rem's desires aside from Rem's relations with Yannul's son was impressive, and, of course, honorably obligatory. But he had promised himself to carefulness in any case.

Lur Raldnor had a girl from the next farm-villa. Her parents probably hoped for marriage with the son of the hero's captain. The girl and the boy cared only for their nights on the Zastis tinder of the hill.

Now and then, riding back in the dawn from Amlan, Rem would meet him walking back from the hill. Raldnor seemed to consider this a conspiracy of sorts. Those were maybe the easiest times of all, and therefore the most difficult.

The practice bouts, the wrestling, the slamming together of blunted iron or wooden blades—or skin—in the yard, that type of innocent physical provocation Rem was used to. The labor, if it was fierce and difficult enough, brought its own relief. Nor, with the bevy of respectable women about, did they strip to fight. In real combat, as a rule, you had mail on your back and leg and arms; to learn to battle weightless in just a loin-guard could prove a disadvantage later on.

With the end of the Zastis months, Raldnor would be going. It was a long road to Dorthar, traveling via the Elyrian port of Hliha. Things were already half arranged. Letters had gone ahead, straight to the person of the Storm Lord, naturally.

Medaci gazed at her elder son, her citrus eyes more still than frozen tears.

One morning there were wolf tracks round the drying mud of the bis pond. None of the birds was missing. The animals of the farm had set up no warning noise during the night. Nevertheless it was thought advisable to pursue the invader. The wolves of Lan became greedy so close to the city, insolent thieves. One canny enough to avoid audible detection could prove a nuisance.

Yannul, who had been out chopping wood with his servants, now sent two of them to get ready for the hunt. The men were experienced in such affairs, grim but not displeased. Raldnor, seeing them start to saddle up, decided he was hunting that day rather than swinging a practice-sword. "Come with me," he said to Rem. "You hunted wolves in Karmiss, didn't you?"

Rem had, one whole long winter in the Istrian hills, hunted and eaten them, too. But for eight years wolves had come to mean something else to him, no longer adversary but terror, nightmare. And he had had the dream again, once or twice, at the villa, or on the pallets of Amlan's Pleasure City.

Nevertheless, they got their zeebas, weapons, food from the kitchen, and set off, catching up to Yannul's men on the hills.

The dog had the wolf-scent all the way, but it was a prolonged trial. By midday they were miles up and over the hills, with only one abandoned cave to show, and that quickly abandoned also by the wolf-dog.

The heat smote down. They entered a wood and stopped to eat in its shade. The two servants diced sleepily. Even the dog

rested, its nostrils alert, but its eyes and tongue lax. It was
useless to move on until the sun moved sideways off their
craniums.

Where the wood ran down the hill was a wide brilliant pool.
Before he quite knew it, Rem found himself swimming across it
with the boy. The light meal was no trouble, but after a while
each of them turned on his back, floating on the buoyancy,
staring up through the leaves to the day and, blinded, shut his
eyes.

"That wolf," said Raldnor, "he must be somewhere near.
We'll come on him before sunset." But then, "I never yet killed
anything and liked it. The chase, yes. And it has to be done. But
not to be liked. I'd suppose it's that way, killing men."

"Men are easier to kill," Rem said.

"More stupid than a beast, do you mean?"

"No. But easier."

After a long while the boy said, "To you, perhaps."

Then nothing.

It would almost be possible to sleep in this water.

Presently Lur Raldnor, less life-weary, swam for the bank.
Ram watched him, the tanned body like a stripe of gold against
the darker stripes of the trees.

The responses of his own flesh set Rem swimming again, up
and down, efficient clockwork. He had no intention of coming
out of the pool, watched in turn, and the evidence of Zastis on
him like a blazon. One could blame changes of temperature and
element only for so much.

When he did wade out, Raldnor was lying on his belly,
head on his folded arms, eyes shut again. Then, as Rem walked
to his clothes, there came an oath worthy of the mess hall at
Istris.

"—*Anack*! Who did that to you?"

"What?"

"There are whip lines across your back. A whip with teeth."

Rem had forgotten. It was a long while since someone had
thought to comment or inquire. Not since Doriyos. . . .

"Asleep on duty eight years ago, in the service of my King,"
he said, startled by his own paraphrasing bitterness.

Without prelude, for he had not heard Raldnor stir, he felt the
boy's hand gracious yet firm against his spine. It was not an
invitation, one sensed that. It was the magnetism of compassion.
Before he could control the reflex, Rem shrugged him away.
"No."

"I'm sorry. It can't still hurt you, can it?"

"It doesn't."

Rem dressed. Raldnor had stopped talking, standing naked at his back, clothed only in blamelessness.

NINE

Beyond the hill was another hill. You climbed it and there was another. They piled behind each other, and then there were the distant mountains.

Rem had gone back through the wood, nodding to the dice-playing servants, and away. He meant to give himself the half of one halved hour, then return. Things would be as they had been, then. Except, obviously, they had been *this* way from the start.

One of the mountains was moving. Like a great ship, it came sailing toward him, filling the horizon. The top of the mountain was smudged by a sunset many hours away. Lower, the hillside rock opened on a solitary ink-black nostril—the wolf's lair? No, not that.

Nearby, there was a hovel in a wretched field. A woman came suddenly out of the hut. She seemed to see him; she waved to him and hurried up. She moved in a coquettish way, but, coming close, he saw her dirt, her age and her pathetic idiocy.

"Would you like to come in the house?"

The world exploded like a shattered mirror. Pieces of vision fell down.

"Would you like to come in the house?"

He could see again. He could see the mountains far off in their correct order, the light of primal afternoon on the hills. There was no cave, although there was a field, and a small cot overhung by fruit trees.

"Lord?" the woman said. "Lord?"

And the woman was still there. But she was hardly old, and not dirty. Her looks were plump and pretty, her black hair held back by a red scarf sewn with beads.

Rem looked down at her. Her welcome was unnerving. It was almost more natural when her face fell, lapsed into terror. She turned and ran from him, screaming.

Out of the hut burst a great brute of a man. As he raced

through the field, the woman darted to him and he caught her, held her, glaring at Rem.

"What did you do to her?" the man demanded. "She means no mischief. She'll have offered you hospitality, that's all. Out here, most are glad of it."

Rem said, "I don't know why she cried out." The hills were slowly moving, not a vision now, only vertigo.

"You must've hurt her. Did he hurt you, Berinda?" the man asked her with urgent tenderness. "Tell me if he did. I'll do for him."

The hills steadied. The sky was cut above them as if by a knife.

Rem walked toward the man.

"She surprised me, I may have looked angry. Not meant. She's gentle, isn't she?" It was the dulcet Lannic word for simple, and the man, accepting its use, grew less belligerent, though no less protective.

"Well, so she is. But she's been a good woman to me. She's given me children, a host of them. Nothing wrong with their wits, either."

Rem went closer. He offered a handful of coins.

"My apology."

The man brushed the coins away. Money was not always wanted in the hills, barter was more use, but the symbol he allowed.

"See, Berinda," he said, "a mistake. Smile now, sweetheart. Smile for me."

And Berinda looked up at the man, smiling.

All these years, searching for her. And he had not known her. Though she had known him, some dark shadow from her unhappy past. Yes, that would be the cause of her terror. Rem was the fall from the ship, the cruel water, the unloving coast—And now, contendedly here, loved and valued at last, a day's ride from Amlan. All these years—

"Berinda. That's a Karmian name."

"Ah." The man did not care.

They walked together toward the cot where she had borne the most of children, all alive. Was one of them—

No. No, this much the gods might give, but no more.

"Berinda," said Rem. She glanced at him, and he smiled at her, without recognition, but friendly, and saw her mislay who he had been in her life.

"We have wine," she said, "honeyed wine from soft fruits."

The man smiled, too, showing off her housekeeping. "She's a rare one for hospitality."

Rem had forgotten the wolf, the hunt, forgotten Yannul's son.

He sat in the clean little house, where two small children came in and out—strange he had not heard their voices, as now he did, ringing round the slopes—and one more crawled on the rugs, and a fourth purred at the breast.

He had seen her last, this way. Feeding a child. Not that child now. None of them were that child.

There was not much talk, the time went thick and slow and timelessly. They made no move to indicate the door to him. Of course, he did not go. The man and he exchanged a few commonplaces. Rem mentioned he was up here after wolves. Something odd, then. The man casting a look at his wife. "Yes, they're wolves round about. We get no harm from them."

As the sun began to go, the man asked for supper, and laughing she put down her sucking child and ran about preparing a meal, like a child herself playing with toys. But it was tasty when it came, if Rem could have got any of it down his throat.

"Eat," said the husband. "We've plenty."

But he could not eat, as he could not leave them. Just as he could not ask her for the past.

Shadows began to come, and a brown candle was lit.

The husband fell asleep. The woman rocked her youngest child, the other children, who had settled indoors like pigeons for the food, grouped sleepily at her skirts.

"Tell us," said the elder girl, "the story about the wolves."

And Rem, a mature man who had lived by three or four trades of death and by the hard edges of his brain, felt his heart stop.

She told them.

As she spoke, in the way of her child, he pictured it. The images came, conveyed by her murmuring. And sounds, and scents, all of it. All.

When the white wolf appeared like a thing of snow on the rock above her, she had screamed and help had been far away, unhearing.

After a while, the wolf came toward her, and she tried to run, but the wolf and its fellows caught her up. They loped around her, shutting her inside a wall of their own bodies. All through this she held the baby, and all through this, as she shrieked and wept and ran and fell to her knees, the baby remained quiet. Finally, the wolves nudged Berinda. They nudged her in such a way that she knew she had to get to her feet. So she did. Then they began to nudge her again, and she discovered they were unroughly pushing her toward some other place.

In abject horror, she obeyed. After a distance of rocks and uplands, twisting, climbing, the heat of the wolves' mouths soaking through her clothing every time they nosed her on, there was a cave. It was a wolf cave, and it stank of wolves and the things wolves had killed. But it had begun to rain, and the cave was out of the rain. Berinda went into the cave and here she sat down for sheer fatigue, and dropped into a sort of dreadful doze.

When she woke, the wolves lay against her. She watched, some slept. The warmth of their bodies was a comfort. The stench in the cave seemed less now that she was more accustomed to it. Berinda, who had grown up in squalor at Xai, had spent her earliest years among the stink of humans, where disease had augmented poverty. The wolves themselves did not smell bad, for they had health. There was the difference.

Later, other wolves trotted in. Berinda was afraid, as if these newcomers might not show the same consideration as the first wolves. But they seemed indifferent. More, they had brought in a kill. Growling, the pack savaged the bloody carcass into parts. At length, a piece of the raw meat was brought to Berinda. She could not stomach it the first day. But the next, when again she was brought something, she did eat it.

By then, she was feeding the child, sitting there in the midst of them. They seemed to respect this duty, and some would stare, wagging their tails like dogs.

With nudgings and tuggings and pullings and whines they managed to conduct her where there was a stream. When the spring began to open the land, she found fruits under the ice and ate them. She offered them to the wolves also, and the wolves ate from her hands.

She was grateful for their warmth in the cold of the nights. She was solaced by their bodies' liveness against her. She had long ceased to be afraid.

For Berinda, "gentle" as she was, was also a wild thing. To her it came, with more facility than to most, to be at one with the wolves. She reacted with the straightforwardness of a child.

And the child too, accepted and accepting, bloomed in the midst of the cave, or slept in Berinda's lap in the weak sun of the hillside. She would even leave the baby among them for short intervals, as she wandered with the wolves or by herself.

When the summer came, four of the wolves showed her that

they were leaving the cave and she and the baby were to go with them.

She was sorry, but the call of the summer running of the wolves infected her, and she did not hang back. They went south. She did not say this, but it was apparent. Also the impressive distance.

All the way, the wolves fed her and companioned her, as ever. Perhaps she had unremembered mankind. It seemed so from her narrative. Certainly the wolves had generally been nicer to her than men.

Thus, when one of the wolves urged her to a spot where a village could be seen among grain fields, Berinda evinced no special wish to approach it.

But the wolf wanted to approach the village, so they went together, playing through the tall stalks of the young grain. The child had been left behind on the slopes.

All at once the wolf and Berinda emerged into a thicket of people, who shouted, either retreating or hurling things. The wolf ran, and Berinda turned to run—and the people took hold of her, rushing her to the shelter of the village.

In vain she tried to free herself. In vain she tried to tell them how she must go after the wolves, to her baby. Her human speech had suffered. They took her noises for hysteria. When, the backlands of Lan being what they were, they did understand and believe her, it was too late. The wolves and the child were gone. Gone forever. She ran about the hills crying for them, to no avail. Washed clean of the wolf smell, her arms empty of love, Berinda wept in the village street and slept in it, refusing kindliness, bereft.

It was here that the man had found her. He was kinless and wifeless, and Zastis was near. The pretty aura of Karmiss was not all faded from Berinda. Something in her despair, besides, touched him. He wooed her in some way, maybe merely by caring particularly and only for her.

She went home with him, timid at first. But his goodness was not an act, not a fluke. Then the magic was achieved, the magic Kesarh had worked with her, better than Kesarh's magic, for this child lived. Her arms were full again of love.

And here she was now, her bright eyes bathed with it, and laughter lines about her mouth.

"And when," said the older girl, gazing up into Berinda's face, "did you find me again?"

It was plainly a ritual question. The dark child believed she was the baby the wolves had taken, who had somehow sorcerously been reinserted and brought forth a second time.

When Berinda replied, it was sure that she thought so too.

"When my womb swelled, it was you."

"But where had I been till then?"

"Riding the air," Berinda said. And the children and Berinda laughed.

Something in the phrase arrested Rem, even through all the rest. The air-borne soul outlawed, waiting—like the ancient Dortharian belief that some souls returned at once, through the medium of their fleshly got unborn children, or the children of their kindred. Hence that insanity of the Storm Lords that not the eldest son, but the *last* son conceived before a King's death, must be his heir. The foible which had granted Raldnor Am Anackire a right to the Koramvin throne.

The dark child looked over at Rem, infallibly guessing he had been an assenting party to the whole outrageous tale.

"In winter," she said, "wolves come to the door and we feed them. From our hands. We're not afraid. Nor they."

He assented to that, too.

The world had given way. To feed wolves like poultry was a little thing.

"There's someone in the field," the elder boy said.

Berinda turned, unflurried, to look at the doorway.

Rem got up.

He went to the door and out, and saw a man sitting a zeeba, leading another, against the whole pane of violet hill sky, staining crimson in the east from star-rise.

"I'm glad I found you," said Lur Raldnor. "We didn't get the wolf, but there's wolf-scent everywhere up here, the dog's almost mad with it." His face was like a stone.

"How long have you been looking for me?"

"Since I went back from the pool and no one could see you. The dog helped."

"But this isn't far from—" Rem hesitated.

"About two hours' riding. We've been longer, circling, trying to get the dog to sort you out from wolf."

"I didn't realize I'd gone so far."

"No."

"Where are your father's men?"

"Just up there. I think we should leave here now, if you can manage it. They've about had enough."

"And so have you, I take it."

Lur Raldnor went on looking down at him. He said flatly, "Whatever I did to offend you—"

"You didn't do anything. Give me a moment, and I'll be with you."

The sour exchange had amused Rem in a way he recognized in himself, a shield up against all that had happened.

He felt empty. Even his awareness of the boy did not mean much now, just something else he must control.

He returned into the cot, perhaps to bid them farewell like any other passing traveler. But they had already dismissed him from their scheme of things. The girl child was playing with her mother's hair, the other children, the baby, the man, slept.

Ram left them, mounted his zeeba, and rode up the slope with Yannul's very polite and very angry son.

Everything was finished. As it had not, somehow, been finished in the surety of death, in the face of mythos somehow it was. The child might have lived. Now, still it might. But he had heard here of what they called *wolf children*. There had been similar prodigies rumored in Karmiss; everywhere, maybe. Orphans adopted by wolf-packs, reared like wolves, running with wolves.

And so, if she lived, that was what she was. More conceivably, superstitious hunters had come on her, rending sheep or orynx or men. Killed her. Long ago.

He could of course go on trying to find her. If he ever did, she would be a wolf.

Eight years of dead ends. And then this ultimate dead end.

It was finished.

They made a makeshift camp somewhere in the hills, slept a few hours, and went on. Beyond terse civilities, Lur Raldnor and he did not exchange a word. There was nothing to say. Rem's quest had been private and stayed private in its solution.

When the villa-farm emerged at the edge of the dawn, he realized what came next. It was the only step which was clear in the aftermath.

"They may be concerned," he said to Raldnor. "They probably looked for us last night."

"Probably."

"My fault. I'm sorry. I'll speak to your father."

"Don't you think I can speak to him myself?" said Lur Raldnor, and for the first time his tone and his look cut like a razor.

Rem shrugged.

"If you prefer."

* * *

"He can't learn any more from me," he said later to Yannul. "You'd already taught him enough to pass very well. Otherwise, he's got presence and a good head. If Raldanash gives him a command, which I take it is what you're predicting, he'll handle it. Better than most."

"And you abruptly found this out during your nonexistent wolf hunt?" said Yannul, bringing him a cup of wine Rem thanked him for, set down and ignored.

"You've paid me generously. Don't throw your money away when you don't need to. He can work out with the young servant—I forget his name."

"You've taken against my son," said Yannul. He seemed quite serious, unhurried.

Rem said nothing, fretting for the door.

"I'm concerned," said Yannul, not looking concerned. "I thought we'd brought him up to be a credit."

"Sir," said Rem, "He'll shine for you in Dorthar like a torch. But I've my own dealings in Amlan—"

"I trust you," said Yannul. "Why don't you trust yourself?"

Rem stopped dead. Everything stopped.

"I beg your pardon," he said. He stared Yannul out and was stared out in return.

"Is it," said Yannul, "that you think he won't be able, well-mannered lad that he is, to say 'No' loudly enough? He would say no, Rem. There's no Ommos blood in my son."

Rem felt the lash of that as if the man had struck him.

The land of Ommos, narrow of scope and heart, cruel predator while able upon the Lowlands, had a name now worse than offal. And at the same time that name of Ommos, whose cult was the sexual union of male with male, had become synonymous with the proclivities of men like himself. Logically, illogically. The Lowlanders had hated Ommos. Yannul would hate it. To Yannul it was perversity and filth. All of it, and everything about it.

"I speak my mind," said Yannul. "But think. You've been in my house some while. With my son. And I knew inside a day."

Something slipped from its moorings inside Rem's spirit. He was worn out. Truth was making a fair bid to revolt him.

"Yes," he said. "Very noble. Well, be pleased I'm leaving."

"I would take it as a victory if you'd stay."

"Why, in the name of the gods?"

"Something. You remind me of someone. My youth, maybe. The best and worst of it."

Rem got to the door, blindly.

"No," he said, "no, I won't take this. I've taken all the rest. Not this." He wanted to end it, but words kept trying to come. He remembered the lashing at Istris, and Lyki's house, and vomiting from pain in front of her before he could prevent it. This was the same. And beyond this, anyway, there was nothing. The baggage trains and killing starving thieves, the Zastis nights in brothels. Not even the dawn star of the child to guide him, however hopelessly, pathetically, toward nothing that did not know it was nothing.

"Rem," said Yannul.

"I've taken my beating," Rem said, "like all the beatings. Kesarh's. Her protectors with their fat hands. Lyki's bloody sticks and pails of scalding water."

"What did you say?" said Yannul.

Rem thrust himself to silence. At last he said, swathing himself in the doorway's glare: "Nothing."

"I caught a name. Lyki."

Why not answer? He never spoke of her, but he had already said too much for more to matter.

"The woman who was my mother. When I was a child, and she wasn't mooning over her days at the Koramvin court, mistress to some Dragon Lord, she used to knock me about. Or her gentlemen friends would do it, to save her delicate wrists." There was another silence. "My father apparently deserted her," said Rem. "I can quite see why. I never knew him. A shame."

He swung round and was in the courtyard when he heard Yannul shout.

"For the sake of Aarl! Wait!"

For some reason, Rem looked back around the door.

Yannul was gray in the face even through the darkness of his skin. Rem checked. Was the man ill? More quietly than he had intended, Rem said, "Truce, sir. There's nothing you can say to make me remain here now."

"Isn't there?" said Yannul. "What if I were to say you're the son of Raldnor Am Anackire, god and hero, and former Storm Lord of Vis?" Yannul grinned even through his grayness. "Would you stay for that?"

There were fireflies stringing necklaces from the shrubbery to the terrace. And there was also Rem, who was Rarmon son of Raldnor son of Rehdon, standing looking at them.

There had been talking all day. He was numb from talking as from yet another lashing. That numbness before the agony came.

They had told him all they could. Too much. He was brimmed over by knowledge. To have nothing. Then to be given this.

The gods must be extant somewhere, after all, playing their board games with men, as the fables said.

Lyki. How often she had muttered of her passionate love-affair with royalty. The hero Raldnor's mistress, of whom he tired. He had preferred the betrothed bride of the King. A year later, Lyki had been part of an abortive plot against his life—how she had hated Raldnor Am Anackire, the father of her son.

Why had she never told him, that bitch? Viciousness—or was her hurt, also, too great? It must have hurt her, a woman like his mother, to fare as she had. To be reduced as she had been reduced.

And after all was said and done, Raldnor had willingly let this son be taken from him. Sown without wish, cast off with the woman. Maybe, as Yannul said, his goddess had possessed Raldnor, blotting out humanity that he might do Her will. Even so, he had planted Raldanash in Vathcri with intent and purpose. Lyki's bastard had been nothing to him.

There was a step on the flags. Rem knew it. His whole body tensed, then relinquished tension. He had ceased fighting, for a little while.

"In one second I can be off the terrace," said Lur Raldnor.

"Never mind."

"If you wanted to be alone."

"Each of us is always alone."

Lur Raldnor, *(my father's namesake)*, laughed his golden laugh.

"Still Rem, despite everything." He moved forward, standing parallel with Rem, but some way off. "Do I call you 'my lord'?" Rem did not answer this sally. Lur Raldnor said, "What will you do?"

"Nothing. Very little has changed."

"Everything has changed, and you know it."

"But only I, and your family, do know."

"I think he almost knew from the beginning, my father," said Lur Raldnor. "The first evening, riding back here, he said to me, 'That man's like Raldnor. The way he was before Anack laid hold of him.' I think he was waiting for you to give the key to it, even if he didn't realize there was one."

Rem observed the fireflies. He felt young and afraid. Fifteen years old. And it was too late for that. He should have had this from the commencement, or not at all.

"By rights," said Lur Raldnor, "you'd go to Dorthar, with

me. Present yourself to the Storm Lord on my father's authority, with myself as your witness. Raldanash is your half-brother. Do you even *see?*"

"Perhaps not," said Rem.

He moved away along the terrace, and Yannul's son followed him.

"Come to Anackyra, Rem," said Lur Raldnor. "It isn't just the war. It's everything else. That place is—like no other place on earth, because of what it was, what's happened there. You have to see it. Walk over it. You were the first-born; by Dorthar's laws you don't threaten Raldanash. It wasn't even legal—forgive me. But you're part of the legend, still here in the world, as he is."

Rem damned the legend, garishly.

"In any case," said Lur Raldnor, "I never did get that knife-to-sword pass as it should be."

"The passage to Hliha could take a quarter of a month. The crossing to Xarabiss is six days. The land journey to Dorthar is a deal longer than either." Rem looked round and confronted him. "In all that time, just suppose I can't keep my hands off you? We may end the most perfect of enemies."

Lur Raldnor looked quizzical.

"I thought the premise was I didn't know."

"If your father knew, he'd make sure you did. So you could be ready, how did he put it? To say 'No' loudly enough."

"I love my father," said Raldnor, "and I revere him. A lot of the time, he can speak for me. Not all the time."

"You're saying you'd lie on your face like my whore?"

"No. I'm not saying that."

Humiliated by his own responses, Rem looked away. The boy said:

"When my mother was younger than I am now, she killed a man. He—your father—made her do it. By telepathy, willpower. It was when they broke Amrek's occupation of the ruined city in the Plains. She's never forgotten."

"That has something to do with this."

"This much. None of us know what there is in our blood, or souls, or minds. But what we are, what we can—or cannot—do, these things *make* themselves known. We don't need to struggle always toward them. Or away. It's like breathing, Rem. If we need it, it happens, without thought. Better, without thought."

The fireflies hung in the bushes, flaming.

Far off, the boy said to him, "Come to Anackyra, Rem."

*　　*　　*

The wolf, which had left its prints around the bis pond, and so drawn them to the hills that day, never returned. It was never mentioned. In after years, if they spoke of it, they would recall it as intrinsic to the will of Anackire, Her messenger. Only Rem would never, he knew, speak of it in that way.

In the end, it was still Zastis when the small party for Dorthar left the villa-farm near Amlan.

A scene had ensued on the hill between Lur Raldnor and his recriminatory Lannic girl. The usual sentences were said. They parted, their irritation unassuaged by love-making. Medaci was gentler. She did not weep, though her eyes were fashioned out of tears. It was Yannul whose eyes were wet.

Rem did not overlook any of these things. He had waited for his fellow travelers in the city. Distance both geographical and psychological.

TEN

Amlan was buzzing with news before they rode out of it. It seemed to be the one sort of news that did travel fast, since it came straight in off the sea-lanes with such marine traffic as still risked the port. The Black Leopard of Zakoris-In-Thaddra had been prowling the shores of Karmiss and Ommos. Kesarh Am Karmiss had gathered his fleet at Istris, and was preparing to meet the swarm of Free Zakorians. Now thick on the water as a fleet themselves, the pirate vessels were reckoned to be nearly fifty strong, though such assessments were certainly exaggerated. They lay off Karmiss' southwestern coast, basking in the sack of Ommish Karith, which once Vathcri had tried for and not taken.

Kesarh's navy, built on past Vis tradition and sound Shansarian knowledge of sea and ships, had also grown in stature and magnitude. It seemed, for the past seven years he had been preparing for such a day, while Dorthar, the hub of Lowland-won Vis, had lain dreaming.

Generally, in the manner of men, these reports were taken as alien to the life of Lan, or else dressed with forebodings. A sea battle of the size now in the wind seemed close to war. Close in other ways. There were dire predictions of the sequel. Karmiss, Ommos, even eastern Dorthar would take the brunt of this, but might not Zakorian strays fare over the water to Lan? Her seas had been unsafe for a long while. Buoyed up with victory or primed to vengeance by defeat, the port of Amlan could prove a tempting titbit with which the pirates might follow the feast. It was a fact, a convoy of King's guard had marched out of the city at dawn, making for the port, watchmen rather than defenders. The harbor and the port road had been shut at noon.

Rem got most of this thesis at the inn before he left. He did not discuss it beyond a sentence or so with Raldnor when they met. The boy appeared informed, and so far only mildly troubled to be leaving in the storm-light of such events. He, and even the servant riding with them, claimed to share Rem's opinion that the battle fleet of Istris would complete its task very ably, and that the routed Free Zakorians were more likely to hit out at the eastern tip of Dorthar in their long flight home, if still capable of hitting out anywhere.

Rem's conviction, succinctly conveyed, was that Kesarh Am Karmiss would not take on such business unless he was sure of success.

Hearsay had it the King would command his fleet himself.

He had some qualifications for the work.

The storm shadows of war seemed lifetimes away on the incandescent days, high-ceilinged nights of the journey south. As they progressed, the shadows paled altogether. When they entered Lanelyr, the tidings of imminent battle evolved only with the caravan they themselves had joined, more garbled and fantastic than ever by then, and so infinitely less believable.

An unforeseen fresh nuisance fell on them when they broke the journey at Olm.

Rem's duties as outrider had brought him into the small town on a couple of past occasions. Five years ago he had spent some days riding about the mountain foothills. There had been one of the false Berindas reportedly living in the area. When he found her she was a mix, and her child too. A brooding sense of the Zor had disturbed him in those hills, that old lost kingdom with its black-haired Vis version of Ashara-Anackire.

Olm he had barely noticed. Nor would have done so now, save that Olm had mysteriously been given word that the son of Yannul had ridden in at her gates. No sooner were they settled at the inn than a messenger arrived, and everything must be moved over to the more than modest palace of the guardian.

It was a thundery velvet-textured night, stars like sparks, the Zastis moon a blown rose.

They ate in the palace hall, vanes in the roof hauled back to show the night, and invite nonexistent air.

Rem realized with slight astonishment that his true identity was making itself known to him, for it struck him as funny to be placed far lower down the long table than Lur Raldnor. The female they had partnered with Rem was the guardian's younger, somewhat illegitimate daughter. She was a strange creature, stiff-backed and fluidly opaque by turns, as if in the process of some curious aesthetic change. Someone had whispered she had aristocratic Dortharian blood, but her mother had been lowly, some Lanelyrian freedwoman. Her thoughts seemed happier elsewhere, and Rem was happy to indulge them.

While comprehending what had been said to him on Yannul's fire-fly burning terrace, and lured by it to an attempt at self-collection, he was made uneasy trying to be easy. He had been told what the name of the country was not. He had been told, as yet, it had no name, but that a name might arrive for it, perhaps unexpected. He had been told he was valued as a man and a friend.

The goal of Dorthar was also in front of him, filling the empty horizon where had been the oblique dawn promise of his quest for Kesarh's child. Dorthar disconcerted him, but it promised something, too, if only the recompense of anger.

He paced out all his ground carefully. The dull dinner and the unsociable Lady Safca were actually a relief.

Before they were shown to guest chambers, there was an entertainment.

It was an embarrassing flung-together allegorical re-enactment of Raldnor Am Anackire's victory over the Storm Lord Amrek, full of gods and fates who did not know their lines.

The son of Yannul had been seated with the guardian's attractive legal daughter. They were intent on each other, to everyone's gratification, and paid little heed to the awful proceedings. The Lady Safca, rather to Rem's surprise, did pay heed.

Presently it came to him that all her attention was centered on one person, a mix girl about twelve years of age.

It was thought blasphemous to impersonate Anackire Herself, and so the girl represented the Idea symbolically, sitting all this while on a little gilded throne borne about by porters. She was dressed as a Lannic priestess, veiled all over in milky cloth, only a high forehead showing, and eyes described by paint. He was too far from her to see if they were light or somber eyes, but the hair escaping under her head-veil was dark. The interesting thing was the fact of the snakes—two of them, wound one each about her bare white arms; live snakes, twisting and coiling, neither they nor the girl demonstrating any wish to escape. The Vis, even mix Vis, even goddess-worshipping Vis, were usually allergic to the touch of serpents. It was obvious why she had been chosen.

Maybe Safca was concerned for this reason. The girl must be a favorite, whatever that might mean. He had noticed, too, a ring gleaming on the snake-girl's thumb, gold or amber.

At length the theater ended. Soon after, they were allowed to go to bed.

Rem bade his female uncompanion good night. He was not, hopefully, significant enough to be saddled with a bed-girl.

However, on the way to his allotted chamber, the servant going ahead up the lightless corridor with a torch, Rem was given cause for doubt.

Suddenly from a by-way another lesser light appeared. It was a hand-held bronze lamp, and the glow of it lit up the under-plains of a slender white face, its eyes downcast but still smudged with paint. She had no snakes about her, though her arms and feet remained bare, and now her head and face were also uncovered.

She was a servant on somebody's errand, he thought, and gave her no further glance. Then, as they passed each other, he felt her fingers brush across his palm. His hand closed involuntarily on some small object.

Without a sound she was gone. He knew better than to look back.

It was not until he was alone in the room that he opened his hand to see. And there was the ring she had worn.

It was amber, clear as Lowland wine, smooth as cream, and yet warm in his warmth from her. There was another characteristic. A sort of peculiar inner vibration. It seemed alive. In a second he had cast the ring down on the floor as if he had touched instead one of her snakes.

A little later he assembled the truth. The Lady Safca had propositioned him. The ring, put on her servant for the theater, had become a Zastis token.

He wished she had had the sense to avoid that pitfall. He could hardly himself send it back and humiliate her further. It would be best to leave the ring lying, perhaps in the courtyard. Valuable, the palace servant who found it would hardly dare not return the jewel.

That it had tingled was simple magnetism, for such amber was magnetic. Or else the Star had loaned it intensity.

He took off his clothes and lay down on the bed.

There was a hollowness in his skull. Safca. . . .

Some knowledge concerning her, or to do with her, was there to hand, but occluded, by light rather than shadow.

Rem dreamed white wolves were running over a landscape shaped from amber. Behind, rode a man in a chariot. He wore black. He held the reins in his right hand, in his left a gold-handled whip that gradually altered to a serpent.

"Where have you been?" said the guardian's younger daughter as the Lowland girl came into her chamber.

The girl looked at her, shaking her head gently. This, in the language of signs which was accumulating, seemed to mean the question was in no need of an answer.

"I wish you hadn't been shown in the hall," said Safca.

One of her brothers was responsible. He had come into Safca's apartment unlooked for, and seen the girl at once.

He had fancied her in his bed, so much was apparent. Yalef liked his women young. His two wives were only thirteen. And this child was so graceful, already she moved and walked like a court woman. More elegantly than Safca, or her sister, or Yalef's two wives.

Safca did not know the girl's age, but was positive that she was not yet nubile. When argument failed, she tried to put Yalef off by the reminder that pale skin and eyes meant frigid Amanackire blood. She also informed him that the girl was dumb, retarded, and had a habit of coaxing snakes into her bed. Yalef was duly discouraged.

When the word came of Yannul's son, however, and the entertainment was planned, Yalef came back and demanded the girl for snake-sporting purposes.

Safca could hardly refuse.

At least the blonde hair had been dyed wood-color again. That had been at the girl's own request. She had written it, so there could be no doubt. The art of writing was something she had to thank Safca for. Perhaps. The woman who taught the girl remarked that she was abnormally quick to learn her letters. Safca, observing the second of the two lessons, which were all that had been required, was filled by awe. It was as if the Lowlander had always known, merely needing to be reminded. . . .

Now the girl came to her and began to comb her hair.

At once, Safca was soothed, her taut muscles relaxing. She

half-closed her eyes, watching the flowing movements of hands and hair in the mirror.

Relaxation did not prevail. Abruptly Safca noticed the amber ring had vanished from the Lowlander's thumb. The ring had been Safca's gift, her own possession, yet she so unfitted to wear delicate jewelry. Now it had been lost or snatched—Safca opened her mouth to demand where it had gone—*or given in turn to another*. Safca closed her lips in a tight thin line.

Had she saved the child from Yalef only to have her make other arrangements for herself?

Jealous and put out of patience by her jealousy, she grew rigid under the soothing caress of the comb.

Next morning, the youthful but august visitor departed, leaving the guardian's elder daughter sleekly lying late a-bed. Maybe a child would result, to be the boast of Olm.

Safca, who had always had a temper if nothing else, threw a piece of pottery across the room, listened to it smash, then shouted for her litter.

The other man, the friend to Yannul's son, had been as uninterested in Safca as she would have predicted. Something in her seethed and bubbled. She forgot the night the snake had coiled all about her. She remembered instead her mother's deathbed, the lack of attendants, the lack of words. The few words which were said. Safca clutched the bracelet on her wrist, and ordered the litter-bearers to a trot, and ran them like kalinxes.

When she returned, Yalef met her in a corner of the outer court. With him was a tall blond man. Filled with dread, Safca did not know him for a moment. Then she did. Her heart quaked.

"The Am Vardath gentleman said you had a girl he'd like to buy."

"No," she said.

"Alas," said Yalef. "I already had her brought and given to him. His servant took her off. She's gone. She was no use to you, Safca. No real use to anyone."

The Vardian grinned.

"Your brother's received what you paid, Vis lady. Twenty parings of patriotic *Olmish* silver."

She had no say, no power. What was she? An illegal daughter. Maybe not even the guardian's work. And if the Am Vardath knew that story from the deathbed—he would spit on her literally, instead of merely by inference.

She tried not to cry. She could not even think why she should

be crying. Was it her jealous rage which had lost her something
she had not properly acknowledged, could only acknowledge
now that she would lose it? But what, after all, was the child? A
magician who could call serpents—

"Why," she whispered, shamed by the Vardian's sneer, "do
you want her?"

"I saw last time her Vis-tan was a fraud, cover for a slave
auction. Her skin's white and her eyes yellow. She's got a lot of
pure Lowland blood. Bleach her hair and she'll pass as immaculate.
There are rewards in the Plains for rescuing their children from
wicked Vis slavers, evil Vis owners. The Lowlanders, after all,
are the elite race. Like my people, the Chosen of the goddess."

Yalef, between nervousness, and pleasure in Safca's discomfort,
only beamed.

Safca bowed her head.

I shall never see her again.

There was nothing much at Hliha, save the shipping in the bay
which ran in and out, organized from Xarabiss or Lanelyr or
Lan. The only built thing, on the upland above the scatter of huts
and tents, was a slim dark stone tower, one of the multitude Elyr
had raised to gaze upon the heavens. Astrology, magic, mysticism,
non-involvement, that was Elyr. She had no Kings. She produced enamels, that was her trade. Her fealty, if she knew the
word, was given to Lan. One ascertained her temples, rare as the
astrology towers were not, were very old. And black, Lowland
style.

The ship put out from Hiha before sunrise, and carved over
the sea toward Xarabiss.

Rem was on deck, watching their flight from an ascending
sun, when he found the amber ring.

There was a reason. He recalled throwing his clothes on the
floor that night at Olm. In the morning he had looked for the
ring, also on the floor, and failed to find it. Reason assured him
the ring had been caught up in a fold of cloth, dropped into the
thief's habitual knife-pocket of a sleeve—whence now it rolled
back into hsi palm. Thief's pocket and still a thief, it seemed.

He looked at the ring. There was no sensitization anymore.
Just a circle of amber.

He could no longer very well return it to Olm. He would give
it to Raldnor to give some girl.

He thought of the amber ring he had given Doriyos.

The amber sun shone over the ship to the water.

*   *   *

That night he awoke with the ring in his hand burning like a live coal. Or thought he woke. But somehow the dream went on. The clamor and the redness, and through it he saw the peaceful deck, the tilted sail, the awning, the other sleepers. At the prow the watch leaned out, and through him and through the Zastis-colored night, blades seared down and up, and great doors rocked, booming.

"What is it?"

Lur Raldnor's voice, wide awake, came through his skull.

He could not speak.

Suddenly his fingers were being prized open. He heard Raldnor curse, and then the ring was gone.

The night cleared. There was only sea and sky and ship.

"The amber," said Lur Raldnor, "it's red-hot."

"Ankabek," said Rem. He started to breathe again. He heard himself speak and understood only as if another told him. "Kesarh's won his battle. The free Zakorians are routed."

Raldnor said quietly: "How do you know?"

"I saw it. Mind pictures. This has happened, something like this—years—Never quite like this. From my father's side, maybe." Rem stared into the merciful, ordinary night. He said, "Zakoris. Routed, turning like a wounded tirr. Not against Lan, Dorthar, Ommos. *Ankabek.*"

Vodon Am Zakoris had lost the battle and therefore, though he lived, his life.

The thirty-eight ships that had turned for home, heavy with spoils from the southwest rim of Karmiss, last-laden from the rich little Ommos port of Karith they had left alight behind them, had met the navy of the Karmian King lying like a sailed city on the afternoon water.

The ships of Zakoris-In-Thaddra were pirates still, but they had always borne the sigil of Old Zakoris on their canvas. That a king sent out his fleet against them, sigiled in its turn with the Lily emblem of the Karmians, and with, at the prow of all their prows, a ship flying the scarlet Salamander of the King himself—that was challenge for challenge. Kesarh did them the honor of offering them war.

They came together then. The black biremes with terrified slaves at their oars and the leopard-bees of Yl standing ready on their decks. The Karmians' lighter, Shasarian-modeled vessels, curved like swans, that Kesarh had favored, who favored almost nothing else out of Shansar, were rowed for pay and glory. Fifty-three Karmian ships; a score of whirling flame-throwers;

half a score of the giant bows which fired their giant arrows of iron to a range of sixty lengths—capable of splitting timbers and breaking masts, at more intimate range capable of slicing a smaller craft in two; six towering fire-catapults; eleven buffer-shot bombards of oil. And packed on their decks close to five thousand fighting men.

Until this time, such an armament and such a multitude had not been sent against Free Zakoris. Fierce as they were, the Zakorians might yet have stolen victory, or wreaked havoc, or at least won space to win through. But there was not only force, there was deployment and preparation against them. Almost as they closed, they were encircled. As their weapons screamed out incendiaries, defensive shots came from the foremost Karmian galleys, knocking two thirds of the blow away, some of it back on the Zakorians. This was a trick not often mastered, but Kesarh's men had mastered it. The machines of Karmiss had been perfected and the gangs trained to the job had learned to use these great weights, poised on hair's breadth slipwires of steel, with the accuracy of deflecting spears. The Free Zakorians' first rain of arson was dispersed, then, and the second rain came from the Karmian side.

As the fire-clouds rose, and the air-borne blades of Karmiss fell again and again, Vodon drove his own galley to engage the royal ship which, flaunting its Salamander, had drifted to the north.

To kill their King would stand for much, when so much else might be destroyed.

Vodon's ship was not in time to reach the Salamander. A pair of Zakorian biremes fell upon her. He saw them grapple her, and knew all at once she was too easy to come up with. By then, so it had been found. The figures at her rail were straw dressed as men.

It was a joke in the middle of carnage. There was another joke, a memory of twenty-eight years before. The invaders were still grappled, disengaging, when the Salamander exploded. She had been filled with oil and primed, slow-burning. In a similar way the sea had been fired at Karith in the Lowland War, to repulse the fleets of Vathcri, Vardath, Shansar.

Wreckage and hailing flame showered about Vodon's galley as they pulled away. The other two, panic and fire, were going down with the Salamander.

Vodon concluded Kesarh had not, after all, come in person to fight. This disheartened him, even as he despaired.

By sunset, it was not only the sun that fell burning.

In the dusk, five free Zakorian ships, scorched and ragged, limped from the maze of steam and smoke. They ran. There was no other word. Vodon's vessel, which had by lot the battle-command, was the third of these. It was instinct by then. For having failed, having shown weakness, there was no place for which to run.

Trailing through the night at the pace of death, they were not pursued, but some of them were in poor shape and the sea drank two of them under. The other three took up men left floundering in the ocean, as reflexively as they had fled. While different men, those who had died of their injuries during the flight, they cast down there, to the courts of Rorn.

But the Rorn gods in the prows, to whom they had offered lavishly after Karith, went hungry now.

When the dawn came, they huddled at anchor, resting the slaves, not from pity, from necessity. Several were dead, and the corpses were unshackled and flung over after the rest. Thaddrian corpses, Alisaarian, Otts, Iscaians and Corhls, came between the sun's path and the water. There was even one blond corpse, a mix from the Old Kingdom, now Vardian Zakoris.

Vodon stood with his two officers of deck and oars, and their two seconds.

Their faces were sullen with knowledge. To return to Zakoris-In-Thaddra would mean death-sentence, and ghastly death, the reward of failure. Their other option was the traditional suicide pact, the recognized exit when contrary odds had proved insurmountable. Vodon, the ship lord, must kill these four men on whom the onus of the lost battle had rested. Then himself, the figurehead. Thus they would assure their families at least survived unmolested, retaining the very little they had. Their names would not be spat on.

They had not got far in the night. The current rocked them, racing in to swell the straits between Dorthar and Karmiss.

The dark men stood looking at the waves. Their hair was black, which, if they had sailed the western or southern oceans, it would not have been. The salt of those seas had a bleaching property, perhaps due to their proximity to the great Sea of Aarl, where volcanoes blew fire spouts as fish blew water.

Vodon brought his mind back to terminus. He made a gesture that they should go below.

Vodon's deck master caught his arm.

"Wait."

"For public flogging across chest and loins, slow dismemberment, disemboweling? No."

"You mistake me. I'm suggesting one more deed before
this."

"What?"

The deck master pointed, away into the straits.

"We must go to Zarduk, or to Rorn. Let's take him a present.
Destroy one of the lives of the yellow men's woman god."

The sullen sodden faces sparked alert.

"The Anack temple."

"Will their King Kesr not have protected it?"

"I never heard he did, Kesr has brought the men gods of
Karmiss back. He gives Anack only offal at the feast."

They laughed.

The watch-horn sounded to the other two ships.

With the tide, they turned into the straits for Ankabek.

The three ships were seen at sunfall, sliding dark out of a
coming night. There had for some while been awareness on the
island of the goddess that eventually religious immunity might
fail. A pattern of actions had been prepared. These were instigated.

The village at the landing was swiftly deserted. Other pockets
of outlying humanity on the island were alerted by the flare of
beacons along the rocky slope, ignited as the first fugitives
passed on their way to the temple.

The Free Zakorians, as they hove nearer, saw these fireworks
across the gathering dark, but flame, so often the emblem of
catastrophe, only stimulated them.

The landing at Ankabek had not sufficient depth of water to
accommodate their biremes. They anchored a mile from the
coast therefore, and put out for the beach in relays of boats.

Long before they were fully landed, the live things of the
island were all within the central temple precincts, men, women,
children, and the animals of their sustenance.

The Free Zakorians scoured the village as a matter of course,
and fired it, before pressing on up the slope.

The priestess Eraz, having dressed herself in her golden robes,
walked the buried corridors toward the Sanctum. Years had
passed since the aura of such robes had been thought needful.
More than eight years. Yet they were as beautiful and as shining.
Eraz herself looked no older than in that hour she had confronted
in her gold the young soldier of the Prince Kesarh. Rem, who
had been called Rarnammon, on whom the Dream of the goddess
lay like a faintly perceptible light. At that hour he was the
Messenger. The Message had required to be given surely. Not

merely words and scenes, but in the coinage of Power. Eraz had possessed the Power to impart, and he the Power to receive.

The future of his body's life continued now, along the lines of invisible brilliance, the roads of the planet's own force. Her body's life would end tonight. She was saddened, for she had learned to love her body, in the rightful way, and to love the form her soul had taken in this body. To imagine leaving her flesh and meeting again with her soul as it truly was, this was daunting, the reunion with a beloved stranger. But, that was only the fear of the unremembered thing. After death, memory returned. She would not fear, nor be a stranger to herself, then.

She ascended, and passed through the final unsealed door into the Sanctum. She was the last to enter. The door was immediately closed and barred behind her.

The gold curtain had not yet been lifted from before the goddess.

The rest of the room was not unduly crowded, though all were present. The men and women of the island, and of the temple. The novices, the acolytes, the priests and priestesses. And the beasts. Cows lowed, their feet covering the bodies of heroes in the mosaic floor. A pet rodent scampered, chased by a child, in and out, a game.

The waste also saddened her. But the souls of beasts and men could not die. There would be other lives for them in the world, or other worlds. Nothing was for nothing.

They looked at her, and she felt the strength of her aura touch, clasp, enfold them. They could not all know these things. Or could not all trust in them. She must hold them now, their mother, as Anackire held the earth, or the Principle, which they had named Anackire, held it. Eraz smiled a little. It was not hubris.

And outside, the Black Leopard raced toward them.

She had felt their aura, too, the Free Zakorians, a thundercloud. Death and agony of spirit, and lust for the agony of others.

Had she, Eraz, contained the Power of one such as Raldnor Rehdon's son, had this room been filled by Lowlanders imbued by that Power, then, no doubt, they would not have been the victims. Yet the place where the hero had worked his magic—the earthquake, Koramvis' fall—had been adjacent to the great Power-source of the hidden cave temple, known to the ancients of Eraz's people, who had set there the colossal goddess statue. That charge, the vitality of Raldnor, combined—Ankabek was not a power-source, though the island lay over one of those lines of psychic power that ribbed the planet: The line that ran to Koramvis from the arcane kingdom of the Zor.

But no, she must not idle, musing on these occult mathematics. They had not the strength to stand against their enemies, either of body or psyche. That strength had been, and was to come.

As she raised her head, there was a terrible booming.

Women in the small crowd cried out. There was not one of them who did not know what the sound indicated. The Free Zakorians had reached the temple's outer doors and had begun the process of breaking them in. Having some knowledge of Ankabek, they would have brought make-shift rams from their ships to do it.

Even so, the noise seemed far away.

Eraz began to speak.

"We are well defended," she said. "The outer doors, when secured, are very hard to penetrate, though they will penetrate them. The Sanctum is enclosed, and it is unlikely any Zakorian may breach the stone's mechanism, even by random accident." She saw their faces, and understood she must not prolong their hope, which was groundless. "Yet," she said, "they will also gain access to the precinct of the novitiates. Corridors descend there and run below the temple, connecting to stairs which lead between this chamber's outer and inner walls. Here there are doorways only of metal, barred only by metal. Through such a doorway you saw me just now enter." She waited a moment, her heart chilled at their faces, now. She said, "Others than they might abandon the central temple. The inner ways which lead to it are complex. They would not try them, might not even search for them. But these Free Zakorians are different. There is shame and death before them. They have, in turn, a madness to debase and to kill. By the desperation of this need, they will discover the way in to us. Hours may pass, but you will eventually hear them against these inner doors, which cannot forever keep them out." Women wept. Children, catching fear, wept also. The beasts were troubled. There was anguish and horror. She must conclude. "We know the leniency of Free Zakoris. To their own kind they are merciless. For us they will have torture unspeakable. I shall describe none of it. Remember only what you know of them. They will leave none alive, but for many death will be slow. They will kill also your children in hideous ways, and your beasts. They will drink blood in the stolen wine. Then they will burn whatever is left." She paused. She said, "The statue of Anackire they will hoist and drag and fling into the sea, though they will tear away her jewels and cut out her eyes, and rip away the curtain for loot. Such spoil will be vaunted in Zakoris-In-Thaddra. They will say they have slain one of Her lives.''

She waited then, once more, until, over the horrified weeping and moaning, the silence of despair came down like snow. And beyond the walls, all at once, she heard the outer doors give way. The sound was appalling. Even Eraz it appalled.

And even if she had not thought life stretched away beyond life for all of them, yet she could not have wished to live to hear that other splintering of the inner doors, which must come.

She looked out at them, and let the Power pass through her, and from her, and so into each of them.

"The soul never dies," she said. "Death is not death. So the rituals of the goddess have taught us. Dying is only change. The flesh is left upon the ground. The spirit is born again out of the husk. And this She has taught us by her symbol and her image which is the snake, who, casting its skin, pours from the husk alive, that we may know we too shall live beyond a cast-off skin, alive and beautiful as the stars.''

She felt them now. Each mind a flame, held within the scope of hers. Their faces were empty of fear.

She motioned with one hand, and the curtain flew upward and the statue of the goddess was at her back, before them.

She let them gaze awhile at the goddess. From the trough below the serpents had gone away. They would be safe in their narrow vasty labyrinth, as no other thing at Ankabek.

Outside, with the crashing of the doors, there had come a muffled roar which still went on. Nothing else was distinguishable. It sounded elemental and subhuman.

Quietly, she signaled again, and a priest came to her, the great cup in his hands. She took it and one by one, dozen by dozen, the faces and the eyes came back to her.

She told them about the cup.

The drug was Thaddrian, once more universal. It brought an immobility, and outer hardening, turning men to stone as inwardly, without pain, they died. Those Vis warriors, standing guard forever in the tombs of kings, had perhaps partaken of that brew. Now it had been distilled and mixed. The death it brought was swift, though still painless. A death sweet as sleep, from one small sip at the great cup's brim.

"If any will not," she said to them, "say now. There is time for you to hide yourselves in the corridors below. The Zakorians have not yet reached them. It may be possible for a very few to find some cranny that is missed, and so escape. I do not promise it. I offer the choice.''

They murmured. They fell still. None of them moved toward the doors.

"Then," she said, "if you consent, come closer, to the goddess. When you drink, give also to your animals. Fear nothing. We shall go all together, a flight of souls like a flight of arrows all from one bow."

The Lowland priest drank first from the cup, as he had offered to do, to demonstrate their oneness, and that the drink was nothing to be afraid of in itself. Having drunk, he smiled at them, and gave the cup into another's grasp. For a moment they watched him, his countenance—that of a young and handsome man—serene, contemplative, without distress; his eyes full of light.

The cup passed. Hands reached for it. They drank, the Lowlanders, the Vis, priest and priestess and villager. The children sipped. The little pet animals were given the cup, the cattle. None refused, as if all had comprehended. Their lips mingled at the brim with the sense of other lips, a kiss, which was also death's kiss. The mixture had no taste. Not even like the taste of water.

The last to take the cup, a priestess, came back with it and held it toward Eraz.

A young girl, black-haired, she wept. There was only sufficient in the cup for one.

"Drink it," said Eraz, "then touch my lips with yours. Yes, it is so strong. I don't lie to you."

So the girl drained the last morsel of the drug, and touched Eraz's lips with hers.

Outside, the roar had ended. Now there began to be a volcanic grumbling from the depths below. They had found the under-corridors. They would soon be at the inner doors.

Within, the stillness was intent, yet soft as powder. Aware of each mind, Eraz was aware as each mind put out its light. In the hall of her brain, the little candles flickered, sighed, faded. Beside her the young Lowland priest was long dead. She could not move her head to look at him.

Sweet as sleep. They had trusted her, they had trusted what lay within themselves. Her sadness was over. Her heart was full of joy.

All the little lights were gone.

And Eraz sank into the moment and the century of oblivion beyond which there waited life.

*   *   *

When Vodon's men brought down the final door, their blood-lust, so long aroused, so long denied, was a single thing, unanimous. Each man was nearly insane.

They spilled in over the door, yelling, yowling, and others sprang in behind them. All were checked.

Whatever they had expected, whatever the villages and towns of shrieking women and terrified men had lessoned them to look for, it was not here.

The floor torches burned. Across the mosaic, in their glare, the great statue of the yellow men's she-demon, upraised on her tail, lifted the serpent stems of her arms. Beneath her, they stood, the people of Ankabek. Most seemed to look into the faces of the men who had broken down the door. Their own faces were calm, almost smiling, the eyes wide, luminous and unblinking.

And there were beasts, too, standing there like the rest, or held in the arms of children. The beasts, the children—all alike—

Another door crashed inward.

Another gout of men rushed roaring into the chamber.

And were checked.

A minute passed.

The Free Zakorians began to shout. Spears were hurled, deliberately short, to dive at the Ankabekians' feet. Not one started, or stirred. Only the folds of clothing stirred at the wind of a spear's passage, or some woman's hair.

"*What is it?*"

"By Zarduk, I don't know—" Vodon half moved forward. "A trance perhaps—"

Suddenly one of the younger Zakorians ran across the temple. He ran straight through the motionless crowd to the place where a tall woman stood, in robes golden as the goddess' tail. Shouting, the Zakorian plunged his knife to the hilt in the woman's right breast. Or would have done. The blade, turning on her breast as if on marlbe, skidded and snapped from its haft. The Zakorian cried out, a different cry. He backed away from the woman, the almost smiling statues with their glowing eyes, the brindle cow, the silken rat on the girl's shoulder, the flesh that was not flesh. Then, screaming, he rushed from the temple.

"*Witchcraft!*"

Vodon choked down a sensation like blood.

"Maybe, but against themselves. Take the jewels. Take the great statue and sink it in the sea. Fire the place. The trees outside. Leave nothing whole that'll catch alight." Turning, he spat. As the passionless human statues watched him with their shining eyes, he cut down his officers, next their seconds, then pushed the long knife into his own throat.

Presently, his men ran over him.

The night flamed redder than the Star could make it. The flame-colored leaves flared to black ashes.

When they dragged the tumbled Anackira to the edge of the rock, they congratulated their gods. They cast her down to Rorn, naked of riches, and blind, for they had gouged out her topaz eyes.

They drank above the bleeding, smoking groves, the wines of the temple.

A wind came with the dawn. It ravaged the blackened trees, blowing off charcoal dust.

Certain of the Free Zakorians did not like this wind. They groaned that it had been full of figures, swirling—a flight of ghosts, like arrows all from one bow.

Dead Vodon's ship foundered as they sailed north.

Only one of the goddess' yellow eyes ever reached Free Zakoris.

At midday in Elyr, the Vardian trader had called a halt. A mile away rocks stood on the dusty sky, and on the rocks two of the ubiquitous star-gazing towers. Here, from a great boulder, a waterfall speared down into a pool.

The Vardian's two servants and the drover sat apart to eat. The herd of fierce Lannic sheep fretted and picked at the dry grass, and nearby, the two herd kalinxes sat bolt-upright, black as basalt. Such guards were trained from infancy, lambs put in with the kittens to be suckled by a female cat. There were no such beasts in Vardath. The Red Star did not burn there, either. Nor anywhere above the Sister Continent.

The Lowland Amanackire were unaffected by the sexual stimulus of the Star. The race of the second continent claimed to be.

The Vardian trader had long since come to think they were unaffected only while they avoided its influence.

He sat outside the makeshift tent he had had put up for himself, looking at the mix-blood girl. She was taking wine to the servants and the drover as he had instructed her. She did not move like a winegirl. She was thirteen if she was a day. Small supple waist, curve of the hips, the little round breasts. And the lovely white skin that never took the sun.

She brought the wine jar to him. Her eyes were lowered. He

had never looked into them. Yellow eyes, of course. He had
noted that from the beginning.

"It's too hot to go on today," he said to her. "We'll stay here
now, till sunrise tomorrow." He knew she was dumb. That
might be an advantage. She had filled his cup and stood meekly.
Eyes lowered. "You're not afraid of me, are you?" he asked.
"Of course not. I'm helping you reach your own people. Safe
from the greedy Vis. Perhaps you'd like to give me something in
return." He hesitated. She made no move. He said, "Lie with
me."

She did not flinch. She did not seem pleased.

"Don't worry," he said, "I know you're young. I'll be
gentle. Am I the first?" She said nothing. He wondered if he
would have to force her to comply. He preferred not to use
force. "Go over to the water and get clean, around the rock
where the others can't see. Then come into my tent." Rather to
his relief she turned at once and went toward the waterfall.
Probably she was not a virgin, and used to being had. Her quiet
was servility not distaste.

It was dark red in the tent from screened-off sun. When she
entered, light came in with her and stayed.

For a moment he could not think what it was, then he sat up
with an exclamation. He went to her slowly.

"By Ashkar! The brutes dyed your hair in that dung-hill
town."

For she was golden-blonde. She was sheer Lowland stock.

And she was beautiful, extraordinarily beautiful. So white,
so golden. Her eyes—golden. They expanded as if with tears,
but it was pure luminosity.

The Vardian trembled with his need. He took the edge of her
dress in his fingers. The fastenings were simple.

He pulled the garment from her. She stood before him naked.

Again, he was almost shocked. Her exquisite high breasts
were capped with gilt. In her navel a drop of yellow resin spat.
The hair on her loins resembled spun metal.

"Don't be afraid of me," he muttered.

"It is you who fear."

He jumped away at the voice. She could not speak—had not
spoken. The words had been inside his skull. The Vardian was
familiar with telepathy, had experienced it with his own kindred,
if mostly as a child. Beyond the initial astonishment he was not
unnerved by the mere fact of mind speech. This mind speech
was, however, unlike any other.

He shuddered. Her eyes seemed to eclipse the world.

Then he fell to his knees. It happened, his body's reverence, before he knew why. On his knees, only then, he knew.

Cast from her light, a shadow rose behind the Lowland girl on the hot red wall. It was the shadow of a being much taller than the girl, though also long-haired and high-breasted, its many arms outstretched and swaying upright upon the coiled tail that formed its lower body.

"Ashkar," said the Vardian.

He bowed to his face as wave upon wave of ecstatic and wondrous terror burst through him, until eventually he fainted.

BOOK THREE—*Cities of Rust and Fire*

ELEVEN

The Xarabian ship reached home port uneventfully, on a smooth evening sea. Next morning, Rem and Lur Raldnor rode inland for the capital.

Lin Abissa was the first true city Rem had laid eyes on for over eight years, and Raldnor's first ever. You could not count Amlan, whose charm was all in her littleness, her impression of a sturdy painted town.

The high slender towers flashing crystal at the sun, the high walls with their parapets, crenellations, bastions, the combination of refined delicacy and obdurate strength—here was Vis, Visian supremacy and beauty, still upright in an altered world.

They entered through the Gate of Gourds. Above it, the banner was flying, Xarabiss' dragon woman. There was a tale of the Lowland War, that the tyrant Amrek had accused Xarabiss of using Anackire as a device. And indeed, there was some resemblance.

With the political unsettlement of the seas, Zakorian spies were apparently suspected. Papers must be produced at the gate. Not everyone had papers. The ecstasy of the first-seen Vis city began to pall in a long wait. Then, when Lur Raldnor's own impressive credentials were produced—Yannul's letter, marked with the council seal of post-war Koramvis he still had the right to use—an escort of soldiery was brought round to conduct them to the palace of the King.

They had reckoned they would get this treatment, (the servant had banked on it), and Lur Raldnor had facetiously postulated a plan of false names.

People on the wide streets turned to look after them. Chariots whipped past, drawn by the fire-swift leaping chariot-animals of the Middle Lands.

169

But it was as they crossed a corner of Lin Abissa's Red
Market that the initial scene of the alteration was impressed on
them.

Members of the pale race, as well as mixes, came and went in
Amlan. But they were Vardians or Shansars. In Xarabiss they
had so far set eyes on one Tarabine merchant, riding in a litter
through the port, the curtains well-back, so all could see him
laughing and sharing sweetmeats with his Vis hataera.

Until now, neither of the Lans, nor Rem himself, had got sight
of a born-blood Lowlander, save gentle Medaci.

The Red Market was lazily energetic in the hot afternoon.
Under the fringed awnings every kind of ware imaginable was up
for sale, even to a row of sequined slaves hung in a flower-
strung cage. The ten guard of the escort were good-naturedly
prodding and cursing the turgidly moving crowd aside, when
suddenly all activity seemed to terminate. Only a drove of cattle
was abruptly hurried, lowing and stamping, into an aisle between
the booths.

The captain of the escort had raised his mailed hand to halt
them, and now held it upright as if congealed in the air.

Clearly, someone of utmost importance was about to enter the
Market.

"Who's coming?" Lur Raldnor asked the captain.

The man lowered his hand. He said, "A Lowlander."

Lur Raldnor raised his eyebrows. "But who?"

"It doesn't matter," said the captain. There was no clue in his
voice.

"You mean you stop all traffic, clear all paths like this, for
any—"

"For any of the pure blood of the goddess. Yes."

Lur Raldnor looked at Rem, shrugged, grinned, and said:
"Proud?"

Rem laughed.

There was hardly any other sound.

Rem had looked for an entourage; litter, outriders, bearers of
fans and parasols, something Karmian.

Then the Lowlander came, walking quite slowly along the
human avenue. There was only one. A woman. She had no
attendants, no accessories.

She was simply dressed, but the robe was silk. Her hair was
the whitest blond Rem had ever seen, snow hair, and her skin
looked as white. On her arms, almost the only ornament, were
bracelets of amber, row on row of them. Round her neck was a

serpent torc he took for polished white enamel—then it moved, and he beheld it was a live snake.

The Amanackire woman barely seemed to notice the crowd. She did not glance at them. Only once her eyes swept outward, to the place where the mounted guard sat their animals, waiting with the rest. Her eyes were not gold, but as with her hair, nearly colorless, eyes that were almost white—like the eyes of the albino snake. The pores of Rem's skin stiffened along shoulders and neck. The captain bowed.

A moment later the woman herself halted. She beckoned to a seller of fruit. At once he and his assistant ran forward, and laid panniers of citruses and grapes before her. She selected, by pointing at it, one fruit. It was taken up and given her. Offering neither thanks nor payment, the woman moved on.

As they rode toward the twisted metal pillars that marked the gateway of the palace, Lur Raldnor said to Rem, "I begin to understand why my father left Dorthar."

Thann Xa'ath was King in Xarabiss now, the oldest of Thann Rashek's eleven sons.

They were assured an audience, then left kicking their heels for two hours in a nicely appointed room with a fountain. Plainly, this was not Olm. At last a servant came to conduct them to a larger room with a larger fountain. The King was sitting at ease, flanked by a couple of guards, a couple of minstrel girls, a scatter of courtiers. There were two Lowlanders. They were not as ice-pale as the woman in the Market, but they sat apart under an ornamental indoor tree, watching, seemingly unresponsive.

The King welcomed the son of Yannul the Lan and his traveling companion.

The portion of court clapped.

Rising, the King took Lur Raldnor over to the Lowland men. After sufficient pause to demonstrate amply they had no need, they got to their feet and greeted Lur Raldnor. One spoke. "We remember keenly all our allies, those who fought beside us. Your father's name is unforgotten." Thann Xa'ath bore this without a murmur. The implication was not veiled. Xarabiss, who called herself the ally of the Plains, had in fact stayed neutral.

"You've arrived at an opportune season," Thann Xa'ath said to Yannul's son. "The son of Raldnor Am Anackire's second most famous captain—our own Xaros—is at court."

Nor was this veiled. The King saw fit to remind the Lowlanders not all Xarabiss had skulked at home.

Thann Xa'ath began to walk about the room, his hand on Lur Raldnor's shoulder. One guard moved smoothly, almost negligently, behind them.

A woman said to Rem, "Do you go to Dorthar, too?"

He told her that he did. She smiled, and said, "I also. In the Princess' train. A tiresome long journey. Didn't you know? Where have you been? In Lan? Oh, naturally, there's never any news in Lan. The King's daughter is just now to be sent to the Storm Lord. Etiquette generally dictates even a High King should come to claim his bride from her father's house. But Raldenash must remain in Anackyra, with all this talk of war—" her patronizing smile grew more intent; she widened her charcoaled eyes at him. "They'll have missed Zastis for their consummation. But I think that may not matter. Raldanash is cold, they say. The hero Raldnor's son! Do you think it possible?"

"As you mentioned," Rem said, "we get no news of any sort in Lan."

He excused himself and went to remind a wine-server of his existence.

But it turned out to be the truth they were now expected to join the cumbersome bridal caravan that would be wending to Dorthar in five days' time.

Xa'ath's daughter had been betrothed to the Storm Lord of six years. It was form. Raldanash, entering Dorthar at the age of thirteen, accepting his first three queens a year later, already had a bevy of wives from almost every country of Vis, and out of Shansar and Vardath also. Xarabiss, lacking daughters old enough for bedding, young enough for wedding, had lagged behind till now.

But it seemed Ulis Anet Am Xarabiss was worth awaiting. She had Karmian blood on her mother's side, that fabled part-Xarabian part-Karmian mixture which had produced the legendary Astaris.

"Well, she's red-haired at least," said Lur Raldnor, leaning on a parapet two evenings later. "And with very light skin. That much I got from her lady. You know, the young one I—"

"I know."

"I heard something more."

"You're getting to gossip just like a Xarabian," said Rem, tickled.

"What else is there to do here, apart from the other thing? This Iros son of Xaros we've not yet met. He's been given the command of Ulis' personal guard. To attend her to and in Dorthar. Which may be unwise."

"Because."

"Because Iros is her lover."

"I thought custom decreed the bride of a king went to him with her seals intact."

"He needn't have deflowered her to have shared her bed."

"If he's so restrained," said Rem, "he'll be able to control his jealous rage in Dorthar, persumably."

"Or Iros may have had her. She's only a subsidiary wife, not chosen to be High Queen. So long as she's not with child, she's acceptable."

Iros was on view that evening. He sat at the King's side through dinner, and afterwards was noted dicing familiarly with two of Thann Xa'ath's sons.

Dressed in the casual wear of a high-ranking officer, Iros was exceptionally handsome, as his father had been in his youth and still was, reportedly. The son's personality, however, was his own. Xaros' reputation was that of a mercurial opportunist, who had won a decisive stroke of the Lowland War with one fortuitous trick. Iros, though he laughed and jested and gave evidence of wit, had the peacock's other side of arrogance and anger. Introduced to Lur Raldnor, Iros' junior by several years, the Xarabian flashed a smile and said, "And are we supposed to hang on each other's necks all night for our fathers' sakes? Or can I simply go back to the dice with a clear conscience?"

"Please," said Lur Raldnor quietly, "return to the dice. I wouldn't dream of detaining you."

Iros flushed under his Xarabian skin. His mouth curled and he said, "I'm glad you understand a soldier's pleasures. But you're not a soldier, are you? You anticipate something in Dorthar?"

Lur Raldnor looked at him out of advantageous Lowland eyes, then said, "Courtesy?"

Iros scowled. "You're saying—"

"I'm saying your dice game is pining for you."

Iros sneered, but could do nothing else but go. He went, and lost the next three throws, as they heard all across the chamber and even over the dancing girls' music.

So, they had seen Iros. Rem did not see Ulis Anet until the night before the bridal caravan set out.

"What's the matter?" said Yannul's son, coming out on the balcony.

"I thought you were with your Princess' lady," said Rem.

"I was, earlier. It's nearly morning now, not worth taking to bed here. We'll be leaving in a few hours."

Rem spoke of the perfidy of timing involved in royal progresses.

"You still didn't say what the matter was. Is it—"

"No," said Rem. "Zastis is finished, and besides, half the palace carries on like an Ommos Quarter. Go to bed."

Lur Raldnor nodded, waited, vanished.

The air was fresh and cool in the last spaces of the night. The unlit darkness made an all too perfect slate on which to draw again the pictures, and the thoughts.

To try to recall the first time it ever happened. The lancing pain through the skull, and then the image within the skull, shutting out all else.

Late adolescence. He recollected exactly the hour and the place—Istris, behind the wine-sellers on Jar Street—he had been drunk. He had put the vision away as a thing of the drunkenness, could not now remember what it had been. Nor the others, the two, three, that had fastened on him. . . . Had they borne any relation to his life or to anything? They must have done. For in the end, prescient, empathic, whatever they were, they had all had meaning. Even the mirage which shut his eyes outside Kesarh's door and earned him a lashing.

He could evoke that one easily. The red-haired woman standing like a stone. And in her womb, the beginning of another life.

And then Kesarh going by on his way to bid stormy farewell to his sister—the sister he loved carnally, Val Nardia, that he would make his mistress at Ankabek. Mistress, and mother of his child.

And at Ankabek itself, in the blind circling corridor of the temple which was now a burned-out husk, the second mirage. Three women, white hair, blood hair, ebony. And the three embryos like wisps of silver steam—

There had been other details. Perhaps, as with the more recent seeings, they had to do with his connection to Raldnor Am Anackire. His—father.

But the vision at Ankabek had told him already who he was. He had been shown the three women who had carried Raldnor's seed. White-haired Sulvian of Vathcri, mother of Raldanash the Storm Lord. Ebony-haired Lyki—Rem's own mother—had she not surely identified herself *with a blow*? And thirdly, the red-haired woman of his former sighting: Astaris.

How many knew that she had lodged in her womb the third child of Raldnor? In all the mythos, there had never been a word of it.

Even Yannul had not known.

The child had been lost, so much was sure. Raldnor and Astaris were gone. Their progeny, if it had survived, had had long years to reveal itself. And had not. And yet somehow the worshippers of Anackire at Ankabek had guessed at its being, its loss of being, looking for the balance to be set right. They had searched for some resembling conjunction of flesh and race. Maybe grotesquely, predictably, they had perceived it in Val Nardia and Kesarh. Blood of the blood peoples mixed with Vis, the sorcerous affiliation of twins, and one other thing, omen of omens—

No wonder Ankabek had held Val Nardia's corpse in stasis, brought the child to term—

Do I give credence to any of this? Do I even acknowledge the engineering of a holy mystery? No. It's lust gone sour, insomnia. How could they breed her for that, and their magic let her end a wolf child?

Since the night he had seen the attack on Ankabek through the body of the Xarabian ship, Rem had kept the amber ring among his slight baggage, carefully not easy of access. To take out the ring now, hold it, wear it, might clarify these things. He did not want them clarified.

After all, he had been given a sign, if he must rest this craziness on proofs.

She had come to the banquet, her last night in her father's palace. Beforehand, the whole place had been murmuring about how beautiful she was, this late daughter of the royal line. How nearly like Astaris, the most beautiful woman in the world.

Rem had not looked to be impressed in any way. As a rule he did not like women. If they were beautiful, he saw it with a grim detachment, or missed it altogether.

Ulis Anet entered the hall with her maidens.

She was lustrously red-haired, as foretold, and her gown was the exact red of her hair with a girdle of red-gold. At her throat shimmered a necklace of polished amethysts, a Xarabian jewelry pun, for the amethyst was the jewel closest in looks to a Serpent's Eye.

She was slim and graceful. Then he realized her figure and her walk reminded him of another's.

And then, she was near enough he saw her face.

Ulis Anet, said to resemble Astaris, was also a replica of Val Nardia, the mistress-sister of Kesarh.

* * *

Yeiza, her skin fragrant from the grasses she had lain among
with Lur Raldnor, knew better than to make a sound beside the
doors to the Princess' bedchamber. She did, however, pause a
moment to listen.

Two voices, but not vocal in love.

Shaking her head, as one party to affairs of great importance,
Yeiza, unable to make out a syllable, crept away.

Beyond the doors, Iros stood, fully clothed in his elegant
attire. A single lamp was burning and Ulis Anet was seated
beneath it, robed for the bed she had not sought.

"Then I'll leave you, madam," he said coldly. "And this is
the end of it."

"You should never have come here."

"The secret passage remained unlocked and unguarded. If
you'd wanted to keep me out you should have left men there.
They might have killed me. Then you'd have been rid of me for
good."

The girl sighed. The sigh caught a flare of purple at her throat
where the amethysts still lay.

"You know I don't wish you anything but well, Iros. But you
should have had more sense than to visit me tonight."

"I should have waited till we were on the road? Come swag-
gering into your tent for all to see? Or waited for Dorthar, till
your white-haired High King tires of you? From what I've heard
that will be swiftly. If he even troubles to bed you at all."

Ulis Anet rested her forehead on her hand. She was exhausted.
They had had this discussion over and over during the past
months.

"Even if," she said, "I am to live as a virgin in Dorthar,
there can be nothing further between us."

"I'm so dear to you."

Her temper snapped suddenly, and she rose.

"Don't be a fool. Do you think I want this match? I've no
choice, and neither have you. You've given me no peace—"

"What peace have I had—"

"What else can I do? Run away with you like a peasant girl
married off against her will to some farmer? I've been given to
the Storm Lord. You knew of it and all that it meant before ever
you saw me."

His eyes blazed with hatred.

"I love you!" he shouted.

Had Yeiza been at the door, this much she would have heard.

"Love. Well, you've a choice in lovers. I have none."

"You chose me, once," he said, more softly.

"Yes." She closed her eyes.

"And if Whitehair takes you, he'll find as much."

"It seems it doesn't matter," she said, "providing there has been adequate interval."

"He values you so highly."

Ulis Anet turned. She walked to a mirror and stared it at her beautiful face, the mellifluous lines of her body. And behind her the handsome and furious demon who had invaded her unsympathetic world. She did not love him, but she had been amorously and tenderly fond of him. She doubted now if she had ever meant as much to him. If the bond with Dorthar had not claimed her, she might have been made Iros' wife, to mark his father's standing. He would have valued her royalty and her looks, and been frequently and blatantly adulterous elsewhere.

Getting no reply from her, he strode to the drapery that hid the secret door. He wrenched the curtain off its rings and flung out into the stone passageway.

Straight-backed, she crossed to the door and closed it. Then she sat at her window, watching the sun begin to come, since it was too late now for sleep.

TWELVE

The Princess' caravan wandered through the heart of summer, slow, dreamlike. They seemed to make no speed at all. Plains gave way to hills and hills to plains, beneath skies powdered by dust or stars. One impressive city enveloped them, then let them go. At night, another would appear far off before them in a valley, haloed with lights.

For Rem it was a time of timelessness. Lur Raldnor was not often nearby. After dark he was with his Yeiza, the Princess' youthful chief lady. By day, the boy was taken up by the royal circle. Ulis Anet had noticed and liked him. Perhaps that was a further move to anger her commander Iros, or further to keep Iros at bay. Xaros' son rode at the head of his column of men, stony-faced. His behavior toward his royal charge was ostentatiously correct, so impeccable as to be suspect. There was now hardly anyone in the entourage, down to the last groom or page, who had not fathomed what had been the relation of the com-

mander of the King's daughter's guard to the King's daughter.
One day a soldier was flogged a hundred yards from the camp,
and left out half dead all through the heat of noon. Apparently he
had been overheard by Iros whistling some song invented upon
some matter.

At night the commander entertained lavishly and grossly in his
pavilion, or organized torchlit chariot-races, making the darkness
raucous. In the cities, he picked out the lushest available women
and paraded his lust all through dinner.

Sometimes, on the upper plains, thunder came cantering across
the skyline, a storm of wild zeebas, shearing away at the last
instant from the campfires.

Rem, walking beyond the tents along the rim of a hill in the
dusk, glimpsed a man and a woman entwined oblivious amid the
fern. Raldnor and his girl. Noiselessly, unseen, Rem avoided
them.

Zastis was done, and maybe it was only that which made this
distancing in him. The urgent frustration of Lan had become like
another's memory, not his own. Yannul's son seemed far off, a
pleasing sight, amiable companion, a hundred years younger
than Rem and scarcely recognized.

Ommos, the ill-famed.

They saw Uthkat on the plain of Orsh, where Raldnor Am
Anackire had routed the Vis, and later the ruins of Goparr which
Raldnor Am Anackire had razed for treachery. History still
moved. Less than a month before, Karith had been burnt by the
Free Zakorian fleet, and troops were toiling across the landscape,
skirting the caravan once its mission was ascertained. The indigenous Ommos were dark, inclined to flesh, their accent so thick
as to create almost another language from familiar words. Other
than soldiery, the whole kingdom seemed bare and deserted, and
the towns looked dark by night.

At Hetta Para they were received. The capital had been cast
down in the War. The new city was something else again, little
more than a town on the outskirts of a wreck.

There was no king in Ommos now, but a man who named
himself Guardian, a Lowlander. The court, if such it might be
termed, was Lowland, too.

The betrothed of Raldanash was austerely and publicly entertained some three or four hours, with a group of her followers.
Then they were all consigned to cramped apartments, or to
anything the area might be thought to offer.

Those who investigated the spareness of the new Hetta Para and the shambles of the old, came back with stories of an Anackire temple of black stone, its portals patrolled by Lowland guards, of the immemorial fire-dancers in taverns of the ruin, boys or women, scorching their clothing from them with lighted torches, and of a Zarok fire god flung down in a pit, Lowland work, on whom the Ommos came ritualistically and fawningly to urinate, making all the while partly hidden religious gestures for mercy to the god.

There were countless delays between Hetta Para and the border.

It was not for another five days that they came to the river and saw the repaired garrison outpost the War had once destroyed, while the bowl-topped Dortharian watchtower belched out blue-purple smoulder to welcome them.

Dorthar.

My father came here, not knowing then, as I know mine, his line or dubious rights or heritage. Insolent, ill-at-ease, in danger, in love with the land and hating the land for its symbols and its shadow.

Rem looked about him: earth, mountains, sky.

What's Dorthar, then, to me?

For the entry into the city of Anackyra, Lur Raldnor had been granted a chariot, and a team of thoroughbred animals, and his best clothes had come out of the traveling chest.

"What do you want to do?" he inquired of Rem.

"What we agreed. You'll be presented. When the moment is suitable, you give him Yannul's letters. At some point he'll read them."

"From what I've heard he may not."

Rem had also, here and there, picked up Xarabian evaluations of the Storm Lord.

"Then politely stress them, indicating the Koramvin seal."

"But you'll follow me into the presence chamber."

"If allowed."

"Where are you placed for the entry?"

"Behind the chariots, somewhere."

Lur Raldnor appraised him and eventually said, "You do know this indifference isn't humbleness on your part, don't you? It's pride. You're already saying: *I* know who I am. Let *him* find out."

The conversation was held by the old white road which had led across the plain under Koramvis. It was dusk and the tents were up. Tomorrow they would be going in to the new metropolis, and down the valley above the ancient watchtower the smoke plume still hung, one tone darker than the darkening sky.

"It's possible," said Rem, "that even when he does find out, he may not care to know."

"Whatever we've heard of him, he wouldn't risk that. He needs you as a friend, not an enemy. Think of the harm you could do him if estranged."

"I've thought. And Raldanash may think. He might consider me worth a tactful murder."

Lur Raldnor grinned.

"This isn't Karmiss."

Rem was taken aback. Had he implied so much about Kesarh's service?

Across the long slope of the valley plain, where the ground rose up to the hills which, before the quake, had been of a different shape, the night-fires of the new city began to gleam.

When the boy had gone off to share the Princess' tent-court, Rem stayed, looking toward the city.

There had been groves of fruit trees and cibba here, burned long ago or cut down. The last battle had begun on this earth. All day, he had noted the superstitious mutter as they approached.

He wondered suddenly if men here alone at night fancied they heard the cries of war and pain, and felt the land start to shudder. He half expected one of the visions to seize on him. But nothing came, and only the lighted lamps of Anackyra shone two miles off, no sheen of ghosts.

The Princess Ulis Anet was dressed in white. Rem, after the first startlement had lessened, had observed her skin was darker than Val Nardia's had been. Clad in the whiteness intended to symbolize her fitness for a High King of the fair races, she looked darker yet, but arrestingly so, like an icon of pale gold. Her ruby-colored hair was appropriately veiled in an openwork mesh of rubies.

Before and behind her chariot came Iros' men, blinding with polished metal. The banners of Xarabiss and the blazon of Thann Xa'ath swayed glittering from their poles.

The caravan had sprouted into the usual elements of show.

Dancing girls clothed only in brilliant body-paint with disconcerting mirrors at their groins, acrobats, and magicians producing globes of radiance from the air. Twelve milk-white kalinxes had been found—or bleached—to draw three gilded carts from which sweets, flowers and small pieces of money might be

thrown to the crowds by girls dressed in the carmine robes of
Yasmis, the Xarabian love-goddess. Before the rule of Anackire,
a statue of Yasmis would have been carried in any betrothal and
bridal procession that could afford one. No longer.

Musicians played. The chariots rolled.

Where the new road went between the fields and orchards, it
was lined by peasants, holding their children up to see, and
young girls casting petals and looks at the soldiery.

A quarter of a mile from the gates, Raldanash's envoy met
them, with a further escort.

For the first time Rem saw the white goddess banners of
Anackyra, and carried amid them the device of his half-brother,
the hero Raldnor's legal son. Raldanash's emblem was a brazen
serpent coiled about a black thunder-cloud, gripping the might of
it surely in immovable coils. The understanding was there for
any with eyes to see.

Koramvis had been reckoned the wonder of the north. Anackyra,
going up fast on the back of her ruin, had had something to beat.

Yannul had left before the city was completed. The post-War
council, mixed of Vis and Lowlanders and men of the Sister
Continent, had held together reasonably well under the original
Koramvin Warden, Mathon. An old man then, initially chosen
for his post just because he was old and therefore considered
safe, the earthquake had spared him and he had gone on to watch
the city reborn over the plain beneath and the forested western
hill-slopes. He had outlived Yannul's defection, and the death of
another who had been, in his way, a friend to the hero Raldnor,
the Dragon Lord Kren. Kren had died the year the boy King
entered Anackyra. Mathon, though, had lived to one hundred
and twelve, an age not unheard of among the Vis, but spectacular considering the upheavals of his era. He had seen the commencing years of Raldanash's reign. He had seen the city finished.
To the end, Mathon had kept his wits and, they said, his
uselessness. Now the Warden of Anackyra was a Vathcrian, a
cousin of the King's from home.

The walls were high and thick. There was something in that.
Until a few years ago, all but the royal area had been unwalled.

White stone, touched with white crystal and white gold: White
fire. Young—she was younger than Rem himself. Beautiful she
was too, naturally. They had donated to her all the glories of
aftermath. On raised terraces her ten goddess-temples blazed
back the sun.

But she did not feel young, or beautiful, or even old under the youngness and beauty, antique Vis crying out in anger at her chains. She tasted of—nothing.

Yet, something there was.

The heat had come early, and there was a curious styptic quality to the air. Rem consoled the neck of the zeeba he rode, gauging its tension, which maybe it had only caught from him.

But there was a stillness, too, which was not possible, for ever since they had got in the gate, the crowds, packed by the road, on balconies and rooftops, had been screaming and calling, and the clatter and music of the entourage itself was enough to deafen a man. Yet those crowd noises, which were at first too loud to have patience with, now seemed engulfed, bat-squeaks in some colossal and echo-less cave.

In Anackyra, as in Koramvis, there was an Avenue of Rarnammon, this one far longer. It was ten chariot-lengths wide, lined by massive statuary—dragons, serpents, and mere human giants. Where the avenue opened out before the terraced approach to the palace, the square was dominated by Rarnammon himself, gigantic above the giants, in a chariot on a plinth. The monument was all gold and gold-washed bronze, with windows for the eyes of saffron glass behind which twin torches were kept lit. In the shadow of this, the Storm Lord would give public welcome to his Xarabian bride.

The stillness was heavy as a blanket, now.

Ahead, the chariots, Iros' smart men, the ruby-haired woman in her car decked by flowers.

"Storm coming," someone said just behind Rem. "Look how the trees're thrashing about."

Involuntarily Rem turned to see. The trees above the walls were motionless. There was no one close enough at his shoulder to have spoken so hoarsely and been heard.

"Magic," someone else said, directly before him. He almost felt the breath strike his face and there was no one so near. "Oh gods—what is it?"

Rem looked up and saw the hills above the city. There were white towers there, but only for a moment. He saw the red spout and gush of powdered rock explode silently from beneath Koramvis' walls. Then the hills ran together and the towers were lifted like an offering to an ink-black sky.

Even as it happened, he was aware it was not real; he felt the zeeba beneath him and kept it in hand. His eyes were open and he knew where he was. Then he seemed to blink, and the hills were calm, the summer morning light spread through them.

He thought, without hurry, precisely, *Prophecy, this time. There's about to be an earthquake.*

The zeeba tossed its head and mouthed the reins. You could see it now, all along the route the animals were growing fractious. Men, irritably forcing them to keep the line, were responding too, unknowingly.

In the grip of it, Rem felt only an enormous distancing, no terror. He understood he would be aware to the second. He rode on, holding the zeeba steady.

The Avenue widened and gave on to the great square. Ahead, the mighty Rarnammon statue, behind that the Imperial Hill, the terraced rise with the palace, and higher, framed in forest, the oldest temple of the Dortharian Anackire. Across the nearer space, the glint of other caparisons, banners, the figurines of the Storm Lord and his officials. And the crowd everywhere, and more running in to pile up against the buildings. Some had even climbed the Rarnammon to gain vantage from its chariot wheels.

Inside the body of the procession there was abruptly more room. Rem found he was advancing between the chariots as they widened their phalanx, and through them.

Before he was quite through he felt the pulse of the earth stop. That was what it was like. The earth's pulse, or his own. Then under the cheering and the hubbub, there came a low strong roar. At first, they mistook it for themselves.

Then bells began to ring, the curiously noted stringed bells brought here from Koramvis. The bells knew the grasp of the earthquake, it had shaken them before. They seemed to be crying out a warning. It was recognized.

All at once the screams of excitement turned to shrieks of horror. The crowd pushed against itself. He could hear the prayer-screams, too. "Anack! Anack!" The Xarabians of the entourage were if anything more afraid than the Vis of the city. This was not even their country that they be expected to die in it. Already all was out of control, beasts struggling and rearing, chariots dragged sideways, men tumbled, and the crowd on every side milling and howling, no one able to move. But the ground itself moving.

The zeeba danced to keep its balance. Something of Rem's iron command came through to it, just negating the primal urge to kick and run. He looked at the sky. A man was falling from the Rarnammon, screeching. He burst down into the crowd. The great statue, however, did not shift, only trembling at its roots, its human cargo clinging to it.

Rem was through the chariots, up to the place where the

rear guard of Iros' soldiery had flanked the procession's gaudy center, its core Ulis Anet's ceremonial car. But something had happened to the order of the procession.

One of the Yasmis carts had overturned. One of the Yasmis girls lay dead where a kalinx, expelled from the shafts and its tether snapped, had torn out her heart and stood now, in her blood and the crushed sweets, irresolute between fear and viciousness. No one had killed it. When the quake ended it might attack again. Rem leaned, met its glacial eyes, and swiftly cut its throat. He rode over the cadaver, the zeeba snorting, and into the clamor of mounted men beyond.

The Xarabians were shouting, invoking gods. A sword, drawn to hack a passage somewhere, into another world maybe, where the earth was solid, slashed blind over his unmailed shoulder and drew blood. Rem turned and struck the sword-waver unconscious. As the man slumped, Rem saw across him to the garlanded chariot of the Princess. The driver was gone and the banners had fallen. Caught in the maelstrom it was pulled now one way now another, the panic-stricken chariot-animals, bred for strength in speed and little else, leaping and cavorting in the shafts, screaming as human women screamed all about. The reins were gone, she could not have taken them up even if she had had the weight to hold the team, which she did not. Beyond this, he saw again the flash of metal; swords were out everywhere. Iros and his captains were cutting a way to her through the crowd, their own men and the naked dancing girls.

The quake was almost done, the earth merely shivering now, like a man after sickness. It needed only moments more for the complementary dousing of panic, a cold depairing relief, to come down on them. The beasts would feel it first.

But before the dousing came, the freakish flailing of Iros' guard had cleared a road before the Princess' chariot. The animals did at once what they had wished to do all along, bolting forward, their screams trailing like torn flags. The very men who had striven toward her went down before them. Rem saw Iros dashed aside, the long glancing rip of his sword across the breasts of the team serving to madden them further.

Rem touched his spurs against the zeeba. That was all it took. It rushed forward pell-mell as the chariot-animals had done.

The chariot raced ahead, the girl holding to the sides. Ghastly addendum, one of the dancers, caught by her own long hair among the spokes of the wheel, was carried some way in tow over the paving. Her silence was due to death. But Ulis Anet made no sound, either.

Before them, the royal panoply of the King. On foot, hemmed in and pressed against the first steps of the hill, they seemed set only to stare, those figurines, until the chariot ran into them.

The bells had stopped tolling.

Rem had been in enough skirmishes. It was familiar in essence if not in exactitude. And he knew what to do.

Only a little thought went mocking through his occupied mind: *Kesarh would have planned this.*

Then he was level with the pelting team.

Swinging over, he brought his sword down on the inside animal's brain, blade and arm with all the strength behind them he could spare. The beast went over at once, taking the sword with it out of his hand. The others were unable to stop, their momentum carrying them in a snarl across their dead fellow, the chariot slewing behind, all in his path. But he had already kneed the zeeba aside, and as she came by, her volcanic hair flying, he caught the girl up and out and across his mount.

They were away even as the chariot went over. Wrapped in a tangle of traces the animals were flung across it, broken-spined in half a second.

It was as well he had kept up the warrior's training of Karmiss, Rem told himself wryly. He glanced with pity at the dead team. Wryness, pity—that was all. He felt no more than that.

He stayed his mount and slid down from it smoothly, lifting the woman after him.

She stared at him. "Thank you," she said.

"An honor, madam."

The inanity struck both of them. Standing on the square, amid spaces of white paving spilled with blood, a broken chariot, dead bodies, they both laughed bitterly.

There was a tremendous soundlessness all about. Then a ragged cheer went up. The Xarabians, having botched the job, were congratulating a foreign stranger on saving precious Xarabian goods.

From the palace end of the square, men were starting toward them.

"Are you hurt?" Rem said to the Princess.

"No. But you're bleeding."

"Some fool with a sword. It's nothing."

"It seems more than nothing."

"I, too, was a soldier, madam," he said for some reason. "I know when I'm hurt or not. But your solicitude is generous."

"The quake. . . . Is it over?" she asked him. He had become

an authority on things, wounds, rescues, earthquakes. He smiled, nodded.

Irrationally, this private conversation in the middle of pande-monium seemed relevant. Though it meant nothing, he could see how beautiful she was, still spear-straight and self-possessed.

But her eyes drifted to the dead dancing girl and away. Her voice faltered now, before she mastered it.

"Perhaps it's an omen. I've heard when my future husband, the King, entered Anackyra as a boy, there was a violent tremor."

Something happened. It was intangible, invisible, deep as mortal illness.

"What is it?" she said.

But at that moment the group from the palace end of the square had reached them.

Immediately Ulis Anet was encompassed. Rem discovered himself cordoned by a mass of men, Vis, Vathcrians. He could pick out none of the Lowland race. And then there was another man, exactly in front of him. He dressed in white as Ulis Anet had been, and a white cloak roped with a golden snake, the scales laid on like coins. His hair was whiter than his garments, but his skin was tawny as young wood. He had the beauty one had heard of, Raldnor Am Anackire's looks, like a god. But there was no discrepancy in height. They were as tall as each other. So Rem looked at him eye to eye, and these eyes were the color of the glass in the eyeplaces of the Rarnammon.

There had been muttering: "A Vis hero! Who is he? Who is this man?"

Raldanash the Storm Lord said to him directly:

"Who are you?"

The city, if it had shaken in augury or not, had given the torch into his hand. He could no more quench it now than walk away.

"My name is Rarmon," he said. "I am your father's son."

In the darkness, the eyes of the Rarnammon statue glowed upward from the plain, looking brighter than all the other lights of the city.

"But," Vencrek asked, "how do we know the Lord Yannul was not mistaken? Or misled?" He looked across at Yannul's son and smiled. "Hmm?"

"You know, sir," said Lur Raldnor quietly, "because he tells you through me that he was not."

"Your loyalties are commendably to your father. But after so many years—"

"My father, sir, is not senile. He spent some time at the side of Raldnor Am Anackire, and knew him well. He saw Raldnor again in this man who is his son. As Yannul's letter explains, the Lord Rarmon was unaware of his own lineage. The woman had never told him."

"Yes, the woman. Surely the name 'Lyki' is not so uncommon in Visian Karmiss. There might be more than one Lyki with a—forgive me—bastard son."

"She had waited on Astaris at the Koramvin court."

"So she said. Or so the—the *Lord* Rarmon seems to have said that she said."

Rem, who was now Rarmon, turned from the eyes of his namesake below. He put his hand briefly on Lur Raldnor's shoulder and said to Vencrek, "Might this discussion be somewhat premature, since the King is not yet here? Unless, of course, the Storm Lord's belief in me is less important than your own."

Vencrek let his smile freeze, then dismissed it. As the Warden of Anackyra, his good opinion was to be won or forced, or maybe bought. He was a perfect example, you saw, of what Yannul had called the 'blond Vis' of the second continent. A butter-haired Vathcrian; Rem who was Rarmon had seen his kind often enough, fair or dark, at Istris.

The rest of the men in the small attractive chamber were of the council. Tradition had kept it mixed. Two Dortharians, someone from Tarabann, a Shansarian, another Vathcrian. It seemed the Lans and Xarabs who had held honorable places here in Yannul's time had probably all gone home. There were no Lowlanders in the room.

Except, Rem-Rarmon ironically supposed, for Yannul's son and himself.

There was the old familiar sound of spear-butts going down on marble. The doors opened, and the King walked through, two guards at his back. He had retained the custom of the Storm Lord's Chosen, an elite bodyguard. They wore the historic scale plate, too, but it was washed gold and marked with Raldanash's device, the inexorable snake gripping the storm-cloud.

Raldanash looked immediately at him while the others bowed. Rarmon offered no more than an extremely courteous nod.

The Storm Lord sat down. All around, the council representatives seated themselves. Before Vencrek could resume the floor, Raldanash lifted his hand.

"Son of Yannul." He spoke Vis, as he had on the square. It must be the fashion here, if not at Karmiss. Even Vencrek used it.

Lur Raldnor went forward, bowed again and was acknowledged.

The boy was impressed, but then his King was impressive. His appearance alone was overwhelming, straight out of the myth. He had presence, too. Even doing nothing, something came across. And he did very little, his gestures few and spare, his face almost expressionless, the beauty and the trace of power speaking always for him. He was a year Rarmon's junior, which gave him anyway inalienable rights in Dorthar.

Rem who was Rarmon was not immune to the incongruousness of it all. He seemed almost obliged to suspend skepticism since the earthquake.

Apparently the damage was slight from that. Six persons had died. In Koramvis it had been thousands. Hordes of people all day pouring to and from the Anackire temples, to offer in thanks or supplication against further activity, were by sunfall the only proof that anything had happened.

But there had had to be some sort of personal proof. Bathed, and clad for form's sake in mild finery, Rem had taken out the ring of Lowland amber. It would go no farther than the middle joint of the smallest finger on the left hand. The finger which, in his father, had been missing from that same joint since infancy.

He had no sane reason for putting on the ring. A silly woman's Zastis token, which had turned out to have psychic properties. It had assumed the temperature of his skin, he could not even feel it now.

"I shall inform Yannul," said the King to Lur Raldnor, "of my pleasure in your arrival here. Tomorrow there will be space to speak with you in privacy. For now, be free in my court and my city. Only one thing I will ask from you." Diverted from his thoughts, Rarmon looked at the two of them. He guessed—or mentally overheard—what was coming, and braced himself for it. "Yannul the Lan," said Raldanash, "in all well-meaning, named you for his lord. The name of 'Raldnor' is frequent everywhere. But I don't recognize it, other than as the name of my father. In this place, therefore, and in any place where you serve me, you will relinquish it." Lur Raldnor's mouth opened. He stared at the King, then decided to keep silent. "You may use instead the name of your father, which is illustrious and well-remembered. Hereafter, you are Lur Yannul."

The boy realized that was all. He bowed a third time and stepped away. Under his Lowland tan he had gone white.

Vencrek stirred. Raldanash looked directly at him, to Rarmon. "And you," he said.

Rarmon waited, meeting the eyes again. It was too easy to

meet them. They were like wells of light, a depthless deep that
cast away even as it submerged. Magician's eyes.

"You said," Raldanash told him, without inflexion, "and
before many witnesses, that by his Karmian mistress, you are my
father's son."

"His bastard," Rarmon said plainly.

"Yes. You're not claiming Dorthar, then?"

"I'm claiming nothing, my lord. Except the truth of who
and what I am."

Raldanash came to his feet.

"You'll follow me," he said to Rarmon.

As they moved, the King with his guards, back toward the
doors, Vencrek started forward and the others hurried from their
seats. Raldanash gazed at them. "Warden Vencrek. Gentlemen.
I thank you for your attendance. This matter I shall deal with in
my own way. Good night."

They went through the doors, which the guards outside closed
on a stationary staring of faces.

The council chambers lay against the side of the Imperial Hill.
A covered bridge, magnificent with carving, ran over a small
chasm into the palace courts.

So far, Rarmon had only seen the guest palace. The architecture of the royal domicile was massive and complex, grouped in
towers and tiers about endless courtyards. It was modeled, they
said, on the previous structure gone to dust and rust in the hills
above.

Presently they walked into a long hall. The flaming cressets on
the columns lit up the sight he had all this while been waiting
for.

There were seven of them, and they looked like incandescence,
the pale hair and skin, the white clothing—he realized now to
wear white was an affectation with them. Not all were as blanched
as the woman in the Xarabian market. And indeed, seated to one
side, there was a swarthy Vis, a squat man in the yellow robe of
the Dortharian Anackire. He looked as impassive as the rest. He
would have some need to be.

The guards withdrew.

Raldanash walked down the hall, Rarmon at his back, among
the standing candles of the Lowlanders.

None of them bowed, curtseyed or knelt, as the Vis custom
was. Each touched a hand to the brow and then to the breast. It
was a noble enough gesture of honor. It had the feel of something ancient, too, which was strange, for it was also the gesture

of a proud people, and he knew their story. Shunned, spat on, persecuted, due to be annihilated and unwilling to resist—until Raldnor told them differently. Now—*this*.

Three were women.

All seven looked at the King, and then beyond the King to Rarmon.

He felt something, heard something, but without hearing. They were speaking with their brains, and presumably the King with them. One trick of the hero-god's genes that had passed Rarmon by. The eyes never shifted from him. Eyes toning through citrine to ice: the eyes of snakes.

The King spoke to him.

"These are your judges."

"What's my crime?" Rarmon said.

"If you gave the truth to me, there is no crime."

Rarmon dissuaded his skin from crawling. *A quarter of my blood is like theirs. It's the same with him—only a quarter.*

"My mind is open to them," he said.

"You have much Vis blood," one of them said to him. "You are not to be read."

The words were so near yet so opposed to his thoughts, he sensed there had actually been some inadvertent communication.

"Your adepts can read the minds of the Vis," Rarmon said.

The comment was ignored. In a body with Raldanash, they turned and went on through the hall. Rarmon was left to follow, a meaningless demonstration of free-will. The Vis priest did not come after them, but only fell respectfully on his face as they passed. Which was a politeness of Thaddra.

Beyond the doors of the hall, a sloping garden-court stretched gently toward the sky. A building blotted the stars, and as they approached it, the smell of the trees was familiar. A black stone temple, in a sacred grove.

It was no bigger than the shrine of some Plains village. When they entered, a lamp hung alight up in the air. There was no statue, no ornament—nothing but the stone, sweating chill even after the heat of the day.

The door shut.

Raldanash walked to the center of the tomblike place.

"Stand here with me."

Rarmon obeyed. He felt a peculiar misgiving. All religions had mysteries and deceptions. What was to be done here? The seven Lowlanders stood about the walls, snow figures on black.

There was a sound. A soundless sound, reminiscent of the

undercurrent in the air before the tremor struck. But it was
nothing so simple as precognition.

Raldanash stood facing him. Rarmon was aware they had
adopted, he doubted spontaneously, the selfsame position, feet
apart, left arm loosely at the side, right arm slightly advanced.
Almost a fighter's stance. The amber ring commenced softly to
burn. There was Power here, then. Matter of factly, he accepted
that the burning was not uncomfortable, ready to remove the ring
if it threatened to grow red-hot, as on the ship from Hliha.

Then a new light seemed to come up from the stone under
their feet, a curl of sourceless, colorless energy. It enveloped
them slowly, rising like water. Witchcraft.

Through the light he saw Raldanash's face, partly translucent,
but no hint of the skull beneath. Instead, a kind of ghostliness,
other faces, all his facets—indecipherable. So, too, Raldanash
would see him. The facets that were Lyki, the facets that must be
Raldnor's; the inheritance beyond that, a line of kings and
priestesses. And his own many lives in this one, the thief and
cutthroat, the captain of Kesarh's men, the lover of boys.

The ring scalded. It was like molten metal. It should have hurt
him and he should have wrenched it off, but somehow the heat
brought no pain, fire to a salamander. . . .

Then the light went out. The ring was only the temperature of
his skin.

Raldanash stepped away from him.

One of them said, behind him, "You are no liar. You have the
atoms of the messiah Raldnor, and through him of Ashne'e.
There is more. The goddess has left her mark on your soul."

Rarmon had no reaction to the words, or very little. He looked
at the King.

The Amanackire began to leave. As the cool night air stole in,
he knew the chill temple had become very close and warm.

"What now?" he said to Raldanash.

"You are what you said," Raldanash replied. Nothing else.

They approached the door as if nothing had happened.

"Which brings me what, my lord?"

"Whatever you wish, under my authority."

Outside, scale plate flashed. Guards with torches were standing on the lawn after all.

"Perhaps," Rarmon said, "a small gift to start with." Raldanash
paused. Rarmon wondered what Ulis Anet had thought when
first she laid eyes on this impossible husband. "Yannul's son,"
said Rarmon. "To some men, my lord, their name means very

much. It's a magic thing, the key to the ego. His father and
yours were friends. Why not let the boy keep his given name?''

"He is," said Raldanash, "no longer in Lan."

"He found that out. You shamed him. Your implication, sir,
is that no man's fit to bear your father's name."

Raldanash, looking almost utterly like a Lowlander, seemed to
show his Vis blood then. He glanced toward the soldiers. He
said: "You say to me 'Your father,' yet you harangue me like a
brother."

"I'm asking a favor. And they told you, those you trust, that I
am your brother."

There was a long, still interval. A drift of scented air brought
with it faint singing from the public temple in the forest above,
some hymn with cymbals and cries. Truly, Dorthar had made
Her theirs.

Raldanash said, "He can't carry the name of Raldnor in my
service."

"Suppose," said Rarmon, "I'd claimed it for myself."

"Do you?" said Raldanash.

"If I did?"

They stared at each other, as in the black stone room. Time
passed again. Rarmon came to see the King did not intend to
answer him, and what this must mean. A challenge could not,
beyond a certain point, be offered or accepted, for they were not
equals. And yet, with an inferior, one need only command.

"Yes," Raldanash said suddenly to him, "I was spoken to in
the temple, as you were not, mind to mind. My soul isn't
marked by the goddess. I'm only the King."

"My lord, I don't understand."

"I'm not afraid of you, Rarmon. I have powers in me you
lack. I have rights you lack. And I was shown, besides, you
were a thief who now steals nothing. But one other thing they
showed me. You will be more than I can be."

Rarmon nodded. "I still fail to understand you, sir. But am I
to take it you want me to leave Anackyra?"

Yet Raldanash only walked away. His Chosen Guard, among
whom the dark race was represented, went shining after him.

Rarmon was still standing there when a chamberlain came out
and found him. The man was eager to discuss the apartments to
be opened for Rarmon in the palace, and other such matters.

Over it all, the wind still brought the singing down the hill. He
did not know the music was because of him.

*   *   *

"More wine?"

The Thaddrian refused, with great politeness. Intoxication would feel uneasy tonight, even on the juices of the High Priest's cellar.

Beyond the luxurious chamber—the High Priest's "cell"—the songs and shouts had finally died away in the body of the forest temple. It was almost midnight. The High Priest, who had sent the servant out long ago, refilled his own cup.

"But," he said abruptly, "You're sure?"

The Thaddrian gathered himself. This was the fifth time the Blessed One had asked him. The last occasion had been two hours ago. At least the intervals were extending.

"Virtuous Father, you sent me as your witness and I waited in the hall. The cressets were bright. They entered. I had less than a minute before the King and the Amanackire took him from the room to the Storm Lord's private temple. Nor did I see him closer than that lamp-stand there, at any time."

"However," the High Priest prompted fiercely. He was himself, naturally, a Dortharian. Once, *they* had been the master race. Filaments yet lingered.

"However, I was myself convinced, as I told you, and as you informed the worshippers, that this man called Rarmon is truly one of Raldnor's sons."

"And yet you say he's unlike him."

"As Raldor was when I beheld him—few men could compare with that. As few women could have compared with her. And yet, the likeness was evident. This Rarmon is a handsome man in his way. The features, from certain angles, are similar to those of the Rarnammon statues. Raldnor himself was said to look like these."

The High Priest assented, and quaffed his wine.

The Thaddrian had at no time repeated his own inner thought on seeing the King enter the hall, the much darker man at his back. A sudden thought, sheer and quite explicit. *It was divided between the two of them, then. The white-haired Vathcrian has the beauty. But the reservoir of strength—the other has that.*

He had been a child when he saw Raldnor Am Anackire. Sunrise in a rioting Thaddrian town, flames and smoke and sunshine jostling for the sky. And out of the chaos emerged something so simple and ordinary, a peasant's wagon making for the jungle forest. And in the wagon two creatures not ordinary in the least. A god and a goddess. Only years after did he learn who they must have been, Raldnor son of Rehdon, and Astaris, the woman he had loved. The clean banality of their exit from the town and the majesty of their supernatural looks combined, essentially, to make a priest of the Thaddrian. To make him argumentative also. Certain aspects of the worship of his goddess bothered him. Mythology should only so far rule the lives of men. The afterlife should be left to itself. Religion would do better to aid mortals in the mortal state, not drug them with hopes of the transcending future. Were they to live only dreaming of death?

"In any event," said the Blessed One, suppressing a small belch, "the Amanackire will have tested him."

"No doubt, Virtuous Father."

"And you were sure?"

Merciful Anack. The intervals were growing less again.

"Most Virtuous, as far as I could tell—"

"Yes, yes," The High Priest gave signs of impatience with both his Thaddrian and himself. The earthquake escapees would have filled the temple coffers. Maybe he wished to go count the loot. The best donation of all had been from a young Xarabian, the commander of the Princess-bride's personal guard. He had been stunned by a bolting chariot in the quake, but recovered sufficiently to come up here this evening. The Thaddrian doubted the lord Iros had been thanking Anackire for sparing his life. He had seemed in a rage, but also wept. There were already rumors he was in love with the Princess. That had an inauspicious quality to it. Raldnor Am Anackire had been the lover of his Storm Lord's betrothed.

"The portents are sound," said the High Priest, rising. It was time to leave, apparently. "Sons of the heroes meeting here, at the hub of Vis. If war's coming, we need such tokens."

The Thaddian prostrated himself and went.

If war was coming. A child could tell—did tell, for the games of Anackyra's children had become factious, the lower streets loud with those objecting to playing Free Zakorians. War, that curse of men. And this a war worse than any. Zakoris in exile had become a ravening demon. At length she would try to tear all Vis apart for vengeance, and if she won her battles, not one stone would stand upon another, not one blade of grass remain that was not black with fire or blood.

The Lowlanders did not shirk. They had triumphed before. Besides, did not the goddess teach that the soul lived forever? What odds if a man died in the flesh? Death was only the sloughing of a skin. Such philosophy had made them passive long ago, and now reckless, and pitiless.

Passing through the temple, he touched the goddess' golden scales with his lips, loving the idea of Her, and sick and tired of men.

A distant storm, low and faint, murmured over the mountains. The transparent lightnings were thinner than watered milk, but now and then they would catch the surface of fluid—stagnant rain held in a broken cistern or some accumulative pool. On the river too, they played, lighting it as once the street torches had done, the lamps of temples and boats, and the tall windows.

Dead Koramvis, smashed in bits, lay at either side.

He had left the chariot back a mile or more, tethering the zeebas—he had insisted on zeebas for his journey, unused to the flimsy chariot-animals, not wanting to risk them on rough going.

Why he had come up here he did not altogether know. Now, with all done, maybe it was an urge to escape. His father had known such feelings, trapped here in his glorious disguise, Amrek's man.

Rarmon had briefly wondered if he would know his route about the ruined streets, Raldnor's genes reminding him. But, considering the state the shock had brought it to, he doubted even Raldnor could have found the way to much.

Only the river, the Okris, was a sure landmark, smeared fitfully with the lightning. A huge bridge had fallen into the water. On the cracked and upheaved pavement, vegetation had had more than twenty-eight years of chance to grow. Here and there, some building still stood in portions, a tower, a colonnade—but the weeds and the vines and the trees had fastened on these too. There were wildcats lairing; he heard their cries.

When the wind blew, powder ran down the lanes, more than dust, the gratings of marble. Rot came from the river. Metal lay rusting. The whole city rusted like a broken sword.

He walked awhile, then stood and looked across the river.

When movement came, off to his left, he turned without haste, drawing his knife. He would have expected bandits to lair here, with the beasts. But the ring was burning. He hesitated. There was no threat, only strangeness. Beyond a shattered arch of pallid Vis stone, there was another arch like a shadow, also shattered, but black. Under the second arch, someone. . . . A girl.

He went toward her slowly. There was no need for slowness, he could not break the mirage, like a web.

All around it was night, but in the second arch, daylight.

She was not looking at him. She was drawing water from a

well. Young, thirteen or fourteen years of age, lovely with her youth and with some other thing. Lowland hair and skin. When she had filled her jar, she set it on her hip. She raised her head, and so her eyes. And meeting her eyes in the mirage, which she had not allowed to happen in the corridor at Olm, he knew her and cried out, so the heart of the hollow ruin felt his voice.

THIRTEEN

A queen had ruled over it once, before the history began that was remembered. Ashnesea, from whose name such other names had evolved as Anici, or Ashne'e. It felt old as the earth. It had seen so much. The splendors of legend, the decline of its people, conquered or cast down, the persecutions of the Vis, the ultimate persecution by Amrek. It had been occupied, garrisoned by men who hated and feared both its inhabitants and it. Then a messiah walked over its black stones, and it saw the beginning of the overthrow of the Vis, the Lowland Serpent, waking. And the first strike of the Serpent's fangs.

It was a ruin still, the Lowland city on the Shadowless Plains, and it had no name, if it had ever had one.

Through its decayed walls animals yet ran in and out, travelers penetrated and departed as they wished. Everything had changed, but it had not. Entering the undefended gates, one would still be overpowered by a sense of enormous age and enigma.

Haut had been intending to make for one of the two or three sizable Lowland towns now flourishing on the Plains, even Hamos, maybe. Then, lying in his tent at Elyr, waiting for the girl to come in and pleasure him, he had considered, if she were good, he might keep her for himself. He would free her first, of course, so there would be no irregularity to annoy the Amanackire, binding her only by love of him. Then she had come in, and he had seen her hair, and her eyes, and next the Shadow of the goddess.

When he regained consciousness, she was gone. He went out, shivering, to determine if she had ever existed. His servants and the drover slept, but she sat by the guard kalinxes, watching the sheep.

He went over to her and when she did not deny him or strike him dead, he kneeled to her and begged her pardon.

Thereafter she rode in a cart with an awning which he purchased at the next village. Sometimes, he asked her what she wished, but she only smiled. However, the smile was enchanting, and considerably better than a flung levinbolt. In the dust, her shadow was now only a girl's. His servants, Vardians like himself, respected her blondness currently revealed, and assumed his care of her was prudence, prudently copying it.

To Haut, the ways of avatars were familiar from stories. The Lowland War had occurred before he was born, but was recent enough for the new paint on the tales to have stayed fresh. It was still an era of wonders. More than unnerved, he was excited to be included in it. In Vardath, too, where priestesses walked and talked with lions, and the telepathy of near kin was fairly frequent, it was simpler to remain easy with the prodigies of faith.

Crossing into the Lowlands, Haut became aware of their destination. She did not tell him, he merely knew. He was a little disappointed, for the ruined city offered scant business to him, and, he would have thought, scantier fame for her. But it went without saying he obeyed.

He did not warm to the city, standing darkly brooding in its shallow valley. That was no surprise either. But numbers of people still dwelled there, and that was a surprise. There was even a venturesome Xarabian quarter, intent on trade. They had revived one of the marketplaces, and re-awarded it its antique Lowlander name of Lepasin. The houses round about had been shored up and repaired. It was the most cheerful area of the ruin, giving more than a semblance of life, and here the Vardian took rooms looking out on the market. On the far side of its terraces, two arcane palaces kept one in mind of decay, but the rest of the slope had gone to grass. The last of Haut's sheep could be pastured there, and sheltered in the overgrown courts by night.

With the day, women began to gather at the ancient watering places, carrying their jars, lending to the morning a further normalcy.

There were still many of mixed blood in the city. Not so long ago it had been their only refuge, when they learned they did not suit either with the Vis or the pale races. The true Lowlanders for the most part were gone—to Plains towns such as Hamos or Moiyah, or away into the Vis world now wide open to them. Those who remained here were of that outer kind, pure of blood, yet more tender of spirit. They were many, but proportionally

few. The Lowland people had found themselves. Mostly, they
were not as they had been. Or rather, they were exactly as they
had been, eons past.

When the girl appeared in the Lepasin, the groups of the
industrious and the idle made way for her. Even here, deference
was paid to the Amanackire, and from her coloring she could be
no other.

When she went toward the old well, two or three women
hurried across to her to set her right.

"Young mistress—don't trouble with that. It's dry."

"Come to the well on the South Terrace, lady. We'll show
you."

The girl paused and looked at them. It was clear she had heard
them, for she smiled a little and half inclined her head. But then
she went on up the steps to the well. Framed by its shattered
arch, she stood as if in thought or daydream.

The women conferred. They were mixes, and did not like to
belabor their point. They waited under the steps for her to see for
herself and come back to be shown the working well the other
side of the Lepasin.

All about the moving market was astir with sale and barter,
but near at hand there was already some interest in the Amanackire
maiden at the dry well.

A young half-Xarabian man left his brother to mind their
booth of painted earthenware and vegetables. He brushed through
the knot of women now gathered under the well. The Lowland
girl had caught his fancy. He walked up the steps until he was
beside her.

"There's been no water in there since my father's time. Didn't
those daft pigeons tell you? Let me take you to the other well."

"Wait," she said gently.

For a moment he was about to answer, then he clapped his
hand to his head, inside which he had heard her. His half-blood
had made mind speech a rare incoherent thing. To receive so
strongly thrilled him. As the hero Raldnor himself had once
done, he fell in love with a woman for allowing him one
moment's sheer telepathy.

When she lowered the bucket into the well, he let her do it,
unprotesting. When the bucket came up, she dipped in her jar.

He had been looking at her, not the bucket, but sounds alerted
him. He looked at the jar, then, and saw it was wet.

Under the steps, the women had seen too. One exclaimed.
They gestured toward her.

Then she offered the jar to him.

"Drink."

The word—but it was not a word—stood bright as glass in his brain. He found he was trembling as he reached and took the jar and brought it to his mouth. Then the trembling stopped and he let out a roar.

Heads turned all about.

The young man was in an ecstasy of incredulous delight, almost fury. "It's wine!"

People came hurrying, questioning, calling.

"A trick!"

"Magic!"

The girl stepped aside, and let them lower and raise the bucket for themselves; taste, vociferate, pour away, lower again and raise again and taste again and shout at each other.

The noise grew into hubbub.

Watching from his window that looked out across the market, the Vardian, Haut, felt himself also begin to tremble once more. He had known the well was dry, the Xarabian landlord had explained that. Haut heard the cries. He understood she had not required his presence, but now he felt impelled to go into the Lepasin, to become involved in what was happening.

It was part of the repertoire of magical religious conjurings intrinsic to his continent, especially to Shansar. The symbolic metamorphoses: A staff or a sword to a snake, air into fire, the blasting of trees into stone, or the bringing out from stone of water, the changing of water into blood for a curse, and into wine for a blessing. As with the rest she had shown him, he was ethnically at home with it. Yet something now made him want to taste the wine, and perhaps to weep.

When he had pushed beyond the door, one of Haut's servants caught his arm.

"You know what's done, sir?" Haut nodded. "They're trying to *buy* the wine from her."

Haut laughed after all, his commercial bone tickled.

You did not buy miracles.

The excitement and coming and going about the well of wine went on until the heat of noonday. The activities of the market were suspended, or carried on half-heartedly. Whoever came new to the scene was told. The dry well did not run dry.

As for the girl, she sat by the well on the topmost step, quite composed, gazing into the faces of those who approached, or away across them all. It was as if she waited, but whether for some sign from the crowd, or from within herself, or out of the sky, was not certain.

Those who knew or had discovered Haut belonged to her, sought him.

"Does she never speak?"

"She doesn't speak aloud. Just within. She's Amanackire."

"Where did she come from? Over the sea?"

"My land? No. I found her in Lanelyr."

He was a celebrity, since he accompanied one. He stretched and basked, not minding it. The wine was yellow, very clear, a Lowland vintage. Everyone had drunk the wine. He had drunk it. Perhaps he was altered.

Slightly astonished, he found he was comfortably dozing on his bench, his back to the wall. It was very hot. Something so strange was happening, but it was quite acceptable, a perfect fit.

The Lepasin was packed like a cupboard. On the upper terraces they reclined on their sides over the cracked stone and bleached grass, under makeshift parasols. People sat in windows and doorways. A handful had climbed the ruinous façades of the two palaces. Haut could even see the noble bearded faces of some of his sheep peering down between the columns.

The sun passed from the zenith.

The girl rose from the top step of the well.

They watched her as she walked down, and across the market. A vast number got up, unbidden, unrefused, and went after her.

She walked about the ruined city, through its scoured shells and dusty streets.

Twenty or thirty paces behind her, the crowd followed. At any spot she seemed to wish to traverse, where sections of masonry might have collapsed and blocked the way, young men, usually headed by a blond Xarabian, would run ahead with yells and laughter and the fume of dust, to design her a path.

She seemed to know history well.

She walked to the house that had once given shelter to a man called Orhvan, who in turn had sheltered there Raldnor—and, unwittingly, the traitor Ras. She went in at the door and through the round hall alone, and out again, and on. She moved into the upper quarter to the house once belonging to the Ommos, Yr Dakan, but did not enter. The Zarok-pillars outside had long since been crushed by mallets. She crossed the city to the stagnant palace from which the Dortharian garrison had held the Plains, rung its curfew bell, planned its rapine and sadism, and where, on the night of Awakening, it had died screaming in its blood at Raldnor's word.

She entered the long cold vaults of this palace and lingered. Only a few accompanied her there, to see her and to see her safe. Men seldom ventured into the building. It was reckoned unlucky by the mixes and the Vis, a thing of pain and sorrow to those pure Lowlanders on the edge of their kind.

There were a few other places she visited. Another house that Raldnor had occupied. The makeshift forge where the first Dortharian sword had been seared with a crude but passionate emblem of Anackire, and still hung on a post, rusting now. The street where they said Raldnor had slain a huge white wolf.

The sun lowered itself on golden chains.

The crowd was footsore, some elated and chattering, some losing the thread, wondering why they had followed her, what she was that they should have done so, the little slight figure of a young girl, who never looked back at them.

The shadows were long spills of cinnabar when she led them again into the Lepasin. The black broken column-shafts of the palaces streaked a carnelion sky, darted with purple birds.

Those persons who had remained in the market had cleared their booths for the night and gone away. Only here and there vigil was kept by a lighted lamp. Lamps had been woken also in the windows round about, where watchers leaned to look forth.

The girl walked to the northeastern terrace and up the steps of the undry well. The glow of the western sky edged her, so she also glowed against the dark stone.

A huge stillness balanced between heaven and earth. The birds had settled, no wind blew. The sunset hesitated.

Something was about to happen. It would be impossible not to know as much. The Vis in the Lepasin afraid and voracious, stood on mental tiptoe. The Lowlanders felt an aching of some old wound of the heart.

The girl lifted her arms.

Haut the Vardian, sometime drover of all kinds of flesh, purveyor of sheep, slave-trader, experienced the floating sensation known in the prayer-towers of the Sister Continent, where the soul could loosen in the body, letting go. All around, the crowd swayed, giving up concentrated emotion into the air. There was a sound now, an unheard sound, like the plucking over and over of a single noteless harpstring.

The girl seemed to contain fire, an alabaster lamp—her hair stirred, flickered, gushed upward, blowing flame in a wind that did not blow.

The crowd groaned. Not fear. It was like a love-cry.

What came next was sudden.

Light shot up the sky, a tower of light, beginning where the girl stood, or had been standing, for either the intensity of the light made her invisible, or she had herself become the light. For half a second, then, there was only the light. Then the light took form.

The form it took was Anackire.

She towered. She soared. Her flesh was a white mountain, Her snake's tail a river of fire in spate. Her golden head touched the apex of the sky, and there the serpents of Her hair snapped like lightnings, causing lightnings.

So tall, so far off, the unhuman face was almost lost, indistinct even as it bent toward them. A necklace of sun-touched cloud encircled Her throat, cloud which, even as they stared, uncoiled and drifted from Her. Her eyes were twin suns. They blinded, they were so bright. The eight arms, outheld as the two arms of the girl had been, rested weightless on the air, the wrists, the long fingers, subtly moving.

The torrential tail of the snake flexed.

She was alive. She gazed at them, and unable to meet Her gaze they threw themselves down, or fell down, losing consciousness.

Anackire remained before them five eternal seconds. Then the sheen of her became, all of it, unbearably effulgent, a searing whiteness which abruptly went out, leaving only the black after-shadow on the dying sunset; presently, not even that.

As some sense came back to him, Haut beheld the girl standing before the well, unblasted by the entity she had released. She seemed in her turn only quiescent, not drained. And he saw at last her face, as it had always been, was the face of Anackire.

Leaving her mistress for the night, romantic Yeiza hoped the antechambers would be roused by the arrival of the Storm Lord. But the candle-flickering rooms stayed calm as stagnant pools. As usual, the doors were not flung open to admit the handsome white-haired King, vivid with his lust.

He might have had his given bride at once, the betrothal permitted that. But startling matters had intervened—the unexpected revelation of the Prince Rarmon, and then envoy from Karmiss presaging dealings so far unannounced. Tomorrow, however, was the marriage day. Yeiza had directed Ulis Anet's maids in laying out the lovely garments, the jeweled headdress, the oils made from all the flowers of love. By tomorrow evening, the Princess' suite would have been moved into another sector of the palace. She would be one of the High King's fifteen lesser wives. And could it be, exquisite emblem of Xarabiss that she was, she would not even have a night with him? It was a fact, all Raldanash's wives, the lesser, and the higher—those blonde queens from the other continent—were strangely and unfortunately everyone of them barren. Some of the concubines had had children, but they were not legitimate, nor did they at all resemble the Vathcrian King.

Could he be impotent? It was also a fact, the King kept no boys to pleasure him, either.

The gods—the goddess—could not, surely, desire the legal line of the hero Raldnor to perish?

As Yeiza came out through a door into one of the garden courts, a man's hand gripped her wrist. She gave a squeal, but the palace nights were full of amorous squeakings. It would require a determined scream to fetch the guard. Before she could take breath for it, she recognized the handsome face in the light from the doorway.

"Lord Iros—"

"Is he with her?"

"You mean the King? It's his right to be," said Yeiza defiantly.

"Not what I asked you, slut."

"I'm no—"

"Answer me, or I'll break your wrist."

Yeiza believed him. She did not care for Iros, though his looks fascinated her. While, in a way, not caring for him had increased her interest.

"No then. She's alone. My lord—you can't go in."

"I've bribed seven men to make sure I can. How do you think I got so far unchallenged?"

"If anyone found you with her, she'd die, and so would you."

"Who's to find us? Not him, for sure. Unless you betray me."

Yeiza gazed into Iros' blazing eyes and quailed. When he dragged her to him and kissed her, she yielded, melting in his heat though she knew it was banked for another. When he pushed her aside she almost sank to the grass. The door shut. Insulted and pleased, she discovered he had dropped a gold coin between her breasts as he caressed them.

The King's regard contained a constant remote familiarity. Nothing had changed this. One sensed it never would change.

"Good evening, Rarmon."

"Good evening, my lord. I regret I was delayed."

"I gather I called you here straight from your chariot. You were riding in the hills?"

"In the ruined city, my lord."

"Koramvis . . . yes. We all go to look at that. But you've been there more than once."

Rarmon said nothing. It was not out of the question his half-brother the King would have him observed. It was too soon in Rarmon's own ascent to arrange similar courtesies. His guards were Raldanash's soldiers. Even hired men from the streets were not advisable at this juncture.

He had not been privately in the Storm Lord's presence since that bizarre night of the Amanackire judgment. He had seen Raldanash, of course, and been publicly recognized by him, to the consternation of the council. Warden Vencrek, one deduced, would also have set his own, more prosaic, investigation under way. Meanwhile, the crowds had cheered, an arresting noise to hear for oneself.

This summons was not entirely unexpected, however. Rarmon had at least heard of the arrival of a Karmian envoy. Though his past had not been brandished, or even elaborated upon, Rarmon had given some outline of it from necessity. Raldanash knew he had been Kesarh's man almost two years.

Sure, enough, Raldanash said,

"It seems I must go east. Officially it will be a progress. The Karmian King has sent a man across to Dorthar, a valued councilor, I intend to meet with in person, near Kuma. War games, naturally. You'll recall how Karmis crippled the ships of Free Zakoris."

"Yes, indeed."

"I'd like your opinion on the policies that are put forward, since you have some understanding of the aims and mind of Kesarh. You'll come with me."

Rarmon gave an acquiescing nod. It had occurred to him, obviously that though the King might care for his advice, he might also prefer to have the bastard brother safely at his side when away from Anackyra.

"There's to be secrecy. The Free Zakorians have spies in Dorthar. I shall leave tomorrow. The more surprise to the capital the better."

Something else suggested itself.

"I take it, sir, you'll spare time to marry the Xarabian princess first."

"Yes. I don't want to insult Xarabiss. I'll be taking her with me, it helps give reasons for such a progress—a show of the land to my new bride. Thann Xa'ath should be flattered. None of the other women had such treatment." Raldanash did not smile. His eyes seemed far away, held by distant things, that looked like vistas neither of concupiscence nor of war. "So I must give you another task, that of messenger to Ulis Anet. Go tonight to her apartments and tell her my news. She's to be ready to leave once the morning's ceremony is concluded."

Rarmon allowed a moment or two to pass. Then he said, "It's late. She may have retired."

"Take a couple of guard with you, and a chamberlain, enough to make it formal. Wait for the women to fetch her. She should be told personally of the journey—but not the Karmian matter. I shall see to that later. And decorous apologies. You understand why I'm asking you to do it?"

Rarmon had ideas. He said, "No, sir."

"Because etiquette demands someone of importance, while the fewer who are privy to the plan the better. Impress this also on my betrothed."

"Yes, my lord." Rarmon waited again, then said quietly, "and if she should wonder why on such a secret matter you yourself—"

Raldanash said flatly, "If I go myself, she'll suppose I've arrived to claim betrothal rights in her bed."

The frankness, rather than funny, was unnerving. Raldanash displayed no trace of anything, no self-consciousness, not even ruefulness.

It would be politic to say nothing.

Rarmon said nothing.

Outside, summoning two guard and sending for the chamberlain, Rarmon was aware of a further notion ranked with the rest. The King did not particularly want his latest wife, if he had wanted any of them. It might be convenient to fob her off with one's dramatically important half-brother. Later, maybe, to discover the two of them, and have both executed. Rarmon could not assume Raldanash had learned his sexual preference, even after the psychic delving of the Amanackire. Incriminatory situations might, in any event, be stage-managed. Then again, Rarmon would not swear the King was capable of that. Actually, you could not be sure what the King was capable of, either for good or ill. His charisma was valid, but how he used such a utensil on the fields of life and kingship was not yet clear.

*   *   *

Turning from one gorgeous corridor to another, the chamberlain found his path blocked by the noteworthy son of Yannul,
who—politely about to make way—perceived Rarmon and hailed
him.

"Can I ask the favor of a word?" Lur Raldnor, now known as
Lur Yannul about the palace, was a picture of casual equilibrium.
His eyes looked into Rarmon's and said *This is vital and must be
now*. Rarmon stepped aside from the escort. He and Raldnor
stood in the embrasure of a window.

"Is he going to Ulis tonight?"

"You mean Raldanash. No. I'm sent with a message."

"Someone cast a rumor and has been spreading speculative
gossip. The King's reckoned to be rushing there to have his
rights. Which is what Yeiza overheard."

"Am I to take it the Princess isn't alone?"

"That damnable clown Iros bribed a way in, through the
garden. To get out he has to leave via the antechambers—guard
changes—and the antechamber route, due to the rumor, is now
awash with members of the entourage."

"I see."

"If there's any hint she's got a man with her now—you know
the laws of Dorthar on adulterous treason. Raldnor just missed
them by a dagger's length, didn't he?" Yannul's son smiled,
then laughed. Rarmon was not unimpressed by this actor's
camouflage. "Can you do anything?"

"Maybe. If neither of them panics."

They beamed at each other and parted. Rarmon with his escort
went on. Minutes later they were at the doors of the suite, the
guards saluting. There were persons in the passage, too, hangers-on
come to gawp.

When the doors were opened, Rarmon saw the interlinking
anterooms were busy with people. Xarabian servants, even clerks
loitering about, as if they might be needed to take letters. All of
them looked disappointed not to have caught Raldanash in the
act. Ulis Anet's ladies, or most of them, were also to be seen.
Luckily Yeiza, young and frightened though she was, had had
the urge to come back.

The chamberlain announced Rarmon unnecessarily. The chamberlain portentously added that the Prince was here on the Storm
Lord's business. Everyone kept a straight face. Spoken in the
theater, such words would have had the tiers in thigh-slapping
uproar.

Rarmon intervened before the next speech. He thanked the

concourse for attending, and dismissed them. His personal authority coupled neatly to his fame, and the rooms were nearly empty in less than a minute. Rarmon then addressed Yeiza, asked her to enter the bedchamber and represent him to her mistress.

There was the chance that Iros, being the impulse-ridden flamboyant he was, might rush from the room, flourishing a sword, sure Raldanash's soldiers had come for him. But the murmurous noise had so far kept him pinned. Yeiza's sinuous entry, drawing the inner door closed behind her, did not precipitate disaster.

Rarmon expected that Ulis Anet would master herself and come out, leaving the guilty evidence within.

He was surprised when Yeiza reappeared and said, "The Princess has not retired to bed, my lord. As the King's brother and her illustrious kin, you may enter."

This was all so absurd that for a moment he suspected the springing of a trap.

Then he walked into the bedchamber, wondering if Iros had been stuffed in a clothes closet, as in the sort of theatrical farce events seemed to be emulating.

But Iros was standing by the far wall in plain view. Ulis Anet, despite the lie garbed for bed, stood facing Rarmon. Yeiza shut the door, and leaned on it.

"As you see," said the Princess, "we are at your mercy."

Her voice was low, but not tremulous as Yeiza's had been.

Noncommittally, Rarmon said, "I shall render you the King's message. Then I'll leave. You need not expect the King himself. In fifteen minutes it will be safe for the gentleman to depart. Using the anterooms, which I shall see are vacant, and wearing the unfashionable cloak I will have Yeiza send him. One more dawdling clerk."

Iros swore, but had the sense to keep his voice down.

Ulis Anet did not take her eyes from Rarmon.

"You saved me from maiming and death during the earthquake. It must affront you to see me take such a stupid gamble as this."

"Those risks you take voluntarily are nothing to do with me."

"And this, my lord, had nothing to do with *me*." She lifted her head and there was a tension to her eyes and lips. Again, unavoidably, he was reminded of Val Nardia, the uncanny physical likeness; but they were not the same. "Lord Rarmon, I feel I might trust you. I hope you'll be my witness before this man that I didn't invite him here, nor do I wish him here. In fact, my lord, I'm invoking your protection against him."

Iros made a sound that was altogether too loud. He was gathering himself to speak or to shout, and Rarmon went to him and struck him across the head. Iros slumped back against the wall. Rarmon caught him by the throat.

"Be quiet. She denies you. You ventured this without her consent."

Iros struggled, but his rage had grown flaccid. Rarmon let him go.

"The bitch can only deny me now, to protect herself."

"Don't call her names. If she'd cared to, she might have accused you of rape. If you'd valued her, you might have had the good manners to admit to it."

Iros rubbed his jaw. He did not like his beauty bruised.

Rarmon said to him steadily, "I'll be waiting for you in the North Walk, beyond the Fox Garden. Should you be late leaving here, I'll be compelled to return. It will then have become a charge of rapine, for which you'll answer to my own men."

"You upstart slime of Karmiss, do you dare—"

Iros faltered in mid-cry. One did not serve with Kesarh and learn nothing.

"Try to remember," Rarmon said, "who I have become here, and what you have remained. You're a braggart and a clot, but you live. I can and will alter that condition if you persist in your folly."

Later, in the North Walk, they met again for the briefest of conversations. It seemed by then Iros had begun to remember what Rarmon had become.

When at length the commander strode off through the topiary, Rarmon leaned on a pillar and watched the moon go down, and eventually the blazing heat of the amber ring went out. It had been burning from the instant Yannul's son spoke to him in the corridors. Why? Some new warning? But one could not think of this and not think also of the child.

Eight years, nine years of age, she had shown herself as a woman of fourteen to him, in the flesh at Olm, a ghost in the ruins of Koramvis.

Where was she? No longer among wolves. What did she want from him? She had vanished when he moved toward her, the spell after all broken by proximity or outcry. Yet still there was the sense of something asked. Or to be asked. And the binding of the ring.

Strange, for he did not truly now believe in her anymore. He had no faith in her goddess.

FOURTEEN

After the King had left her, Ulis Anet sat a long while under the dying lamps, still as any other object in the tent.

It was a hilly road, to Kuma, and she had begun it in her bridal finery, the wedding flowers still fresh against her cheeks. When they settled their tents for the night on the rim of the hills, a scene spangled with torches and stars, to which she was becoming inured, a wedding gift arrived. A collar of golden kissing birds and clusters of fruits in rose-quartz and sapphire, with heavy earrings to match. It was all very proper, and more than adequate. She knew then he would be bound to come to her, and so he did.

The lamps had dimmed, the perfumes been sprinkled and the flagons of wine put to hand. Her women had arrayed her for the nuptial bed.

He arrived with an escort, men with torches, singing the marriage songs of Dorthar, perhaps of Vathcri, too, for there were foreign words mixed with the bawdy ones.

When they had gone, and the women gone, Raldanash was alone with her for the first time, in the closed and perfumed tent.

She had seen his beauty in the first chaotic moments on the Imperial Square. Instinctively, she had not responded to the beauty, as to anything positive. There could be no allure in it, it offered nothing. She knew he had not come here to make love to her, and she was right.

"I see you comprehend, Ulis," he said at last.

She might have reigned her tongue, but she was angry, not specifically with him, with everything, a restrained courteous anger.

"No, my lord, I don't. But I know what is required of me."

"Nothing."

"Yes, nothing."

"I'm sorry," he said, "if that dismays you. It was never my choice, to bring you to a sterile pairing. We are both victims of policy." He seated himself then, and said with no show of concern, "Because of policy, I must spend some time with you tonight, and for most of the nights of this journey. It would be

209

thought odd if I did not, and might disgrace you. I realize such a sham may be offensive, but I think you appreciate the need. When we return to Anackyra, you'll be able to make such arrangements as you prefer. Providing you are discreet, I shan't tax you."

"You're telling me I may take lovers, my lord?"

"If you wish. That's only fair, Ulis, since I will never be your lover."

She marveled, even while she anticipated nothing else, at his coolness.

"You're contravening every conjugal law and tradition of Dorthar," she eventually said.

"Perhaps."

"Is it," she said, "that you cleave only to your fair women, the Queens of Shansar and—"

"I cleave to no women." He almost smiled. He added, "And no men."

Without warning she shuddered. She felt herself to have moved beyond her depth, and yet something prompted her to go further.

"You'll think me impertinent, my lord," she said, "if I ask you why."

"You've every right to ask. Since all I shall offer you for these hours alone will be conversation, I can at least be honest with you." He paused. He said, "There is a custom of the lands over the ocean, limited usually to priests, a giving of oneself to the goddess. It entails chastity, and chastity of the emotions. One does not make love, one does not love—anything—save the goddess and the earth which is Her expression. This offering was also demanded of me. I don't mean that I was asked or instructed to do it. I mean that I knew in myself I belonged to this persuasion. In Vathcri, such men are called Sons of Ashkar. They are considered holy, and can sometimes work sorcery.

"Conversely, the moment I could reason, I grasped I was to leave my homeland and become High King here in the north. I was taught the responsibilities of kingship. To continue the dynasty my father founded was a necessary part of these. But it makes no difference. The voice within is always stronger than any cry without. One has only to listen. Raldnor's line ends in me."

"You could," she said, "never bring yourself—"

"I've felt desire," he said. "At Zastis, I was often tormented by desire. That's past. I have mastered it, now."

She could not contain her astonishment.

"This is some riddle, my lord."

"No. The Vis have no organized cult of celibacy as a source of Power. The Lowland people, the Amanackire, have always had it. To some extent, my people also. To repress the sexual energies of the flesh is not some horrid fruitless penance, such as a Vis priest might set a wrong-doer. Libido is a power that may be transmuted, stored, used as another power. The Amanackire have long been famed for secret carnal temple love. Time out of mind they knew how to structure the act of sex and wield the pleasure-spasm as a lightning bolt of magic energy. Contained and channeled, such energy is equally valuable. Is it so curious that the mechanisms employed in generating life itself are also capable of generating an alternate force of creation?"

The nakedness of his speech, coupled to his impassivity, disturbed her. She said nothing else on the subject and he, surprising her again with his social abilities, guided them into a discussion of Xarabiss. During the two hours he spent with her, he also mentioned the true purpose of their journey to Kuma. She had known there must be something.

When he left she was numbed, but as the numbness wore away Ulis Anet was repelled to find herself aroused and tingling, as if at Zastis. The very sexual power he had described seemed conjured in the tent, a hungering cheated elemental.

Kuma too had been sacked in the War. Smudges of old conflagrations were bandaged by flowers and streamers. The town was almost as much amazed to see royalty bursting in upon it as Anackyra had been amazed to see her Storm Lord riding out. On the second day, a hunt was arranged in the eastern hills. The guardian protested, distraught. Last year there had been something of a drought in the region. Game was scarce. But the Storm Lord proved adamant in his fancy that game abounded and in his wish to pursue it. A third of the wagons went off with the hunting party, the royal pavilions, even the Queen, with a scatter of her Xarabian guard, and various ladies. If Kuma guessed itself a base for other more important adventures, the guardian remained unenlightened.

High on the heat-burned uplands, the imperial party was split again. Leaving the tents to blossom like flowers beside a shallow river, the King, his bastard brother, and some twenty-five guard, rode full tilt away up the slopes, the racing chariots roaring through the dust. For such ardent hunters, their tactics seemed rather poor.

*   *   *

From the peak of a brown hill it was possible to look out toward the sea, miles off, the great glitterings of a sleeping snake, under a sky of cobalt. It was also possible to look down into the valley below, and behold another hunting party. There was one dark tent, men and zeebas straying about.

The King gestured, and the banner of Anackyra was unfurled.

The second party answered promptly with their own device. It was not the Lily of Karmiss. Over the black cloth poured a scarlet lizard-beast.

Rarmon who had been Rem felt muscles clasp together all along his spine. He turned a little to Raldanash, but the tent flap was just then pulled aside. A figure came out and stood in the valley looking up at them. It was Kesarh.

The chariots sluiced forward.

"My lord," Rarmon said decidedly, "this isn't some counselor. It's their King."

"You recognize him?" Raldanash seemed unmoved. "I had a suspicion. He fought with his fleet, apparently, dressed as a common soldier. He likes the heart of things."

They were over the brink, the vehicles lightly bowling into the valley.

Had Raldanash done more than suspect? Conceivably, he had known.

Rarmon, with no way out, geared his mind grimly to the confrontation.

Twenty yards off, the chariots pulled up. The white banner-bearer advanced, planted his standard and called out:

"Sir, you are in the presence of Raldanash, son of Raldnor son of Rehdon, Storm Lord of Dorthar, Dragon King of all Vis."

There was no show from the other side. Kesarh walked forward, and rendered the Storm Lord that grave slight inclination of the head which one king owed another.

Eight years had added to the physical power natural to the man Rarmon remembered, and taken nothing of the style away. His build, like Rarmon's own, remained a fighter's, the body had stayed slim and lithe, and tough as iron. Between the right cheekbone and the eye there was a little scar, hardly the length of a child's fingernail. No other marks were displayed. The eight years had done something to the eyes themselves, to be sure. They seemed more deeply set, blacker, their gaze less penetrable, though the strength in them was flagrant now, and the evaluating watchfulness. Every last scrap of youthful formlessness seemed gone. Kesarh had become only himself.

He wore black, as ever, and unblazoned. Black-haired in the black he faced white-haired Raldanash in his pale leathers. That was almost theater again. They were two pieces of a board game.

Raldanash dismounted from his chariot.

"I hope Karmiss is well-governed in your absence."

"I see I'm identified," said Kesarh.

"My brother," said Raldanash, "recalls you."

Rarmon, too, had left his chariot. He began to approach them. It seemed one of the game-pieces was using Rarmon himself as a game-piece. Kesarh's eyes were moving by the Storm Lord, finding Rarmon, fixing on him. Yes, the eyes were truly Kesarh. They could drive you to your knees. Rarmon walked nearer. Kesarh had recognized him now. Rarmon knew there would be no change of expression. As he came up by Raldanash, Kesarh said, with only the merest inflection, "Your brother, my lord?"

Raldanash did not reply, leaving the blade for Rarmon to pick up. Rarmon said, trying to keep from his tone the clichés either of explanation or insult, "Raldnor Am Anackire's bastard, by his Karmian mistress."

Kesarh went on looking at him. At Rarmon who had been Rem, who had merited ten lashes from a whip called Biter, who had milked snake poison at Tjis, who had ridden back with the rags of Val Nardia's death too tardy to be of service, who had taken Kesarh's daughter aboard Dhol's ship. And who had not returned.

The black eyes said all this to him. They told him they had forgotten nothing.

Then the smile came, the brisk charm now and then awarded a servant.

"Yes," Kesarh said, "I thought Karmiss was in it somewhere." And to Raldanash, "Shall we go into the tent and talk business, my lord?"

The front of the tent had been looped aside, and afternoon light fell in on them. Thirty paces off, the guards, white and black, maintained their stations.

Kesarh had brought one aide to the table, and a clerk to take notes. Raldanash's two men sat or stood beside their lord. Rarmon was left to sit farther up, his role as observer unspokenly stressed.

The wine was Karmian. Rarmon noticed the grapes had improved.

For an hour the discussion maundered. The victory of Kersarh's ships was examined and approved, even the massacre of Ankabek touched on—"An impious cowardly act. The goddess will be paid in blood," Kesarh remarked. He did not bother to glance at Rarmon anymore, who knew very well, and had probably detailed to others, the depths of Kesarh's love of Anackire.

The Storm Lord in turn allowed his aides to name predations of Free Zakoris on Dorthar's coasts. A system of northern and eastern coastal defenses, out of use since the War, had been re-established. There was no startling revelation in that.

Old Zakoris, for twenty-nine years under Vardish rule, was tossed on the table and regarded. It had of course no bargaining worth at all. Vathcri and Vardath were in firm alliance, and the Vardian claims, staked undeniably in battle, siege and surrender, could not be quashed. Yl Am Zakoris, in any case, was now beyond the appeasement of a returned diadem. All symptoms indicated it was the entire continent he lusted after, when he should be mighty enough to snap at it.

The second hour commenced.

Raldanash's seated aide, taking a cue from Raldanash, desired of the air how many ships were left to Free Zakoris after the disastrous rout.

"Reports indicate ten ships escaped us," said the Istrian aide. "These were the devils who destroyed Ankabek. Since the sacred island had been given military defense by King Kesarh, there could have been no less than ten in the offensive."

Raldanash's aide said ingenuously, "I'd heard Ankabek had no military defense. Having refused it on religious grounds," he appended sweetly.

"You're misinformed. A detachment of soldiery guarded the island, and a naval garrison was situated on a high vantage point of the Karmian mainland, looking across the straits and ready to put out should the goddess' beacons be lit."

Kesarh's resonant voice cut effortlessly through this small under-play.

"Yl did not, besides, spend all his ships in the sea-fight. A quantity were left at Zakoris-In-Thaddra. The Thaddrian forests are prolific. They don't lack for timber."

"We've picked up word from Thaddrian sources of a second fleet of one hundred vessels," said Raldanash's aide.

Kesarh said, "My own sources indicate Yl has two fleets now stashed in deep-water bays along the northwestern shore. One hundred ships is certainly the tally of the smaller of these fleets."

This was news. Raldanash's aide scowled, and looked at the Storm Lord.

"Your sources are impeccable," said Raldanash.

"No source is ever that."

"What tidings do your sources give you," said Raldanash, "of the Southern Road?"

Kesarh smiled, and poured wine for the Storm Lord and for himself, flustering the mobile Dortharian aide, who should have seen to it.

"You refer to Yl's fabled highway being hacked through the jungle toward Vardian Zakoris?"

"And therefore toward the western limits of Dorthar."

"Ah, yes. Yl uses it as a punishment for malefactors. The jungle resists every inch of the way. In ten years, only ten miles of road were secured. Even then, to keep it open, the slave gangs work day and night, or the forest would swallow it again."

"Outposts of Vardian Zakoris have sighted smoke and burning forest," said Raldanash's aide. He waited to be stopped, was not, continued: "They look for rainy weather, and then fire the trees. The rain prevents it from spreading. But it clears the ground remarkably well."

Kesarh's face was blank. Looking at him, Rarmon read the blankness: Prior knowledge, obviously.

Kesarh said, "Your highness understands that Karmiss, one of your nearer neighbors and your devoted vassal, would move instantly to take Dorthar's part."

"Dorthar thanks you," said Raldanash.

"And with Karmiss," Kesarh said gently, "you may anticipate the support of Lan and Elyr."

There was a lapse. Raldanash's aide looked to his lord, then said, rather too loudly,

"Lan keeps no army. Elyr is a wilderness."

"There are, however," said Kesarh, "young men in Lan and Elyr both able and eager to assume arms. A war-force will be levied."

"The Lannic King has informed you of this?" said Raldanash.

"The Lannic King has accepted my brotherly advice," said Kesarh. The stillness in the tent seemed to press hard against its walls of owar hide, even against the open wall of air. Kesarh drank from his cup, then nodded to the Istrian aide.

"The Lannic King," said the Istrian, "feared incursion from Free Zakoris, and begged succor. Fifty-four days after the route of the Zakorian ships, my Lord Kesarh sent such generous help as he might spare."

The lapse came again.

Suddenly Raldanash's seated aide sprang to his feet. He was a mix, darker than his fellow, a good three quarters Dortharian. He glared straight at Kesarh and said hoarsely, "Storm Lord—he's saying Karmiss has occupied Lan."

"Sit down," said Raldanash. He had not changed.

The aide sat. His hands were shaking.

Kesarh offered Raldanash the wine flagon. Raldanash moved his cup aside. He said, "Lord Kesarh, whatever you are saying, we would like it more plainly."

Kesarh's profile, as Rarmon studied it, was faultlessly composed. He might have been some merchant-prince debating trade.

"Very well, Storm Lord. I am, patently, your servant." They all hung in the silence, and he let them hang. He said, "I was asked by Lan, who irrationally possesses no means to defend herself, to provide that defense. My ships now patrol her coastline to protect her from attack by sea. I have deployed men inland in case the naval cordon should founder."

"How many men, my lord?"

Kesarh smiled at last.

"Enough."

"Then Lan is invaded," said Raldanash.

"No, Storm Lord. I was invited to enter. I intend that Lan herself will now form her own army. When she's secure, Karmiss can withdraw her strengthening arm."

Nobody laughed.

"It was done," Kesarh went on, "without subterfuge. Karmian maneuvers might at any time have been observed. Possibly the defensive naval patrols which were inaugurated, following the horror at Ankabek, confused any watchers there were. The onset of the mercy mission to Lan may have been misconstrued as only more of these. Deception is not, however, my aim. Even before rumor reached you, my lord, I've rendered the story in person."

"Well?" Raldanash said.

Rarmon demurred. "It turns out you hardly need my judgment."

Chariots moved across the slope. The sun had grown heavier and swung low.

"No, I don't need your judgment. But perhaps I should be interested."

"He's played the game so long, it's in his blood—acquisition, conquest. He wanted Karmiss and got it. Now he wants more. He enjoys the getting. And he's good at it." Rarmon had never spoken so freely of his former master. He had no basic loyalty to Raldanash, and questioned himself, to see it there might still remain some tug toward Raldanash.

"What is it that he wants?" said Raldanash.

"The world, one mouthful at a time. But that's the future. For now he's dangerous because he has two roads to choose from."

"Dorthar and the Middle Lands," said Raldanash. "Or Zakoris."

"Yes, my lord. Exactly. He can ally with you, or send offers to Yl. He has the weight now to tip the balance. Dorthar caught between Free Zakoris and a Karmian Lan could grow uncomfortable. He's shown you his hand. He concluded you'll have scanned it correctly and will make a bid for him."

"Yes."

"Your advantage is that Zakoris has, at the moment, little to tempt him with."

"Yl has a new counselor in Thaddra, a manipulator and strategist. They may find something to offer Kesarh. Aside of course from the ultimate partnering force whereby to take the world."

"Yes, they can always offer that."

"You reckon him so hungry?"

Rarmon said, "He was hungry all his youth. Suthamun threw him crusts and bones as if to a dog. It's a disease now, the hunger. It'll take a world to stop it."

"You speak of him with great sureness," said Raldanash. "As I supposed."

"You knew he'd be here today, and not some minor prince."

"It had occurred to me."

"No, my lord," Rarmon said. "You knew."

The King's charioteer shook the reins, and Raldanash's chariot moved to join a black vehicle which stood against the stormy sun.

There were more of Kesarh's men about than formerly. They must have been off on the farther hills. Even so, to stay here, negligent and at ease—that was an ominous display. They would not dare lay a finger on the Lord Kesarh, not even poison him at the sumptuous bucolic supper to which he had been invited, regal friend of Dorthar that he was. The very carelessness of his demeanor told them that his plans were properly shored up beyond any haphazard villainy one evening could see to.

The thunder began as they rode over the first hilltop.

It was not until the storm broke and the rain lashed down that Rarmon's thoughts flung before him one extra facet. He wondered then as the chariot tore through sheets of water, if he should somehow warn Raldanash. There was, he noted, even a fleeting impulse to inform Kesarh.

Rarmon let both stimuli fade with a sense of conscious divorce.

Eight and a half years were gone. It might anyway mean nothing now, Val Nardia's red-haired double seated before Kesarh at a banquet table.

Long after sunset, the rain swept down on the splendid little makeshift camp by the river.

In the King's pavilion, fifty-six dishes were presented. There were even dancing girls from Dorthar, and Kumaian girls to serve the wine. But the officers had not brought their ladies, and the Storm Lord's minor consort was also absent.

His message had come with the lighting of the lamps. Raldanash politely commanded her to avoid the pavilion. The occasion was festive but no longer social.

By the time the first concordance of dishes was carried out empty and the next relay gone into the great tent, loud with music and lights, she had heard the talk, Raldanash's aides having been unable to contain it. Unbridled gossip scarcely counted. All Dorthar must presently learn.

Politics did not interest Ulis Anet, since she was required to play such a cursory role in them. She had felt no curiosity. Kesarh Am Karmiss was a name. That it promised to be the name of a tyrant and foe made her the more averse to contact with him, but even that merely in a desultory way.

Yet she was restless, and the confining tent, from which she had dismissed her women, did not please her.

Outside one of Iros' men stood guard in the rain.

She considered her life as it was to be from now on, and to her humiliation found herself weeping. She had anticipated nothing; it was foolish to mourn because she had been wise.

The man stood brushing water from his cloak.

"Good evening," Rarmon said, "Biyh."

"Magnificent gods, Rem, I never though you'd know me still."

"And you're still not thinking, Biyh. I'm no longer called 'Rem.' "

The soldier from Istris faltered. Resentful, then resigned.

"Yes, you've come up in the world. I'm sorry, my lord."

"Well," Rarmon said, "you're here from Kesarh. What does he want?"

"To see you."

"He saw me at dinner."

"Privately, Lord Rem—Rarmon."

"No."

Biyh goggled at him. He had been another Nine in Kesarh's secret army. Unlike Rem, he had not particularly gone up in the world, being yet a soldier and a go-between.

"But my lord—" he broke out.

"Your King," said Rarmon, "is aware how it will look if I'm come on skulking to or from his tent. I'm no longer in his pay. Be so helpful as to remind him."

Biyh continued for a moment more, unbelieving. Then he went back into the rain.

Rarmon sat in the chair and waited.

There was a chance Kesarh might want to kill him, but assassination was unlikely here. This ground was diplomatic and acute, too brittle to withstand stray murders.

But the intrinsic information had not yet come. It could not be evaded.

He knew what Kesarh would do.

Less than half an hour later, two noisy torches evolved from the splashing night. Shouts were exchanged with Rarmon's own men outside, one of whom tried to come in and was got from the way. Instead one of Kesarh's guard strode in, set down a great jar of wine and withdrew. After him, Kesarh entered.

He seemed to fill the tent with an electric darkness. The impression was aphysical but overpowering.

This was how Rarmon had seen him last, at Istris, removing a wet cloak, the focus of the lamps, and the shadows.

"Our approach was well-lit and not quiet," said Kesarh. "Your King doubtless already knows I'm here, and that he's been let know it."

Rarmon indicated the wine jar.

"Doctored? Or do I only merit a knife in the back?"

Kesarh looked at him.

"Stand up," he said.

Slowly, and without emphasis, Rarmon stood.

Kesarh's face gave no hint, no clue.

He said: "Now tell me where you left my sister's child."

Rarmon gathered himself who he had been, what he might be now, ordered these men and gave them speech.

"In Lan, my lord."

"Where in Lan?"

"Pirates took Dhol's ship. You'll have heard of it. I got her to the shore. The girl went off with her when I slept."

"You say you failed me, then. Did you search?"

''I searched.''

Kesarh gave him space to go on, eventually said, ''And found what?''

''Wolves.''

Rarmon brought out the word, and the claws of some fateful inexplicable thing closed on him. Why did he mislead? Because the supernatural alternative would not be acceptable? Because he hated Kesarh, or because he was still bound to Kesarh?

Perhaps Kesarh did not care, the child simply a loose end to be tied or cut away, no more. As Rarmon was a loose end to be killed or forgotten. Or killed and forgotten.

''And you didn't dare come to me and tell me this,'' Kesarh said at last.

''As you point out, I'd failed.''

''And then, after all, you discovered your heritage. And were able to convince Raldanash. I've heard he isn't partial to women. Is that it?''

They were in Istris. This could be no other place.

Rarmon said nothing, and presently Kesarh took up one of the gold cups from a side table, and filled it from the wine jar. He drank without interest or thirst.

''Obviously,'' he said, ''it's suggested itself to me you may already have known who you were in Karmiss. That you may have been gathering some sort of information to bring as a gift to your Lowlander-Vathcrian King.''

''No,'' said Rarmon.

''On the other hand,'' said Kesarh, handing him the tasted cup, ''you could remain in Dorthar and send information as your gift to me.''

The rain was slackening. A train of thunder wracked the sky and ended twenty hills away.

''Lord Kesarh,'' Rarmon said, ''I've already proven an inadequate servant. Don't dismiss what else I am. He and I are brothers.''

''Yes, you always were a prince, my Rem. Thief and cutthroat and mercenary. And prince.''

''And the son of Raldnor Am Anackire,'' said Rarmon.

Kesarh's eyes stayed on his, and then Am Karmiss reached out again and took back the cup Rarmon had not drunk from. Deliberately, Kesarh poured the wine on to the rugs. Tossing the cup to the table, he walked out of the tent.

Kesarh, Lord of Karmiss and Protector of Lan, returned across the Dortharian side of the encampment, toward the more modest

Karmian bivouac over the river. His torches scrawled smoke behind him. The rain was finished.

The Storm Lord's pavilion stood near the narrow stone bridge. Close by they had put up the tent of the latest surplus royal bride. The arms of Xarabiss glinted, catching light; the flaps had been pulled back to let in rain-washed coolness. Encased by the dark lamp-shine inside the tent, a woman sat reading.

The silhouetted image momentarily distracted Kesarh. Then was set aside.

In the last hour of that night season the Lowlanders called the Wolf-Watch, Kesarh came out of sleep and lay, his eyes wide on blackness.

He had been dreaming of Val Nardia's witchcraft baby, or maybe only of the dead Prince-King, Emel. Kesarh could not reassemble the dream. It was already gone. But it had left him strung and tensed as if for violent action.

He rose, and drank from the ewer of wine and water.

While he did so, he painted for himself on the dark the face of a dying blond boy, and observed it, without remorse. Emel had been afraid, and had seemed to guess, even at nine years of age, that he was not expiring of plague but from something more contrived.

Beyond the palace, the crowds were already shouting for Kesarh. When Emel sank in coma, his regent left the death-bed. The next Kesarh saw of the child was the box of spices in which he had been hastily packed. The weather had reached its hottest. Kesarh malignly awarded Suthamun's son a Vis tomb in the Karmian Hall of Kings, rather than Shansarian cremation. A draped coffin became necessary, the embalmers Raldnor Am Ioli had dispatched declaring a strangely poisonous corruption consumed the body, rendering their work impossible. These mutterings were swiftly quieted. Instead, when Kesarh spoke the funeral oration, the rabble wept. A month later it had shrieked him to the throne of Istris.

Emel's memory dissolved.

It was the other child which had waylaid his sleep.

When Kesarh left the tent, the first pre-dawn pallor was in the sky. Men were already beginning to move about. At sunrise, the Karmians would depart. Aims were achieved. Dorthar had been assessed, and shown she was prepared to come courting.

Kesarh walked away from both campments, along the bank. Trees grew and tall, thick-stemmed reeds with tasseled heads.

Night clung to the earth. The river, swelled a very little by the rain, ran shallowly over its stones.

Kesarh stood among the trees, looking down at the water.

The memory of the child would not go away. It was ironical, he had cared nothing for it. He had taken fewer pains with it than he had taken with Emel, whom he had killed. Even the sorcery had lost its impact, become unimportant. Years back, hearing of Dhol's wreck, he had thought it dead.

Something glimmered in the shadow on the opposite bank.

So Kesarh looked up and saw, across the twilight and the low race of folding water, Val Nardia his sister.

The initial shock was nothing, like a blow, no more, for she might be unreal, imagined. But then awareness rushed to fill the void. The crepuscular sheen described her, the river held fragments of her reflection. She existed. The second shock was not sudden, a smooth rapid draining, just such as he had felt when told of her death. It left him hollow, and hollow he moved off the bank into the river.

It seemed she took half a step in retreat as he crossed toward her. But the half step was meaningless. The river was a symbol, crossing it another. She must remain, and remain she did, poised on the low shelf of rock, watching him, until he walked out of the water on to the rock and stood over her less than a foot away, and took her arms in his hands and felt silk and flesh and mortal warmth. Light was sinking through the treetops and the red of her hair, red as that Karmian flower, was the first color to come alive in the world.

"Ulis," he said.

Hearing him speak her name, Ulis Anet could only stare at him. She seemed paralyzed, or enchanted, and could not even attempt to pull herself from his grasp.

She had lain awake all night, stifled by the tent, too tired to rise, her nerves too quickened to allow sleep. In the hour before dawn something had sent her in flight from the tent and the King's camp. It was ill-considered, the deed of an adolescent. She had even left the guard, and concluding she sought the King, the guard had not argued. Now, alone and unprotected, she reached the margin of this emblematic river, and from the black wood had come a man clothed in black. That he was one of the Karmian's officers she decided at once. Her own position was horrible. She meant to withdraw immediately, then she saw, even over the distance and in the dark, his eyes.

That was how he held her, merely by looking at her. His intensity, a compound of exceptional personal force directed solely at her, deprived her of volition. Stupidly she stood and awaited him, until he came out of the water on to the rock and took her by the arms.

The human contact was vital. Appalled at her own willingness, she gave in and let the power that streamed from his overwhelm her. She did not know him, but she had heard yesterday's descriptions, and suddenly she recognized him as the Karmian King. In that moment he spoke her name.

His voice was a low rough sigh. Dimly and unreasonably she sensed that, while he was a stranger, she was not.

She could say nothing, do nothing.

"You're not," he said, "a ghost. So how are you here?"

His voice was level now, but the intensity sheared through it as through the black, devouring eyes.

Not a ghost—I am someone dead for him, she thought. Still no words would come. She shook her head, and felt the grasp of his hands tighten on her.

"She's lying in a mausoleum at Istris," he said. "You can't be her." And, with a peculiar shift to mildness, almost casually: "Who are you, then?"

Her voice came from her, before she realized she could speak.

"You called me by my name."

"Ulis," he said.

Begun, the words came flooding, titles, meaning nothing at such an hour: "Ulis Anet Am Xarabiss, daughter of Thann Xa'ath, wife to Raldanash." *Is that,* she thought, *who I am?*

His color had come back. The power persisted, beating on her like a dark sun, but the look which had been almost madness, that had ebbed away.

"One of the Storm Lord's wives," he said. He did not relinquish her, not the grip of hands, or eyes.

"But who is it," she said, "that you believed me to be?"

"Not believed. That you are."

"No," she said, and for the first time struggled.

He meditated upon her, hands not slackening, until again she gave in.

"You must have been a child," he said, "when she died. You're the age now that she was then, Ulis Anet, wife of Raldanash of Dorthar."

"Let me go," she said, "my Lord Kesarh."

He smiled a little, and his hands were gone. The marrow of her bones seemed to go with them.

It was an effort to turn from him. She constrained herself to do so, and then to move through the trees away from him. She

knew herself the focus of his eyes, they mesmerized her, even
now she did not see them. At the edge of the open hill she must
look over her shoulder.

The sun had risen, he was blacker now than the shadows of
the trees. It seemed to her he could have summoned her, drawing
her soul toward him by means of some invisible nexus.

Once more she convinced herself to turn away.

The steps she took toward the Storm Lord's camp were leaden
and without strength.

Storms emphasized the journey to Anackyra.

The titbit rendered the Storm Lord in a black tent on the
Kumaian hills, was now vehemently debated in the capital.
Zakoris-In-Thaddra loomed on one side, Karmiss-In-Lan tow-
ered on the other.

Two such blades might close like pincers on the Middle
Lands.

A dozen days after Raldanash's arrival in the city, a convoy of
three ships put out on the Inner Sea from Dorthar's small western
port of Thos. Their destination was the Sister Continent, and the
bulk of their cargo was news. But it would be an embassy, to
and fro, of months. Such ballast was precarious at best.

Storms tore Anackyra's sky, and her council chambers.

Yannul's son, standing in the princely apartments of Rarmon,
said with desperate quietness, "He means to leave Lan spilled in
the dirt under the Karmian's heel."

"Raldanash's enemy is Free Zakoris," Rarmon said. "Dorthar
won't expend her might against Karmiss. She dare not. Move
troops out to Lan and Yl's navy would come in on Dorthar
behind them like high tide."

"So Lan stays a chattel. You must be proud of your old
master, Rem."

This gauntlet was taken no notice of. "What do you mean to
do?" was all Rarmon said.

"Go to Lan, what else? No letters can get through, nor have
they. My family is there, and he's given me little enough here.
My father tried to warn me. I should have listened."

"Would you listen to me?"

"You?" Lur Raldnor looked at him with youth's blasting
disdain. "I don't know anymore which you run with, sir."

"None."

"Kesarh went to your tent with much show."

"I left him no choice but to make a show of it. Which is how
you, and the King, learned of the business."

"Maybe. You must forgive my bad manners. I'm angry, you see. I do know this. Raldanash can strip me of my name but not my blood. I have his leave. I'm going home."

"When?"

"Tomorrow." Lur Raldnor took one long breath, and was altered. "I'm sorry," he said, "You wouldn't even be in this corner of the earth if we hadn't argued it." His eyes were steady and clear. Rarmon sensed an invocation of that night in Zastis on Yannul's terrace, the fireflies, and some feeling that was gone and would not come back. "Rem," Lur Raldnor said, and now it was oversight not sarcasm, "you do understand that you put this mile of space between us, and not I? I've been listening since Amlan. You had only to call on me. You never have."

"You never told me what you were offering me. The one thing I'd have taken I don't think you could give."

"There were other things. Perhaps you didn't want those. Just something like sex when you needn't look at my face or remember I can reason or that I'm alive, as you are. I still recall that time you said it was easier to kill a man than a beast."

They stood without speaking then, until Lur Raldnor turned for the door.

"It'll take forever if I have to sail from Xarabiss. But they say ships are putting in at Karith again."

FIFTEEN

Under the heel of Karmiss, Lan shone with unaccustomed armaments. The unusual dust of marital passage contended with indigenous rain. The major garrison installed at Amlan currently occupied one of the larger warehouses of the port. A second detail was beneath tentage in the palace park. Elsewhere, substantial droves of Karmian military were lodged at every significant town. The highways between were patrolled, for Free Zakorians would, if they came, come to any spot and in any disguise. In the smaller villages, men were robbed and women abused in case they might hold Free Zakorian sympathies. Such offenses of the soldiery were localized, but severely punished by the Karmian High Command, when they could be proved. Which was very seldom.

Ships sailing to and from the port of Amlan received an escort that safeguarded them from Zakorian attack. The east harbors of northern Xarabiss, and of Ommos, were open again. As yet, from political tact, escorting Karmian galleys did not venture inside a five-mile limit of the Middle Lands.

There were other limits.

A Lannic curfew was in force, in order to regularize traffic and commerce.

The sound of that bell, clanging across the dusk, turned the blood of Yannul to ice. The first time he had heard it, Medaci had come running to him and sobbed in his arms like a child. The sound was too well remembered from the Shadowless Plains, Amrek's curfew rung every sunset in the ruined Lowland city, the message of the mailed fist, and the edge of steel to come.

Now, standing at midday in the old audience chamber of Lan's painted palace, Yannul reviewed the insecure scenes of his young manhood with uneasy foreboding. He had looked for peace with the years, at home.

Presently his host came in, Kesarh's Chief of Command in Lan. He was the mix type made fashionable by Raldnor of Sar, dark-skinned and blond. He had the hero's name, too. And all the Vis patina of display.

Wine and cakes were brought. They sat down before windows that gave a fine panorama of dripping feather trees and sodden tents, and a Karmian unit at drill in the mud.

"It goes without saying," said Raldnor Am Ioli, "you see why you've been asked to come here."

Yannul looked at him blandly.

"The great hero of Lan," said Raldnor Am Ioli. "We had some difficulty in finding you, though you live so close. But the King was eventually persuaded to reveal your secret."

"And how is the King these days?"

"His doctors assure me the fever's broken."

"Something you may have guessed," said Yannul. "Lan is barbaric in its royalism. The King and Queen have an almost sorcerous significance to us. A sudden death would be—upsetting."

Karmian Raldnor laughed.

"My dear Yannul, are you suggesting my Lord Kesarh has left any orders that your King and Queen should be murdered? That's not kind, sir, to a benefactor. Your King himself invited the Lord Kesarh to send troops to Lan."

"Our gratitude," said Yannul, "flows like the rain."

Karmian Raldnor was not without wits. He said softly, "But the rain's stopped."

There had, of course, been no invitation, save the invitation an unarmed country always offered to a predator. Karmian ships had docked at the port after their epic sea fight, been lauded and welcomed. They then lingered, for fear Lannic prophecies of stray Free Zakorian marauders should come to pass. After a while, a small party of troops marched to Amlan's walls and offered its assistance to the King. He had not been so ingenuous as to accept it, but, with some Karmian influence already at the gates, they were let in. The crowds had cheered them, and thrown flowers. Ten days later, a thousand Karmian infantry and four hundred cavalry with chariots had landed, and swarmed along the port road. Their fellows had the gates by now and ushered them through into the capital. They were a preliminary. Inside a day, Lan was Lan no more.

Kesarh himself had not bothered to sail over. He had matters to see to elsewhere. The invasion was just his goodness at heart.

"Well," said Karmian Raldnor, refilling Yannul's full cup so it spilled, "what we desire of you is a small piece of spectacle."

"My days as an acrobat are over."

"Oh, I think not." They smiled at each other. Raldnor Am Ioli said, "there's been unease. We shouldn't like it to spread. Your King, as soon as he's fit, will address his subjects. I'd take it as a favor, sir, if you would be there, and add some encouraging words."

"Encouragement to what?"

Raldnor Am Ioli sighed.

"You're a respected, almost a mythical figure, Yannul. You know about policy. Assuage the people. Explain, Karmiss is their friend. That you yourself accept this as a fact."

Yannul said, "Yes, it's stopped raining, hasn't it."

There was a prolonged pause.

Karmian Raldnor said, "Think of all you enjoy, sir. Your villa-mansion and the land. Your wife—one of the Amanackire, I believe. Your sons. Treasures. It would be a pity to let it all go."

"You're threatening me?"

Karmian Raldnor said nothing.

"As you mentioned," said Yannul. "I'm something of a hero in Lan. I told you how we are about our royalty. In a way, an aspect of that applies to me. Destroy me, and you could have trouble all the way to Lanelyr. I would deferentially remind you also that there are Shansarians, Vardians and other men of the second continent in this country, who stood by Lan's neutrality in the War, and have since evolved flourishing business concerns on our soil; it would anger them to see those disrupted.''

"The Lord Kesarh is himself half Shansarian."

"The Lord Kesarh, half Shansarian though he is, has tended to forget, I think, that simply because the Sister Continent is invisible from our own, it has not ceased to exist."

"Now, I believe, you're threatening me," Karmian Raldnor said.

"Not at all," said Yannul. "I'm only telling you that when the King publicly says whether it is you've asked him to say, I shall be indisposed."

Raldnor Am Ioli, returning to his well-guarded palace apartment, evinced mild irritation.

In the long term, such stumbling blocks as Yannul would not matter. But here and now one could trip over them and go sprawling. Raldnor was anxious to impress Kesarh, though not from any of the fear-admiration the King seemed able to induce in his soldiery. Raldnor had not forgotten the cryptic tidings he had awarded himself in that council chamber at Istris: Once you were of no use to him, he would leave you to burn.

Raldnor Am Ioli the opportunist, had so far followed Kesarh's dark planet into the ascendant. Raldnor had taken pains along the way to cement his luck. He had also learnt a lesson or two from Kesarh himself, and in this manner had come to execute some bold strokes in the line of insurance. Finding himself sent on this mission to take Lan and Elyr, Raldnor had decided that in his absence from Karmiss, certain routine but exhaustive investigations would be made into his affairs. He had accordingly left everything immaculate, and brought the only incriminating element with him, a touch of utter simplicity, or genius.

His thoughts turning on this eased him, and he consigned Yannul to later deliberation.

Raldnor went out into a private corridor and so walked into a modest room flung with Lannic cushions. In their midst, teasing a kalinx kitten, was the figure of a sullen girl. Her long blonde hair was plaited with ribbons, her fair skin had paint and ornaments upon it.

"Mella, if you tease that cat, it'll bite you."

The girl looked up and grimaced at him.

"Why must you—"

"You know I'm thinking of your well-being."

Mella gnawed her mouth. She pulled the tail of the kalinx and was rewarded by a dagger-thrust of claws and teeth. Leaving the victim screeching, the kitten fled past Raldnor and down the corridor to a tiny window that provided escape.

Raldnor looked on. The remaining furious creature licked its wounds. Mella was known by his men to be a young mistress brought from the estate of Ioli. She was pretty in her way, and though her breasts were small and her feet somewhat on the large side, Raldnor was entitled to his personal taste in bed-girls.

"How long must we stay here?" Mella inquired eventually.

"You're bored? My humble apologies. You know why I brought you, and you've some idea, I hope, as to the sort of action I have to take to ensure Kesarh's purpose."

"*Kesarh,*" said Mella. Her reedy voice was imbued by loathing.

"Yes. For now, Kesarh's purpose. You'll have to be patient, as I've often warned you, before you can indulge your hate of him."

"And what of my hate for you?"

"Why should you hate me?" said Raldnor calmly. "I'm your savior. You should be grateful."

"Grateful to have *this* done to me?" Mella's torn hands suddenly dragged down her bodice. Raldnor looked away. He found the sight faintly revolting, though he had once traveled in woman-hating Ommos, and been shown such things as a commonplace.

"Yes," he said, gazing at the frescoes on the wall, "grateful. Because it's kept you alive."

"And will it," said Mella with dreadful fifteen-year-old scorn, "give me my rights?"

"Keep your voice down. There are Karmian sentries beyond that window out there."

"But will it?" Mella shrilled, and broke into a repulsive jeering laughter.

"Again, I've told you, such things can be managed. But your best safety lies for now in reticence. Or do you want to lose your tongue with the rest?"

Mella paled. Tears sluiced from her eyes and the paint ran. She sniveled at Raldnor's feet. What an amalgam the thing was!

Medaci turned from the little garden and the ephemeral pale sun came in with her hair.

"And must it be so?"

"I think it must."

She sat beside her husband and Yannul took her hand.

"It seems so strange," she said.

"I promised you peace, here."

"Is there peace anywhere?"

They stayed still awhile and remembered aloud to each other the past. Yannul understood the litany. It seemed to cry, We have survived all that and can now survive this.

But it would be hard to go away, to abandon the farm and the land, abandon Lan itself which in his youth he had abandoned cheerfully, knowing he could always come back. Fighting by Raldnor of Sar, Yannul had not been so certain of that. Yet he had lived, and taken his golden-haired girl with him at last across the sea and home. There came the first shock, then. The old farm in the hills was empty, most of the roof down, wild bis nesting in the walls. And, beyond the well, the marker of his mother's grave. Finding one of his sisters in another valley, wed to a stranger, he heard of sickness and hard times, his two other sisters dying, one in childbirth. One of his brothers had gone to join the Lowland army, but did not get there, or if he had, was dead in Ommos or Dorthar, never having made himself known. More likely robbers or shipwreck had been responsible. The other brothers went north, hunters and seekers of the savage wilds. Yannul never found them. All this had been a series of blows across his heart. In the thick of danger himself, he had somehow never reckoned his family anything but safe. In the dark cold nights, they had beamed there for him, in Lan, a distant beacon that could never go out, his mother happily heavy with child as she seemed perpetually to be, his sisters singing and squabbling round the loom, or nursing birds fallen frozen by the door, and his brothers boasting that one day they would eat at the King's table in Amlan. Well, Yannul had done that very thing. When he remembered remembering that, the blows had seemed to break his heart.

It was Medaci who comforted him. Not only with her words and her touch. By her presence. It came to him that though he had lost his kindred, still he had kindred. He had been enamored sexually of Medaci, fond of her, protective, but in that moment of revelation had begun to love her.

And then his country gave him riches. The villa-farm arose, clasped in the indigo hills which, as Rem had long ago concluded, seemed to hold everything of note in Lan. So there was largesse, and love; presently the boys came. Life heaped them with harvest.

When the shadow began to creep out of Free Zakoris they acknowledged it, for shadows must be acknowledged, and put it aside, for neither must shadows be allowed to drive out all the light.

The Karmian initiative was not looked for.

It was like snow in summer. The end of the world.

"Basjar's a good man," said Yannul now, "half Xarabian, a demon for finance and tricks, but trustworthy. He'll keep the farm in perfect shape, if nothing happens. If the worst happens, he'll salvage what he can and keep it by for us." Medaci smiled. Basjar, Yannul's agent, had always paid courtly love to her in his Xarabian way. She liked him. He was kind, lethal only to enemies. "To find Vardians to make the journey with is also a stroke of fortune," said Yannul. "Karmiss is still careful of the yellow-haired races." He had arranged their travel plans yesterday, as soon as he received his invitation to the palace. He had comprehended what that would mean, and had not erred. It would not take long for the blond Karmian to decide that, though Yannul might not be slain, there were other forms of coercion.

The Vardish caravan would wend southward at sun-up tomorrow, and they, Yannul, Medaci and the boy, would accompany it. She was Amanackire and his younger son, fair but for his dark eyes, could pass for it. They would be honored and protected all the way to Lanelyr. In Elyr, Karmian development was still haphazard. Once into the Shadowless Plains they were on the Middle Lands, where Karmiss dare not stake a claim. As yet.

They discussed these things and then Medaci said, "what if Lur Raldnor comes back?"

"The last letter placed him safe in Dorthar. The King would have more sense than to give him leave to return. Raldanash will have work for him."

"But he might not listen to the King."

"He'll listen. Raldnor knows we'll take care of ourselves. He'll keep where he is and wait for news. When we reach the Plains, we can send word."

"Yes," she said.

She did not cry. Her eyes were only full of yearning, still fixed on her garden sweet with lilies, and shrubs which blossomed at night into fireflies.

The sudden picture came to him again, and Lowland ruin in the snow, blood on the streets and dead Dortharians, and the Amanackire passing like silent wolves with gleaming eyes. And then Yr Dakan's house, with its own dead, Ommos this time. In the round hall, an indescribable thing hanging half-in, half-out of the Zarok god's oven-belly. And nearer, crouched by the table, Medaci. She had stared at him, then jumped to her feet, running to the doorway, trying to escape by him. When Yannul caught her shoulders she screamed. And then she had flung herself

against him. "Why was I made to kill him?" she had cried in
terror, her tears burning through his clothes into his skin.

She had, with her doubt, rescued his sanity that night, and
perhaps he had rescued hers.

But he knew, even in flight from the new oppressors, she was
afraid to return to the Lowlands.

The army of Lan was already being formed.

Any Vis, or man of dark enough mixture, was from the
twelfth year eligible. Or vulnerable. The levies were taken by
demand, where necessary by force.

In Amlan, and the towns, a public exhortation was employed.
All suitable candidates were ordered to report to the local Karmian
station. Those who did not give up their sons or themselves and
could not buy exemption, received a visit from Karmian soldiery.
A parcel of carpenters' lathes were chopped up on the cobbles, a
chain or so of extra zeebas appropriated by the military, a few
score beer jars smashed. That was normally enough to set an
example. Youths and men arrived at the recruitment centers and
became part of the Lannic militia. The lit Torch emblem of Lan
was displayed over each makeshift barracks, under a great scarlet
Salamander.

To civilization's outposts—the little wild villages swept across
the uplands, through the bowls of valleys—Kesarh's troops proceeded and merely took. Men were dragged from their fields or
out of their beds, and hauled, stunned and roped, toward a
soldier's life, leaving their women and children to wail and
perhaps to starve behind them.

One witnessed such sights on the way south. In the north,
rumor said, it was worse.

As the Vardish caravan came down toward the borderland of
Lanelyr, it skirted a burning village. Out on the hill a couple of
women had been raped to death. Several men, too old to interest
the levy, lay about broken. Other women and livestock were
being herded away to pleasure and feast Karmian warriors.

The Vardians refused to intervene. Not much, in any event,
could be done. The Karmians were many. The dead were dead.

Beyond the scene, those mountains which were the spine of
Lan, stood blind against the sky.

In Lanelyr, in the guardian's house at Olm, Safca was dreaming.

In the dream, a Lowland girl stood at her window, with a
golden moon behind her head.

Come and see, said the girl, but without words.

Safca approached the window with diffidence. She had never thought to meet the Lowlander again. Safca looked where the girl indicated, and noticed her window had a vista in the dream it did not have in actuality, looking out on the great mountains beyond the town. A huge snake was winding up the hills toward them, glittering. Then she saw it was not a snake, but streams of lights.

"Where are they going to?" Safca asked the Lowland girl.

The Lowland girl told her.

Safca was disbelieving, incredulous.

Then she saw that on the mountain tops the golden moon had become the shape of a luminescent woman with a serpent's tail. For some reason, Satca laughed with delight.

When she woke she was still laughing. She found she knew the Lowlander's name.

There were only fifty of King Kesarh's soldiers in Olm. Two stone houses had been given them—the occupants had fled. Their captain had required quarters, for himself and his most immediate officers, in the palace. The levy began on the first morning, and the guardian himself went into the marketplace and instructed the Olmians to cooperate. Karmiss was aiding Lan toward a proper self-defense that was surely needed. There was no rebellion. The influx had been expected for days, and Olm's population grown even smaller from the resultant exodus. Those who were left had already given in.

The Karmian captain was pleased with the guardian. The Karmian captain now shared the bed of the guardian's legal and prettier daughter. The man made frequent proud allusions to his rise to power from lowly and insalubrious beginnings on wharfs of Istris. But the guardian's legal daughter offered no objection, even seemed inclined to show off her lover.

Yalef, the guardian's eldest son, had run to Elyr with a pack of gambling friends and some acrobat girls.

Safca, catching the blaze of the Salamander lifted above the palace gate, remembered her old anger at the men of Shansar and Vardath, her inchoate wishes for Vis valor to return. Here it was. She writhed with shame and disgust.

There was another reason. Discreetly offered, by her third brother, her own person for the duration, one of the Karmian sergeants had said, "The bitch is all shanks and no breasts, and where've I seen that face? On a jug without handles."

She daydreamed of killing the man throughout the evening. Then, asleep, she dreamed of the Lowlander, the mountains, the lights, and Anackire.

In the morning, anticipated nowhere and with nothing to do, she considered the dream.

There had been, along with the chatter of the Karmian invasion, more frivolous tales of Lowland magic on the Plains, flower-garlanded crowds emanating from the black ruined city, lights and manifestations. One story, brought by a trader, had held Olm's marketplace agog. Wolves loped with these mystic bands, it seemed, harmless and amiable. And there were snakes, naturally, wound round them with the flowers. Safca, recalling the great snake the Lowland girl had given to her, that she herself might be wound in it, had trembled. Was it that the girl had reached the Shadowless Plains and there led these occult revels? Was it that the girl, telepathic and powerful, had sent a vision to Safca?

Why? It was madness.

At length, Safca summoned the dream-diviner, a toothless crone who dwelled in a hut near the town gates that no one had held against Karmiss. Years before, the crone had interpreted a dream to Safca. Safca had never been sure she accepted the verdict. The woman heard all kinds of gossip, and was clever at guessing. Now it seemed she had guessed some other thing, and fled; she was not to be discovered.

It had been quite apparent where the lights of the dream had been going, even if the Lowland girl had not told Safca. At the heart of those mountains lay the ancient kingdom of Zor, rarely visited, difficult to come at over reeling passes, which in the cold months were inaccessible.

An almost faultless refuge.

Something bizarre began to happen to Safca. It was like a low sonorous vibration in her blood. She did not know what it was. She realized she had felt something of it in the vicinity of the Lowlander.

Now, Safca listened to the thrumming of her soul behind her bones.

All at once, the room where she was seated began to go. She was frightened, and called it back. But the voiceless harp string thrummed on and on.

Outside, the Olmish conscripts were being drilled in the square. A Karmian officer with a stick lashed them when they faltered, like slaves. Some days ago, one had been brutally whipped.

Down below, her sister chirruped, plying the Karmian captain with candied fruit. The two Corhlish monkeys, who were afraid of him, whimpered in a corner.

Safca became aware she was seeing and hearing things that were not to be seen and heard, physically, in this room.

"*Ashni,*" she whispered. That was the name of the Lowland girl. It had been left with her, and this had been left with her, though she had not known.

The room wavered again.

With a pang of terrified elation, this time, Safca let it go.

The veiled woman at the door of the makeshift barracks was carefully examined for any weapon. The two guards who examined her were very thorough and joked, enjoying it, telling her to enjoy it too. If it had been Zastis, she would have had more from them. They did not bother with her covered face, but probably would not have recognized it. Her bribe they accepted graciously. She had not been foolish enough to wear any jewelry, save the plain little necessary luck bracelet on her left wrist. To go in and entertain her man for the night seemed quite a sensible request. Such things had happened before.

The low stone hall into which the woman picked her way, the door of which was bolted behind her, contained two thirds of the recruited Lannic army of Olm, about two hundred men.

Many were elderly and should not have been involved, sport for sadistic Karmian leaders. Some were very young, children. Some were merely soft, unhappy, and a few of these lay weeping. They were all the fodder of war. But there was a core of men, itinerant hunters, wagoneers, builders of houses, even Olm's own guards, strong men lying awake in anger.

Safca took out the stub of candle the guards had permitted and kindled it. Then taking up one of the empty lamps, she lit it in turn.

Men roused all about.

Even as the race of excitement, uninformed and random, spread over them, a Karmian came from behind a pillar, one last enemy she had not reckoned on. There was of course mixed blood in Kesarh's army, though not many blond men at Olm. This one was, which made things seem worse.

"What're you doing?" He caught her arm.

Safca, half blind with fear, raised her veil and smiled. She put her free hand to her hair, loosening it from its pins.

"The lordly captain sent me to spice your night."

Her voice shook so it was a wonder he heard it. She shrank, even in this extremity, lest he should think her too unappetizing to be of use, but he grunted and began to pull her back behind the pillar.

"All right. But why light the lamp, brainless mare?"

He was already busy pawing her groin when she brought

herself to do what she had known she must, and ran her hairpin in through his ear. The noises he made were muffled but hideous. They did not continue long. It was a fighter's gambit she had heard Yalef mention, years ago.

Once the man fell, Safca fell beside him and vomited, trying to expel the heart from her body.

When she came to herself, one of the Lannic recruits was holding her head. She struggled away, and he said, "Lady, we saw. Did the guardian send you to such debasement, to play whore to our jail? Don't fret. One of us'll say we did it to him." And there came a dull mutter of agreement. She looked up, her veil clutched to her mouth, and saw thirty or so men grouped around. "They're only sending us to feed Free Zakoris," said the Lan. "Better to die here." Across his shoulders she saw the tail ends of whip marks and realized why he was too feverish to sleep, and too resentful to want life.

Safca got to her feet with help from the pillar. When they handed her water, she drank it.

"There's no need," she said, "to die." They stared at her warily, knowing before she could tell them, the way the desperate sometimes will, that she was a messenger of reprieve. "If you've the courage, you can take the Karmians unaware and slaughter them."

"But, lady, rid ourselves of these, and others will come. We'd be hounded, taken. And our families killed without mercy."

"There's one place they can't hound us to," she said. They waited. "The Zor."

There was a great stillness.

A merchant's son said to her, "The trek up there is hard. Impossible. How many would survive the journey? And what's at the end? Ruins. The cold months are coming. We'd perish. We'd lose everything."

"You've already lost everything," she said, startling herself with her own crispness. "Kesarh Am Karmiss took it. Let's attempt freedom. Or would you rather end in battle—battle with Leopard Zakoris, or with Dorthar, or any other land black Kesarh thinks he can engage?"

The growling noise came again, stronger.

The man drunk with fever said, "She's risked her life to tell us this."

Safca said, slowly, her voice gone deeper, thrilling herself, and them: "I had a vision. The goddess Anack instructed me to do this."

In that moment she had them. She saw herself surrounded by

men, some of whom were young and noble, and their faces were
full of light that had come from her. She had never before caused
any man to look at her in this way.

The jailer was already dead and someone took his sword.
Minutes after, Safca's frenzied screams brought the guards from
above to unbolt the door, and she had the dubious joy of seeing
them cut down.

Untrammeled, Lans swarmed through the stone house. There
were sword racks farther up. They slew every Karmian they
found, and later, spilling in the street, slew others. In the house
across the way the Karmian soldiery had got wind of violence
and put up barricades. Even as external Lans were beating these
flat, the Lans inside, catching also the scent of what was happening,
perhaps even by some sort of telepathy, took the invaders from
the rear.

So it must have been in the Lowlands, Safca thought, the night
about her full of running flames, cries and shouts. But before
even the curiosity of this idea, which compared Lans to the
Amanackire, could unnerve her, she was picked up bodily and
carried by blood-stained men into the marketplace amid the
torches. Someone was ringing the curfew bell. All about, Olm
was gushing forth into the night.

When the Karmian command came from the palace they were
murdered to a man.

High on an upturned cart, then, Safca must address the horde
of people, their frightened faces, or the victorious faces of those
who had already torn free.

What must I say?

But she already knew. She held out her hands to them and was
unbearably moved by the night, the fires, the depth of what had
sprung from her.

"Anackire," she said, and there rose a peculiar sighing sob
from the heart of the crowd. "Anackire has come to us, as she
came long ago, and to all those who are oppressed. Anackire is
in the mountains, the black-haired serpent goddess of Lan."

Within five days they were ready, and traveling. Provisions
and persons had come from some of Olm's villages around
about, villages that had seemed deserted and bare since the
advent of Karmiss. Most of Olm moved toward the mountains.
They even had a Zorish girl, a snake dancer, to act as their
guide.

Those who would not go with them they left behind with
token injuries, so the Karmians who came later might hold them

blameless. The guardian was one of these. Even as the riot of
townspeople evacuated Olm, he was scribbling dispatches, left-
handed, for Kesarh's High Command at Amlan, the other arm in
a sling. He had begged the Lan with the sword to slice deep.
Now the wound was festering nicely. No one would be able to
blame the guardian.

The roads that led into the foothills were gentle. The rain held
off at first. The Free Lans came on late flowers and wove
garlands, and sometimes sang as they moved toward the Zor.

The rain, that was not necessarily Lannic gratitude, was coming down again when the Vardish caravan made camp in the
hills. A cold wind was blowing, too; summer ending, with the
world.

There had been trouble at Olm, they had been informed of it
earlier. Just before sunset, a detachment of Karmian soldiery
went clattering by, riding in that direction. The caravan took
heed and crossed Olm from its inventory of stops.

It was a wretched night.

Huddled in one quarter of a wagon with their curtailed
belongings, Yannul sat watching Medaci make beautiful bead-
work with a slender bone needle. Their younger son was down at
the fires under the awning, dicing with a Vardian boy.

Suddenly there was fresh clatter and noise. Three riders erupted
into the wagon camp, dramatically fire-lit through the lines of
rain.

Yannul thought for a moment they were Karmian pursuers,
and his hand went to his knife. Then a man's voice roared out:

"We mean no harm. I bring word to any Lan who may be
here."

There were no Lans that he could see, but undeterred, the
spokesman shouted again: "The word is this—one part of Lan
stays free. Any who would join Free Lan, come a mile east, to
the rock with four trees. We'll wait there one hour. A caution.
Those who seek us seek in friendship. This—" and the man
whipped out a sword, cleaving water—"waits for the tirr of
Karmiss, or for any traitor."

Then the zeebas wheeled. The men were gone, leaving the
Vardians to yell.

Yannul's younger son was running toward the wagon from the
fire.

Yannul said, "That was a Karmian sword. Karmian mail he
had on, too."

"What is it?" Medaci said.

"I don't know. A small uprising. Olm, maybe."

She looked at him, her lovely eyes all flames and rain.

"Go then," she said. "See."

Their telepathy was erratic and always surprised him. He kissed her, left her to explain to their son, and went to get a mount.

He followed the three Lans so close they paused for him a quarter mile from the camp, swords out, frowning.

Riding up to them, he thought, with a kind of dull laughter, *This is Raldnor's time all over again.*

"Halt. Who are you?"

"My name's Yannul. I'm a Lan, like you."

"Yannul."

They looked at each other. One said, "He would be the right age. His hair's long. They say he wears it that way. But he's in Dorthar."

Another said, "Don't be a fool. Of course it's him. I saw his son at Zastis, in Olm. Talked to him. This *is* Yannul."

They got around to asking Yannul, then.

"Yes," he said, "I fought with Raldnor son of Rehdon." They sat tense as drums and stared at him through the river-running night. "Now," Yannul said, "what's *your* story?"

After a while, they crowded under an overhang. He heard it better there, what had happened at Olm, and about the princess who was a priestess, to whom Anackire had sent a dream. They were going to the Zor. The main party were up in the foothills. But Olmish riders were still going about the villages, stirring others to follow.

Something of their vehemence struck tinder in Yannul; then it died. They were already entreating him to add the weight of his figurehead to their enterprise when he felt himself step inwardly away. *I'm past all this. Heroes and miracles. I want the south, and security for her and the boy, and quiet.*

"And your woman," one said, "your wife—she's Amanackire."

He said something, afterward he could not remember what, but it sobered them down. He explained he wished them well. He said he was going to the Middle Lands.

One of them muttered, "Raldanash'll need him. The Black Leopard of Free Zakoris one side, the bloody Salamander the other."

There were some soaked awkward courtesies.

Not long after, he rode away, back to the Vardian wagons.

Medaci was seated under the awning now, by the fire, with

their younger son, whose dark eyes shone. Yannul shook his head at them. Sitting down, he told softly what he had learned, what he thought of it. No Vardians came up to pry. Traders, they were inquisitive but also uneager to know too much of anything. Vardath's main force was elsewhere too, after all.

"There are scarcely a thousand of them, mostly women and children, I'd surmise. If the snows come early, and they do up there in the mountains, they'll die. More dignified than death for Karmiss, perhaps. Still death."

"But Yannul," Medaci said. "Yannul, Yannul."

"What?"

"Your country," she said.

"My country's all this, not a sad little rebellion herding up a rock."

"Your country," she said again. "It's everything you are. It's almost your soul, Yannul."

"Oh, yes. That's why I left it. That's why I fought with Raldnor for *your* people, when mine wouldn't raise a sword."

"And like your soul," she said, "it was a part of you, wherever you went, or fought."

"Then it'll be with me in the Plains. Or Xarabiss. Or wherever."

"No," she said. "The day the curfew sounded at Amlan, you held me. You said, Lan is Lan no more."

Yannul looked away. His eyes were full of tears and he chided himself.

"But the heart of Lan stays free," she said. Something in her way of speaking made him gaze back at her. "We have no country," she said. "The Amanackire, the Lowlanders, we are a race, but the land is Vis—we have no growing root, no physical soul but the vagrant spirit of our people and the star of the goddess." He waited almost breathless. She had never spoken like this before in all the years he had been with her, lain with her, seen her carry and bear his sons, loved her. "But you made my people your people, Yannul. You made me your sister and your wife. And your land became my land. Yannul," she said, it was only a whisper now, "the Zor, Free Lan, the mountains. Let's go with them."

She looked a girl again, no older than that day he first saw her in Dakan's house. He was still gazing at her dumbfounded when their son said, "If Anackire called them, She won't let them die. Can't you see that, father?"

"Yes," Yannul said vaguely, "I suppose I can."

*   *   *

They traveled through the ashes of the night and all the next day. Yannul mastered the tracks and by-ways up into the higher foothills, which would take zeebas, and which must be taken on foot and the zeebas led. He had never come this way himself, but, a wanderer in his youth, he had been educated and not forgotten.

They had kept from their baggage only what was highly valuable or incorrigibly sentimental, paring down from the other paring down at the villa. The rest they sold for non-perishable foodstuffs. A group of the Vardians began to evince signs of wanting to accompany them, but had been dissuaded by their fellows. Farewells were coupled with good wishes. *Ashkar go with you!* some had called. Having acquired the tongue of the other continent while he was there, Yannul had spoken all along to the caravan in its own language, for which they respected him.

On the second night they ran into the three Lannic riders who had come to the wagon camp. They had now a bivouac of their own in a tall cave. There were five or six village men too, and seven women, and a quarrelsome pig. Everyone but the pig welcomed them heartily, without explanations.

They moved off before sunrise. The rain and storm winds, though making their own path treacherous, would help deter hunters. Apparently the Karmians were out on the lower hills, searching.

The guardian of Olm had been stripped of his drawers in the marketplace and given four blows with a rod. It had not done him good.

The first mountain flank, blue-gray, the hide of some primeval petrified beast, stretched dauntingly before them. Beyond, other mountains rose, a wall against the air.

There would be a pass, old as the hills themselves, partially choked by boulder-slips. Higher yet, there was an almost legendary way, carved hundreds of feet by nature, leveled by men. It was possible to get in and out of the Zor. The Zorians did so themselves, if seldom, peddlers, magicians, snake dancers, snakes.

They struggled all day, men, women and zeebas, to climb that initial flank. The pig struggled not to climb it. At last, lamenting, the seven village women let it free. It cantered away, burping with rage, in a torrent of sliding stones.

They got over the flank in the sunset. The rain had paused. The sun descended blazing and red at their backs, laving the mountains before them.

After the sun had gone, pieces of it were seen to have remained, trapped in cracks and on spurs above.

They had reached the lower pass, and found the sprawling camp of Free Lan.

Safca started, nervous and defiant, meeting Yannul the hero. Even a momentary unworthy jealousy had filled her, for she had been both the mascot and the commander until now. They fury at herself—to be so petty. She seemed two persons, always at odds. But at least she was teaching herself how to have dialogue with her other self, to reason with it and tell it to be quiet.

And Yannul was an impressive man. The Amanackire woman had pleased the Olmish refugees, who paid her instant reverence. Safca was more able to accept this herself. Medaci reminded her somewhat of the Lowlander she had known, though they were very unlike in all things but coloring, and even that was not really the same. The guardian's daughter did not mention the one named Ashni. It did not seem yet the time.

When eventually Yannul said, "You did so much, risked so much on the strength of a dream?" Safca challenged him across the fire: "Lord Yannul, so did you."

His fine eyes fell. He looked tired and lined under his splendor.

"And I seem still to be doing it."

He felt himself a faint distrust of Safca, an antagonism. He did not know what it was. She seemed honest, if impassioned, and had shown him so much honor he smiled.

Later, curled up with Medaci under an invented tent, he said, "Anack used to be a goddess of peace. Then She was a war-goddess. Now She instructs women to take up hairpins and knives and kill with them."

Medaci shivered, and he was sorry. He was all too conscious that, in avoiding the phantoms of the Shadowless Plains, they had entered a situation uncannily similar. Olm, too, had slain its occupying garrison, and now sought to hide in a ruin. But then Medaci said, "That was Safca's interpretation. So it was interpreted to us by Raldnor, in the past. To meet the sword with the sword. Perhaps we were wrong. Perhaps it's another way Anackire shows us, but we never see it."

He thought she fell asleep then, but after a while she said, "There was a story my grandmother told me, why the goddess is depicted with eight arms instead of two arms."

"I'd heard it was from the spider," he said. "Eight-armed, because the female spider is greater than the male."

"No," she said, laughing a little. He was glad of her laugh.

"The story is this. An innocent came by chance into a grove on the Plains and found Anackire seated there. Being an innocent, he was not afraid, and the goddess was kind. They talked and presently he asked Her why, in Her statues, She was shown as eight-armed, seeing She was before him in the grove with only two arms. And Anackire replied: 'It is because you are innocent that you see me in such a way. But the statues are carven by men who have seen me through other eyes.' Then the innocent apologized, saying he didn't understand her. Anackire answered, 'My words you do not understand. My Self you do.' "

Yannul lay a long time, holding her, listening to the small noises of the exhausted camp. What she had said grew warm and drifting. Again he thought she slept, until she murmured, "Lur Raldnor." But then she did sleep, and he soon slept, and forgot.

Five days along the pass, having negotiated fallen boulders, crawled through apertures, climbed over tremendous rock heaps, coaxing or forcing the zeebas and what livestock remained to them, they came out on an open platform of stone and were able to look down the long fraught way they had already come. It had not been an auspicious day. One of the unstable slips they had had to climb had tilted. A man was flung into a ravine below the pass. Although they had got the zeebas free, the cart had slithered after him, laden with flour and salted meat. At least, they did not scream as they fell. The man's wife kept up for several miles the high desolate keening that might be used to mark death, until Safca, walking back to her on blistered feet, had reasoned grief to silence.

When fires were lit at dusk on the platform of stone, some Olmians looked down across the stony sides below. They were even able to make out the flank of the first mountain they had scaled. Before too long, they were also able to make out the many campfires spread along the entry to the pass.

"Karmians," said Yannul.

The Lan who had been an officer in the Olmish palace guard, next a levy recruit, now a captain of this unmilitary march, considered. "They're five days behind us."

"They're also lighter. We've got children, women, beasts, baggage. I've had dealings with a man who served Kesarh Am Karmiss. He said little, but his reactions were eloquent. If I were in Kesarh's army, I wouldn't want to let him down, either."

They resumed progress two hours before dawn.

Yannul consulted the Zorish girl who was their guide. She was a strange creature, with black whiplike hair—snakelike hair, as her movements were snakelike. The Karmians had butchered her snake at Olm from superstitious dislike. One heard, the snakepits were gone from the temples of Istris. Very little was known of a Zor dancer's relation with the serpent partner, but it had long been accepted among scholars as a spiritual one. The snake could be a familiar, conceivably a friend. The girl was full of wordless anger and woe, and this added to the difficulties of stilted speech. The Zor spoke the Vis tongue, but wound into some older or parallel language, its accent more appealing but less understandable than the guttural slur of Ommos, Zakoris or Alisaar. To make matters worse, the girl had never seen her own land. Her mother bore her in Lan and taught her there the snake dance. Though she knew of the passes, Vashtuh had never used them, until now.

"The upper pass, do you remember how far it should be, Vashtuh?"

"Ten days, and then ten days," she said. Or he thought she did.

"How do we find it?"

"A cave. Through the mountain."

It rained. The rain turned to hail, daggers flashing through the air, striking starbursts of pallid fire from the sides of the mountains that now went up sheer to either side of them. Sometimes stones fell, causing minor abrasions and substantial panic.

They knew the Karmian detachment was behind them, knowing them to be ahead, though the route curved—it was no longer feasible for one group to glimpse the other.

Moving almost constantly now, they realized, however, the Karmians would have encroached on the separating distance.

The Lannic officer organized fifty men who were willing to block the pass, delaying the pursuit, maybe annihilating it. They approached Yannul, who had the diplomacy himself to approach Safca. "We saw the Karmian campfires," he said to her, "those we *could* see. Fifty-one men will hold the pass for fifteen minutes. And they'll be fifty-one men we've lost."

She accepted him as counselor and with his personality to back her, refused the others leave to act.

On the twenty-third day, worn out, some sick, all sick at heart, and the hail again smashing about them, there was no evidence of the cave Vashtuh had said signaled the higher pass. Only the rock walls going up sheer, the somber peaks beyond, no longer blue, and the memory of Kesarh's men on the road behind them.

Shortly after dawn on the twenty-fourth day there was a new

mountain, directly in their path. A stone-slip had come down there, probably the year before, dislodged by snow. There was no way round it, no way up or over it. The only use it would serve would be to put their backs to when the Karmians arrived.

"I had a dream," said Yannul's younger son. "I saw the other side of the mountain. There's a huge valley. It must be the Zor. It must mean we'll find a way through."

Yannul did not say anything. He could only have said, "That's the closest you'll come to it, now." He had other things on his mind. He was wondering if, in the final extremity, he should kill them, his wife and son, to save them from atrocities the Karmians might inflict. One did not hear of such atrocities too often, save from Free Zakoris. The Amanackire were sacred. But maybe not here, where none but Karmians would live to tell of it. Kesarh had ousted Ashara-Anack from eminence in the fanes of Istris. Besides, Yannul recollected the burning village the caravan had negotiated. No, the Amanackire might not be sacred here.

But to kill her, to kill the boy—Yannul's throat scalded with bile. He did not know what to do, so he went on listening.

"There *is* a city, you can see it far off. It's big, but fallen. Black stone, like in the Lowlands. You said the Lowland city was black, didn't you, father?"

"Yes," said Yannul.

"But the valley was fertile. There were fruits growing, and I saw sheep, and orynx. And a river."

"They say an abandoned city is like a broken sword," said the Olmish officer. Yannul had not seen him come up. "It rusts, rots away. But it wasn't like that. It felt alive. There was a light there. Did you see that, too?"

"Yes," said Yannul's younger son. "A kind of flame on the ruin, when it got dark."

"A city of fire then," said someone else. "Not rust."

Yannul's belly clenched.

"You're saying you had the same dream, the two of you—and my son?"

"Maybe. What about you, Lord Yannul?"

Yannul hesitated. At the back of his mind something stirred. In sleep he had thought it was the Lowland city, and had been puzzled because—because *a river ran across the plain*—

A hundred feet away, Medaci was standing by Safca. Beyond them, a man was running along the pass from the lower end.

Yannul got up and went over.

The man gasped for breath and said, "My zeeba fell. Dead. I

ran for miles. They're almost here. A hundred of them, more. They saw my mate. Spear shot got him. Didn't see me. Not that it makes any difference, lady. I dreamed of it all last night, dropping asleep in the saddle, seeing the valley. But we'll never get there now.''

There was a wash of sound. They had all had the dream apparently, but many were only just discovering. Mind-speech was not recognized among Lans. A mental link of such magnitude was unconscionable, therefore sorcerous, therefore, at some level, absurdly acceptable and accepted.

Safca climbed one of the tumbled rocks. Standing higher than the rest of them, she raised her arms.

Yannul looked at her, the philosophical part of him awed, the man amused.

When she became a priestess, this unbeautiful woman changed. A sun seemed to rise behind her face, her whole body, and to be channeled out upon them. She must have looked like this the night they killed the Karmians at Olm. Transfigured.

Suddenly he heard a woman from his past speaking inside his head. "None of us could harm him. He is his god's. And the gods protect their own." She had been referring to Raldnor. Raldnor walking back from the forest of the second continent, branded by Anackire.

Safca began to cry out to them. She was telling them the goddess was near and would save them.

The wind and the bad weather had stopped, and she was clearly visible, audible. It was no trance, no rolling of the eyes, wriggling, salivating, howling. She was in command of herself, disciplining herself instinctually that the wondrous energy might pass through her and to them, unsullied.

It was not her power. Someone had trained her. Or gifted her—

It was like something of Raldanor's. Something he might have passed on to his sons. But Rem had been the son of Raldnor. Beyond that princely and striking but quite human aura, the often striking, not always quite human good looks, Rem had had nothing of this, or seemed not to. Raldanash, seen as a boy, had been more of Raldnor's way, yet he was heatless as dead coals. Raldnor, even Raldnor as a god, had never been that.

Yannul had loved Raldnor as a brother, but with more love than he had ever felt for the loved brothers of his flesh.

The love had never gone, though Raldnor had left all their lives a generation ago.

Why think of this now?

The Olmians were moved by Safca, electrified. But Yannul had not even heard her. Yet he heard something. Something that had no sound.

He had heard it previously. On the plain under Koramvis, the night before the last battle. The silent strumming of the air, the earth, over and over.

Power.

He felt suddenly young as he had been then, afraid as then, and with a new fear astride the first. Something would happen. He could not see why it should, but it would. Energy, power— and death. An avalanche, perhaps, tearing the mountains out by their roots, burying the Karmian soldiery who hunted them, simply because they were ordered to do so, would commit atrocities upon them because they were scared and cowardice invented evil.

He partly turned. They were all turning, to face toward the lower end of the pass, from which the Karmains would come.

Yannul glimpsed his son. The fine young face was open and savage with strength, a man's face, a demon's. Yannul wanted to shout. Whatever they confronted, this was no answer. To meet sword with sword, prevent death by death. They had killed Koramvis and the might of the Vis, and the world was altered, and had brought this, more killing, more pain. Endless. A circle of fire.

"No," she said. Who was it now? The hand slipped into his was cool and sure. "In the Lowland city, Raldnor made us kill. I recall so well. In my sleep I've lived it again and again. But this isn't like that."

Medaci.

He was himself now like a child, and clung to her hand.

The wind rose, then.

And around the slight curve of the mountain pass, the Karmians appeared.

The Karmians had had a harsh journey up from the foothills, but had suffered no casualties. They knew preseverance was expected of them.

Their leader, who had been appointed to his post months before by Kesarh himself, was yet galvanized by the meeting, and had imparted some of his dedication to his soldiers. The plan was to slaughter all male Olmians. The women would be sent as slaves to Karmiss, or put to similar work with the army of occupation.

Coming up around the pass and seeing the huddle of humanity

before them, their backs literally to a wall, the leader kept his
zeeba to a walking pace, allowing the entire Karmian force to fill
the pass and so to fill the sight of the Olmians. From here, he
would presently command his javelins into position. They could
take out a random selection of the rebels as a precedent, before
the detachment moved in to a more tidy execution.

Before this could be arranged, the leader noticed a man standing on the stone track, exactly between rebels and soldiery.

It was odd, since he had not seemed to come forward from the
rebel side, and certainly could not have climbed down the mountain steeps unseen. From some cave, maybe.

The leader held up his hand to halt the column. There was a
problem here. The man was a mix Vis, almost black, but his
mane of hair was blond-white and even from here, the eyes were
seen to be pale and peculiarly brilliant.

Unwillingly, the leader became aware of muffled exclamations
and curses behind him. He even fancied he caught the phrase of
a frightened prayer. As this went on, his own skin started to
crawl along his neck. Then he knew why. The man on the pass
ahead of them wore the dragon-mail of Old Koramvis. He was
tall, had the look of a king, and the face of a god—

Behind the leader now, they were kneeling, some of them.
Zeebas were shying, officers bawling for order, their voices
cracked with shock.

The man on the track was Raldnor Am Anackire.

The leader strove to control his mount. He would have to do
something, but what?

Then everything was taken from his hands.

Behind the figure of the god-hero, a gleam began to burnish
the air. Gradually the world faded, leaving only this gleam,
which touched the sky. A second figure formed within it. It was
the figure of the serpent goddess, Ashara-Ashkar-Anackire, the
Lady of Snakes.

Rather than screaming, the men of Karmiss had fallen utterly
quiet, and motionless. The leader was caught in this same weird
grip. He did not feel afraid. He felt a terror, but it was almost
ecstatic.

The colossal apparition had not completely solidified. She was
translucent. Despite that, She was not as they had heard or ever
been shown Her. Her skin was dark, a Lannic skin of brass. Her
hair was black, and the great tail black-scaled, with a coiling
gold design across it, shimmering and alive. But her eyes were
amber, and fixed upon them, from out of the sky.

Her eyes did not blast them. Her eyes turned them.

It was not unpleasant now, merely easy. They moved about, and those that needed to remounted their animals, which had become docile. They rode away.

They had gone three miles back along their route at a serene unhurried pace, before the leader, trotting now to the rear of his soldiery, came to himself with a violent start.

Only then did he hear the dying rumble of the avalanche, which had blocked the pass, between the rebels and themselves.

SIXTEEN

When the figure hurried out at him from the colonnade, Rarmon reacted faster than his own guard. But the man dropped to one knee, bowing, an obeisance of Visian Karmiss.

Rarmon's guard was standing in close, hand to sword, by then. He nudged the man.

"Get up."

"When," said the man, "the Lord Rarmon tells me."

The guard looked inquiringly at Rarmon.

Rarmon said, "Get up, then. And say what you want."

The man rose. He was Vis and very dark. More than that. Though he had none of the accent, he had a look of Zakoris.

"What do I want, my lord? A word in private."

Rarmon had been coming from exercise, across the courts of Anackyra's Storm Palace. This spot was a thoroughfare, a hub of much of the palace's traffic. The fountain and the scented vines also ensured aristocratic loiterers. For a sudden meeting it was in itself far from private. Without looking about, Rarmon knew their tableau was already well-observed.

He said to the guard, "Step back." To the man he said, "What nation are you?"

"Yes, lord Prince. I have Zakorian blood. But I'm half Dortharian to sugar it. I feel the war councils of the Storm Lord. A paid informer against Yl."

"A traitor, in other words."

"No, lord Prince. I was born in *Vardian* Zakoris. My King's Sorm of Vardath, Dorthar's ally. And I serve Dorthar."

"Who sent you to me?"

"One you, lord Prince, betrayed."

Rarmon looked at him. The man's eyes flinched away, but returned. "Who would that be?"

"A mighty lord, who'd not forget your worth, though you forget his bounty."

"I see. You are then a Vardish Zakorian, aiding Forthar, and acting for Kesarh Am Karmiss. Does all that never make you dizzy?"

"My lord. I carry the messages of those who pay me."

"What's the message?"

"None, as yet. I'm to sound you. Would you gladly receive a messenger from the Lord Kesarh?"

"He knows not. I told him so. Then why are you here? To display the bastard brother in conversation with a Zakorian spy?"

The man took one perfectly coordinated backward step.

"Wait a moment," said Rarmon. The man waited. "Since this will be going into the annals of court gossip, I must try to cleanse my reputation. Go to Kesarh for recompense if I loosen your teeth." Moving forward with the swiftness of a cat, Rarmon struck the man and sent him staggering. Pitching his voice to travel, Rarmon called: "That's all I have for Zakoris."

Not looking back, Rarmon continued into the colonnade and so to his apartments.

Vencrek, the suspicious and unliking Warden, might have primed the man. A test on all fronts—current loyalty to Dorthar, past loyalties to Karmiss. One trusted it was a test, not simply the machinery of discredit.

Discussion of war had been continuous all month. Kesarh, in possession of Lan and Elyr, and received delicate offers without response, offering in turn only cordial and empty communications. He seemed abruptly disinclined to be wooed, after all. Dorthar already attempted to reconstruct her campaigns, in the likelihood the east must now simultaneously be dealt with too. Both the oratory and the military deployments had acquired a muddled and bombastic ring. Raldanash's composure began to look like indifference, the old passivity of the Lowlands.

For the Lowlanders themselves, you saw them sometimes, passing through the palace or the streets, just such pale all-indifference to everything. Men stepped aside, bowing, keeping a distance. Children were prevented from playing outside Amanackire houses in the suburbs. They were not only respected, but plainly feared. More, or less, than the Black Leopard of Free Zakoris, Rarmon could not be sure.

It rained. The leaves rotted. Anackyra was full of gloomy forecast and idiotic bravura.

Last year at the end of the hot months, Rarmon had been Rem, riding hills that were then Lan's own, looking for Kesarh's child. . . .

Dorthar had given Rem very little, that was his. The luxury and the title and the apparent power were ultimately weightless and meant nothing. In the war, he would have an honorable and exalted command and maybe die. Nothing, again. Dorthar had given him nothing.

Once or twice he wondered if Yannul's son had got home. But Yannul, and Lur Raldnor also, inhabited the land of the past.

The man who waylaid Yeize, chief lady to Ulis Anet, was not a Zakorian.

He stole upon her as she, with other women of the connubial courts, was hastening down the Imperial Hill from the Anackire Temple. It was early twilight, and dry, though a brisk wind ran from the northern mountains, rattling the forest trees above. But the man murmured to Yeize, whose heart was full of romance, and she was quickly drawn aside. The others, deeming in an assignation, went on.

Some hours later, preparing her mistress for bed, Yeiza snipped a small lock of blood-red hair, under the plea it grew awry. Later yet, when the Queen withdrew to her inner chamber, Yeiza was able to appropriate one of the silver ribbons plaited into the red hair at dinner.

Initially, the girl had been outraged at the idea of stealing anything from her lady. However, the go-between was very charming and persuasive. After all, his master, who had sent him on this mission, could be expected to return a trinket with interest. While, as long as the token was something recognizably the Queen's, it need be of slight significance.

The ribbon was, Yeiza thought, an apt and artistic choice. Even if the go-between had not forced payment on her, to do this service for her poor neglected mistress and the elegant lord Prince Rarmon could have been a pleasure.

Since Lur Raldnor's departure, Yeiza had been frankly bored. Her mood was further soured by a growing disconsolation that Iros was now seldom in person about Ulis Anet's courts. Yeize had decided, with great poignancy, that she was in love with Lord Iros. She was sure she could win him—had he not often shown himself attracted? But not with the Queen as a rival.

On the other hand, here was Ulis Anet, pining for want of attention. Yeiza, who oversaw the appointments of the bedchamber, knew quite well that, though he had been closeted with his new wife, Raldanash had not lain with her. After the hunt at Kuma, Ulis Anet grew strange, withdrawn and listless. She seemed not to know herself or care what went on, observing form, but no more. She was like someone recovering from a debilitating illness. Except that she did not recover.

Since the night Lord Rarmon had saved her mistress from disgrace, Yeiza had astutely guessed he loved Ulis Anet. Had he not already heroically rescued her from her runaway chariot after the earthquake? Had he not banished Iros from her vicinity? As for Ulis Anet herself, it was equally obvious she had conceived a passion for Rarmon. She had trusted him with her life, allowing him to find Iros in her bedchamber. She had come back from Kuma, where she had so often seen him, like a creature without a soul.

The man in the twilight had proved Yeiza's clever deductions were correct. His master, Rarmon, required a token from the Queen. She had so far refused from loyalty to Raldanash, though, as the go-between stressed, Rarmon was the one lover who could protect her and offer her the honor she merited.

Presently, the conspiracy became more personal.

Suppose the token could be gained without Ulis Anet's knowledge? Her guilt would not be roused, but the Lord Rarmon would assume himself at liberty to come to her. Once two such persons were alone together with privacy and a bed, who could doubt nature must take its course?

Yeiza did not doubt. She even suspected in this the connivance of the Storm Lord himself. She had heard talk by now that all his women were left alone at night and encouraged to remedy the matter as they wished.

She had also noticed how this apartment connected by a garden walk to a number of deserted courts before reentering the outer environs of the palace. For clandestine visitors, the way was fortuitous.

Nor did Yeiza forget, going out to deposit the lover's token with Rarmon's servant, to leave the door on to that walk unlocked.

Iros Am Xarabiss, commander of the guard of Xarabians attendant on one of the Storm Lord's lesser queens, checked drunk and ill-humored at the foot of the Imperial Hill. He had been trying tonight to buy his way instead into a position of battle command, filled by a rage to kill Free Zakorians, which conveniently masked for him his septic rebuke at the hands of Ulis Anet. But the bribery had not gone well. He felt himself insulted. He felt himself seen through. He, who was the son of

Xaros, hero of the Lowland War. The wine had flowed angrily at an expensive inn.

Up in the air the fire-eyes of the Rarnammon statue blazed. Below, the man stood bowing in its shadow.

Then something was extended, and slipped into Iros' hand.

"Do you know this tress of hair, my lord?"

Iros stared. The pole-torches of the city gave excellent light.

"And the ribbon," said the man. "You may have seen her wear that at supper."

"How did you come by it?"

"No need for alarm, my lord. My mistress could assure you of that. She asks you to attend her this evening."

Iros lurched forward. The man drew back.

"Ulis—" Iros said. His tongue was thick, and his head, but his heart raced now to clear them.

"You're to go where the paper tells you. Be there by midnight, my lord."

Iros did not even look at the paper until the man slithered away across the square. Breakers of huge emotion were rocking the commander. Now she would heal his lacerations with love.

He had never really doubted she must return to him as soon as she was able. He held the lock of hair to his lips, breathing in its fragrance, a lust on him like Zastis, already planning all he would say to her, do with her.

Only when he peered at the paper was he rather aggravated. It seemed a long and curious way to go for prudence's sake.

Ulis Anet woke in a vague dim horror that had no source. All about the night was quiet. The aromatic lamps burned low, flickering. A bird fluttered its wings in a jeweled cage.

She had dreamed of a sailed boat, black on a dying sunset sea, rowed toward a shore of snow. One man sat behind the sail. She could not make out his face.

He held her in his arms.

She left the bed. She was afraid—or was it fear?

A masculine voice spoke from the doorway, startling her so much she could only turn to him slowly, almost calmly. There were two of them, white-cloaked, Raldanash's elite guard.

"Forgive me, madam," one of them said again. "You must come with us. Dress quickly. There's little time."

She did not move. Consternation had not yet reached her.

"What is it?"

"The Storm Lord's received word Free Zakorian assassins

have penetrated the grounds. These courts are vulnerable. The royal women are being escorted to safety."

"Very well," she said.

They retreated, and the curtain swung to.

Her pulses were clamoring now. Still it was not fear, and still the aura of the dream had not left her. Nevertheless she dressed swiftly, took up a mantle and went out to them in the antechamber.

Beyond the rooms the darkness was silent, as it usually was in this quarter of the palace. The men walked one on either side of her, tense and watchful. It would be possible to imagine a cutthroat in every shrub, behind every pillar. They reached a wall and a gate was opened. In an archway, a covered carriage waited. No guards were in evidence here, although this was one of the exits from the palace grounds.

"But where will I be taken?" she said.

"Just get in, lady. For your safety."

She obeyed them. They did not follow her. The door was fastened shut and instantly the carriage was moving.

They were proceeding uphill at a jolting heavy gallop—toward the Anackire Temple?

Presently she found the window-spaces of the carriage were also immovably covered and she might not see out of them. The door had been secured from the outside.

She was a prisoner, rushed toward some unknown fate. She suddenly thought: *Can Raldanash mean to have me murdered?*

The ruins of Koramvis were eerie and desolate by night. Iros left his chariot, and walked down to the edge of the River Okris. The directions on the paper were explicit, the standing house with the tall tree in its courtyard quickly located. He ascended the river terrace, stumbling on the misplaced flags, and pushed open broken doors.

There was a stairway, and at the top a hint of the faint topaz glow of a lamp.

He grinned with relief, and his excitement came back to warm him.

Iros mounted the stair, went through the shadows and into a salon. And found, in the light of a single bronze lamp, that he had been surrounded by men in coal-black mail. Men who showed their teeth. One of whom said, "Not exactly the feast you had in mind, eh, Xarabian?"

He tried to draw sword, but someone stopped him. Iros himself was not in mail, and someone else drove a knife through his ribs into his heart.

He was not quite dead as they dragged him down the stairs, but he was no longer an arrogant officer, no longer a proud peacock. He was a boy, sobbing in his soul for Xarabiss and the laughing father who had carried him on his shoulders, and for light, and for life.

But poised in the air all he saw were the hard stars of Dorthar, and the black river of Dorthar gaped for him, before his passage cleaved it.

The jouncing jolting ride seemed to last forever, the zeebas galloping in fits and starts, as was their wont. When the carriage stopped and the door was opened, she saw the upper foothills of Dorthar's mountains had come closer. Jumbles of masonry informed her further. She was on the outskirts of Koramvis, far above Anackyra's plain. There seemed to be the remains of a wharf, and beyond that the ancient river.

Beside her were soldiers. Two others riding up were those who had conducted her from her apartment; they were no longer dressed in the garb and blazon of Raldanash's Chosen Guard.

She stood and looked at them all. She was not afraid, only very cold, with the esoteric awe of these men a child may sometimes experience for adults.

One approached her, offering her a cup with wine in it.

It was incongruous. She did not accept the cup, but she said, "Is it poison?"

"No, lady. We've had instructions you're not to be harmed, only cherished. But there's some way to go by river. This will help you to sleep."

"I don't want to sleep."

"Yes, lady. It'll be tedious for you otherwise. And you might make a fuss."

"You're not the Storm Lord's men. Where are you taking me?"

"No questions now, lady. Drink the drink."

One said behind her, "Or we may have to put you to slumber another way."

"You were told not to harm me," she said frigidly, wondering how she could speak at all.

"It won't harm you. A slight pressure to the side of the throat. But not pleasant. Better to do as we ask."

She stepped away from him. There was nowhere to run. She allowed the other to give her the cup. It smelled herbal under the wine, nothing more. Poisons surely, did not smell this way? Besides, what choice.

When she had drunk she let the cup fall. A man picked it up. Another picked her up in turn. The drug was imperative and already she was will-less, helpless. She remembered when she had known such a sensation before. She admitted where she must be going, then, and felt a curious shame.

By the time they rested her in the boat, the woman was unconscious. They knew better than to sport with her, though she was alluring, beautiful and young.

They rowed upstream.

When the dawn began to show, they were many miles away.

Raldanash sat quietly, listening.

"Events are but too blatant, Storm Lord." Vencrek posed. "Guards who claim to have seen nothing—obviously bribed to be elsewhere. The two of your Lordship's own guard killed and stripped naked, hidden in bushes. Patently their garments were used as disguise for the Xarabian's men. The tracks of a carriage were found, going up into the hills toward the ruined city—My own men have scoured the area without success—a decoy, perhaps. Others have gone the opposite way, to investigate the roads south into Ommos and Xarabiss."

Raldanash said, "And your conclusion, Lord Warden?"

Vencrek stared at him. They had known each other as children in Vathcri. For a few seconds, Vencrek was too exasperated to remain suave. "Raldanash—this Vis bitch has made you a laughing-stock—"

Raldanash did not respond. There was nothing to be seen, no jealous fury, no passion, not even embarrassment.

"Pardon me, my lord," said Vencrek. "Your honor is dear to me. You asked my conclusion. Very well. There can be only one. Your Queen Ulis Anet has adulterously run off with her commander, Iros. It's widespread knowledge they were lovers prior to her marriage. He boasted of it and raged about her loss through half the wine-shops and brothels of Anackyra."

The limited number of counselors who had been admitted to this scene murmured gruffly. One, a Vis, said, "Your lordship should solace himself that they've nowhere safe to run to, and must be discovered. Dorthar's antique laws, I'd recommend, should be observed. This Iros to be publicly castrated and then hanged. The woman—"

"Yes," said Raldanash. "I know the justice given a straying royal wife. Spikes and flames."

"Leniency would be a mistake," said Vencrek. "If she were

of the race of the goddess—from the countries of your birth, or the Lowlands, maybe then. But she's Vis."

The Vis counselors shifted uneasily.

Raldanash said, "You haven't taken her yet." The beautiful kingly head was turned. He looked across the chamber at his half-brother. "What do you say, Rarmon?"

"Do you want my agreement or my opinion, my lord?"

"Whichever you think most useful."

"Storm Lord," Vencrek broke in, "the Lord Rarmon himself has some questions to answer to the council."

Rarmon regarded him. "Upon what?"

"Your dialogues with Free Zakorians."

"Which dialogues are these?"

"Storm Lord," said Vencrek, "this isn't the moment—"

"If you're accusing me of something, Lord Vencrek," said Rarmon, "any moment will do to make it plain."

Raldanash came to his feet. They all looked at him.

"Lord Warden, you may convene full council for two hours after noon. Until then, I thank you for your energies on my behalf. Good day, gentlemen." Then, almost idly from the doorway, "Rarmon. Attend me."

Presently, in one of the glorious rooms of the palace, the Storm Lord sat down again and pointed Rarmon to another chair.

"And now," said Raldanash.

"Your lordship has, I believe, taken delivery of the statement I sent him."

"The Zakorian informer who waylaid you in the Fountain Walk? Yes, I do know him; he purports to be ours. But apparently other things have been going on. Free Zakorian letters brought to you. Signals exchanged in passages. Some spy's dispatch intercepted, which mentioned, albeit obliquely, yourself."

"And you think I'd be such a dolt as to do such things here, at your elbow?"

"Perhaps," said Raldanash. "But I doubt it. Another man, maybe."

"You continue to trust me," said Rarmon.

"I sense powerful forces at work against you, in this."

"Do I have your permission to disorganize them?"

"If you can. But these may not be the powers of men alone."

Rarmon seemed to hesitate.

He would not let himself reach to the amber ring, to contact the fierce yet painless burning.

Raldanash said softly, "and Ulis Anet?"

Rarmon recollected himself. He said, "The flight of the Xarabian Queen is a little too pat."

"Yes. It parallels, also, the saga of Raldnor and Astaris."

"Such an ideal, of course, might have appealed to Iros. But she didn't want him."

"She was informed," said Raldanash, "that she might welcome any man, providing it was done discreetly."

Raldanash, even in this admission, showed nothing at all. Rarmon gave in, and closed his right hand convulsively around the ring. And wrenched his hand away. Though it did not sear the finger that wore it, the other intruding hand seemed scorched. Raldanash had not missed any of this, but made no comment.

"It's a fact," said Rarmon, "everyone knew of Iros' obsession with your wife. And anyone could have learned of it. Someone has therefore abducted her, probably against her will. While the coincidental disappearance of her commander has been arranged to suggest that he and she have fled together. I imagine his body is feasting carrion birds up in the hills. Or fish in the river."

"Who would want her so much?"

"There is one man. To my knowledge, he never saw her. But it may have happened. Kesarh Am Karmiss."

Raldanash made no protest, did not even ask for reasons.

"Then he no longer cares to pretend friendship with Dorthar."

"Enough to give you another story to believe, should you wish to. Iros took her."

"I see."

"I can arrange a private search for Iros' body, and any evidence left lying about up there. And you could send fast chariots to cut them off. They'll have used the Okris, I think, to go east. Kesarh must have a ship still standing off from Dorthar, ready to take them aboard. Of course, if you do apprehend his men, you'll have no choice but to break all ties with Karmiss. He could have foreseen that, too."

In the hour before sunset, the Anackire Temple swam in a dark golden gloom. The Prince Rarmon had previously come here on two occasions of formal religion, included in the Storm Lord's party. The ceremonies were Vis, noisy and exotic; even the mystic flamboyance of Ashara had not gone to such lengths. But now the place was hugely stilled, smelling of incense and cibba wood, only the cup of flame burning under the great statue.

Climbing the paved avenues up the forested hill, he had been half reminded of Ankabek. But there was nothing of Ankabek here. Though the more extreme rituals were not practiced so close to the palace and sacred prostitution was left to the other fanes of the city, this place was simply impressive in the way of mortal things. The marvelous statue, marble, gold and precious gems, was taller than the Anackire of Ankabek. It touched the intellect and appetite, not the heart.

A yellow-robed priest appeared around a screen, and bowed low, as Ashara's priest would not have done.

"I regret, the young woman's dead, Lord Rarmon. It was a subtle venom. We were able to alleviate her pain and lend her courage, but we couldn't save her life."

Poor Yeiza. She had been caught in the plot, ventured too far from shore, drowned there. Seeking sanctuary in the temple when she saw how things were going was her only act of wisdom. He could assemble the rest of it: Some token stolen from Ulis Anet to persuade Iros to the meeting. No doubt they had paid Yeiza. An Alisaarian trick maybe, a coin with one razor edge, and poison on it. She had not investigated the little wound until too late.

"I'm sorry," Rarmon said. But her death was a proof, too, as much as anything she could have told him. "You did right to send for me anyway. I'll see Anackire's well-gifted."

"Thank you, Prince Rarmon."

Abruptly Rarmon recognized the swarthy little man. He was the Thaddrian who had been among the Amanackire that night of the testing, the Thaddiran who, in his childhood, had supposedly witnessed Raldnor and Astaris riding into the jungle forests.

"I've already a gift with me for the goddess," Rarmon said. "Or for you."

He drew off the amber ring, cool now, and held it out.

"No, my lord," said the Thaddrian. "I can't take that."

"Why not? Lowland amber is valuable and considered holy."

"Nor can you give it, my lord." Despite the squat body, the priest was dignified, almost gentle. "It's geas, Prince Rarmon. You can't lay it down. It can be removed by the one who set it on you, no other."

"It's only a ring."

"That isn't so. It has Power. A gift for you, not to be given elsewhere."

"I thought you believed in the pragmatics of worship."

"Yes, my lord. Magic itself can be very pragmatic."

"I'll merely leave it lying on Her altar, then."

"No," said the Thaddrian. "It isn't the ring you're trying to be rid of. It's your destiny. Which is unavoidable."

Rarmon found he had replaced the ring. He said, halting, gaps between the words, "Is that what I feel, hanging in the air about me like a storm? I don't believe in Anackire. I don't believe in gods."

"My lord," said the Thaddrian, "Anackire is the symbol. The externalization of the Power inside us all. The face we put on beauty and strength and love and harmony. As writing is the cipher for a sound we only hear."

"You stand under the effigy and say that?"

"And see," said the Thaddrian with a monkey's grin, "She doesn't strike me down. Truth is never blasphemy when the god is Truth Incarnate."

Rarmon turned and walked between the pillars, and out into the pillars of the forest. The storm-warning of destiny pursued him.

It had rained, and the marks the carriage had made going in and out of rough ground were washed away. Rarmon sent his five men along the darkening south bank of the river. They found things, evidence of bandit lairs, a lover's tryst—but not the one they searched for—and disturbed a nest of wildcats. Torches were lit and bobbed about amid the ruins.

The council had detained him through the afternoon. It had been necessary to parry Vencrek's added allusions to Free Zakorian friends, in person. But to leave this trail till morning would have left it colder even than it was now. Finally, by an old standing house, one of Rarmon's men came on a chariot with a team of fretting animals. The chariot-prow bore the sigil of Xarabiss.

In the house they discovered a lamp, upstairs; dregs of recent oil. There was a black stain on the floor, equally recent blood. They went out on to the terrace.

"He's in the river, my lord."

"Yes. I think so."

"Luckless bastard."

Rarmon sent the chariot cityward with two of them. One of the other three went down by the tree in the yard to urinate. He did not come back.

Rarmon checked the last two men, who were for rushing to see. From the side of the terrace they discerned, around the tree bole, a booted leg sprawled in the relaxation of death.

"Bloody robbers—"

"Robbers wouldn't dare kill palace guard so close to the city."

There was a gasp above, a man spontaneously taking air to jump, and Rarmon flung himself aside.

A figure crashed down, crying out as it hit the edge of the stone terrace, but taking one of the Dortharians with it.

The second Dortharian sprang round, thrusting his torch at another running figure while he jerked out his sword. His hair alight, the attacker plunged aside screaming, but two more had the Dortharian between them, blade immobilized.

Someone must have struck the screamer quiet. His noises ended in time for Rarmon to hear the snapping of the second guard's neck.

Behind him, the first Dortharian had also stopped fighting.

"Throw down your sword, Prince," someone said. "You can see it can't help."

The spilled torch had been rescued. It gave enough light to display the dozen or so men clustered about. They wore the black-washed mail of Karmiss, but unblazoned.

"We knew you'd come here," said the voice. It was familiar. "Your erstwhile lord, Kesarh, can read your mind like a Lowlander." A man sidled forward. He was not wearing mail but black owar-hide. It was the accosting Zakorian. "Yes," he said, "I've decided after all to renege, to give my loyalty to my own old master, King Yl Am Zakoris. Your Kesarh helped me to decide. Not shocked are you, Lord Rarmon?" He gestured at the Karmians. "Take his sword, knife, any other weapons. Give any jewels he has to me. I'll have that ring, to start."

Aid would not come. Even the other two guard would have been caught and killed by now. Rarmon offered no battle. It would have meant death and he was not ready for death as yet. Even so, they pushed him to his knees before ripping the weapon-belt from him. Someone kicked him in the back, a blow like thunder. He fell into a pit of blackest nausea, and lying on the paving, was aware of the sword removed from one hand, the ring of the geas torn from the other. Then a yell. Of course, the ring had been burning. He heard it hit the stone somewhere and shatter like glass.

The Free Zakorian swore.

Vencrek was not, this time, the first with an accusation. Instead, a parchment had been fastened to the gate of the council halls. It read:

Nobles of Dorthar, you should never harry a wolf. He has

run to his brothers in Free Zakoris with news of all your strategies of war. And he laughs at you as he runs.

After the river, there was a traveling-chariot. After the chariot, another oared boat out to a dark galley standing like night on morning sea. They had continued to drug her, she saw these things in snatches. On the ship they drugged her also and now she was glad, for the brief voyage was storm-flung.

When she woke from that she was on land again. She conjectured which land it must be.

But this last awakening was dreamlike. She was in a house, ornately built, overlooking savage gardens of wild and disconcerting loveliness. Beyond, a cultivated valley undulated to the horizon.

As the physical weakness of the drugs left her, she took note of her surroundings. Every appurtenance, everything her rank had made her used to, was supplied, even to the nourishing and decorative food, the costly unguents, and trays of jewelry.

Two women attended her. They behaved as gracefully as any of her attendants had ever done, and answered freely, except when she put questions regarding where she was, and who had placed her here in this attractive cage.

"But I'm in Karmiss," she said.

"Look at this velvet, madam. How well it suits these pearls."

The pearls were black, Karmian riches. Yet they would never reply exactly.

But then, she did not need to be told, that was only some vestige of pride—to pretend herself ignorant and afraid.

His men guarded the house, which she came to see was a mansion-villa. Though she might go anywhere in the tower which she had woken to, the rest of the mansion proved inaccessible. The garden, too, was only to be enjoyed from a balcony. She saw distant figures in the fields, but no other servants. It was a relief. If any might have heard, she would have felt obliged to cry out.

Four days went by. Each seemed twice its length. At night her sleep was feverish. Her body ached, but not with any sickness. Sometimes, attempting to read one of the books, or wandering the tower, or seated on the balcony, she seemed to sense some stir in the house—a scarcely audible conversation, a footstep sharp on a walk below—and her heart would spasm with a kind of agony, thinking he had arrived. But her response was never justified.

On the fifth day toward sunset, however, every symptom was

shown her that he was indeed imminent. The women brought fresh and surpassing clothing, complex jewels. They were agitated as they contrived to dress her hair. In the chamber where she ate, the braziers now necessary had been lit and perfumes added. Extra candles appeared and were set on fire.

"We must hope," she said tartly to the women, "the Lord Kesarh won't be late."

When they were gone, she paced about in the violent and disquieting afterglow.

She had, captive that she was, no choice but to receive him. But no, the ease of that was false. It had all been made easy for her, but she found at last she could not lie to herself. Since infancy, she had been molded to her existence. Given to the Storm Lord six years before, she had looked for nothing save those things her molding assured her were hers by right. But Raldanash did not want her. She had had some warnings. She tried to be stoical. To remain so, faced with a life of such stoicism. Then, in the darkness of that dawn near Kuma, Kesarh had crossed the black river like the river of arcane myth which separated the living from the shades, and bound her to him by his shadow across her face, the grasp of his hands, the will behind his eyes. Kesarh, unlike Raldanash, had wanted her. And she. Yes, she had wanted to be wanted by Kesarh.

And her integrity was revolted.

Very well, she must receive him. But like this? Garbed and gilded for him like one more dish upon his table—

She ran to the mirror and wiped her face clean of cosmetics. She took down her sculptured hair and shook it loose. Shedding the gems and the velvet, she took up the dress she had traveled in, which they had cleansed and returned to her when she asked for it—she had not then known why—but which was dulled by the journey, no longer gracious, in places even torn.

She was only just in time.

As she stared at her transformation in the mirror, the outer door was opened and then firmly shut.

She learned then that she could not move.

So it was in the mirror's surface that she saw him come through that chamber with the candles and braziers and table, and stand framed in the doorway of this.

You have seen him, she thought, *turn and confront him. He's no more than you behold in the glass.* But in the glass he was enough to take her breath from her. Somehow she made herself turn. She avoided his eyes, looking directly through him.

He said, "I thought the women were to dress you." She could not stop her ears, His voice came into them.

"They did everything you wanted," she said. "Now I've done as I thought fit."

"Yes," he said. There was no irritation, no mirth. No expression at all.

He went back into the outer room, and she was impelled to follow him and to say: "Am I at last to have an explanation for your atrocious act against me?"

He wore black. They had said in Dorthar that was usual. He seemed all blackness against the flaming wax. He was pouring wine, which he now offered her.

"No."

He drank the wine himself, straight down, all of it.

"You are," he said, "on the estate of my counselor, Raldnor. At Ioli. Soon it will be expedient to move you elsewhere. I apologize that, as yet, I can't receive you in my capital of Istris."

"I'm your hostage against Dorthar," she said.

"No," he said. "Just mine."

"This insult to the Storm Lord could mean war."

"There will be war anyway. Nothing like this ever caused a fight that wasn't already spoiling."

"Why," she said, "did you—"

"You know why."

She met his eyes not meaning to. He and she were yards apart. She looked aside from him and her blood seemed full of water.

"I recall for you some woman who died."

He said nothing.

I, too, should have died, she thought, *before I submitted to this*. But the idea was empty, a fallacious ritual. Even to her it seemed sickeningly coy.

There came a plea outside the door, and he told them to come in. Unknown servitors appeared; a lavish meal was set out. That seen to, Kesarh sent them away.

He indicated the table.

"And chance some other drug or potion? No, my lord."

"You mean to starve yourself for virtue's sake."

Their eyes met again.

"Don't suppose," she said, "I can willingly accept anything of yours."

He came toward her then, crossing over the bright room as over the lightless river. He did not touch her. He said, "Starvation's a slow, comfortless way." He drew the dagger from his belt and offered it as courteously as he had offered the wine. "She killed herself," he said. "Why not you?"

Ulis Anet did not look at the dagger. It had no value for her. She knew she could never employ death. The words meant more.

"Who was she?" she said.

"My sister."

She tried to shrink from him.

"You offered rape to your sister? She preferred suicide."

"What else?"

She gazed at him, striving to see through him to mockery or rage or pain. But she could not; he was like Raldanash in that.

Only the heat beneath the cold darkness was not the same at all.

She must not attempt to force his hand with her, push him to violence or the rape she had mooted like an invocation. Again, it would be too easy. She could give in to superior strength and need not blame herself.

"Allow me to withdraw," she said.

Even that might exacerbate. She had sounded cool and meek, colorless—she lowered her eyes. It was difficult to do.

"There's no need for that," he said. He was dangerously urbane now. "I'll dine elsewhere." He walked to the door. She did not look up. She did not know that in the modest gown, her long hair down her back, face unpainted, she was more than ever an image of Val Nardia, that morning when she had departed for Ankabek. By the door, he said, "Tomorrow I'm sending you to a house nearer the capital. It's pleasant, and there's a decent road. Anything you want can be got for you."

"Let me have passage back to Dorthar, then," she said to Raldnor Am Ioli's mosaic floor.

"Forget Dorthar. When the war's done I'll give you Karmiss." The astonishment of it made her, after all, stare at him.

"Yes," he said, "My first Consort, Chief Queen of Karmiss, Lan, Elyr, and any other ground that's then in my possession. Did you think I brought you all this way to serve the wine?"

The door was opened and once more firmly shut.

Kesarh had left her alone with the dinner, and with her thoughts.

Far from his estate that night, Raldnor Am Ioli stood in his bedchamber at Amlan, reading dispatches, while a nervous Lannic girl crawled under the bedcovers.

There had been reports of rebels in Lanelyr killing the occupy-

ing soldiers, escaping up some mountain and now safe behind a
convenient rock-fall. Strange stories had apparently attached to
the phenomenon. He supposed he would have to look into it, at
some juncture.

He was getting lazy, was Raldnor.

One area, however, where he had remained careful, was the
discretion with which he bedded the local girls. This one had
been smuggled in and would be smuggled out before sunrise. It
would not do for Raldnor's soldiers to become informed that,
though he had brought a favorite mistress all the way from
home, he never went to bed with her.

Some, of course, might have liked to. For some, Mella's sort
would always have attractions.

Thinking of his insurance, this most brilliant hazard of his life,
Raldnor set the dispatches aside.

Mella.

There must come a time when Kesarh would overreach himself and the heavens crash down. And that would be when
Raldnor the King-Maker would lift his gem from the rubble.

The embalmers, who were not embalmers, had got their trade
in Ommos and were accomplished. Their covering lies of corruption and poison Kesarh himself had silenced. The child, stupefied with medicines that were not quite those Kesarh had
authorized, had slipped into a coma that did not actually preface
death. It was an empty box Kesarh had glanced at, sufficiently
scented with foulness from a recent and genuine plague-corpse
that he did not investigate further. Why should he, anyway?
Raldnor had been trusted to perform murder before and seen to
it, impeccably. A vacant weighted coffin was buried in the Hall
of Kings.

Hygienically and caringly cut, the boy regained consciousness
a eunuch. He grew up in the backlands of Ioli, soon female
enough to pass for a woman save in the most intimate of
situations.

Given intelligent handling, one day the Prince-King Emel
might regain the throne of Istris.

Though, being what he was, it was unlikely he could keep it.

The dreadful truth would be found out, and Raldnor, who had
waited so long in the wings, could stride across him into glory.

Kesarh had enfranchised Raldnor. Raldnor did not brood on it,
but he was no longer the same man who, hearing the slaves
shrieking in the blazing galleys at Tjis, had been honorably
dismayed. Learning it was workable, a certain latent cruelty had
come to Raldnor's surface. He could now indulge, along with a

taste for power Kesarh had taught him by example, the callous-
ness and the infliction of pain which, to Kesarh, were tools not
toys.

Raldnor himself enjoyed his sadism, as the Lannic bed-girl
was about to discover.

BOOK FOUR—*The Black Leopard*

SEVENTEEN

It would be snowing in Dorthar. It did not snow here. The summer lasted longer, here. Winter never came.

They had crossed by the ancient Pass through the mountains. The Dortharian side was well-guarded, the frequent lookout towers hewn from and perched on the rock, bristling with spears. Even coming down into Thaddra there were Dortharian outposts. Caal the Zakorian was known, however; he had been this way before, with a council seal of Anackyra on his person, and all the correct passwords. It was quite true he was a spy for the Storm Lord. In Free Zakoris he was reckoned a spy of King Yl's. In this way, Caal got about pretty adequately, sometimes alone, sometimes with servants. He had two guards this time, and a slave.

The private guards were of the light Vis darkness most common in Xarabiss or Karmiss. The slave was a little darker, maybe a Dortharian. He was also disobedient or slothful or careless, for he had been recently beaten. His face was a mass of bruises and old blood, and his strong back, where rags of clothing revealed it, showed old whip scars. He was chained at the ankles too, with just enough slack between the chafing irons to plod. He carried the baggage, while the first guard rode ahead. The second guard and Caal rode behind the slave, and now and then Caal flicked him with the starchy-tongued flail generally kept for flies.

Coming off the Pass, they reached Tumesh, then moved roughly westward. The best mode of travel through the jungles of Thaddra was by poled raft along a selection of her several rivers, such roads as there were being half-choked by growing plants. Before Yl and his armies made their strike into Thaddra these roads had been cleared more assiduously, but for a couple of decades, Thaddra had preferred inaccessibility in all directions. Finding rivers and rafts, Caal's party pressed gradually on.

The sun seemed to come in black through the great trees, the roping creeper and colossal ferns. The water was like treacle, poisonous to drink, and full as a soup of reptiles. Faintly visible sometimes through gaps in the foilage, Vis' northern mountains drew away.

By day they broiled. The nights were cooler and feverish with nocturnal life.

But in Dorthar it would be cold now, snowing, now.

The initial beating had been allotted for purposes of disguise. "You see, my lord," Caal said, when they had got up into the foothills above Koramvis, "someone might recognize you. But with your face swollen, blood all over it—well, even your own brother'd have trouble."

He was already chained, but the five Karmians held him, for good measure. He still used a couple of tricks they had not looked for, and one had fallen over screaming with a shattered kneecap. But the leg-irons told. Eventually Rarmon gave in and let Caal proceed with his beating. It was pointless to put off and so prolong the inevitable.

Caal reminded Rarmon, as he punched and slashed, of the blow Rarmon had awarded him in the palace.

When the camouflaging marks began to fade, the beating was repeated. There were, too, other pastimes later. Each night, making their camp, they would tie Rarmon some distance from the fire. Caal would bring him a share of food, and leave it on the ground just out of reach. After first attempts to take the food, Rarmon desisted and did not bother with it. Since Caal had told him he had been paid to present this captive in Free Zakoris, as Kesarh's gift to Yl, and since Karmians remained with them to make sure of it, he would have to feed his prisoner sometime, and did.

Caal was disappointed in Rarmon. He resorted to other less subtle tortures. He was limited in this, too, by the need to keep his goods basically unflawed. He hit on the trick of making a shallow cut in Rarmon's thigh or arm and stanching the blood with salt. When the cut was almost healed, he would open it again, exactly along the line of the original wound. Sometimes, he used vinegar instead of salt.

The Karmians, men Rarmon had never known, sat by the fire dicing, ignoring it all. They had no interest in Caal's hobby, and no disapproval. They were risking their lives, going into Yl's kingdom, but Kesarh had ordered it.

"You wish you were untied, I expect. Like to kill me, I

expect,'' Caal said. As they approached Free Zakoris, his Zakorian slur was slinking back. He no longer called his slave Rarmon, but Raurm. "Like to kill me slowly, eh, Raurm, bit by bit."

But Rarmon had no desire to kill his tormentor. He felt only the familiar gray hatred and aversion and that terrible acceptance of both, and of pain, in which Lyki had seemed to tutor him. He did not resist anymore, even in his thoughts. For you found that through abnegation, the beating always ended sooner.

It was all so similar, the dark sunlight, the thick sweating vegetation—breached less and less by squat hutments, barren fields—the rivers and the forest paths where he and the guard and Caal himself worked with knives to get through; even the tortures were similar. Rarmon had long lost track of time. He was aware only that winter must have the Middle Lands and the east. Perhaps they had been two months traveling.

Then there began to be burned clearings in the jungle, wooden towers with guards, river fords patrolled, and narrow dirt roads that were passable. Watchwords came to be needed. The men who demanded them were black or blackly brazen, mostly blow-sculpted of feature and thin-lipped. Caal's party was approaching the outskirts of Free Zakoris.

Yl son of Igur had got his kingship in the usual Zakorian way, fighting with Igur's other eldest sons. Yl won the contest by breaking his brothers' backs. He had taken three hundred wives to his throne with him, and crowned his first queen for slitting the throat, while heavy with his child, of a swamp leopard. So Zakoris had been, and still was, here in the northwest.

When Hanassor had capitulated to Sorm of Vardath, Yl, with some nine thousand men, their women and brats trailing after, had pushed a way through Zakorian swamplands and over the low mountains that bordered southern Thaddra, down into the jungles beyond. He lost three thousand men as they went, in rear-guard battles against Sorm's harrying troops, or merely devoured by swamp fever or the treacherous variety of landscape. Countless women and children perished, too. In accordance with Zakorian ideology, the sick and the weak were sloughed from their flight.

Thaddra was a lawless land. For centuries she had paid lip-service to Dorthar and to Zakoris. What had kept her secure was her lack of riches; she had nothing to offer an invader. Now, however, she acquired other values. The host of petty kings she supported here were too small and too parochial to oppose Yl.

He annexed the coastal region and the great forests adjacent, planning for the future: Timber, and oceanic access to the shores of Dorthar and those lands farther east and south. Zakoris had always been a country of ships. Naval war and piracy were her heritage; the latter had, even in peace, continued.

Between building their galleys and raiding in all directions for things they lacked and for slaves to man the oars, they lay with their women and their slave women and got sons. Every man of Free Zakoris was to fight. From ten years of age they were schooled to it. The daughters they produced had also a task, which was to bear more sons. There were no warrior women now, or women to serve the ships. They were precious vessels, now. In Zakorian tradition, homosexualty, which denied increase, was rewarded by a multitude of appalling punishments. In Free Zakoris currently, the crippled, unless they could prove some use, were slain, and unhealthy babies left in the jungle for wild beasts to eat. Barren women were flogged at the fire-altars of Zarduk, to appease him, until life left them with the blood. But before each major enterprise they would burn alive for him a perfect boy, to show they were in earnest.

The heart of Zakoris-In-Thaddra was a city of wood and stones and mud-brick, westward on the north coast. Ylmeshd had none of the stark grandeur of Hanassor. It stood above the jungle forest, on a sunset smeared with smokes. Beyond, a second forest of spars lay for miles across Ylmeshd's three deep-water bays, the dying sun crucified on their points.

Caal retrieved the garments of a Dortharian prince from the baggage and Rarmon was requested to put them on, for their entry into Ylmeshd. This necessitated removal of the leg-irons, but escape was out of the question. Rarmon made no attempt at it. Dressed, the irons were fastened on again, the finishing sartorial touch.

Torches burned on the gate-arch which, like the wall, was of piled stones mortared by clay. Whole trees made the gate itself.

Save for its size, Ylmeshd was not like a city. Hovels leaned on hovels like cells in an ant-hill. Hordes of soldiers marched to and fro, in hardened leather—mail was scarce. Forges rang and glared at every intersection. There seemed to be no women out of doors, no children, though babies cried behind hide-curtained doorways.

Acting guide, Caal had called the attention of the two Karmians to a temple of Zarduk and another of Rorn, the sea god. Both were no more than caves in the headland, closed by massive doors. The palace dominated on a rocky rise, darkness and sea behind it. It had a stone tower, and stone walls like the city.

There was no break in this wall; a ladder was lowered for them to climb once the guards on the wall-top acknowledged their business.

The palace flew the banners of Old Zakoris, the Double Moon and Dragon. But before the entry there was a wooden pole and atop it a leopard of black metal, crudely shaped in the posture of springing: Symbol of the new regime. It rattled dryly in a wind from the sea.

Inside, the palace was dark and guttering from isolated torches. They entered the King's hall. Wooden trunks, uncarved, held the wooden roof. The floor was dirt flung with skins.

At the far end was a dais with a great ebony chair they said Yl had had brought on his flight from Hanassor. Possibly, the statue had been brought, too. Rarmon had glimpsed a version of the fire god in Ommos, and this was substantially the same. The idol had no body, but was a formless log surmounted by a snarling convulsed face—a mask that could be interpreted as rage, orgasm, or agony. The open belly leaped with red fire. Its energy, and a smell of roasting pelt, indicated some sacrifice had taken place not long ago.

They waited until Yl Am Zakoris came in behind the ebony throne, and down the steps.

For a Zakorian, he was light, bronze-skinned, but he had the threadlike lips and the twisted flattened nose, through the right-hand nostril of which a golden chain passed to link a zircon in his right ear. He was a heavy man, ugly and aging, but not tired, and not strengthless. He grinned. It dazzled. His teeth were full of gems.

There was a shadowy group of men behind him. Even in the ill-light you could just see, one shadow was not quite like the rest.

Caal, now all Zakorian, was on his face. The two Karmians knelt. Rarmon stood. No one had thought to push him down. When the guards who had come in with them took hold of him to do so, Yl called, "No, let him stay as he is. Let me look at him. Is this a king's son? Ralnar, the scum of the Serpent Woman." And Yl spat on the floor.

He came slowly to look. He was tall, but no taller than Rarmon. Raldnor, the scum of the Serpent Woman, had give his height, at least, to his sons.

"Do you know," said Yl to Rarmon, "who sent you here?"
Rarmon said, "I was informed, Kesarh Am Karmiss."
"Yes. The message I got informed me also, it was Kesr. A friendship token, before we crush Dorthar between us. And I

was told you could supply Free Zakoris with the battle plans of your King. The one on the floor there,"Yl said confidentially, indicating the prostrate Caal, "will only have been allowed to learn so much. But you. You were privy to the Storm Lord's councils, to his heart. If you're his brother, as Kesr says to me in his letters you are." Yl stood breathing in his face. Presently Yl said, "I suppose we'll have to use our Zakorian arts on you, to make you render the strategies of Dorthar?"

"Not at all," Rarmon said. "I'll tell you anything. The Storm Lord will know quite well where I've gone or been taken, and will alter his military gambits accordingly. Anything from me will therefore be useless."

In the shadowy group up by the stair, the unlike shadow laughed.

"Yes," Yl said. "Come here, Kathus. Come and see, too. You knew the Lowland Accursed. Is this his work?"

The man came down. He, like the King, was in late middle age, but slender, quietly dressed, and couth. His complexion was far lighter. Most of all, his movements, his very walk, were different from those of any other of Yl's coterie. He glanced at Rarmon. The glance itself spoke only of un-Zakorian things. But he said, "It might well be. Certainly, Dorthar has accepted him as such."

The voice of Kathus was a surprise. It had a little of the slurred accent. Some touch of Zakoris after all, then.

The two Karmians had grown bored with homage and stood up, trying to offer letters to Yl. Caal remained as he was.

The Zakorian guards, at Yl's order, took Rarmon away.

"Drink, Kathus. Drink deep."

"Thank you, my lord."

Yl, but not Kathus, drank deep.

"Thinking of Dorthar, Kathus? Her blood and entrails and ashes?"

"Vengeance," paraphrased Kathus, imperturbably. His face was scarcely lined, for he had trained it from his early years to eschew expression. "And, of course, your promise I should rule Dorthar in your name. What there will be left of her."

"And now you think Kesr of the Karmians will have Dorthar from me, when he and I have mown the white-hair half-breed into the muck?"

"I think Kesarh's too useful, not to agree with all he may wish."

"And then kill him and give it you?"

"My lord," said Kathus, "I can be patient. Both of us know that skill, by now. Kesarh's young and runs swiftly. And may stumble."

Yl liked Kathus Am Alisaar, who had once been a prince and intriguer in Dorthar. It was in the way he liked a new weapon, or woman, or an animal that could do clever tricks. Kathus was wise. He had been helpful, making sense of the written aspects of a diplomacy Yl required but had no forbearance with. Kathus had fashioned an intricate network of spies. Yl's blunt Zakorian counselors had not survived the flight to Thaddra. Kathus was the most sophisticated thing in his kingdom.

"Then counsel me," said Yl.

"You return Kesarh's envoys. You repeat the false vow that you'll rebuild Ankabek—he doesn't give a damn for Ankabek or Anack, we all know that, but he forgives your men the island's spoiling, so you must play, too, and regret the offense. He's shown you · the other side when he destroyed your fleet off Karmiss, recall. You thank him also for your present, Raldnor's bastard son. That's the letter. The military dispatch goes separately and we've already discussed that. What, by the way, will you do with Rarmon, son of Raldnor?"

"He would have made a burnt sacrifice to Zarduk," said Yl. "But Kesr mentions Raurm has lain with men. I can't offer the god such filth."

"How irritating."

Yl grunted.

They had come into the King's chamber off the Throne Hall. Yl's eyes strayed across the room to the niche where there reposed a gigantic topaz. It had been a goddess' eye, at Ankabek.

"The bitch watches," he remarked. "Zarduk," he said to the eye, "wears your gold. No use to look for it." He stared back at the topaz, and seemed to forget the talk in hand.

Kathus reminded him.

"My lord, if I might suggest. Rarmon. Since you can't burn him alive, he may be useful elsewhere. Further inspiration for your soldiery, a warning to your slaves and those by whom we are scrutinized. It should be told publicly who he is. He should be publicly abused. Keep him, as a figure of obloquy. There's also the information he can impart."

"It's useless. The White-hair will alter his plans."

"My lord," said Kathus, "he will naturally do that. But to learn the original formula will suggest what the alternatives may be."

"Ah. Sharp, sharp. Raurm shall be questioned tonight."

"Give me charge of it."

"You judge my captains too rough?" Yl was amused.

"I can't be sure he has loyalties to anyone, even Raldanash. But he refused to assist Kesarh—Kesarh would otherwise have retained him. This needs inducement. He isn't to be wasted."

"What means?" Yl had become brutally curious. While not titillated by cruelty, it sometimes made him think.

"He's been whipped in the past, knocked about all the way here. It asks something different now. We must remember, too, Kesarh didn't bother to try persuasion. Kesarh seems to have assumed him unbreakable."

Kathus, the regicide, walked quietly downward through the sloping corridors burrowing under Yl's palace. It was interesting to him that the King of Free Zakoris had made his house less penetrable than his city with its high ungated wall, while under it he utilized the natural cave-system of the rock, reminiscent of Hanassor. The ships which had lain in caverns under Hanassor, had also been better protected. Though it seemed unlikely much harm would come to Yl's present duet of fleets, two hundred and thirty vessels of which were in harbor, before summer opened the war. That was how close war was.

Long ago, Kathus had journeyed through the world, seeing how it changed after the Lowland War. In so doing, he used up the widespread caches of wealth he had formerly set by for himself against catastrophe. He returned to Alisaar where Shansar held sway, and turned from it. For a while, he manipulated affairs in Iscah and Corhl, and earned some prestige in the tiny city of Ottamet. These were all very minor exercises. He had Zakorian blood. At length, he went to Thaddra and to Zakoris-In-Thaddra. He did not tell Yl too much about himself, only enough to make himself precious. He never mentioned that he had murdered, albeit on a battlefield, the Storm Lord, Amrek. The deed, actually in retrospect, struck Kathus as a flight of fancy, almost poetic. It had served no purpose for himself. He had been younger and maybe, despite his own training for himself, had wished, in that wild aftermath of quake and defeat, the trumpets of history loud across the darkling plain, to sear his own mark forever on the scroll of events. But Kathus was not a poet. Yl's taunting assumption that Kathus wanted revenge on Dorthar was itself poetic, and therefore wrong. Kathus merely wanted ownership. He had always wanted that.

He had by now entered the series of caves that were partitioned for dungeons.

He spoke to the guard. When the guard had removed a sliding

stone, Kathus was able to peer into a narrow chimney. About seven feet down were the head and shoulders of a man, the one they called Raurm. The chimney was not wide enough for a prisoner to sit; even to brace himself by knees and back, and so lift the weight of the body from the legs, was out of the question for a grown man, though a child or a small woman might have done it.

The Alisaarian prince now known as Kathus stepped aside, and the stone was slipped back in place. The only light below came in via the grill when the stone was off. The chimney would now be in darkness again. The prisoner had been lowered into it by hooks passed through the ropes that bound his body, for the grill, like the stone, was removable. Food and water could be lowered in the same manner. So far, they had been omitted.

Raurm had dwelled in the chimney one night, a day, a portion of a second night. It would seem to him much longer, although not yet like eternity.

Kathus was fascinated. At this stage, when the stone was withdrawn, they usually shrieked and begged, staring and straining toward the hopeless hope of light and space. But Raurm had not even glanced up.

"At noon tomorrow," Kathus said to the guard. "As you were instructed. It's clear?"

"Yes, Counselor."

Musing, Kathus went away, to drink unpleasing Thaddrian wine. And wait.

After the darkness of the cellarways, the midday light in the upper rooms hurt his eyes. His guards had left him in a small bright chamber, unbound, and presently Kathus entered.

Rarmon was aware this was not a reprieve. In the dark undercaves he had been allowed use of a primitive bath, and fresh clothes were thrown in on the floor for him. To relax to the relief of these things, because he knew they would not last, was an act he resisted.

In the chimney, it was harder to resist. Physical endurance he possessed. The discomforts that swelled, minute by minute, hour by hour, into atrocious pain, these he made room for. But in such confinement a man became his own tormentor. Thoughts, memories—mind-devils. They danced about him in a space where he could barely shift from one foot to the other. Rarmon did not know how long he could master these other aspects of himself. How long it would be, therefore, until he went mad.

Kathus had seated himself and now observed Rarmon with an unfathomable expression. The he waved him to a chair.

"Thank you, no."

Kathus nodded.

"Because your legs will strengthen the longer they're forced to support you, the less respite they're given. I see you think you'll be sent back."

Rarmon did not speak.

Kathus pointed to a dish of fruit, a pitcher of wine.

"To eat will also strengthen you." Rarmon did not move. "You decline?"

"It seemes rather futile."

"You could have found means to kill yourself on the way here, but refrained."

"An oversight."

Kathus smiled.

"Once I had your father brought before me in a comparative position, my prisoner. You may be amused to hear, I found him less adroit than I find you. But then, he was younger, too."

Kathus clapped his hands. Zakorians did not employ effete summoning bells.

A man entered, set down writing materials, and went out.

"You will," said Kathus, "outline the Storm Lord's proposed campaign for us. A general plan should do. Specific questions can be settled later."

Rarmon crossed to the table. He dipped the pen and wrote one brief line.

Kathus rose and took the paper.

Rarmon had written, *At this time, anything I tell you will be disbelieved.*

"You're accustomed," said Kathus, "to being ill-treated. It began with your mother, no doubt. I knew your mother. I've seen you in your cradle, when the women called you Rarnammon. Actually, you were born, with a great deal of clamor, under my roof. Guard."

They entered the open door and took Rarmon back to the chimney.

A little later, the fruit and wine were lowered to him, and contrived to be left hanging.

The temptation was too great—not so much the temptation of eating as of having something to do. As he gave in, he felt a terrible despair, unknown to him until now. But after he had eaten he slept, and though there were dreams they were no more than dreams, and constantly half-waking, he escaped them.

*   *   *

When his legs had grown numb again and the spike that filled his spine had again reached up and pierced his skull, he was taken out once more. Once more there was the bath, and the fresh clothing. It occurred to him Kathus, whose apartment had had certain un-Zakorian refinements, only wanted him dusted off, as it were, so as not to soil the furnishings.

Rarmon limped up the stairways. When Kathus arrived the exchange was brief and the paper and ink already waiting. To sit down was now more agony than to stand, but Rarmon had to take the chair or he would have fallen, bending to the paper.

He had prepared a reasonable theory of Dortharian deployments, a fake. It might not be believed, and he must remember it, since probably he would be invited to repeat the format on many occasions. He had never intended to give them Dorthar's true war-plans for, having those, the alternatives could be more easily mooted. Rarmon had no loyalty to Dorthar, she had not seemed to touch him. Nor was there a sense of kinship with the man who was his brother. Nevertheless, Free Zakoris was a midden. Even through a haze of exhaustion and blood, he had seen the skeletons of a score of exposed babies lying just off the road, a little heap like discarded rubbish. The concept of Free Zakoris astride Vis offended him. It went deeper and less deep than that. At this stage it was native of him to resist everything. Rather than grow confused, his allergy had become obsessive.

Lowered back into the chimney, he caught himself trying to impede the passage by twisting his body, trying to stop the inevitable descent. He forced his bootless intuition into abeyance and let himself drop the rest of the way.

Later, or perhaps in not só much more than a few minutes, the wine and fruit came down, and a meat gravy. He accepted it all, tilting the bowls into his mouth by angling them with his face.

Soon after, he threw up. Even as he puked—desperately, painfully, the upright position hampered it—he realized some emetic drug had been mixed with the wine or broth. When the spasms ended he stood in his own vomit, as in the rest of the bodily filth, and he began to want death. It was a passionate want.

For some time it filled his mind vividly, sending away even the haunts and horrors of his own inner brain.

Then this flame also died, overwhelmed by another less intellectual passion, equally intense. Thirst.

He fought off the thirst as he had not fought off the wish for death. He scrambled to recapture the ghastly memories that had ridden him earlier. He marshaled them against the torture of the thirst. But the thirst won.

It began to seem to him that if he called to the guards above the grill, they might let him have water without medicine in it. He knew this was not so. But his voice started to make hoarse croakings on its own, meaning to disobey him.

Then the thirst went away very suddenly.

He was not thirsty.

They were hauling him up again. When they stood him on the stone floor above the chimney he keeled over, stiff as a tree. They dragged him. There was no bath, now; he was not going up to Kathus. A man stood against torch-light and told Rarmon the tissue of lies he had written was seen through, but the Lord Kathus permitted him a further chance of redemption. Here was pen and paper. Now it must be the truth.

Rarmon wrote, *You had the truth before. It stays the truth.* His hand, writing, seemed miles from his eyes which saw it.

"No," said the man. "This won't do."

Rarmon was offered wine. He took no notice of it.

They returned him to the chimney and let him down. It was always done quite gently, smoothly. As his feet went into the stinking slime of human excrement that lined the pit, Rarmon thought: *I've only to continue to insist, remember the deployments as I set them down. They seem very clear. I could have done it, then. Eventually, they will accept my statement. Or,* he thought, *I could write a different thing each time. Valueless. They might kill me then.*

But the dream-desire of death did not return.

Presently, a bowl of milk was lowered. He had the resource to butt it with his head, causing the bowl to shatter on the wall of the chimney, and the milk to be lost before he could gulp it. It might have been wholesome, of course. Maybe it had been. Maybe—

The thirst returned, redoubled. He almost screamed with it. He rolled on the chimney. He beat his head against the stone, meaning to crack his skull like a bowl.

But it was the stone which gave way. He paused in surprise.

Beyond, there was darkness. And in the darkness, far off, a miniature fleck of light.

Rarmon slumped back. He stared into the fissure beyond the stone, at the infinitesimal light. It was hallucination. The thirst was real.

Yet the light was approaching very swiftly. He could not look away. The dark caught no shine from it, no illumination came into the chimney. Then he saw why. It was not light but whiteness. And then it had form. And then it was a girl.

She walked quickly toward him out of the stone where she could not be, all the time getting larger. Her pale hair fluttered as she walked, and the edge of her dress at her ankles.

All at once, she was only a few feet from him, and she held out to him a dish which was filled with water.

She was not tall, a young girl, sixteen, seventeen years old. Her face was grave. Her eyes were suns. She—but she shook her head at him, and lifted the bowl higher.

He was aware of the dirt and fetor, as if she were really there to brave it. He smiled at her, shaking his head in turn. It would be useless to drink the sweet water which was a mirage. But she would not go, and she went on holding up the dish to him. Her arms must ache. Reluctantly, he lowered his head toward the dish; there was room to do this since the wall had given way. Then the water was against his mouth, cool, tangy, tasting as it did from the little falls in the hills above Istris. Chiding himself, he drank. He felt it go down, pure and bright, cleansing him. The dish was empty. He was no longer thirsty, but that had happened before. . . .

"Rarnammon," said Kesarh's daughter, Ankabek's looked-for child.

"I know," he said, "but you're only nine years old."

"No," she said. "Remember how long I lay in Astari's womb, and then how long I waited, of the world, but not in the world, to come to term in the womb of Val Nardia. I'm older than you, Rarnammon."

"Nine," he said, "and not even here."

"Here, I am the symbol of your will. You have the power in you to survive all this, but you've given the power my shape. As others give the power within them the form of Anackire. But it might be another god. Any that they credit—if the Power is there to raise that god."

"You're saying gods are the creatures of men?"

"No. That men themselves are gods. But, fearing their own greatness, they send it from them to a distance, and must give it other names."

He stood in a chimney of torture in Free Zakoris, waiting to die, and spoke philosophy with a sprite he had imagined, nor did they speak in words. But her eyes—flame and sea and light and shadow, and all things, and Nothing.

"Ashni," he said.

"I am here."

He did not argue any more.

"What now?"

"Let go," she said. "Trust yourself."

"Yes," he said. He shut his eyes to rest them, and continued to see her, as he had known he must, behind the lids. "But then."

"Then. You will bring yourself to yourself again, at the proper hour."

"Is there any more water?" he asked, not because he needed it. But she was gone.

He opened his eyes. The walls of the chimney were sheer and closed. The stench of waste and illness and fear were thick. But he had no thirst. He was calm. He considered.

Raldnor and Astaris. They had passed from the world into a psychic inferno, blazing, going out. The child in the womb had not been part of that, or it had not wished to be.

Anackire.

Anackire. The island of Ankabek had known. Looking, not for another child in the required image—for the same child.

What was that phrase Berinda had used, in her cot on the hill? "When," had said her daughter, "did you find me again?" "When my womb swelled." "But where had I been till then?" "Riding the air," Berinda said. *Riding the air.* The third child of Raldnor Am Anackire had not been born from Astaris' womb. It had been—freed. And then, the spirit of the child had lingered, riding the air, in some dimension of the earth and not of the earth. Until there came about a correct conjunction of race and flesh and of the physical soul—two who were also one.

He could see this, since the restraints of normalcy were gone. And, what now? he had asked. She had answered explicitly.

He was not thinking of her as a woman, for he would not have trusted a woman. He did not even think that she was, peculiarly, his sister.

The water of illusion or magic had gifted his throat sufficient moisture that it could cry out. At first it was hard to give himself up. The roarings were acted. But even as he heard the guards above begin to stir and shout back at him, he found the courage to let the rational man leave him and the madness which was the god come in.

And light filled his head like a sun.

"Your Alisaarian *potions*, perhaps, were too rough," said Yl.

"A purge. Nothing else." Kathus did not show his exasperation. But Yl, like a beast, could nose such things. "However, lord King, he'll still do for the display I recommended."

"Led about Ylmeshd, to be pelted by stones." Yl picked his jeweled teeth. "You hate him."

"Not at all. I'm sorry his sanity snapped. I'd never have suspected—but it's no sham. He's been thoroughly tested, and the madness is a fact. I begin to suppose Kesarh understood the breaking-point rather than the lack of one."

"Ah." The hand that had picked the teeth settled on a bare-breasted concubine kneeling by Yl's couch. "But he does not die here?"

"The longer he lives in wretchedness, the better an example he provides."

Yl, his hand between the girl's legs, said slyly, "And you don't hate him? Or do you only hate the father, as Free Zakoris does?"

Kathus bowed and took his leave.

At the back of the palace, in an open yard, he could distinguish the awful sounds of the madman. The madness was proven. Weighted chains were needed now. Yl had postulated a scheme. Raurm could be sent to Yl's pet Southern Road, the interminable track being burned and hacked through to Vardian Zakoris and Dorthar. Fettered in some cart, Raldnor's son could howl above the slaves, frightening them to nicer efforts. As Yl suggested all this, he watched his Counselor's face with lazy eagerness: *You do not hate him? How much do you not hate him?*

Kathus hesitated, listening to the sounds of the madman. Amrek had been unrewarding. Raldnor had cheated Kathus over and over. Now Rarmon cheated him. Only Raldanash was left.

Hate? He did not deign to hate his fellow men. His tastes were refined. But as he had grown older it had set into his bones, partly ignored and always unacknowledged, a sure hatred of this endlessly unfinished game.

EIGHTEEN

In the cold months, dawn could walk to Istris over ice in her bay. But under the white mask, the city's pulse beat loudly; she was not asleep. The snow, in Kesarh's era, was always a time of refurbishing and preparation. There was nervousness this year, too.

The rabble could be turned like a weather-cock, by gossip, by oratory, or by a sudden dispensation of largesse. The merchant classes could be bribed. The upper echelons could be bribed. But there were the fools, the overly avaricious, and the honorable men who foresaw, in this obscure tack of the *Lily* toward Zakoris, something to make them shudder. It was only a rumor beyond the palace, for genuine rumor did circulate in the capital along with the paid sort. But even ignorance knew that, ally or enemy, when this spring unlocked the eastern seas, the whole body and ego of the *Black Leopard* would ride them.

The dispatches from Lan, expectedly, were late. Probably nothing would now get through till the thaw, for Raldnor Am Ioli was proving a lax, ill-organized governor.

To make Raldnor the figurehead of the annexing of Lan and Elyr had served a dual purpose. The eastern lands were to be shown the whip, first. Raldnor at least would do that. Indeed, his dealings had been as harsh, unjust and haphazard as predicted. Presently, a more lenient guardian could be introduced. The conquered would respond, appeased—and lulled—by soothing ointment on the wounds.

Meanwhile, the gambit got Raldnor out of Karmiss, where he had been building far too high on his good luck. Appointing a temporary Warden in Raldnor's stead was sensible tradition, no more. Such an authority must at all times be resident in Istris. To investigate Raldnor's affairs in his absence was also a tradition Raldnor himself might have anticipated. Kesarh had found everything scrupulous, and this was strange. One knew what men like Raldnor were liable to do with power. To uncover no tiniest indiscretion gave one to suspect the whole garden had been tidily raked over, to hide some larger blemish.

The reprimand was decided, and lay to hand. With certain tools, one was aware, from the moment of taking them up, that they must eventually be discarded.

Raldnor, like many others, was induced by the snow to hibernate. And the sea was between them. He would reckon on nothing.

Kesarh spent an hour with his council, during which he established Raldnor's removal from office in Lan. There was no adverse debate. Nor had any of them met a Lannic-looking adventurer on the back stairs leading from the royal apartments. Kesarh had never forgotten the use of such stairways.

Altogether, he forgot little. He had preserved the face of the Outlander far better, for example, than Suthaman had preserved the face of Vis participation. But the Shansarians, Vardians,

Vathcrians who occupied key positions in Kesarh's army, council and court, had been carefully purchased. Bought to a man,
they were always ready to recall the King, too, was half their
blood.

Even the goddess, despite what Free Zakoris was encouraged to
suppose, had not been cast down. In the days of his regency Kesarh
had restored Her and that house which She Herself had struck in
her wrath against the line of Suthamun. The second statue resembled almost exactly that which the Shansarians had set up. She
was just a touch smaller, more eloquently female. Being a
woman god, it was not, surely, so curious she had become more
of a deity for women. Her naked breasts, hinting at carnal
pleasures, had finally reconciled Her with Yasmais, whose temple She had so long inhabited; this was not strange. By the third
year of Kesarh's reign, the lower city had got to calling her
Ashyasmai. Emboldened, other gods had reclaimed their dwellings in Istris. Kesarh, who believed in none of them, gave them
all gifts. To Ashara-Ashkar-Anackire-Ashyasmai, he gave black
pearls. Woven so thickly in her gold hair, it seemed from below
she had become a brunette.

Though Lan was sluggish, by midday dispatches had come
from those who scanned the west. They had less to say of Yl,
the Leopard's guts, than of its Alisaarian brain. It had only
been viable to treat with Free Zakoris since the advent of
Kathus.

From Dorthar there was nothing of note. The ships which had
sailed from Thos for the Sister Continent, might get home before
the snow's end, for the southern seas were milder. *Then,* there
could be news. Kesarh had sent his own envoy that way, having
maintained spurious brotherhood with Shansar for years.

Under the dispatches lay a closed letter without a seal.

She had written to him before, half a month ago. Her writing
had not been like his sister's, but upright and bold, growing
wilder at the finish. She had asked him again to return her to
Raldanash. As if Raldanash would accept her, now.

Kesarh took up the letter. He was older, and had learned. At
no point had he sent word to her.

At no point had he taxed himself with why he must have her.
She belonged to him and so she was here. The rest was only
interim.

He slit the wax and read.

He seemed for an instant, then, almost to be searching within
himself, as if trying to locate some distant memory, something

he had felt, or thought to feel. But either it eluded him, or it had never existed. This much, since he was alone, might be told from his face.

It needed two-thirds of a winter's day to reach the village, an hour more to gain the house. It was a villa, high-walled and well-appointed, with a garden courtyard. It had been one of Prince Jornil's many country nests.

They had cleared the road, but the snow was falling again, and the wind had risen. When he left the zeebas and his men and went into the upper house, he did after all think of Ankabek, the lamp trembling in the wind above the door, the black passageways beyond. And suddenly of the dying flower he had given her, on her pillow, scented with her fragrance not its own.

He waited in the salon while the servant ran to fetch her.

In less than three minutes, she came down.

He recollected the previous occasion, the ruined dress and unpainted face. Now, all had been arranged, even to the colored lacquers on her nails and the diamond stars in her hair.

They were nearly identical—but not the same. The more like Val Nardia, the less she was Val Nardia. The flower from Ankabek crumbled.

The wine came in before she had greeted him. She did not greet him at all, but said, "Is the room warm enough for you, my lord?"

He replied, "We'll be in your bed."

She looked at him for the first time, in terror, and said, "Wait. Please, wait."

"I've waited. You informed me the wait was over." He picked up the wine flagon, and walked across the floor. She was between him and the stair. He took her elbow almost in passing, bearing her with him. She did not resist, but she caught his arm with her other hand.

"Give me time."

He stopped, one foot on the bottom stair, which was of elaborately veined marble. He had never seen the house before. He turned from it to her, that he had seen almost all his life, one way or another.

"What did your message say to me?"

"That—I was alone here."

"A single sentence, like a pining trull."

"Yes," she said. "I am ashamed of it."

"But it was set down with ink."

"I'm afraid," she said. She looked away, beyond him. "Let me explain myself," she said. "Let me talk to you."

"No."

He went up the stair, and she went with him. No servants showed themselves. She walked before him into the elegant room, hearing the firm shutting of the door behind them.

He had chosen the house for her, no doubt randomly, yet it was so apposite—secluded, charming—that she had been soothed. She persevered, in the beginning, constructing letters to him asking to be let go, refusing the glory of being jointress to his empire, which she was certain, she said, he had mentioned merely to pacify and entertain her, not to be believed. Only one of these letters had she sent. And then regretted it. Raldanash would never claim her again. Nor could she escape to Xarabiss. Her father, whom she hardly knew, would not receive her.

During this time, however, she regained her self-esteem. She might hold her abductor off until he grew bored, and forgot her.

But she sensed this would not happen, that therefore she was safe to consider it.

She saw that she must not, herself, give in. And so, sequentially, she did give in.

There came an evening when the snow seemed to have lasted a year. She had drunk an extra goblet of the white spirit they fermented on the estate, and she had written a different letter—*I am here alone*—and they had carried it to him. Why should she fear him? She desired him, fiercely. It might as well be Zastis. *What* did she fear? That his dead would come back and haunt her? But she was not wary of ghosts.

When it was too late, the letter in Istris, she was appalled, as she had foreseen—mocking herself, then. She thought he might not leave the capital. But each day she prepared herself for his advent. When he did not come she watched herself languish. He was here, and she shook with horror.

There was one defense left to her, had always been, and she assumed it. Unfastening the clothes that had been put on her not two hours before, she let them drop to the floor, and breaking the ribbons of her sandals, stepped out of them. Clad solely in jewels, she went to the bed and lay down on it. She looked at the ceiling all her sleepless nights had made familiar. She said, "Then I'm to be quiet and have only one function; I'm your doxy, my lord, as you said. Your harlot. The price you paid is on my wrists and knotted in my hair. Commerce. Do what you want."

But as she said this, even tensed with self-revulsion, there came the heavy, languid stirring in her loins. She closed her eyes and did not open them until she felt the heat of him beside her.

He was naked, now, as she was, the tawny nakedness flared with jet-black hair, that came from the mixture of race. The excellent body had few scars. It had fought too well and been too cunning to get many. She had seen men who wanted her, before, but from his readiness her gaze removed itself. She stared up and saw instead his face was only intent, in control of all of him, even the blaze of sex.

Abruptly, what had gone before was meaningless. She could ignore it as he did, leave it lying on the floor with her clothing and his.

She did not ask him if her nudity also was like Val Nardia's. It was.

The slim figurine of this girl, lightest gold as Val Nardia's skin had never been, the eyes darker, the hair darker if as rich, was Val Nardia seen through a lens of pale amber.

Her arms were around him, caressing, gathering, pleading.

He found her mouth, and the hollws of ears and throat and hands. The beautiful breasts were young and flawless, as he remembered, their tips eager and hard now as pearls.

There had been many women of many types. But the scent of this girl was her scent. The glide of fingers, plains of flesh, hers. The strong hidden mouth, taking, filled. Hers.

Raising himself, he saw the long primal spasms beginning like waves under the surface of her, how her eyes emptied and were shut, the winged lids drawn tight, (Val Nardia's), and the throat arched—as her throat was arched. He felt again the frantic drowning grip of limbs and hands, the drumbeats of her groin. The agonized cries were known.

When she was still, he stilled himself, looking down at her. But when he began to lift her again she was lazy, almost unwilling, as Val Nardia had been. And then quickening into tumult more avid even than before, and the summit was there, the ascent which was the fall.

Of Kesarh's hungers, sex was probably the least. Possession he valued. This night was necessary to him, and there would be other necessary times of lust, and of sure comparison. To give this girl the High Queen's portion of the empire he meant to make himself, that would establish her, the jewel in the jewel. He would look at them, his lover's double, the world he owned, and perceive he had not been cheated.

But of Ulis Anet he took no concern. Her words, her thoughts, her life, could not interest him.

*   *   *

At daybreak, he left her.

Ulis Anet, cold without his heat, stood in a window glaze by
ice, and watched men and zeebas turned black on snow and
sunrise.

She understood now why she had been afraid. She had had
demonstrated the narrow scope of his need for her, even as she
helped him to enslave her flesh. These things might not have
mattered if he had been some other man. But he had turned his
devastating personal armament against her, as against any he
wished to use.

She did not even see the rising sun. His darkness blotted out
her sky.

She despised her sentiments hopelessly. It was like some
tavern song.

They had been singing Karmian songs in Amlan, raucous from
the Salamander barracks, which now took up one side of the
Palace Square. You kept clear of that by day. At night, the
curfew left the roads empty, but for patrols.

The traveler, who had just successfully dodged one of these,
scratched at the door of an inn.

A shutter in the door went back.

"No trade. Go home before the Am Aarl catch you."

"Basjar."

"Yes, he's here. Who wants him?"

"Raldnor, son of Yannul."

"All of the goddesses! Wait. We'll open up."

Hauled into the inn and inspected by the proprietor who had
known him, Lur Raldnor, deaf to questions about Dorthar, was
next taken to a private room. A few men were drinking under the
candle-wheel of thirty spikes that only wore four candles since
the Karmians had rationed them. The biggest man was Basjar,
the Xarabian.

They drew aside into an alcove.

"You found my message under the hearth stone."

"Yes. Where Medaci used to put them. In Anack's name—"

Lur Raldnor had gone the Lowland kind of pale, that was like
bloodloss. He looked only fifteen again and peculiarly old.

"No," said Basjar, "they live, all three of them. Yannul
thought it wise to travel. From the way the Karmian riff-raff left
your farm, you'll agree he may have been right. I sold much of
the livestock before they could get their bloody paws on it. All
the money, and most of the valuables are secure, bonded in

Xarabiss where Kesarh's tribe can't reach. Your father's only lost the land."

"He loved the land."

Dasjar shrugged woefully, a very Xarabian gesture.

Lur Raldnor had been awhile trying to get home. He had let the servant remain in Dorthar. The man had no family, and did not fancy Lan's current dangers. It should have made the journey lighter, but did not. In Ommos, shipping seemed a myth. Giving up on it, Raldnor had ridden after all for the Xarabian border. Near here, he met seven men, who robbed him. Reaching the first port penniless, he must lose further days hiring out as a laborer to get cash to pay his passage. Finally, when he would have killed to get it, someone had mercy and let him work his way on a shallow skimmer which was risking Lan to set up prostitutes for the soldiers. The seas were rough. The girls lay retching along the rail, wishing to die. Lur Raldnor rowed, or bailed, seasick too and numb with cold, wishing the ocean would die instead.

When he got to land, and so to the farm, he had wandered for too long amid the nightmare. The walls still stood. But they had fired the roof, urinated into corners, killed orynx in the yard. The snow hid nothing. Every exquisite memory of childhood, which the villa-farm had held in crystal, lay about mangled. And he had deduced his mother, father and brother were murdered. He almost never thought to search under the stone.

Basjar sat by quietly for the moments Raldnor needed, silently and with complete dignity, to weep. Then wiping his eyes on his sleeve like a boy, he said, "Where are they?"

"They went with a Vardish caravan, to be sure. Yannul's goal was the Lowlands. Hamos, most likely. I sent my letters there for him."

"She wouldn't have wanted the Plains," Lur Raldnor said. "Damn Karmiss."

"I'll drink to that."

They drank to it.

Next morning, funded by Yannul's agent, and with certain helpful papers and seals, Basjar had been able to supply, Lur Raldnor bolted out of Amlan, pressing south through the snow as Yannul had once done. And thus, bypassing Lanelyr, Olm and the Zor, rode on toward Elyr and the Shadowless Plains.

His namesake, Karmian Raldnor, Guardian of Lan, had himself no plans for travel that season.

There were, at the onset of the siege snow, three thousand,

five hundred Karmian troops split between the port and the city
of Amlan, and, though he could not work sorcery on them by
glance or voice, as could Kesarh, they liked him. He let them do
almost as they wished, and gave them "bounty" for it. This
bounty came from extortion elsewhere, but this did not upset the
mixes and Vis who served under him. Commanders in other
reaches of Lan and Elyr also had a glowing opinion of Raldnor
Am Ioli. He could flatter, and he would pay. They committed
crimes, and he forgave them. He caught them out in swindles,
and understood. There was also the matter of Karmian rations. It
seemed Kesarh had not cared to let his warriors have quite
enough, prepared for them to go without in Lan. Raldnor, who
had diverted or withheld supplies, now distributed them as his
own gift. He saw that women and liquor were brought in. And
while preserving a modicum of policy in Amlan, near riot was
now and then allowed elsewhere.

Eventually, discipline would have to be reinforced, but he
would be able to blame Kesarh for that.

Someone knocked loudly.

Raldnor, lolling on a couch, snapped his fingers. A Lannic
page ran to open the door.

Brushing through door-curtain and page, one of Raldnor's
Karmians appeared. He had been at the port garrison yesterday.
Now he was here, boots and cloak thick with snow.

"There's an Istrian ship lying off beyond the ice, Guardian.
Boat rowed in. This packet for you, sir."

Raldnor, with inevitable foreboding, broke Kesarh's seal.

The contents were slight but Raldnor was a great while over
them. When he looked up, he was yellow.

"Something wrong, Guardian?"

He had let them get impertinent, too.

"I'm to go back to Istris." Patently, the letter had implied
rather more, none of it reassuring. The sergeant winced. He, a
parasite of Raldnor's monopolies, did not like the drift of this
either. "The new command must be on that ship."

"Didn't see anything of it, sir."

"No, perhaps not. But they'll be halfway down the infernal
road behind you by now."

There was a commiserating, awkward pause.

"The lads'll be sorry to see you go, sir."

Raldnor, who had started to weigh, gave up, and flung his life
in the balance.

"Damn it. I'm going nowhere."

*   *   *

When he was seven years old, Emel had been wakened in the night, dressed and whispered over, and borne to the map-chamber at Istris. The Warden had given him sweets, and let him fall asleep again. But when Kesarh kneeled to him, Emel stood up very properly. Afterwards his nurses murmured how good he had been.

Now, in the dark, lights burst into the bedroom, he was wakened, and Raldnor his protector loomed alone against the door. Emel must get up and get dressed and come somewhere and do certain proper public things, as before, long ago. But Raldnor had none of the women's gentleness, and though strict instructions had been rendered previously, the bindings hurt, and the male clothing felt insidiously false. Emel was frightened tonight in Amlan as he had never been frightened in Istris. Though, as he now knew, he had had every cause to be.

He was nine when, in another sort of sleep, the Ommos knives had cut him. Afterwards he was cosseted. Drugs had spared him much pain; he had not learned to have any positive sexual desires, and did not mourn heterosexual loss. He had had six years since to grow used to what he was, and now it seemed ordinary. Only at Zastis had there ever been, sometimes, a slight bother. Emel-who-was-Mella did not know that his lovers died, every one of them, when they left him, only that he was never allowed to see them again.

It was Raldnor who taught him, by inference, to resent his new body, which was hermaphrodite, impotently weaponed, and flowered with small virginal breasts. Raldnor had, particularly since Lan, impressed on his charge that, if he should ever have his rights—his kingdom—Emel would have to act the man again, in disguise. The breasts must be bound. There were medicines which, if taken regularly, would lessen such tokens, and raise a little down on the beardless face. And this was how he must walk and stand, sit and speak and be. The instruction had been endlessly repeated, always with tacit cruelty. Emel had come to know his inadequacy by example. He writhed at the girl-name of "Mella." He hated Raldnor, and he hated Kesarh, Kesarh the more, for he had loved him once. But everything, the lessons, the hatreds, the potions and bandagings and disguise, were all far off. Bored to tears, Emel only wanted to be home in Ioli. He did not really want to be a man and a king.

And now apparently, long before it was reckoned on, he must.

He threw an hysterical tantrum promptly. But then Raldnor struck him, thrice, and Emel knew there was no recourse.

Sniveling, he did everything he was told, and did it well.
But Raldnor did not say he had been good.

The houses along the Palace Square which had become the
city's Karmian barracks had also been aroused. Men packed into
the courtyards at the rear and filled the plot of open land that
went up behind, climbing trees, walls, the roofs of makeshift
stables. Assembly was a Shansarian custom. In the great halls of
Istris it was feasible, but here the enormous quantity of soldiers
was crammed too tight for comfort. The cold gnawed and the
torches flared. The air crackled with oaths and sparks, smell and
urgency. In five minutes the situation was charged; something
would have to happen.

Presently the lord Guardian entered the courts, guarded, and
with some servant by him done up in a cloak. One or two who
got a closer look were titillated to see the face of the big-footed
mistress-girl from Ioli.

Raldnor was not Kesarh, and did not try to be. He knew the
tension the overcrowding and the hour would create. He knew
also he had turned his troops into a rabble, and that a rabble
could be manipulated.

They applauded him, too, clapping, calling, banging their fists
on their shields and their spears on the stone flags. They liked
him. He had flattered them. He had given them drink and
trollops and cash, let them run amok and told them they were
fine, the backbone of their country. He spoke and they listened.
He had always said things they liked to hear.

Raldnor Am Ioli announced first that Kesarh, who could not
even see that enough food was sent them, now recalled their
commander to Istris. They did not approve, and displayed their
disapproval, noisily. Raldnor, having thanked them, secondly
announced why he dared not go back. Kesarh had, obviously,
fathomed Raldnor's secret. It had had to come. He had balanced
his life on a line for nearly seven years. For the sake of justice.

He had seen to it wine was going round, to 'keep off the
cold.' Now they waited all agog, like babies, for the story.

Raldnor related it, if not with charisma, at least with some
flair. He gave them the regency and the plague, and the plot
against the Prince—King Emel. He gave them his own revolt,
unable to slaughter a child. He explained his rescue. He even
awarded them, had to under these circumstances, the fact of
Emel's being kept by him, clad as female. But he left out, of
course, that such a ruse would soon have been a failure but for
some extra means. He omitted the Ommos knives.

That Emel symbolized the old Shansarian rule was a drawback, and had always been. But Raldnor was himself a mix, and here in Lan the troops' love affair with Kesarh had soured even for the Vis. In the end, the superstitious currency of pale hair and skin and eyes might tip the scales.

Raldnor was still, whatever else had altered, that opportunist who had pounded out to muddy Xai and flung his dice on Kesarh's table. Still an audaciously clever and perceptive man whose cleverness and perception would sometimes cause him to act foolishly and blindly.

"Gentlemen," he said now to the disorderly vandals squashed in the space before him, "I'm in your hands. And your true King is in your hands. We are dependent on you, on your awareness of what's right, your love of country, your loyalty, and your mercy." And then, turning to the muffled being at his side he said, so they all heard, "Don't be afraid, my lord. These men are noble. They won't harm you."

The cloak came off on cue. Emel had stayed tractable. He knew better than to make another scene. He stood, very young, face washed, hair lopped, in good male raiment. His fixed terror resembled pride. He did not, in the wine-smoke and the torch fumes, look like Mella anymore. There was a look of his royal father, instead. They even forgot the reedy voice, since Raldnor did not let them hear it.

"Emel son of Suthamun," Raldnor said to them. And then he knelt, in the Vis-Karmian way, at Emel's feet.

There was a long, long noiselessness, during which Raldnor held his breath. Then one by one, group by group, battalion by battalion, almost two thousand men began to applaud.

Kesarh's replacement Guardian, riding into night-black Amlan with thirty men, found nothing amiss on the streets. The garrison seemed wide-awake, and far better regulated than the sloppy mess at the port. He was politely saluted and conducted inside the palace. In the corridor leading to Am Ioli's apartments, doors flung wide and an attack occurred. The men of Lan's new Protector tried valiantly to fight, but were hampered by the narrow aisle, sea-and-snow-fatigue and shock. Raldnor had not been supposed to panic. Even if he had, no one had foreseen the whole inland garrison going over to him. How had he managed it? If they wondered, they died wondering.

At length Kesarh's replacement Guardian was peeled alive off the wall, disarmed and deposited in a room.

There was a dispatch. It purported to be his own, and it

informed Kesarh of the success of his replacement's mission.
Raldnor invited him to sign it.

"How long do you think you can keep this quiet?"

"Until the thaw. Long enough."

"If I sign this, I'm dead."

"So you are. And dead if you refuse. The difference being
only in the manner."

Kesarh's replacement Guardian signed. His body was come
across two nights later, stripped to the skin and lifeless, somewhere in the hills.

Meanwhile, the Karmian ship pulled away from Lan's icy
shore for her long, weather-slow voyage of return. She was
laden with one dispatch, lightened only of passengers.

There followed a series of wildnesses in Amlan. Celebrating
soldiers, as the east had found, tended to commit arson, rape and
burglary, and to cast spears at anything which ran.

Raldnor let the festivity continue. He was busy preparing his
approaches, so the rest of Karmiss-In-Lan should come over to
him.

Ten days after his sparkling coup, while striding across the
royal gardens, he was suddenly set on by a yelling Lan with a
knife. The man fled before the undisciplined soldiery could catch
him. His entry and getaway seemed professionally managed, if
the assault itself was rather desperate. Actually, he had intended
to kill Raldnor, as Kesarh had suggested, riding disgraced to the
ship along the port road. But Raldnor had not obliged in this.
The assassin had had to be inventive. Either way, it looked like
the work of an incensed patriot, which was what Kesarh had
wanted.

Raldnor Am Ioli lay in the snow, eyeing the soldiers who
came to pick him up. At first they thought he would speak to
them again. But his eyes set. He had said forever all he was going
to.

They bore him in with the dramatic dignity the undignified
demand at such times. Uproar in their wake, they went on to
break the tidings to King Emel.

NINETEEN

On the Lanelyrian border of Elyr, something strange had happened.

He had sheltered in a deserted steading through the night. The weather-shy Karmian patrols were few and far between, but he had spotted a big, dull star up in the hills that might be a burning village, and taken no chances, setting off again before the sun rose.

Near dawn, then, Lur Raldnor saw two wolves, their smoking jaws clamped in some edible death. They stared with red eyes and red drooling mouths, but as their spit steamed in the snow he realized, with a sudden shift of perspective, that it was not a carcass they were devouring but a crimson flame which ran along the ground. Then as he watched, too amazed yet to doubt, they vanished and the fire with them.

Days and nights of snow could confuse the eyes. Mirages were not uncommon. But the image stayed with Yannul's son, those petals of flame spilling from the jaws of wolves, not harming them, and not harmed.

Some reports stated Kesarh had put just short of eight thousand men into the east. Others said it was nearer ten. In the little stretch of Elyr there was scant evidence of them. And yet villages lay empty, doors swinging, a broken pot lying to catch fresh snow, everything human melted away to the secret places, the hollow hills, the ancient towers. Once he heard the whirr of a wheel, a spinning-loom such as was used here and on the Plains. But it was the wind moved it. If he came on edible food he ate some, not all, and left payment under their hearth stones, in case they should ever come back. Each time, he felt a dread. The world was tumbling toward darkness and chaos. Who could ever stop it? Who could ever come back?

Only last summer he had dreamed of standing in the way of the shadow, driving it off. Victory, through passion. It was Rem—Rarmon—who somehow, distanced, no longer by him, had shown him the futility of the dream. The sword could only

295

beget the sword. And yet, to lay down the sword was only death by other means.

Prosaically, it disgusted him, too, that having got in such a fix to secure a ship from Xarabiss to Lan, here he was racing almost full circle to the northern Plains, Hamos, and maybe on to the border of Xarabiss again.

The cold and the whiteness and the silence began to break his heart. He was soul-sick. He sat the wretched exhausted zeeba under the dark silver sky of noon, looking off into pallor and nothingness.

He had begun to speak aloud to the zeeba by then, and now he said to it: "I shan't find them."

And he went on sitting there in the emptiness a great while, the blade of the wind in his face, but not moving, saying over and over, "I shan't find them."

In the area now where he should have made a definite turn to the west and north, he saw he had no faith in this direction. Hamos lay that way, and another Lowland town whose name he had forgotten. He knew, unreasonably, his family was not there.

He discovered he wished to go southwest. This was also unreasonable. There was hardly anything to the south. Except, of course, the old Lowland city. And they would never have gone there. Medaci could never have borne it. And yet.

Yannul had gone by this route, returning from Lan in the Lowland War, riding through the drifts and the cold, with the answer his country would neither hinder nor help.

Lur Raldnor turned south.

It was a kind of drawing. Difficult to do anything else.

But the city was another mirage. Sometimes he saw it, transparent blackness between the winds and the white earth.

Signs of habitation were less frequent than the phantoms of snow-sight. Once he passed a hovel with an old woman standing in the door. He asked her for food, if she could spare any. She gave him a folded lump of bread with meat in it. When he tried to pay her, she shook her head. She never spoke. A pure Lowlander, he wondered if she had only ever used the mind speech. He had had this with his mother, as a child; in adolescence—that age of the clandestine—the open door had partly closed between them. Just sometimes some bright joy or flash of hurt would break through the door. To the stranger, he could not speak within.

He inquired after the city.

She pointed, without words, southwest. So he went on.

*   *   *

The snow blizzard started in the middle of the day.

There was no shelter.

At first, he tried to ride through, but his beast was faltering. They would be beaten, and their sight put out. The zeeba might die, and he, too, might die. Dismounting, he tied cloth over the animal's head, and bound his own eyes. Then he led the zeeba, a blind man, cautious and with a terrible essential leisure, through the frenzy of ice and wind.

After a while, there was no longer any pain. He could feel nothing. And then there was a slight pleasant warmth, which he knew from tales, told round safe home-fires, was the preface to freezing. When the zeeba sank down, he coaxed it, caressed it, tried to lift it up. It lay in his arms. If he stayed on it, the snow would cover him. And yet he could not seem to let go, its fading body heat, its flickering life, needful to him. Then the zeeba died very quietly, almost restfully, against him. Lur Raldnor laid it down, got up, and stumbled on, forgetting the pack and the saddle, eyes wrapped, not conscious of where he went.

Medaci would know if he perished. He could sense her, his mother, somewhere hidden and inaccessible, as if behind an enormous stony wall. He could not reach her or be reached, yet when the snow killed him, she would feel—what was it they said?—a silence like the ending of a low soft sound, a little area of dark, as if some constant, long-unnoticed light went suddenly out. Yannul would know it, too. Not coherently. It would come to him slowly, maybe taking months.

Would Rem know? There had never been a hint of mind speech between them. Rem, so guarded, even the brain and heart. . . .

Lur Raldnor had loved Rem-Rarmon—as he had loved his family, but the love was of a different kind. He had never been able to mistake it for the love a man might have for kindred. But neither was it the sexual love Rarmon would have recognized and tolerated. On the journey to Dorthar, Rarmon had gone away from him. In Anackyra itself, Yannul's son had seen Rarmon cater to another man, who was perhaps only his true inner self. Curiously, Rarmon grew to resemble the Storm Lord then, so than it was possible to tell, despite all physical differences, that they were brothers. This was, too, like that thing Yannul had said of Raldnor Am Anackire—the mortal man leaving him, the embryo of a hero, or a god, beginning.

Yannul's son saw something, inside his blindfolded eyes. A primeval forest, a sweep of a bay beyond, thick and motionless with ice, and the sea sealed with it. The black stems of the trees were also cased in ice, and the jungle foliage above had rotted, leaving skeletons gloved with snow. He knew the scene from the descriptions of others. The forests at the Edge of the World, the brink of the south. A landscape no longer suited to the climate of the Middle Lands, somehow enduring against all odds such extremes of cold. Even as he gazed inward at it, a red-eyed tirr darted over the whiteness, unmatched, poorly equipped to survive—surviving. A symbol.

The ground gave way. Lur Raldnor fell. He was in a drift of searing snow. Inner vision went out. He thrashed about but could not get loose. It became less awful to keep still.

He seemed to come back from somewhere a moment or an hour later to find someone was digging him out.

Lur Raldnor tried to greet his rescuers—there seemed more than one at work—but his mouth was numb and useless. He could just raise his hands and get the protective cloth away from his head.

The wind and the blizzard were done. Some travesty of daylight still lingered. So he could see with no difficulty the five wolves who were scrabbling to prise him from the snow.

He let his hand drop to the knife in his belt. He might be able to fight them off, although he seemed to have no bones, no coordination. He watched them, depressed more than afraid, waiting.

They were grayish, a couple nearly white. The low temperature blotted out their smell.

He came from the drift abruptly, almost as if propelled from below, and then two of them had him and he cried out, frantically wrenching at the knife. And a long narrow paw came down on his wrist. It was extraordinary, so like a human action that it stayed him. He stared into dark golden eyes that matched his own. The paw slid off him. The two wolves were pulling him over the snow and he let them. And then they went up a little hummock of ice and he saw the sixth wolf.

Lur Raldnor started to cry, and could not help it, though the tears burnt. Because the wolf was beautiful and it was part of the legend, and he knew it.

It was the size of a Shansarian horse, and so white it deadened the snow.

The five wolves were pressing against him, tugging, pushing. He found he could get up. He understood what he was meant to do, just as they seemed to understand he was weak and must be aided to do it. The great white wolf lay down and he crawled on to its back. And then, fluid with its strength, it rose up under him.

This was no illusion: The furnace of its body, the rough softness of the pelt, the peculiarly wholesome stink of its breath.

Then the wolf ran.

It ran for miles, and somewhere the sun set, and night came, so pallor went to shadow and shadow to blackness. Then there came a descent, a shallow valley. Weird shapes, trees spun with ice, something beyond, a barrier more solid than the sky. A wall, a broken chasm. The moon was rising and he wondered what it was for a moment. Then he remembered, and then he beheld a ruined mansion symbolized against it.

But there began to be lamplight. He had not associated that with the Lowland city, he had visualized it in the way of the stories, its fires concealed in fear.

And then he had been sloughed very gently and painlessly, and he was lying against a timbered door. The wolf, which he could still see in absolute detail, reared up against the door, touching the lintel with its brow. A paw struck the timbers and they resounded, once, twice. Bemused, Lur Raldnor lay under the arch of its body. Then the arch swung away. He turned his head on the snow and saw the white wolf pass between two buildings. It was gone.

The door opened. Even from their way of going on he knew they were Xarabians. They exclaimed over him, and then they exclaimed again and grew noiseless, for all around the white was pocked by the huge pads of the gigantic wolf.

As he began to lose consciousness, he noted they did not seem afraid or disbelieving, only full of awe and frightening, emotive exultation, as he had been.

They looked after him very well. Inside two days, he was sitting down in the round hall with them, aware of the romantic formula of his situation. They were a mirthful troup, traders, gypsies once. There was even a honey-skinned daughter, who liked him. He had not had a girl since Yeiza. There had been no time, no inclination either, in the chase across half Vis which had ended up, all amazement and sorcery, here. No one had commented on the wolf-marks, however. It began to be reassuring to block that from one's mind. For he guessed the prodigy had put an onus upon him. He was correct.

On the third day, someone knocked.

They had been playing a throw game in the firelight, and

Raldnor was relaxed since he had now promised to cut wood for them tomorrow, the only payment he could so far render. Then into the room returned the uncle who had gone to open the door, looking constrained, and with him two of the Amanackire.

Everyone stood. Raldnor came to his feet also, not willingly, but so as not to bring trouble to his friends. He had never forgotten the market at Lin Abissa, the Lowland woman, and the throng making a road, making offerings, as if she were a goddess, nor a kind one. And in Dorthar, he had seen others, some as white as she had been, even to the eyes. Ice to look at and ice in the soul. They passed like cold air. There had been whispers of abnormal powers, not only telepathy, or that ruthless passive endurance with which the Plains People had become synonymous. Yeiza herself had once told him that some of the Amanackire were reckoned shape-changers, could heal unblemished from grave wounds, and even fly. Lur Raldnor teased her into laughter at that. The most sophisticated Xarabians could be credulous. Yet, he had never effaced her telling of it, either.

The visitors did not approach. They waited for him—everyone knew it was for him—in the middle of the room. The Xarabs were gestured, mildly enough, back to their fireside. And went.

Lur Raldnor walked over to the Lowlanders. They were both men, and though blanched, their eyes were not white. They looked at him, without menace it must be admitted. But then, without anything.

"If you're trying to speak within to me," he said, "I can't."

"But you have done so," one said.

"With my mother," he said. It was a personal thing, he did not like to tell them. At the same time they stung him, for he had their blood and wanted to prove so.

"Yes, Medaci. You are Medaci's son."

"And, as my hosts will also have informed you, the son of Yannul," Lur Raldnor said fiercely.

"Are you fit, now?" the other man asked.

"Where is it," Raldnor said, "you want me to go with you?"

Then he stepped away from them, catching his breath with a silly little sound. For they had shown him. It was there only a moment, the picture of the terrace, a palace with snapped-off pillars, and through the gaps as well as open space.

He mastered himself, and said, "Why?"

No mind-picture, no intrusion, now.

One of them said, "You wished to fight, once."

"What? You mean you're organizing an army again, to take on Free Zakoris? Or is it against Kesarh?"

"No army," the man said.

"A fight nonetheless." The other smiled. For the first, Raldnor acknowledged they were neither of them much his senior. As he got used to them after the dark Xarabians, they looked less like ice, more the shades of light he had seen so often in his mother, and his younger brother. He himself was winter-pale, wind-burned, no more. And he had learned early on how he could use the color of his eyes.

He shrugged, to gauge them.

"We," said the paler man, "are not your enemies."

"Some of our people have chosen remoteness. We remain. The world is our mother, as Anackire is the world's soul, to us. To see the world at war again, the scars opened on themselves, new scars made, the sweep of Zakorian hate which is insanity, the hunger of Karmiss which is cruel. These are the enemies. Not men, never men, but the evil dreams of men."

Lur Raldnor began to feel a desolate fatigue. He remembered what he had thought in Elyr, the hopeless resignation worse than fear or rage. The world tumbling into chaos, and no one to prevent it.

"Oh yes," the paler of the two Lowlanders said, tackling the thought Raldnor had not spoken. "Even in that, there's more than one path to extinction. But other paths, also. Ashni passed by our village. We came here. Very many came here."

"Like the other time," the second man said. Now he grinned. "Raldnor's time. But she's the daughter of Raldnor."

"Ashne'e?" Lur Raldnor questioned.

But they said the name over, and he heard the slight difference.

"Ashni."

The paler man said, "Come and see."

"This woman you say—"

"Ah, no. She's gone already, into the north. Each of the cisterns of the world's power must be woken and tapped. Her's is Koramvis."

Then, at last he saw how they looked at him, and he went cold.

"You've been told about the great wolf."

"Yes."

"You expected me to come here, as you did. Why?"

But he knew.

Even the Xarabians did not seem surprised when, solemnly and irrevocably, the Amanackire each touched forehead and heart, the arcane reverence the Shadowless Plains now gave to a lord or a priest, those upon whose fate they saw the Choice of Anackire.

Although in fact it was never given to those who, like Raldnor, Ashne'e, Ashni, were in essence themselves considered to be aspects of the goddess herself. Since the goddess asked nothing, needing nothing, being everything.

They went out into the street, and crowds were standing there with torches. There was no element of the macabre or the portentous. It felt almost frivolous, like a party going to a wedding or a feast.

The Xarabians followed them out.

They walked, hundreds of people, through the snow towards the ruined palace and the magic well.

Later, almost into dawn, lying alone on the border of sleep, he thought: *Can it be so simple—ingenuous?*

And somewhere, maybe from some other drifting mind in the dark city, or from some cave within himself, the affirmative.

Men are drops of water in the ocean of life. And yet the vast ocean is only that, myriad drops of water. One single thought, crying out: This shall be! Or crying out: This shall not be! And the vast ocean is altered.

They had said something like this to him, not in words. He tried from habit to put it into words now, although the words would lessen it, make it unclear.

The palace had been warmed by the torches. What occurred? They had stood on the ancient mosaics, and drunk yellow wine which they said came from a well. . . .

There were Xarabians, Elyrians, Dortharians even, and mixes of all types. And the Amanackire, spread through the crowd, like a silver string holding everything together.

Lur Raldnor had always had the telepathy of the Plains. Now those who had elected themselves, or been elected to educate him, began to do so. It was not hard to learn, after all. But then, it was not really learning, only recapturing.

Was he important to them because of these obvious things, Lowland blood which brought the mind speech, Yannul's blood which was proximity to what had gone before? Even, maybe, the significant name of Raldnor, which now was his, and had always been his, though one of Raldnor's sons had attempted to strip him of it.

Sleep moved over him.

He would not be having the girl now. Sex, the magic power, would be retained and channeled. Strangely, already he did not want her in that way. He could think back to Yeiza, or to others, and there would come merely a glimmer of the senses, cerebral, no longer governing the flesh.

Of course, the cold and loneliness of the journey, the hardship, the being lost, the closeness to death, these had enabled him to enter the occult aura of the ruin. The magician's purgation before sorcery.

Floating now, as if in the sky. Murmurs of awareness all about him that were not sound, and glows like candles that were not seen.

He remembered how Ashni had gone by them. It seemed to him that, laboring in Xarabiss, desperate to get to Lan, he had caught rumors of something bizarre, and paid no heed—Men and women moving through the last coppery summer days and over the starry hills, something about music and song that were not audible, and sheens and rainbows invisible, and wildcats, wolves, serpents dancing, and flowers in long yellow hair that did not wither. And yet perhaps there had only been a group of travelers walking in the dust, riding carts past the villages through the still ear of night. Which was the vision, the mirage, which the truth? Were both the same? Or could it be that something which had not happened at all had yet happened, because the mind perceived it where the eyes would not?

He thought of a primeval forest in the snow, persisting where it could not persist, centuries.

He was asleep, now, and sleeping, he looked about him without eyes, to find Medaci.

Presently he did find her.

She was as utterly before him as if they had met in sunlight in a little room. But such things were equivalents, as spoken words were the equivalents of the speech of the mind.

In a response then, which was the equivalent of a quiet touch upon her shoulder, he asked her attention, and received it. She was not nonplussed. She seemed unastonished to behold him, safe and where he was, and meshed in the Dream of Anackire. But her gladness in him was as he recollected.

He took her hand and they stood together in the sunlit room smiling at each other, in the love that could only be when no door, however thin or partly ajar, intervened.

He might never see her again. He knew it, and so did she. The fires that would be awakened, a million times greater than any which had gone before—that Waking of the Serpent, to this a taper to the sun—such fires might overwhelm them. Ankabek had been the first sacrifice. Undemanded, unintended, yet now a facet. To die for this would not be required, yet it might come to be that one *would* die.

For, as he had believed in the beginning, it was to be a victory through passion. Except it was a different passion than the one he had taught himself to serve, with a sword and an angry heart.

As sleep settled more deeply, he relinquished Medaci's hand, and she was softly gone.

He was on a golden barge then, winged by a solitary shining sail. It was his life, and he powered it by his will and sent it flying over the bright water toward morning.

Yannul the Lan, leaning on one elbow, saw his wife smile in her sleep. Sleeping, she looked so young, younger even than when he had met her. Then she spoke his name and her eyes opened.

"What is it?" he said.

"I dreamed of Lur Raldnor."

"Was it a kind dream?" Superstition and a desire for her peace mingled in his words.

"Yes. Before—there was a shadow. I was afraid. But he was with me, he told me. Not only a dream, Yannul. Mind speech. We can be easy about him, now."

"Good," he said. Almost absently. He found that accepting an unvaried diet of supernatural things tired him. It had been the same with Raldnor of Sar, except that the tiredness had expressed itself in other ways, the ways of a young man.

Medaci was already asleep again. He lay back beside her, and watched the walls of the wagon change color as the dawn began to lift the sky.

He reminded himself it would be a Zorish dawn. They were inside the Zor, and had been so half a month, since getting down the mountain.

After the miracle, the manifestation of the Lannic Anackire—it was useless to pretend it was not a miracle or a manifestation—the Karmian soldiery had ridden off, plainly tranced. An avalanche then blocked the pass. One did not know if any of the Karmians had been killed or injured. It seemed they would not have been. The power of the goddess had been merciful this time, if quite ruthless.

The pass trembled as the rocks fell. Other rocks fell behind them. When the fume settled, when the psychic stupor wore off and the resultant insane rejoicing and hysteria were at last controlled, the Zorish girl Vashtuh stood shouting at them. Her dialect had become incomprehensible, they had to go and see for themselves before they found the way into the mountain, and so into the valley of the Zor, was now clear.

It was partly a cave, and partly a tunnel, man-hewn, maybe. On the far side the mountains cascaded down, hung at intervals with wild white curtains of water.

Their descent was not so simple. They lost a couple of men even here, and a goat later, for though there were occasional paths, they were treacherous. In that manner, the religious bravura wore off. They had unconsciously reckoned themselves invulnerable since the magic on the pass. But natural accidents could still happen, apparently.

Eventually, they got to the intermediary slopes of the valley. Even here, the magic faltered. It did not seem exactly as they had dreamed of it. Rain pelted and thunder rocked about the sky. They were very miserable, like children promised sweets and then shooed into the yard without supper.

Safca, with black-ringed, red-rimmed eyes, spoke encouragement, bullied and cajoled. She never gave up as they floundered and crawled through the first acres of mud and drenching. Though the legitimacy of her nobility had been in doubt at Olm, she seemed a veritable king's daughter now, royal to her limits, and slightly mad. The girl Vashtuh, too, was full of savage pleasure at beholding her roots, so she went up and down the lines, wet as a fish, grinning. She said something to Yannul and he nodded politely. Only much later did he translate and understand and say to Medaci in bewilderment, "Vashtuh says the snow won't fall here, only the rain does."

They believed it presently when one morning the sky had grown dry and luminous, and they saw the heads of the mountains they had left behind thickly daubed with scintillant whiteness, and only the rain ponds on the ground. It seemed the valley ran very low, under the eastern snowline, cupped by its palisade of rock and granite, protected. They might drown but would not freeze.

That night, there were songs at the fires again.

They came to realize the dream they had all had was not a lie, but rather a sort of précis of the facts.

They did not see the river for some while, but before then they had come on the riches of the valley, the fruit yet heavy on the trees and bushes, the animals which roamed everywhere and would provide meat.

When the river did come in sight, there was something else, a stone town. It was Lannic-looking—like Amlan, though far smaller. There had been, until now, only cots, a couple of deserted villages overgrown by bare creepers and deep in rotted leaves. The town gave signs of occupancy.

Yannul wondered if the town was what had swelled in the stories to a city, but Vashtuh insisted not. Her mother had come from this place. The city lay northeast, beyond the river.

There were indeed people in the town, and some system of government, but rather resembling that of Elyr, mystic and mysterious. A group of black-haired men came and talked with them on the incline below the town. Vashtuh acted as interpreter, a necessity, for the dialect was well set in here. Beyond odd words and phrases, the men of the Zor and those of Lanelyr could not make sense of each other.

In transpired, nonetheless, that the Zor no longer counted inself a kingdom, merely the testament to one. Free Lan was welcome, although it was asked that they observe a space between any site they wished to mark out and the existing properties. Meanwhile, refuge in the town was available. There were a number of vacant domiciles, not completely incapable of sheltering them; or the houses of those now absent might be ultilized, though with respect for the owners, as was their custom. The produce of the valley was for all.

Plainly, the Zor did not quite trust them, nor they the Zor, but proprieties were maintained, sympathy existed and might expand. The Free Lans, who had watched Karmiss march in and manhandle them, were but too aware of how an influx of foreigners could be viewed. They took care to be amenable and just.

The first night, a percentage were entertained by Vashtuh, who had reclaimed a tumbling house on a slaty outcrop teetering over the river. This had been her family's dwelling; there were others who had joint claim to it also, uncles and cousins her mother had mentioned, out traveling the valley or the world beyond, who might come back at any time. A long stone table, scrubbed by Vashtuh for her guests, was also laid with five unoccupied places—at each an ivory knife unearthed from a chest, a candle, a stone cup lovingly polished by hundreds of fingers and lips—for those who might momentarily return. This was the custom of the Zor, and though there had been similar traditions in Lan, never had one felt the precipitance of possible arrival so strongly.

Free Lan would settle by the river, there was no argument on this. In summer, maybe, there would be other imperatives, to seek another venue, to leave the valley again and reconnoiter the outer landscape. But they had traveled a great distance. They had achieved liberty and a fair measure of hope for survival. For now it was enough.

"But I," said Safca, "must go on to the city."

The Lans listened with deference. Safca was their priestess, she had been the spark for their revolt at Olm, the focus for Anackire on the mountain pass, turning aside their enemies, opening the gate into the Zor. They did not want her to leave them, and if she commanded it they too would feel obliged to go on. She did not, however, command. She expressed her own need, and asked who would accompany her.

Her foremost officer, the man who would have died trying to hold the Karmians back, if she and Yannul had allowed it, frowned in the fragrant, mild winter air, and asked her why she must continue, and how she was sure the city existed.

"I know it does," she said. "I know I must be there."

"But why, lady?" He indicated the men standing around gazing at her. "You brought us out of Lan. You invoked the goddess and She rose up before us—" This cry was smothered in a burst of acknowledgment.

Safca flushed darkly, her eyes bright. She loved to be loved, having formerly been left short of love. When she could be heard, she said, "It's the goddess who informs me I must go on."

Silence, then. This was indisputable. The officer said, "We'll follow you."

"No," she said, "I invite those who feel the need to reach the city, as I do. Others would be useless to the goddess. She wants only those who respond to her design."

"What is this *design?*"

She spread her hands. The wind tossed her hair. In such moments, she began to look beautiful, not as a woman could be beautiful, but like the spires of the mountains, the stands of proud trees.

"I don't know. But I am part of it. Ashni made me part of it."

They had been told of Ashni, the child-goddess who had lived among them, unrecognized, at Olm.

The meeting broke up. Next day Safca had her transport, wagons from the town, very light and peculiarly carved, with covers of dyed, waxed linen. There were no zeebas in the valley, let alone horses. The Zorians used the gelded rams from their flocks, and Safca's party would do the same. When she left, crossing one of the tilting plank bridges over the river, less than twenty persons were moved to go with her.

"Why are we doing this?" asked Yannul.

Medaci said, "Because I'm drawn, as she said, toward the city."

She tried to explain this drawing to him. He could not grasp it or did not want to, but she wished to follow Safca northeast, and he went with her. Their boy was happy at last. He had struck up a friendship with a Lannic lad of the same age who was also part of the expedition. They rode together on a cart drawn, this time, by two stout but willing pigs.

It still rained days and nights at a stretch.

Yannul, the damp in his bones, cursed the enterprise. He did not believe in the city, yet it assumed vast metaphysical proportions.

He lay on his back now, thinking of him, his sword-arm aching and complaining, remembering how the Karmians had not been hurt, only sent packing, too tired to decide any more if he was angry or excited or afraid or bored. When the riot started outside, he plunged from the rugs, dragging his knife up with him, charging out of the wagon and dropping almost on top of his younger son, who was standing there calling him.

"It's all right, father. It isn't war."

Yannul shook himself. He had been half-asleep after all. He lowered the knife, noting his son found him lovable and heroic and funny all at once, and wanting to cuff him or hug him for it.

"What, then?"

"Come and look."

So Yannul let himself be conducted a quarter of a mile, and once there, looked.

The woods they had traversed all yesterday opened to the east on a burgeoning sunrise, soft-colored and hazy. At the foot of the sunrise spread another river, a band of water with the sky in it. And there above the river and just below the dawn was the arcane city of the Zor.

A ruined city. A broken sword. . . .

Before they got there, before they crossed the second river, they came on a chain of villages, spread all along the near bank, separated by yards, or a mile from each other, as far as the eye could see. People, it seemed, resided in the proximity of the ruin, if not within it. An odd arrangement. They had to pass between two of the villages, going to the water, and then by or through others as they rode the bank looking for a bridge or ford. Men and women, children, some sheep, wandered out and stared at them. Yannul and a handful of the other Lans attempted speech, but they had no interpreter now. It was useless. Groups vehemently pointed, however, *that* way—which was upstream. They knew the strangers wanted to go over to the city and were aiding them, without involvement.

Finally there was a large oared boat, in decent repair, tied to a tree. This was the method for getting over.

Four of the Lans rowed the first installment across, and kept at the work until relieved. Although the passage was brief the endeavor took a long time. Not only had human beings to be ferried, but bleating and disgruntled beasts, and necessities from the wagons, which they had had to abandon by the tree.

That the nearest pair of the numerous villages would rob them was probable.

Then the disparaging chatter died down. Deposited under the walls of the Zorish city of Zor, something swept their minds of trivia. It became silent, except for the cawing of the wind around the angles of the stone above.

From outside, the city was a dark bulk, a high bulwark of black stone, infrequently topped by the black tip of a tower.

From the distance, the city had looked whole, though they knew it could not be. Nor was it whole. The walls were cracked, faulted, in spots they had come down, but tumbling against each other had formed new walls, jumbles that remained impenetrable.

They walked, the little troupe of people, along the walls searching for a way in.

Yannul put his hand on the back of Medaci's neck. "I'm here with you."

She smiled at him and he saw she was not frightened. Despite the knowledge that this was the Lowland city in replica—for that was precisely what it was; not now but as it had been, centuries ago.

One of the children running ahead found a gateway. There might have been others. There was no gate, just the echoing arch.

Broad terraced steps went down beyond. Streets folded away. Towers ascended. There stood a pillared building on a rise. A long window burned, clasped in the stone. They gestured to it, for the colored glass was not all smashed.

"Safca," Yannul said.

Medaci shook her head. Their Olmish lady was far off, tuned to some voiceless song of the city.

She walked before them.

They went after.

Overhead, the towers, unleveled if broken, made shadows without shadows on the sky.

"Am I afraid?" Safca asked of herself. "No," the other element of Safca answered gently, the element which was mother and teacher to the lesser element; her solely human self. "No, not afraid. The power of this place is very strong. But you're here for a purpose. You can feel that. The purpose is also the Power."

Something led her, it was no trouble to give in to it.

How long had she been walking in the city? Perhaps several hours. The others must be exhausted. She was not.

Suddenly, she was aware of having reached a destination. Safca glanced about her. In some fashion, she had been anticipating some mighty thing, a colossal statue, maybe, or an edifice that was unearthly and fearful. But no. It was a small carved door in the side of a wall. She touched it, and it gave at her touch. Safca was surprised after all.

She looked down into the eye of a great pool. There seemed to be a cave beneath the ancient street, conceivably some entrance into an under-channel of the river. Then she heard the murmuring exclamation around her. She looked again and saw why. Catching embers from the daylight, she beheld jewels and metal, a hoard such as legends spoke of—

Safca went into the cave room, down its sloping floor, mesmerized not by the worth of the treasure but by its fabulous presence.

The others spilled in after her. Daylight and struck flints shot diamond and ruby eyes across the dimness. There were whispers: Here was wealth to succor Lan against her enemies. Secondary whispers—No, this was a sacred trove, would carry a curse if plundered, had you not seen the carving of the snake goddess on the door? Safca was intrigued at herself, for she had missed it altogether.

It was the pool which had caught her attention, and still did so. She went to it and looked in.

"Make a steady light," she said quietly, "and bring it here."

Someone did. By the glow of his flaring lamp, they stared down into the pool.

Its floor was a great pale stone, which had been cut into. The tracery of letters went on and on. It was one huge book. The water, rather than eroding, had somehow preserved. The writing was Visian. They could read every line.

*   *   *

When night came, black as the city, they had located a huge old house on a hill. Some mansion of the past, its round columned hall was intact. No one lived in the city, or none they had come across. A tirr's nest was long unoccupied, mummified, even its stink was dead. They had seen no tirr in the valley at all. Perhaps these beasts, venom-clawed and ugly beyond reason, were no longer prevalent.

They made their fire, prepared food and ate it. A wine-bag from Olm was opened and shared. They had reached their objective. When the little heap of children slept, a stillness that was in them all came to the surface of their skins and eyes. There was only the crackle of the flames, then, the dance of light on a bead, a woman's hair.

Safca had gone away behind a stone screen many hundreds of years of age. She lay still there, and heard their stillness, with all that time locked in the screen between them.

She had been celibate since Zastis. It was curious. She had known in the mountains she might have chosen a man from among her captains, and he would have lain with her in an excitement and desire no man had ever felt for her before. Because she was special, because she was holy. But of course it was this very thing which had made sex unnecessary.

And now.

She stared up toward the faroff ceiling, the ebony rafters, young a thousand years, perhaps, before her birth.

Could she contain the force, the fire, which might come? She had known Ashni. But she herself was only mortal. She might die.

Then again, the design of the goddess, if so it was, might fail. But she could not make herself think that. Faith was paramount. Safca's faith was utter.

Out in the long hall, Yannul and another man were checking the livestock roped in among the pillars with their straw. The animals, also, were silent. When Yannul turned, he found his younger son, and the pure-Vis boy he was friends with. Somewhere along the road they had sworn blood-brotherhood. Yannul had noted the white scars on the side of each of their arms. Now they gazed at him. His son, the spokesman, said, "Is it true?"

"What does your mother say?"

"Yes, and ask you."

"Then yes."

They strolled back toward the fire.

"The magic must be very powerful. What will happen?"

"I don't know. What happened on the pass, maybe, but more."

"Like what happened under Koramvis when you were with Raldnor Am Sar?"

"I don't know," he said again.

Odd that the knowledge should only have been here. He suspected it had actually lain in other areas, but was now destroyed or lost. Passages on the stone in the pool had made no sense. Others were memories, and legends. The Am Dorthar had always boasted that they had come from heaven, riding in the bellies of pale dragons which burned the ground black with their fiery breath. The writing in the stone had also mentioned this. In the beginning, which was before the beginning as they remembered it, the people of this continent had been universally white-skinned and pale—Lowlanders. But the Vis races, dark, avaricious and clever, had come from elsewhere—out of heaven. Something had gone on that the stone did not properly reveal. There had been a fall, from strength as well as from the skies. The Vis had in some way degenerated, mislaying some mighty power, not sorcerous, yet uncanny. The pale races had already sunk from their personal apex. It seemed they had been witches, but had abused the gift, which finally withered. They gave in to the invaders, who in turn gave in to their own weakening.

These items were peculiar. Mythos. Then the writing in the stone postulated other things, other myths, which belonged here, in the upheaval of the present.

"The Lowlanders have always had such beliefs," Medaci said to him, when the fire had almost died. "Wells of Power, that might be tapped. And lines of Power that linked each well, painted invisibly over the earth, the water and the air."

"Did they say where these wells could be found?"

"Some of the priests were supposed to know. There was always reckoned to be something close to Koramvis, and the story of a hidden temple there, made in the time when only yellow-haired men held the land."

Koramvis. The stone tablet in the pool had called it Dorthara's Heart. And here, that was Zor Am Zor. And the Lowland city, which the stone called Anak of the Plains. And one other situation, which the stone specified as Memon. And then came the reference to a second country, southward, beyond Aarl Sea, that must be the second continent. And here there was a fifth Power source, at a place the stone named Vathak. One imagined this was Vathcri where, disgorged from the ocean, he had ridden with Raldnor Am Anackire, and where Raldnor's white-haired son had been conceived and birthed. And one saw too, with a shattering clarity, that the doomed tower ship which had borne them to that alien shore, through storm and fire and mutiny and murder, and despair, had driven all the way along or beside the line of invisible force which ran between Vathak-Vathcri and Koramvis, Dorthara's Heart.

Yannul wanted to laugh with anger. He was close to weeping, too. The supernal authority which had picked him up and flung him through the mirror of destiny, that monster clutched him yet, had never let him go, or any of them, live or dead.

He tried to dispel his tearing emotions by rational comment.

"But Memon," he said. "Where is that? It isn't a city, whole or ruin. Not even a town that I ever heard of. Some dot of a village, perhaps, seething with psychic broth. May all the gods help them."

He put more wood on to the fire. It was damp, and sputtered. Maybe the spiritual force of the planet would be like that, now.

From the valley, the world, the snows, the nightmare invasion and prologues of war seemed nothing. But his other son was out there, in the thick of it. And the two sons of Raldnor Am Anackire.

"And she also," Medaci said, having read his thoughts with an exactitude that no longer shocked him.

He stirred the fire grimly, the stick gripped with his sword-hand.

"Ashni."

And the sparks became a leap of solid light.

TWENTY

Across the east and the Middle Lands, the cold had cast its spell of white sleep. Through these drifts and canyons of alabaster there presently came struggling a knot of riders, their chariots foundering, their beasts often breast-high or almost to the throat, in snow. Reaching Dorthar, they struggled on. They struggled to Anackyra, and into the Storm Palace of the High King, where they stood, their faces raw, their eyes dull, and one of their number bandaged, having lost fingers.

They brought Raldanash news. The news was bitter, like the journey.

Alisaar, won by Shansar in the Lowland War, had been credited an ally to this Storm Lord, son of the man who had first led Shansar into Vis. Now Alisaar had proclaimed herself. Neutral. The formal message had not yet come, but it would come. The Dortharians who brought the story in advance gave it in their own words.

"It seems Kesarh made secret overtures on first gaining the Karmian throne. He's half Shansar himself though he shows it little enough. Shansarian Alisaar is a provisional ally with Shansarian Karmiss. Now Kesarh seems to favor Free Zakoris. Alisaar can't move. She has Vardish Zakoris next door, the Middle Lands over the Inner Sea, Free Zakoris able to get at her on the other side, and Kesarh sending presents and swearing undying love—and most of that from Lan which he's annexed."

"Alisaar will fight, my lord, but only for herself. Whoever moves up on her will be shown violence. That means Vardish Zakoris and Free Zakoris alike. Or Dorthar."

The news, though bitter, was not quite astounding. Already the majority of Shansarian officers had resigned their commands throughout all Vis.

Warden Vencrek, speaking to the mixed council of Anackyra, exposed the threat that underlay Alisaar's dilemma and resolve.

"We," said Vencrek, using the Vis tongue, but laced by many now-popular phrases from his birthplace of Vathcri, "have sent our messengers to the Sister Continent. It appears we shall be blushing before the snow is done. I'm sure you're aware, gentlemen, that if Kesarh had the sense to keep fresh an alliance with Shansarian Alisaar, he will have done the same by Shansar itself." And the council muttered, although it had known to a man what was coming. "If Karmiss, who still sends us words of friendship—that we discredit—" said Vencrek relentlessly, "if Karmiss, I say, has retained a treaty with Shansar-over-the-water, and we can assume she has, then Shansar must take Kesarh's part. Kesarh leans to Free Zakoris, the Black Leopard, the sworn enemy of Dorthar. In that case, the second continent now stands thus: Shansar becomes the foe of the Storm Lord's people of Vathcri, and of Vardath who holds the kingdom of Old Zakoris in Vis. At the least, Shansar will refuse to aid her original ally, Dorthar. At worst, Shansar must declare war on Dorthar, and on Vardish Zakoris. And so in turn on Vathcri and Vardath themselves. And Tarabann, into the bargain. With the crisis as it exists, Vardians or Vathcrians would themselves be imbeciles to send troops here and leave their own ground unprotected. We can therefore expect no support from the second

continent, gentlemen. All we can expect is a possible escalation
of the war, once it begins, and the decimation of the southern
Homeland, even as Vis herself is ravaged.

"Kesarh, by his fiendish maneuvers and his lack of integrity,
has set the whole world on its ear."

In the aftermath of this speech, the cries of outrage died and
left them empty.

Here was chaos to rival and surpass that of any former conflict.
And now, there would be nowhere for any of them to run. Rich
and poor, serf and master, they would all be caught in it.

The foundations were giving way. Rarmon had betrayed them
to Free Zakoris. Raldanash sat before them like a cool white
stone.

Where were the heroes now?

Into the small room the dusk came crowding, full of shadows
and unheard sounds. Beyond the high window the sweep of the
uplands showed above the city, and on the deepening sky the
mountains built of the sky.

You are not ours, the mountains called faintly to him, *no son
of our mornings; conceived in other shade. We will not conceal
you, nor keep you safe*.

Raldanash, sensitive to the alien contour and expression of this
land, had long ago ridden its hills, sought out Koramvis, stared.
Now he stared inwards, away from Dorthar, and away from Vis.

He was remembering Vathcri-over-the-ocean, her lenient winter season of winds but rarely if ever of snow, her hot months
when the valleys flamed golden with grain. He saw the red-
walled city, a tiara of towers almost ninety feet above the plain,
and the red-walled palace. And there at the center of the cameo
of walls and valleys and dark trees, his white mother, whose
name had been Sulvian, while she lived.

Sulvian was beautiful. She and he were alike in that, and, in
that continent of snowlessness, alike in the snow-color of their
hair. As he grew, he believed that they had only each other. She
had had a brother she loved, an uncle who could have served as
a father to him, but Uncle Jarred had gone with Raldnor to the
War, and perished in a burning sea, leaving no trace, nothing to
mourn save recollection. And his actual father, Raldnor, Elect of
the Goddess, he had not come back, nor been looked for.
Sulvian had always comprehended it a vain thought, that she
might behold her husband once more. She had promised Raldanash
that he would see Raldnor, in her place.

When it began to filter to Vathcri after the War, the word of
Raldnor's disappearance, metamorphosis, transcension, Sulvian

had set it aside. He would return to Dorthar. He had been at such pains to have Dorthar—of course he would return. Raldanash had been about five or six when he noticed her trust in this supposition had undergone a change. She commenced, very slowly, to wean her son from the wish she had herself implanted in him, and which they had shared, that one day, when he must leave his home and all he knew and sail to the foreign kingdom to be its heir, then Raldnor his father would await him, and welcome him. She had been used to say, judging his apprehension though he did not voice it, "You won't be alone, with your father beside you." But his father would not be beside him after all.

Raldanash, though a child, perceived she was more wounded by this than he himself. She had always understood she had been used—the alliance, the seal of the male child. She had loved Raldnor but without requital. She had turned to love her child instead. But, of course, the child also was a temporary solace. In early adolescence he would be sent for.

He thought of his mother now, as he saw her on the very evening he had gone away.

His heart had been wrung with trepidation and the first-blood of severance. He was just a boy. She, her luster already hollowing, her pale hair wound with gems, stood framed by the gems of stars standing in the sky beyond the colonnade.

"I shall send for you," he said, trying, for he was so young, to be older.

She smiled.

"I'm always with you," she said, "there or here, or anywhere."

It was not until days later on the ship, the land sucked away like an indrawn sable breath, that he felt the hidden omen of her words, and knew she would soon die. He would have wrenched the ship about if he could. But already the discipline of his position, and those other elemental disciplines inherent in him, had taught him how to resist and how to endure. So, he bore it, all the way to Vis. He bore it through the arrival alone, the pomp, the earth tremor that rendered him its terrible homage. Through the ceaseless labor to achieve what was asked for, everything novel and to be learned and no harbor anywhere and no rest, for even asleep he dreamed the worries of his state, how he was to rule, the man he must become. He bore it, too, when they brought him the fact of Sulvian's death, and laid it softly as a flower at his fourteen-year-old feet, before upward of fifty bystanders.

His court judged him cold, aloof and soulless. His dignity and dry eyes insulted the tenets of Vis. Women keened for their dead. Funeral processions were frantic. This youthful outlander, he should at least have put his hand to his brow, fumbled his sentence of acknowledgment. But Raldanash had no outward theater save his looks. He was stabbed in the mind, and bleeding, but none of them were allowed to observe it.

Cold King. Lowlander. Amanackire.

In his way, he had loved the idea of his father, too, Raldnor, the waking sunrise, the messiah. And to this hour he could still vividly recapture Sulvian's face and voice, her whole demeanor, as she spoke of Raldnor to their son. To lose such a father totally, and to watch Sulvian's loss over and over in reverie, these things did their work upon Raldanash, even if never seen to do it.

Like Rarmon, he knew that his father had never valued him. To inherit the temporal kingdom with such knowledge was hard.

In the end the imagery of Raldnor, the very name of "Raldnor" began, at some most private level, to offend and so to disturb Raldanash. Knowing himself as others might not have done, for this reason he had banned use of the name in those who were most often about him. Raldanash was aware, how in the depths of things, it might now and then be possible to confuse intrinsic aversion to a name with its bearer. Those he stripped were not informed of his logic. They took the act to heart, as did Yannul's son, and were insulted.

The window closed with darkness. Someone came to light the lamps, and then the frost-bitten messenger bowed his way in.

"I am sorry," said Raldanash, "about your hand."

The messenger was dazzled and knocked off balance. The King was never humane, he had heard.

"My own fault, Storm Lord. I was careless. But it isn't my swordhand, thank the goodness."

"And this other matter?"

"Highness—" the messenger hesitated, uncertain. Then launched into his story with awkward brevity. It had seemed relevant. Now he was less sure.

He had been in Ommos, investigating the movements of Ommish troops and their reactions to the rumors he himself had helped spread of Free Zakorian infamy. When the cold started to gnaw off his fingers, he took refuge at Hetta Para where the Amanackire guardian ruled the sketchy new city, and the wrecked elder capital festered under the snow.

There had already been some murmurings in Xarabiss. They concerned a Lowlander priestess, or witch, depending on who told them, or their point of origin. There had been a peasant's story of a spirit or even a goddess. She traveled north, and some said she rode a golden chariot drawn by white wolves, and some said she rode in a wagon hung with amber and glowing with an amber luminescence. One or two such mutters would have meant nothing. In troubled times supernatural madness frequently took hold. Gods and dead heroes were seen walking about, calves with two heads were born, loaves bled and water changed into wine or urine. However, these tales of a blonde priestess had decided similarities. Eventually, one began to glean a picture of some holy woman of significance on the road, as it seemed for Dorthar itself.

Then, in Hetta Para, going at nightfall into the unsavory lower quarter of the old city, he had seen, across great mounds of rubble and burnt-out houses, a section of the alleys below moving and bright with torches. Sensing the momentous, for this end of Hetta Para was a dubious sink, the messenger got down and blended with the crowd.

He followed it into a pit, and then considered if he had been wise. First off, he had believed they revived their worship of Zarok—the cousin to the Zakorians' fire god. A statue, formerly flung down into the pit, was upright, and its oven-belly red with fire.

It was only after the crowd had inadvertently pushed him nearer that the messenger beheld the god, whom he had seen depicted previously, was altered.

"It was no longer ugly, my lord. I can't explain it. Something had been done to the features, and the teeth—it wasn't like itself. But that wasn't everything." The messenger shook his head slightly at the recollection. He said, "There was part of a broken wall behind the statue, about sixty feet high, before the roof had sheared away. All up the wall there was a mark, a sort of scorch, very faint, but the torches showed it." Raldanash asked nothing, so the messenger said: "It was most of the shape of a colossal anckyra, the tail, the torso and the arms up to the elbows. . . . eight of them." The messenger, who was also a spy, had uncharacteristically failed to probe the crowd. He had merely stood in the pit while the crowd did, and come out when it came out.

But by the time he reached the northern border and caught up with his comrades, he had added to his collection of stories. The witch-priestess performed miracles. Some of these involved manifestations of the Lady of Snakes, eighty or ninety feet high. Someone had declared the woman was the daughter of the Storm

Lord Raldnor. The Dortharians had got no sign of her, but he guessed she and her people—for she went in company, if not with giant wolves, serpents and docile playful tirr—could already be here, in Dorthar itself.

When the man was dismissed, Raldanash also left the room.

He passed through the palace, its halls and courts, out into a snowy sloping garden, and so to the private temple he had caused to be built ten years before.

The grove itself was fleeced with snow, and the blackness of the temple stood out under it in slabs. As he entered Raldanash remembered, with a dull insistent clenching of the brain, how Rarmon had been proved to him here. Rarmon who now, like Raldanash himself, lay dashed in the uppermost hand of Anackire.

The lamp was lit. Raldanash stretched himself on the stone floor, and prepared swiftly for the trancelike meditatory state, in which the priests of Vathcri, and later the Amanackire themselves, had trained him.

He had long been sensitized, as the Amanackire were, many of them, sensitized to such an imminence. It had been abstract, until now.

Presently, drifting free, he gazed across the mists of inner sight and made out a slim flame, pale golden, like the eye of some inexplicable creature from another dimension.

Where the river curved and fragmented, heavy and curded now with ice, an ancient watchtower, only a stone shell, marked the northwest reaches of the Ommish-Dortharian border. Not far from here, almost three decades ago, the traitor Ras had crossed, on his mission to destroy the Lowland offensive. He had gifted—not even sold—his people, out of hatred for Raldnor, to Amrek's Counselor, a man named Kathaos, who now went by another, like, name in Yl Am Zakoris' service.

In and about the shell of the tower was a small encampment. Rough walls built of gathered stones lent added shelter to the three or four wagons crouched in their lee. Zeebas and men stayed mostly within the yawn of the tower, from which a drizzle of smoke rose up to a smoke-colored sky.

At a glance, you saw none of the attendant magic, no hint of miracles and sorceries. The bivouac was comfortless and gray. No wolves danced in the snow.

Haut the Vardian, one of his servants, and a Lowland man from Moiyah who had joined them near Xarabiss, were returning from a hunt. They had found nothing, which was not unusual. The sheep had all been eaten, save a couple of ewes kept for

their milk. The slaughterings had been curious. The girl touched
the animals' foreheads and they fell asleep, nor woke when the
knife sliced through them. Ashni herself did not eat the meat.
She lived on mysterious things, maybe roots and grasses and
now, it seemed, the snow. Yet her slightness was the burnished
slenderness of health not wasting.

They had been speaking, out on the cold white slopes of
Dorthar, about homelands—Moiyah, on the edge of the Inner
Sea, blue-walled Vardath over the ocean. They remembered they
were human men, for all she had changed them. But she had
brought a great stillness into their lives. And even though they
had spoken in words of home, those words were uttered only
within their echoing brains.

They were familiar with strangeness.

So, as they reached the outskirt of their camp and saw the
smoke rising, they did not balk at the other sight, that of a
phantom walking before them through the snow.

One she has summoned, the Moiyan thought aloud.

Or one seeking her, Haut answered.

The vague dusk shone through the man, and his hair was like
frost. Because of that, they knew him.

Raldnor's spirit?

His son.

They proceeded, a respectful distance in his wake. He was a
King. But they did look for the tremulous cord that must anchor
the psyche to the body during life, and believed they detected it.

Raldanash, in his psychic condition, did not wonder, although
never in the past had he ranged so distantly from the body. Nor
had he ever been strong enough to project his own image in
tandem with his awareness. That power would come from her,
her magnetic power, like amber.

He sensed the men behind him, and their ability to accept. But
they were as ghostly to him as he must be to them. The world
itself was ghostly. Only the golden flame burned before him, the
flame that was the girl.

He had already learned, without tuition, all she was, or all that
he could understand she was. The soul of Raldnor's daughter in
an envelope of flesh, older than the flesh, reforming the flesh so
that it had hastened, growing to the likeness of a young woman,
perhaps eighteen years of age. Her consciousness was older.
Older even than itself, for she had in some way remembered
those insights that the soul forgot beyond the spiritual places of

its freedom. That she was also his sister he barely noticed. Of all
the reasons to approach, it was the least.

Raldanash's physical soul entered the shell of the tower. He
glimpsed fires, men and women and animals. A few—Lowlanders—glimpsed him, and fell quiet. It seemed she must have
wished for them to see him, it was no ostentation. So he passed
through them gently, and going approximately to the twist of the
stair, ascended.

The small piece of a chamber that remained at the head of the
tower, open all round to the darkening sky, was softly brilliant
with her light.

Ashni. She rose to greet him, and with an odd sweetness of
gesture put her hands in his. He felt her touch, though he could
feel nothing else that was real, save the silver cold and the
flowing water of the wind.

Her beauty was not like his own, not like the beauty of
Raldnor and Sulvian and Astaris. It was the beauty of fantasy,
more than pearl skin and topaz hair. Her eyes were not eyes at
all, but sheer windows that showed the lamp beyond. Her
strength—Raldanash had read a strength like this in Rarmon,
but there it was banked; events rather than will must unfetter it.
The strength of Raldanash was dissimilar. Rarmon was a sword,
and Ashni a sword of fire. But he . . . he saw it now. His
strength was the mirror of bronze or glass, taking the sun's
reflection, multiplying heat and flame. He saw, and he saw the
mirror blaze, and buckle, cracking, shattering. This, then, was
the mirror's fate. He would die.

Her touch gave him comfort. It was not that she was pitiless.
She had told him only what he had guessed, long long ago, on
the plains of Vathcri, the hills of Dorthar. *Like a candle, some
are given life to die,* the proverb said.

For some reason he thought then of Jarred, his mother's
brother, consumed in the burning sea.

Ashni held him, and the terror ebbed. She began to talk to
him, not in words, or even images, but in a manner that filled his
vision, hearing and heart. And it was also true that in some way
she revealed the past, so he beheld Raldnor and Ashne'e, Koramvis
in her glory, and other subjects of a time before time, at
which he marveled, and which afterward he mislaid.

In the end, he knew death as a little thing, and in the end also,
raising his eyes which were the astral eyes of his physical soul,
he was not amazed or discomposed to find Ashni as she really
was, a summer being limned by gold, taller than heaven where
the stars were branching in her hair, her eyes like suns, her

plated tail coiled with a wonderful economy, the tower miles
below them both: Ashnesea, Ashkar, Anackire.

But he employed words then, finding himself in conversation
with the goddess. The first word was only: "Why?"

The answer blossomed in his soul's mind. It said:

*I am the symbol and the name. In Ommos I am Zarok. In
Zakoris I am Zarduk and Rorn. Outside the world, I am all
others. In sleep, the dream. Beyond death, the emblem of
awakening.*

"And what is that awakening?" he asked Her, though he had
been shown already.

She answered: *Yourself.*

And in the Zor, Safca dreamed of a pillar of light which did
not burn.

But in the Lowland city Lur Raldnor dreamed of a black
monster and a red, and Rem in the midst of fire, and his face was
a screaming skull.

TWENTY-ONE

Six miles from Ylmeshd the land rose into the southeast, a
climbing hip of ground woven higher yet by the reeking, fuming
jungle, blood-splashed with raucous birds and lizard-eating flowers.
Here, even in the cold months it was never cold. And here, too,
began that Southern Road which King Yl desired should one
day, loaded with men and chariots, break through to Dorthar and
Vardian Zakoris.

But it was a sort of fable. The road was made and the jungle
reclaimed it. It was not likely it would see completion before the
battle had been joined on other, more accessible, fronts. It served
to scare the Dortharians and Vardians. It served to punish those
who had displeased Free Zakoris.

Somewhere in the morass of the first twenty miles of Road,
slave gangs were clearing the undergrowth.

There was stone paving here, which had been laid a pair of
years before. Already it was split with seedlings. The slaves,
naked save for leather loin-aprons, hacked and slashed, their
salts pouring from them in the heat, and now and then scarlet

threads, at the whips of the overseers. A fallen slave was kicked. When she failed to get up, she was slung into a ditch at the roadside. It was forbidden that the guards enjoy her, for she was dying and to waste procreative seed was unlawful. They did not bother to cut her throat; time would see to things.

Farther on, where the great ferns and vines had been torn up, human ants labored to replace cracked stones.

Farther on again, a tree had rooted in the road. It was roped, and the ropes extended through iron harness across the backs of two huge beasts, palutorvuses, giants from the steamy swamps of Zakoris, and the margins of Thaddra. One was rust-red, the other blacker than night. They hauled blindly, streaming hair like water, flinching from the flails and goads as at the stings of insects. Behind them the mighty tree creaked. A root sprang from the stones.

A little way up, in the feverish shade just off the road, other antics were in progress. A holy man, itinerant and perhaps insane, rocked in his delirium. He had divined the possibility of rain and was now courting it. The guard did not make fun of him. When they wished for it, they had another lunatic to mock.

The cart was out on the road, wedged by the boulders against its wheels. The sun slammed down on it, disguising nothing.

He had been howling earlier, but now seemed asleep. The head had fallen forward, matted with black hair and beard. The copper skin was welted and streaked by sweat and filth. The cart was filthy, too, despite the withered garlands still decorating it, and there were chips and scratches where the shards the crowd flung at him in Ylmeshd had missed their mark. The enormous weighted chains roped him round and round, binding him to the cibba post bolted into the cart. Pinned over his head was a piece of wood with letters branded into it. Not everyone could read them, but most could guess. *I am Prince Rarmon Am Dorthar, Son of Raldnor Son of Rehdon. Behold my glory.*

They had been beholding it nearly a month. Hearing it, too. He had a good couple of lungs. The words were gibberish. It was more entertaining when he thrashed in his bonds, unable to get loose. The smell of wounds and rage enthralled the Free Zakorians. This was what they would do to Dorthar as a whole, and to the yellow men who had shamed them.

Sometimes they fed him, and he was given water every day. Yl wanted Raurm Am Ralnar to live a long while.

At night when he railed at the moon, they had ceased taking the whip to him. He did not quiet. The only man who went near to try knocking him insensible—the madman had gone for his throat and bitten through the neck vein. The guard expired in minutes, hiccuping blood. Now, when Rarmon bawled they cursed him, but nothing else.

Fifty yards away, the tree tore from the road in a fountain of soil and stones. The palutorvuses stamped, and the prisoner in the cart lifted his head.

His eyes were yellow, like the eyes of the Lowland witch Ashne'e, his grandmother.

The Free Zakorians would have put out his eyes, but Yl— Kathus—had decreed he should not be maimed. It was said he would be paraded in the war, and must be recognizable to the foe.

The undergrowth along the sides of the road was to be burned off. Much farther south, in the choked valleys between the mountains that squatted by Old Zakoris, stretches of forest were often set on fire for clearing. An outpost of the Road was well-advanced there, mostly in order to alarm the Storm Lord's spies. Between that area and this, the rampage of the jungles had been scarcely breached.

Rain was frequent at this season, and they coincided their fires. The deeps of the forests were never dry, full of exhalation and sap, but here in the opened places the trees would flare like kindling, needing some check.

The madman in the cart, if he had even noticed, had presided over two such ignitings and quenchings. The air first perilous with flame and flaming splinters, next the thunder, deluge, and dense strangling smoke. Thirteen days back, a bevy of slaves had been trapped among the thickets and burned, the storm too late to save them. If their screams evoked any ironic memory in the madman's tumbling thoughts, he did not demonstrate. He stood silent in his chains, then and now.

They could not hope the swamp-giants would be so peaceful. Every palutorvus loathed fire. As the sky about the trees began to threaten, men had climbed up and hooded the beasts, smearing their hairy trunks with salve to veil for them the stink of burning. Now they were being fed titbits. The half-starved slaves were too resigned to look on with envy. Gangs of Alisaarians, Iscaians and Thaddrians worked this plot. There had been a gang of mixes, too, but they were dead. Men with the fair blood generally did not last long at this enterprise under this western sun.

The holy man who divined rain came to, and stood up, snuffling thirstily. He held out his hand displaying three fingers. "This much time, no more."

The sky was swollen, seeming to touch the treetops. The Zakorians received their order and pounded along the slave lines. Men and women ran forward, touching bright tongues of light against the forest. Suddenly, like a wave, an invisible curling, soaring thing dashed up thirty feet into the branches. Charcoal fell. The slaves skipped away and bunched together on the middle of the track.

Birds hurled shrieking into the sky.

A white cicatrice of lightning slit the clouds. Timing, it would seem, had been commendable.

Thunder rang. The swamp-beasts shook their hooded heads. They were dumb and could not vocalize distress. They had, despite prevention, scented fire.

Walls of transparent flame reared either side of the road. The slaves huddled, offering prayers, groaning, while the holy man pranced, lifting his thin paws to heaven. The overseers began to swear in fear. For the rain did not come.

Thunder sounded again, directly overhead. Two lightning bolts crossed the sky and seemed to meet, exploding—somewhere in the forest a tree jetted into new fire. A blazing stem sprawled across the road. The slaves screamed and milled. The guards roared for the water barrels to be released, and struck out with their lashes, to little avail. A flash of water became steam as the fire drank it in.

Fire was everywhere. Even the sky was full of it—raining fire not liquid.

Retreating from the holocaust, a Free Zakorian stumbled against the madman's cart. Looking up, he saw the dark golden eyes reflecting lightning. The Zakorian backed away. He remembered which line this man inherited, the very legend over his head proclaimed it—a Storm Lord.

Just then, between the terror of fire-forest and electric sky, a final night-black terror tore loose on the Southern Road.

Someone had been careless at the tethering. Now, savage with its panic, blind in the hood but smelling only conflagration, hearing only the gongs of heaven, the younger palutorvus had broken from its traces. Men scattered away. One not sufficiently swift was tossed, pulped like ripe fruit, as the mighty feet trampled over him.

Scorched, sightless, stupid with fear, the palutorvus bore on. Lightning stabbed into the forest. A white instant showed the giant beast, seeming massive as a mountain. Slaves jumped desperately aside, into fire, which for a moment seemed preferable.

The only motionless impediment was the wedged cart and the man shackled within it.

The stampeding palutorvus hit the cart it could not see. The wooden sides burst apart, the wheels whirled across the stones. The cibbawood post bolted to the floor of the cart snapped away, catching as it fell between the monster's limbs. It seemed Raurm Am Ralnar, bound to that post, would be trampled like the Zakorian. Something else happened. The chains, producing slack as the post was ripped out, had become tangled in the animal's matted under-hair and the trails of rope which were the remnants of its tethers.

Unable to rid itself of this senseless thing, hung at its belly like weird young, the palutorvus veered desperately sideways, plunging abruptly off the road. The last of the cart disintegrated before it. Directionless and crazed, the beast drove against the very wall of the inferno, and parted it. Into the burning jungle, itself burning, the giant lurched, the post and the chained man dragged with it, and was gone.

When the rain began it sank in a heavy curtain. The madman lay beneath it, and let his body drink.

The animal which had carried him had rushed for many miles, a great voiceless engine. The mobile tent of its body had shielded him from the fire, the forest. And the jungle had given way before the animal, as the fire had ultimately given way. In the thick moisture-mist of the jungle's gut, the incendiary lights had died from its back. Somewhere it had sloughed its burden, or the claws of the jungle had torn the burden away.

He had been stunned through much of the flight, by repeated blows, smoke, speed. Only now, under the downpour, did he recall he was alive. Then he turned on his side, for the rains of the north and west could drown a man on his back. He thought, too, to open his mouth and let it drink with his flesh and his bones.

The madman was yet a madman. For him, there was neither past nor present, and no future. His brain was all mosaic. Here an icon which was a girl, hair like rubies, here something like a black wall, and the sea beyond. Or there a merchant who was begging to be spared the blade's edge. Or a silver coin, spinning. It did not irk him. None of it had a name, a start, an end, a purpose. None of it demanded anything of him.

But now, although he did not begin to reason, yet there was some sort of curious change. What was it?

The madman came to his feet and looked about through the shadowy forest, washed by rain as if by ocean.

When the rain stopped, he was walking. It did not concern him where. Sometimes he touched the trees, interested by them. Sometimes he touched his own face. His hands had been wrapped in chains, which were gone, all but some bits of metal still adhering, clanking about him, not constraining him at all. The madman did not theorize upon this. How the post, uprooted, discarded, had uncoiled the chains, and he, rolling from under the great beast, had uncoiled them further. The securing links had given way when the bolts in the cart did so. He had only needed eventually to crawl out of them, as out of the creeper under the trees.

He had forgotten the Zakorians also.

The bluish storm sun went down behind his left shoulder, but he did not note it. Black monkeys with faces like white butterflies watched from the terraces of the boughs sixty feet up. He saw a mask, half black, half white. He saw a man with black hair, and a black pearl.

There came to be a particular shadow, very tall and dense. While he did not recollect it, he sensed acquaintance.

The palutorvus shambled between the trees which, at some juncture, had relieved it of the blinding hood. Too long a captive of men, it grazed the sap-laden leaves, sighing, lost.

When the smaller creature advanced, the palutorvus turned to it, expecting guidance, the goad or the sweetmeat: Order. It had been trained to bear men, even on its back, and despite the smart of its blisters, it soon knelt. The man did not mount it for some time, staying beside it, touching it. But then the man did go up on to the great back, catching at vines to aid himself.

The palutorvus rose with a feeling of calm, appeased.

Some conceivably involuntary pressure was interpreted as a command.

Riding the primeval beast, the madman slept, dreaming still the mosaic, and the moon filled the forest.

Days and nights were swilled from the world.

The beast moved onward, sometimes pausing to graze the foliage. The madman, too, grazed on the leaves and grasses. Some were fragrant, others musty, or bitter, and these he spat out.

He saw a blue enameled snake embracing an indigo tree.

He saw the sun, and believed it had wings and was a child. Or the moon, and it had a boy's face and closed eyes.

Sometimes there was water, and he drank, and the beast sluiced up the water and bathed both of them.

He felt its sadness. He pitied it. But he did not know he felt pity.

Days and nights.

It seemed he had lived for hundreds of years.

The madman dreamed he was on a river. Someone cut him with a knife, a shallow cut, and the cut healed. But then he was cut again. And then on the sixth day—in the dream—there was a challenge.

He had no password; he simply stood looking at the three men, seeing them with more than his eyes. They breathed out oaths at the color of his hair, which—in the dream—was nearly white. They told him they would take him where he wished to be.

When he woke up, the madman laughed.

The palutorvus grazed the leaves.

They had come over five hundred wandering miles and did not, either of them, know it.

And they went on.

Rarnammon, hero and king, had built a city in Thaddra once, but it lay in ruins.

The jungles clung close to the valley where the city rested, and had entered its streets. It was a white city but the jungle blackened it. Its name was lost. In forgotten antique tales, Rarnammon, whose own name had, in the beginning, been only Rarn, called it for his birthplace. Which was, depending on the version, Mon or Emon, or Memon.

It had, for centuries now, been the lair of thieves and outlaws.

Tuab Ey, sprawling like a cat to soak up the sun on the high roof, shaded his eyes and began to credit what he had taken for an illusion.

A piece of the jungle-forest was indeed progressing along the wide pale thoroughfare thirty broken walls away down the slope. But it was not, after all, a fantastically moving plant. It was a shadow-beast.

"Look, Galud. What is that?"

Galud, unhandsome, as Tuab Ey was not, scowled from under their awning of sacks. Galud was sun-shy, for he had Tarabine blood, but he had also the long clear sight of his unknown sailor father.

"By my half-wit gods, a palutorvus."

"I thought," said Tuab Ey, "such beasts were all extinct."

"Farther south, the swamps're full of the things. The Free Zakorians use them for dray-animals." Galud and another man spat, as even Thaddrian cutthroats would do at mention of Zakoris-In-Thaddra.

"It looks big," said Tuab Ey nonchalantly. "It looks as if it's coming here. Shall we run away?"

His men laughed at the ritual idea of their young leader in retreat. He was junior to most of them, but fierce as a kalinx. Pretty as one, too. Tall and slim, he had a lot of Dortharian mixed in his genes. His bandit garments were tattered, revealing a compactly muscled cinnamon skin that had collected only a handful of thin and seemly scars. The raging noon sun on his hair found copper—there might be a Lowland strain somewhere, though his eyes were black as the trees beyond Rarnammon's ruined city. The earring in his ear was new. It had been carved from the tooth of a man, a Thaddric freak nearly half again his own height, that he killed in a fray in a town to the north. The freak had been friends with a petty king of the region. Tuab Ey and his men had prudently departed.

Galud said, "There's a fellow up on that monster's back."

"I thought so," said Tuab Ey.

The palutorvus, ambling through a crumbling arch, knocked down most of the wall on either side. It came into a garden, once the pleasaunce of princes, and began to eat the vines. The man partly lying on its back seemed unconcerned. He did not glance their way. He could not be of their kind. Each renegade holed up in nameless Memon established his territory. Only two days ago, they had fought a rival pack of robbers to keep this tottering palace. The dead bodies, all the interlopers', had been flung down a handy dry well, over there in the garden where the palutorvus was feeding.

Tuab Ey was leaving the roof.

Galud, and the other lieutenant, the One-Eared, fell into precautionary step behind him.

"Your animal is grazing my pasture," said Tuab Ey, looking up the long hill of the palutorvus, to the man on top. "I trust you're going to pay me."

"Tuab," said Galud softly. "Can't you see? He's crazy."

Tuab Ey had begun to consider it. Thaddrians tended to be

superstitious of madness—the Smitten of Gods was what they called the insane. But the Dortharian sophistication of his father made him only scornful. Scornfully, then, even as Galud and the One-Eared affected religious signs, Tuab Ey shouted up the length of the beast: "Are you getting off, or do I throw a stone to *knock* you off?"

Then the man turned and looked down at him.

The madman's hair, which was black and curling, reached his shoulders, and he was thickly bearded. The sun had been searing the rest of him very dark, but he was not one of Yl's nation. Unless Free Zakorians ever had gold eyes. Even here, there had come to be a wary respect for the yellow races. Their goddess could rise on mountain summits to terrify Her foes. With luck, a lot of luck, She might destroy the Black Leopard of the Zakorian-Accursed.

"Well," said Tuab Ey. "I'm waiting."

But his tone was more dulcet. The madman's Lowlander eyes disconcerted him. A thing he was not used to.

Then the madman altered his position. The palutorvus, taking this as a desire to dismount, which perhaps it was not, kneeled impressively. The madman, taking the kneeling in turn as an enablement to dismount, did so.

The watchers were struck by his limber strength. He had the grace of the professional fighter, and they recognized it at once.

Standing before them, he was taller than Tuab Ey, therefore taller than the others. Even covered in human dirt and the debris of the forests, he was imposing, well-made, coordinated. The loin-guard was familiar to the One-Eared, who had inadvertently served a month with Free Zakorian slave gangs. The thief muttered this knowledge to his leader. But his leader seemed not to hear, only staring at the madman. Finally, Tuab Ey said, "Give me that wine."

The One-Eared unhooked the flask from his belt. Tuab Ey, not taking his gaze off the madman, received the flask, uncorked it, held it out to him. The madman was a while accepting. Then he drank sparingly and handed back the flask.

Although he did not speak, he no longer looked mad, merely unusual.

"Come, then," Tuab Ey said. His father had actually been an aristocrat absconded after some nefarious act in Dorthar. Tuab Ey now and then reverted to odd displays of breeding. "Be our guest. Follow us. Your—er, your transport will be safe enough here. I doubt if any of our neighbors will try to steal it. The meat, they tell me is awful."

He walked off, and his lieutenants went after him.

Sure enough, the madman followed.

In the great hall of Tuab Ey's appropriated palace, sunset, then dusk, recolored the wall paintings. The ancient hearths were unusable. A fire leapt brightly on the smashed mosaic, its smoke going out adequately through the smashed roof. When it rained, the fire tended to perish.

The nights grew almost chilly in winter. Sometimes snakes or lizards stole up to share their fire. Tuab Ey did not let his men harm them; they amused him. Once a tribe of apes had got in. Tuab Ey, imitating the chief ape's threat-behavior exactly, grunting and jumping up and down, had frightened them off.

Now Tuab Ey sat cross-legged, watching the madman, who sat himself a little apart from them and from the fire. He had been offered food, fruit and vine-shoots, and meat from yesterday's hunt. He had eaten little, and none of the meat. He had been shown the cracked cistern in the courtyard, freshly full of rain. The bandits washed in it when they had the mind; Tuab Ey, the aristocrat's son, bathed there every day. The madman got into the cistern and cleansed himself. One of the robbers they had slaughtered two days before had been tall and athletic. His clothes were offered the madman, who donned them, ignoring, or uncaring at the knife rent over the heart.

Now, dressed as a bandit, by a bandits' fire, the madman who, perhaps, should have been at home with such things, regarded the air, seeing sights invisible.

Tuab Ey rose, walked to the madman, and sat down again.

"I've a razor and fat, if you want to shave."

The madman did not respond.

Tuab Ey went on watching him.

One of his men said, "Tuab's in love with the Smitten of Gods."

Tuab Ey said, "Each to his own. Is it the frieze of naked girls in the fifth court, or the seventh, that you lie under and play with yourself?"

They laughed. They started to talk about women they had had, or boys.

When the madman got to his feet and walked out, they looked, but that was all. Only Tuab Ey, smiling at them like the proffered razor, went after him.

And like a kalinx, only Tuab Ey pursued his guest up and

down the palace, over the ruined stairs, across the subsiding
terraces. When the madman paused, so did Tuab Ey. And when
he continued, Tuab Ey continued.

Rarnammon, said the stones of nameless Memon.

Rem, Rarn, Rarmon, Rarnammon, said the heights and depths
of the city at every window-place and balcony.

The wind soughed through the forest and through the vents of
towers.

Rarnammon, said the wind.

In each chamber, the wall paintings came alive. He saw
the orgiastic feastings, the women in their gauzes, the men with
the leathers and draperies of another time, the chalices wide
enough to swim in, brimmed by wine. He heard the moaning of
unremembered instruments, and the love-cries of those who
coupled on the cushions—sounds which never change. He beheld sacrifice to a dragon-headed god which grasped lightnings
in its hands. He was witness to an army, marching like armored
smoke through the boulevards of the city, war music clashing
and the sunlight of ghost-day rebounding from spears and chariots.
Rarnammon had taken the continent of Vis and made it one,
every land of Vis bound in fealty to himself. He was the first to
bear the title 'Storm Lord'. Yet his eyes were Lowlander's eyes.

The madman was Rarnammon. A golden-eyed Vis.

Tribute was brought to him, endless streams of men on their
knees or faces, heaps of jewels, bars of metal, weapons,
slaves—He felt the heat of noon on his skin in the chill of night,
and the female kiss of silk against him, where the rough cloth
lay.

"Storm Lord," they said.

But he walked through a colonnade, and saw in at a window.
A woman was rocking a child in a cradle, passionlessly, for
something to do. And the child stared at her with an aloof
distrust to match her own. It was Lyki. She was young, and the
child was himself. And then he saw her again, in some other
surrounding—a tent it seemed to be, and she clutched the child
he was to her, hating him and in need. And someone had said:
"If I were to say to you, Lyki, that I would spare your life on
one condition, that condition being that I take your child and rip
it open with this sword, you would let me do it, for this is how
you are made." And now that someone who spoke, who was
Raldnor his father, said to her, "Your death would be useless.
Therefore, you shall not die."

And then it was raining, and he passed through the gate of the red house on Slope Street, in Karmiss.

It was not difficult to traverse the house, and reach the tiny anteroom and so the bedroom. The merchant was not there, out or away. Lyki lay in the bed. She was colorless, her darkness, even her dark hair, seemed drained to monochrome. She pleated the coverings with her fingers, her mouth turned in and down as he had always recollected it. For a moment she seemed flaccid, something cast adrift on the shores of life, soon to be reclaimed by the hunger of the sea. But then she caught sight of him, and she revived.

"So," she said. "*So.* You steeled yourself, you put off all the more important things, and came after all. Well. I never thought you would. Money, yes. I thought your guilt and shame might drive you to that. But to waste your precious person on me. *Well.* I am amazed."

He stood before her, knowing her. Still.

"Well," she said. She grimaced, feverish with her excitement and her spite. "An honor. The Prince Kesarh Am Xai's own henchman, and here in my bedchamber. Did you bring any more ankars? The physician's no good. He prescribes this and that, but it doesn't help me. *He*—" she meant the merchant, her protector— "has gone off to a tavern. He swears I make his own illness worse with mine. Well," she said, "men have always treated me badly. And you, my son, you never loved me. Never."

He moved forward, coming up beside the bed, and looked down at her. She was near to death, he had seen this expression on other faces, a concentration beyond her will on some inner perspective, which was death itself.

"You look older," she said. She seemed suddenly afraid. "What has he done to you? How can you look older? At Zastis you were here, whipped, disgraced—for more than a year I see nothing of you and then you crawl to me, vomit on my floor, put me to difficulty ad expense—"

"Mother," he said. He spoke quietly, but it stopped her. Perhaps she had never heard this in his voice before. He himself did not quite comprehend it. Compassion, forbearance, but not pity and not hate.

And then she began to weep. The tears gushed from her eyes, and he wondered that she had the strength left to cry.

"I beat you," she said. "You were wicked and deserved it, but I beat you. I should not have beaten you. I shouldn't have hurt you so."

"The Amanackire say, What we have done is the past; reiterate the deed, or dismiss the deed."

"No. I beat you. I hurt you. I'll be punished."

"You were punished," he said. "Do you remember him, Raldnor son of Rehdon, Elect of the goddess? Do you remember in that tent under Koramvis the night before the last battle? He told you what no mortal thing should ever have to hear, he told you he saw the evil in you, as if you were the only creature in the world that had evil in it. And because he made you know your littleness and your viciousness and your selfishness—which is in every one of us, mother, and in him, in Raldnor, too, when he was a man—because he made you know all that, where most of us can keep ourselves from knowing and so hope for something better, you hoped for nothing of yourself, and became simply what he had told you that you were."

She stared through her tears. Her mouth was open, as if she would gasp in what he said to her.

"It doesn't matter," he said, "anything you did to me. You gave me my life. What I do with my life is my concern, not yours, nor can you be blamed for it. But I thank you for the giving."

"Rem," she said, "I'm dying."

"Wherever you go," he said, "you'll be free of this."

"Are you dead?" she whispered. "Rem—have you come to lead me?"

He knew from the name she called him, and the name she had had for Kesarh, from the room, from the sensation of the atmosphere and season, that he had retrogressed, eight or nine years. She had died in Karmiss long ago and he had not heard of it. As he had ridden on Kesarh's business to Ankabek, Lyki had finished her battle with the earth. And probably he only imagined this. It was not possible to go back. She had ended alone.

But he said, "There's nothing to be afraid of. The other side of life is only life."

She frowned, taking the words into herself. She was still puzzling when the final breath went from her. And then her face smoothed over, as if she knew it all. He closed her eyes. Her lips remained a little parted, but no longer wizened or turned down.

He stepped away, and saw Doriyos standing in a colonnade, holding out to him a cup of wine.

But when he took the cup it was Yannul's son, Lur Raldnor, who had offered it. Then the cup touched his lip. He tasted not wine, but water.

"You will bring yourself to yourself again," said Ashni. "At the proper hour."

A skin seemed to tear, across his sight, across his entire body. The dismemberment was painless but total, and the whole of it lifted away and was gone.

He lost nothing, only this, which had come between him and existence. He understood who he was and how he came there, all that had been, everything he had participated in, even the death of Lyki.

And he understood also who the elegant bandit was, standing with him in the rain in the colonnade. So he drank the wine, which had a wine taste now, and nodded.

"Thank you, Tuab Ey."

"Ah," said Tuab Ey. His eyes were wide, but he added flippantly, "And who in Aarl are you?"

"Your guest."

"Called?"

"You may not accept my name, seeing we're here."

"Try," said Tuab Ey, and waited as if he would wait forever.

And having become himself, he said quietly, "The son of Raldnor Am Anackire, the brother of Raldanash, Storm Lord of Dorthar."

The wide eyes could widen no farther, so they half-shut.

"I've heard of you. Rarmon Am Karmiss."

But he said: "My name is Rarnammon. After the King who built the city."

"You lost your prey, Kathus."

"No, my lord. Free Zakoris lost him."

"Zakoris," said Yl, "does not trouble too much."

Kathus showed nothing, which was not uncommon. He was able to conceal disappointment, if he was disappointed. He had lost Raurm son of Ralnar in the moment Raurm's sanity gave way. The plummet into Thaddra's jungles was only a formality.

When the fire smothered in the rain, those that could do so went in search. The blundering track of the palutorvus was at first very evident, but later less so. They picked up fragments of chain and wood. In the end, there had been a succession of clearings, and here they were deceived and the trail eluded them. By Yl's order, the overseers were beaten with rods, but not put to death. From this, you told he did not rate the misadventure very highly.

"Probably, my Kathus, the beast headed for the swampy ground, and the Prince was sucked under there."

"Probably."

"We shall see to it Dorthar receives tidings of demise. Yes?" Kathus acquiesced.

They had gained the end of the stone corridor that ran beneath the palace at Ylmeshd. A great door of trunks braced with bronze was hauled aside. The King and his Counselor entered the cave temple of Rorn.

Free Zakoris had decided to honor all the old ways.

Three male slaves were to be drowned in the sea pool before the god's altar. The King would not officiate, these were minor ceremonies.

The thickset priests, naked to the waist and kilted in long folds of leather, waded into the pool. As they forced the struggling men under and held them there amid a chaos of churned water, Kathaos Am Alisaar looked on, impervious, polite.

Violent murder did not oppress him, and he was not superstitious. And yet Free Zakoris offended him aesthetically and in most other ways. He had sunk to this, and knew it.

He pondered idly, as the churnings in the water faded, if Dorthar was worth such dealings in brutish mindlessness, or if he would even have Dorthar, when everything was said and done. The long game had failed him so far. Why not once more? Was the extraordinary happening in the jungle a foretaste of failure—as a similar happening had been, almost thirty years ago?

There was a sudden tiresome inertia on him. He knew no trade but this, intriguer, game-player that he was. He could not live any other way, so was condemned.

Shaved if not shorn, the man with a king's name, who claimed to be the son and brother of kings, began entirely to resemble one himself. He moved among the robbers with ease, yet they were aware of a superiority—nothing he set on them, only something which was. If what he had told Tuab Ey was correct, then he would be used to command. Grudgingly, they acknowledged it, and grudgingly, growling a little, gave him room, picked no quarrel. The passing of the madness was wonder enough. And he could obviously handle himself if it came to a fight. Altogether they fared better with the palutorvus, which they regarded as a symbol of status to their adversaries, and had made into something of a pet.

Rarnammon, anyway, was not much with them.

He walked about the ruined city, almost as if seeking some hidden thing. This interested them rather. Maybe there was a cache of gems or gold or arms he knew of and they did not. But seeing Tuab Ey tended to go about with him, and Galud not much behind, they must trust to that.

In the first days, Rarnammon quartered the city. Tuab Ey acted as a guide, for he had come here more than once, alone or with his pack. The land rose and fell in the valley, and the ancient streets ran up and down in humps and hollows. Here and there were the bandit nests, standing houses or mansions that had been possessed and now held long enough to merit the chief's label upon them—Scarecrow's Villa, Jort's Wall. When cook-smoke went up, they were in residence. To the west, where the jungle had encroached most vehemently and only a few frames of masonry stayed upright, there was a small leper colony. It had its own well, and kept to itself for fear of instant spearing. On the white alleys, the ochre figures moved weightlessly, dying shadows without faces.

At noon, seated on a high terrace, Tuab Ey pointed out a certain flower that was commencing to nose its way up through the paving.

"The year's turning, Rarnammon. Over the mountains the ice will be starting to heave and crack."

"And when the sea's open," said Galud, who was watering a pillar, "the Leopard moves north, east, west and south."

"The war will get here. But you'll be going back to Dorthar to meet it?" said Tuab Ey.

"No," said Rarnammon.

Tuab Ey said lazily, "He'll need you, won't he, your illustrious brother?"

"Yes," said Rarnammon. "Not necessarily beside him."

"Enigma."

"Fact."

"Well? I'm your host, remember. Tell me."

Rarnammon, who was looking down, a long slow look, at the city, smiled. He did not say anything.

Galud stood scowling at them, and then walked from the terrace and some way off. He supposed they were lovers and was jealous, although his own coital inclinations did not run that way.

Tuab Ey stretched himself out for the sun.

"So, you won't tell me anything."

"I shall find a suitable place and remain alone there. Wait."

"For what?"

"I don't know. I only know what I've told you."

"You're a mystic, then."

"Maybe."

Tuab Ey moved on to his belly, leaning up on his elbows. He stared at Rarnammon until, feeling the powerful gaze, the elder man turned.

"You said alone. Or shall I come too, and act your page, lord King's son?"

Initially he did not know what Rarnammon would do now it was said, and Tuab Ey experienced again the unaccustomed, uncanny sensation that was like awe. But then Rarnammon grinned, and the grin made him very young.

"A mystic remains celibate," he said. Tuab Ey found himself grinning too, charmed or provoked into it. And then Rarnammon turned away again toward the north. "My father was in Thaddra," he said. "If he didn't transmute into fire or ether, then he's still there, somewhere. Part of the stones, perhaps, or the black light through the trees."

Tuab Ey shivered in the bright heat of noon.

"My own father," he said, "had dealings of escape with a slave-trader, whose name was Bandar. Bandar, whom I saw as a child, was a fat and insalubrious oaf. He had one story he always forced on everyone. How he carried Astaris into Thaddra as a slave—not his fault, of *course*—and she was pregnant with Raldnor's child." Rarnammon did not glance about at him, but he was listening. Tuab Ey continued deftly. "There was another story, of a wolf child, in the northern forests—you know, a baby left with wolves and reared by them to be a wolf. Except wolves are scarce this side of the mountains. More likely wild dogs. But the child was said to be supernatural, white as pearl and winged, with a star on her forehead—" He stopped because Rarnammon had softly laughed. "Well, I never believed a word of it," said Tuab Ey, and gave himself up again to the sun.

TWENTY-TWO

The eastern ice began to break. It was like the sound of the earth tearing apart.

In Dorthar, as the marble world gave way, mankind began to move more plentifully on its surface. Through mud and milky rains, a small caravan ploughed toward the capital, Anackyra. Then skirted it, made on toward the hills, Koramvis, the Lake of

Ibron, where they said a mighty statue lay asleep; Anackire, dreaming. . . . The poor wagons were escorted by soldiery of the Storm Lord, which seemed to have been sent to meet them. In the villages and towns they passed, the blazon of the Serpent and Cloud was sighted and remarked upon. Occasional strange rumors flew back and forth. A poisoned well had been found clean, after the caravan had stopped beside it. A woman going out to mourn her dead returned without her sorrow. Someone sick had been cured, after the shadow of something, a cart or a snake, had gone over him as he wandered at the roadside.

A group of Amanackire were seen riding toward the hills above Anackyra.

There was a faint shock on the plain, in the city. Nothing gave way. Many did not feel it.

Vencrek, privately approaching his King, with whom he had spent time but never precisely known when they were children at Vathcri, said, "Raldanash, you can tell me anything about these tales of a priestess given royal escort to the ruin up there?"

Raldanash said, "The tales are true."

"Who is she?"

"A priestess, as you said."

"There's a lot of common talk—"

"Yes," said Raldanash, with one of the rare flashes of humor, "there often is." And then, quite lightly, conducting the Warden to the great table-board which described, approximately, the surface of Vis, Raldanash began to discuss with him the strategies of war. They shifted the small carved galleys, and the units of men and cavalry about, with wands of ivory. Such plans of attack as offered had been revised since Prince Rarmon's traitorous withdrawal—or abduction. Spies had brought word he was dead. This too might be a lie.

Although he had got no answer to his curiosity, Vencrek succumbed to the charisma of his King. While some part of him stood sophisticatedly aloof, the cousin from Vathcri was yet flattered and warmed to play war-games alone with Raldanash. It did indeed, rather disgracefully, become a boys' game in the end. Drinking the mulled wine, briskly deploying the ships, the Lord Warden consented to be Free Zakoris, and sometimes Karmiss, to the Storm Lord's Dorthar. When Vencrek lost he let out a boy's roar of outrage, and then caught the joke. "By Ashkar. Let's hope they play as messily as I do." And heard Raldanash laugh, which was more of a rarity even than wry humor. And remembered he loved him, a male love, not sexual,

love of the blood, love of the honor and the steadfast integrity of
Raldnor's son.

And when, later, Raldanash fell asleep before the columned
hearth, as if immensely tired, Vencrek looked at the beautiful
unhuman face, touched and almost angry at being so trusted.

In Ommos the Dortharian garrison had been increased. Four
and a half thousand of the Storm Lord's men augmented the
Ommish defenses. There was also a company of mixes, almost
two thousand strong, and freelance mercenary units, Vathcrians
and Tarabines, though the pure Shansarians had gone away.

Ommos was afraid.

The last war had raked her over. Like Zakoris, she too had
been scourged and shamed, but Ommos had none of the valor of
Yl's long wish to fight back, only the suppuration of puny
hatred. She feared the Sister Continent men who were there to
help her, as she feared her own Lowlander Guardian and the
white-haired King in Dorthar. The hero Raldnor had remained
anathema to Ommos. No one loved her and she loved none.
Only in corners, where a peculiar radiance had brushed in passing,
had the mood softened and strengthened in different form. In the
alleys of Hetta Para some still spoke of a long-haired religious—a
boy, the dream must be translated—who was tolerant and kind to
them. Zarok had been shown in another guise. The image of
Anackire, which had likewise been shown and which, some said,
had left an imprint on walls, had also in a mysterious way *been*
Zarok. It was explainable as a female alter ego, which they
could respect at last, the cloak of the god.

But these pockets of retention and strength were small. Ommos
had never been fertile soil for things of light. A fire-worshipper,
she had lost even the light of her fires. They were dulled by
blood. She was like Free Zakoris, too, in that.

In Xarabiss, Thann Xa'ath had not hung back, as his father
had, waiting to see how the cat might jump before he moved.

Then again, the fiasco of Ulis Anet's escapade with her guard
commander had brought considerable embarrassment. Though
Xa'ath did not entirely accept the case as presented—there were
other notions, (she had in some way annoyed Raldanash and
been quietly smothered?)—yet he was obliged to observe diplomatic rules. Thann Xa'ath must act, therefore, as if owing an
apology to Dorthar. He brought his army smartly into the field,
and dispatched a vassal's token four thousand troops to Raldanash,
to deploy as he saw fit. They were on the march before the snow

was gone. Slung with spitting braziers, they tramped through the endless rain of the thaw. Thirty men were lost in a boiling river near the Ommos border. But it had been necessary to bustle this spring.

Thann Xa'ath had insufficient imagination to dwell on the price of defeat. He operated the engine of war pragmatically. His court, ostensibly, kept pace.

But out in the crystal cities, in their theaters, pleasure-houses, wine-shops, the talk and the imagery were more honest, or more illuminating. The plays put on were froth—farces, with often a bitter sting in the tail. Acrobats walked wires above the mouths of starving tirr. Escape; dancing with death. Conversation conveyed actual peril. Seers cried aloud in the streets that doom approached. No one laughed. All would be beaten flat, rinsed with blood, with flame—ashes.

There was nowhere to run to.

Even so, as the spring unlocked the roads, they streamed away, to villas, to farms, to remote plains and isolate hills, aristocrat and beggar alike.

Perhaps here, or there, the black and taloned paw would not find them out.

It was a curious fact. Most of them boasted a victory for Dorthar and the Middle Lands. None of them seemed able to trust in it.

Free Zakoris wanted, and would *have*. Karmiss, the unknown crouching thing, would go for the throat of whichever went down.

A few privately commandeered vessels put out to sea, making on battered sails for the Sister Continent. The weather was uncertain. No word came back from them. Nor any word or ship from those who had voyaged from Thos at the summer's end.

Southward, the southern extremity of Vis: The Lowlands. It had remained generally a kind of desert, still. And here, the mantle of the snow yet held awhile. On the wide plains the villages had drawn in to themselves as they had always done, tight, unburgeoning pads behind their stockades, revealing no aptitude for spring, let alone politics. Closer to Xarabiss, the towns of the Plains—famous Hamos, coastal Moiyah and part-built Hibrel, having molded to the northern spirit, and the ways from over the ocean, had formed their armies long since. Dortharian and Vathcrian war leaders had drilled their men winter through in the stone courts. Even a band of Shansarian berserkers had remained, a couple of thousand men, at a camp a mile or so from Moiyah. There was a small Shansar fleet as well, thirty swan ships, ice-choked on the beaches there. But gossip said they would, troops and galleys both, be off to Shansarian Alisaar, when once the seas relented.

It was also known that with the thaw Dortharian troops would be garrisoned at Moiyah. She had come to represent a key position to the west and would certainly be threatened. So far the numbers were not noised abroad.

Of the arcane city, the ruin, nothing much was said. It was thought to be no prize either for Zakorian Leopard or Karmian jackal. Already fallen, hiding no treasures, unstrategic—it was left to its own devices, its own silences.

Report suggested certain villages of the southern south had packed up and traveled there wholesale, as had happened three decades before. For sanctuary, presumably.

An itinerant hunter, having come northwest to Moiyah, enlisting under one of the Vathcrian commands there, regaled his battalion—Lowland men, men of the other continent, mixes, Xarabs—with an inexplicit memory of something seen in or near the ruin, over the snow.

He was strongly called to account by his Vathcrian captain.

"I can't say, sir." A Lowlander and a peasant, knowing the linguistics of the dark races, his childhood spent with little speech, much telepathy, he seemed now calmly at a loss. "It was sunrise. The light hit the flank of the city—or maybe it was some other thing—it was far off, sir, perhaps only rocks or trees. But there looked to be great towers of gold."

The Vathcrian, who was younger than the hunter, anxious and furious at the war, needing to fight something he could see and hack, rejoined:

"We're up against a hell of a thing here, soldier. We don't need visions and dreams and make-believe. We need guts and an army. No snow-mirage ever won a war. Do you understand?"

The hunter who was now a soldier said that he did.

Only later did the Vathcrian realize he had inadvertently communed in his home-tongue. The Lowlander, ignorant of it, had got the sense by reading his mind.

Across the Inner Sea, Alisaar, the Shansarian fortress, stared in all directions. Carved ships patrolled her waters, up and down, up and down, over and over, like clockwork things. The snow had only sugared her eastern and southern edges, as always. But the voracious winds of the cold months had lashed her. In the Ashara temples Shansar had set up, prophecies were made and auguries read. A secret worship had commenced, native Alisaar going back to her own gods, if she had ever left them.

Across the incoherent border, Old Zakoris, Sorm of Vardath's dainty from the Lowland War, had also manned every perimeter. The three brief lands, Iscah, Ott and Corhl, had been sworn to vassalage twenty-five years before, and were substantially under Vardian influence. But Alisaar had become an unknown element to the south. North, the watchtowers eyed the Thaddrian borders; mountains, forest. Particular attention was paid to that threat of Yl's South Road.

Where Vardian Zakoris mountainously touched Dorthar, the passes were held by mutual armies. On the Dortharian side, the Storm Lord had instigated several Vathcrian companies, who now tended to squabble with Sorm's Vardish men. One forgot, but Vathcri and Vardath, at home, had once been traditional enemies themselves.

In Old Zakoris, the Zakorian race had prospered under Sorm. He had not deprived them of their religion either, and the fire and water gods still exalted there, if no longer in some of their more brutal rites. Nevertheless, Zakoris was Zakoris. They had the same blood as the Black Leopard of Zakoris-In-Thaddra. Soon they would be called upon to slaughter their racial brothers, even, in some cases, their actual brothers. They had not deserted with or to Yl, which to the Leopard must be the unforgivable crime. A conqueror, he would give no quarter. The Mother-Kingdom would be destroyed. Not one stone would stand upon another, nor one skin upon one set of bones.

And so, belatedly, several did desert, somehow evading the watches and patrols, getting over the mountains or through the jungles into Thaddra, hurrying to Yl's standard. Others simply ran—to Alisaar, to Dorthar—where they were betrayed and arrested instantly. Or into Thaddra also, but merely to be lost, as Thaddra's custom was.

But it could not be told enough: In the end there was and would be nowhere to run to. This war was a wave, the world an open shore.

In Thaddra the sea was never obdurate. Snow, to Thaddra as to Zakoris, was only an infrequent crown upon some distant miles-high mountain.

The Leopard, feeling the spice-wind of spring, stretched itself.

The two great fleets, one hundred and three ships, one hundred and twenty-seven, flexed themselves in the deep-water bays. Farther northeastward, a scout fleet of fifteen vessels peeled off from the larger units, sentinel, waiting. With the coming of softer weather, others already drove toward the eastern seas.

On the South Road, the cadavers of slaves made paving. It would never be done in time, yet the whips bit and the flames ate up the trees. Charred birds made sacrifice to Zarduk.

In Ylmeshd the minor ceremonies were ended.

The cave of Rorn was already flooded by a valve, and sealed, left afloat with drowned beasts and men, who would now decompose to the satisfaction of the god. A young priest of Rorn, inspired by the drugged incense and the cries and the gongs, had flung himself down from a high ledge as the sea started to come in. Independent immolation was always pleasing to a deity. The omen was good.

As a heavy sunset began to consume Ylmeshd, King Yl entered in turn the temple of Zarduk, by its city-door.

It was already midnight in the cavern, but as Yl advanced— preceded by priests, followed by his kindred, his commanders, a tail of slaves, and a black-lacquered box, windowless and man-sized, borne high—brands burst into tall red leaf.

The last fire was uncovered as curtains of black hide were dragged away. Zarduk appeared, a carved stone, twelve feet in height, massively underlit by his own fiery intestines. He was finer than he had been, for they had gilded him recently with much melted gold, hung him with golden rings. It was his portion of the loot from Ankabek.

He did not have the ancient ugliness of Ommos, this engoldened fire god from the west. He possessed not only a head, but shoulders and a torso. His hands were sculpted flat against the skirt of his garment, seeming to grasp the furnace of his vitals.

They brought swamp leopards to him, ten of them, and ten men cut their throats. The blood steamed and stank.

Yl, himself clad in the pelts of black leopards, a collar of rubies, a pectoral with onyx and sardonyx, moved to the hewn step before the god. He took a knife from a priest, and slicing his own arm, the King let fall his blood into the hissing flames of Zarduk.

A growl of approval rose about the temple. Priests came instantly to stanch the wound.

Yl went to the statue's side, and the priests brought him the mask of hammered brass that he must now put on. When he was adorned in it, had been amalgamated into it, he became an entity of the god, a priest himself. The gathering saw as much, and did him reverence. Yl pointed, and a slave approached, carrying an enormous topaz. It was dirty, the topaz, or obscured from within. It did not glitter in the torchlight or the glare of Zarduk's guts, even when laid on the ground where the length of the god finished.

Yl poured wine now, over the topaz, as if to wash it.

It did not change.

Yl pointed again. The closed black box that had followed him in was brought forward and put down, and its hinged doors were lifted up.

After a few moments, a figure came from the box.

It was a youth, perhaps sixteen, slim yet strong. He was, at first glance, true Zakoris, velvet black of skin, hair and eyes. But there was a handsomeness in the features Zakoris had almost weeded out. The nose had never been splayed, the nostrils were proud and wide, winking with gold. His lips were full, a thing not racially usual; nor was he scarred.

There were golden circles round his ankles, arms, wrists. Otherwise he was naked.

His eyes, dreamy, almost blind—a narcotic—were fixed on nothing.

Drums beat. From behind the Zarduk, two girls emerged, fire on their hair and polished flesh.

They danced, invited, writhed. They ventured to the naked man, caressed him and drew him down, against the skirt of the statue.

The Zakorians looked on, soundless. This ritual too, was old as the Old Kingdom.

A girl lay under him, her hair across the Topaz, in the blood and wine. He parted her thighs, pierced her. As he strove, the red light of the oven of the god strove with him, along his back, buttocks, legs. The other girl stretched against him, her body moving with his, her fingers and her mouth urging him, pressing him to the brink, inexorable.

As he arched, both women arched with him, two curious shadows flung from his silhouette against the light. Orgasm, the magic energy. When he sank down, the women slid and rolled away, and like shadows still, faded through the light and were gone.

His seed was holy. The girl he had chosen to mate with would be examined in due course. If she were with child, this omen also would be propitious.

But now the priests came and turned him, so his face was toward the cavern's ceiling. He stayed as motionless as if he slept.

Again, the priests had given Yl a knife, broader than the other.

Despite what they had fed him, as the knife went in, the sacrificial victim shrieked—but if with shock or pain was impossible to devine. The cries, oddly remote and unhuman, went on, for the first blow did not kill. This, like the rest, was ritual, old as the name of Zakoris. The viscera, disengaged, were flung into the belly of the god, a bizarre juxtaposition. The cries faltered, stopped.

The dying body still twitched, however, as they poured the oils upon it. It was proper some life should remain—Yl had been skillful and swift. A torch was cast. The image of the victim erupted in a gout of flame.

At last, the Free Zakorians shouted.

Zarduk had been honored and would remember them.

Beyond the burning sacrifice, against the burning statue, filmed now with smoke and gore, the topaz which had been the Eye of Anackire looked on.

In Karmiss, there were tiny golden flowers craning to drink the rain in the garden courtyard. Ulis Anet, bending to gaze at them, knew the harbor of Istris, now less than half a day away, would be open.

She had had a premonition Kesarh would come here today, perhaps tomorrow. He had ridden out one further time during the long snow. She had not expected him. She was given over to despair that afternoon, lying in her bed, unable to tolerate any physical evidence of self which arising would force on her. One of the attendants ran in first. And then he—like a storm from somewhere—moved into the room and filled it; electricity and darkness. "Stay where you are," he said. He even smiled. "What could be better?" He was eager and clever and demanding, just as before. Her own hunger and its release seemed to obliterate her, the death-wish inherent in sex. In the night she woke and he was already gone. She rose and cursed him, true curses, Xarabian and coarse. He had sent her many gifts. She found the latest of these and dashed them all over the room. Some days after, when she failed to menstruate, she thought she was with child and was shaken by an unconscionable horror or triumph, unsure which. But at length, the blood began to come. She made plans to bribe and connive and somehow to get away when the thaw freed the land. She would go to the Lowlands, seek asylum in some obscure temple of Hamos or Hibrel. Val Nardia had been a priestess.

But then she predicted this return, today, tomorrow. Very strangely, she knew she was somewhat telepathically receptive to him, though he had stayed unaware of it, and unreciprocative.

There had been the macabre dream in Dorthar before his men took her—the sunset sea, the shore of ice, she in his arms. She heard much more now her Karmian servants were used to her. He had come back with his dead sister from Ankabek, some soldier had said, holding the corpse as if it slept.

When he arrived, she would welcome him cordially, with all the coolness that could mean. She would not lie with him. If he forced her, she would evince no pleasure even should her flesh condone.

It would mean little to him. Symbolically, for herself, it might redeem. Momentarily.

She had contemplated taking a lover during the long snow alone. Some attractive groom or guard. Kesarh would discover. He might be irritated. He might have the man punished or executed: She did not want the guilt of that.

Often she brooded on Raldanash. Or on Iros. Someone had let slip that Iros had died.

She had learned a great deal about Val Nardia. Ulis Anet was uncertain now if she had questioned so constantly, or if they had only constantly volunteered to inform.

Occasionally, she theorized to herself that she could attempt to murder Kesarh. But this idea was too melodramatic, like everything else, and vexed her.

She watched most of that day at the windows which looked toward Istris. The sky grew tawny, and she did not think he would come after all.

Fifteen minutes later, as they were lighting the lamps, there came the give-away flurry all through the house. She went down to meet him. He should not find her spread out for him tonight, or even malleable.

She was prepared, and when he walked in, she thought, *you see, he's just a man. You are obsessed by him, but he has not allowed you to love him. It can be borne.*

But she avoided his touch and his eyes.

The dinner was served then, in the salon. They spoke desultorily of basics, the needs of the house, the climate. If he was amused, he did not display it. She felt his glance on her, and now and then the intensity of a prolonged stare, which she did not meet.

Inevitably, learning so much of Val Nardia, she had copied her, some of it without knowing.

The dinner ended, and he had not mentioned the bed upstairs. He walked to the hearth and leaned there, drinking wine.

"Tomorrow, I shall be sailing for Lan."

"Lan?" she said, courteously, as if she had never heard of it.

"There seems to be some trouble."

She said nothing, did not care. He had invaded Lan, probably Lan resented it.

"The forthcoming war no longer seems to interest you," he said. "They say on the streets, Free Zakoris could destroy Istris in an hour. The whole island in six days."

"But you are the beloved of Free Zakoris."

"Ah. You do listen, then."

"I shall pray," she said, "that the sea is tempestuous for your crossing."

"It'll take more than salt water to drown me," he said. He emptied his cup and she came solicitously to refill it. "Val Nardia," he said, "often had her hair dressed in that same way. Did they tell you?"

She raised her head and met his eyes then, and said quietly, she did not know why, "Her shade comes to me and instructs me, how to resemble her the most."

"Bleach your skin," he said, "and say 'no.' "

"I shall," she said, "say no."

The blackness of his eyes, live as something pale and molten, bore down on her.

"What a pity," he said, "to have ridden all this way only for supper."

"There are several pretty girls in the house. One of them even dyes her hair red."

He smiled slightly. He seemed to be jesting with her as he said, "Or I'll take you anyway. I sometimes enjoy a little opposition."

"Of course. Do whatever you wish."

"You aren't like her," he said, "at root. Not like her at all. When you consent, when you refuse. When you most remind me of her I can most perceive it's a reminder, nothing more."

"Why am I here then?" He said nothing. She said, "Yes. A man loses a jewel of great worth from a ring. He replaces the jewel with another which, though flawed, will complement the setting. He values it less, but there. The ring is to be worn."

"And she," he said, "could never have thought to frame that so wittily." He drank the rest of the wine. "You know where I'll be sleeping, if not with you. Send some girl along. I leave the choice to you."

An hour later, she herself went to the guest chamber.

In the morning, she told herself this too did not matter, that to prevaricate was senseless. Her body had been pleasured. Why not?

But she could no longer rely upon herself, traitor and liar that she had become.

And to admit this, in itself was another form of traitorousness, as she discovered.

They breakfasted together in the salon. She disliked the normalcy of it, her position fixed: His mistress, with all that title's most dismal connotations. Already, she heard the going about below, his men readying to leave.

When he rode away, what? Another long vacancy, further peering after his sister's phantom, impotent plans.

"Do you," she said, "ever remember me when you're elsewhere?"

He acquiesced amiably. It was a woman's question. He seemed deliberately to miss the sharper point.

"Yes, Ulis. You're my haven."

"From what? The cares and toil of state? But you are in love with those." With the little knife she sliced open a fruit, and looked into the stained glass of pulp and seeds as if to read portents. "Perhaps I should give you some token to remind you of me. A lock of hair. Like the hair that was sent to Iros, to mislead him to his death." She said: "You went to great lengths to obtain me. Am I worth it?"

He rose. He nodded to her, said he must be off, remarked that she was beautiful, and that essentials the house required would be delivered in his absence.

Something absurd happened. "Get out," she said, and her voice was like a cough, and she had snatched the little fruit knife off the table.

She saw she had his attention. He was nonplussed. *She* had done this, maybe—Val Nardia—

But then he turned and walked toward the door. And Ulis Anet hurled the knife after him. It was a wild cast, aimed for no vital spot. It went through his left sleeve, hovered, and dropped spent on the rugs.

He paused. He did not glance at the ripped sleeve, the knife. He moved slowly and came back to her and she, out of character, lost, stood before him waiting vulgarly for some blow. He did not lay a finger on her. Only the eyes struck down. And a few words.

"Tame yourself, lady," he said. "We lack conversation as it is."

"I didn't mean to do such a thing," she said. She was void of expression, or excuse. "It serves no purpose."

"None," he said.

Soon, the door closed, and he was gone.

The trio of ships, thrust by the rain-speared wind, made speed. Then, as Lan's bladed coastline came near, they began to throw a shadow in the north. The tall, knife-edge shape of three Zakorians bore down on them. The Karmian vessels flew merely the Lily. The Zakorians hoisted no flag, but their sails had relinquished the Double Moon and Dragon of the Old Kingdom, and of old piracy. Each wore now the sigil of the Black Leopard.

Kesarh's captain, standing in the bow, said, "Are they after a fight, my lord?"

"You forget, the Lily and the Leopard are fast friends."

The ships hailed each other peaceably. Thereafter they moved together on the last of the day's journey into the rocky shelter of the land.

An orange sun went down behind them, and through the burnt, wet shade on the sea, a parcel of Free Zakorians rowed over. Kesarh's galley took them aboard.

"We thought your King was here," said the Free Zakorian commander.

Kesarh, mailed, unjeweled, without device, said, "Did you? Never mind. I have his authority."

The Zakorian was not a fool, not deceived, but neither prepared to argue with conviction. Tall and brutalized, he had one memorable adornment. The left eye, which was gone, had been replaced by a smooth ball of opal.

"King Yl sends greetings then, to your King, through you."

"Thank you," said Kesarh. "I'll remember to convey them."

"And I'm authorized to offer assistance."

"In what capacity?"

"There is awkwardness in Lan." This polite, sarcastic phrase delivered in the Zakorian slur was nearly laughable. Kesarh did not laugh.

"What awkwardness is that?"

"Karmian troops in Lan have rebelled against King Kesr."

"King *Kesr*," said Kesarh, "would be most surprised to hear this."

There was a stasis. Then the Zakorian said:

"My galleys will escort yours to the port of Amlan."

"No," said Kesarh. He smiled gravely. "Karmiss holds Lan. The entry of Free Zakorian warships into her harbors at this time would be regarded, by the King, you understand, as an act of aggression against Karmiss herself."

The commander had not really believed he would get any other answer.

They exchanged brusque civilities, and the Free Zakorians went away.

In the hour before dawn when the Lily ships began their pull down the coast, the three shadows dogged them, too far off now to be hailed, or accused, simply a very positive menace.

The official word from Lan had been uncomplex. The new command had taken power, Raldnor Am Ioli was ousted and would consequently be disposed of. But much later, other words drifted in, even over the snow and ice—Kesarh's roundabout skein of spies had seen to that. Details were obscure, yet it appeared—though Raldnor had died—he had won over the troops at least in Amlan and her port. Some puppet leader was now set up, a blond Shansar, who had captured, somehow, their cloddish imagination.

For Kesarh to lose his grip on Lan at the onset of the war could be fatal. He had used Lan as ballast, and needed it. Despite the kudos of his navy, the strategic excellence he had crowed from in Dorthar and by proxy in Free Zakoris, was irreplaceable.

And the Free Zakorians, their own spies active—intelligent in a way they had never been till Alisaarian Kathus had taken over their reins—had also caught a whiff of decay.

Three and a half thousand soldiers were quartered at Amlan through the snow. To go in with less than three hundred men at his back was Kesarh's gamble, also a necessity.

The Free Zakorians, for one, must now be in serious doubt. You did not race to such a confrontation with such a miniature force. Could their information be wrong? To Karmiss-In-Lan, the look of it would be much the same. This was no punitive expedition. Kesarh was going, not to assault, but to woo them. Maybe they recalled, no one played the suitor better.

In the foredeck cabin the physician, having opened Kesarh's mailed sleeve, viewed the inflamed and ragged wound in his forearm.

"So slight a cut, but refusing to heal. It bothers you, my lord?"

"Yes. It bothers me."

"I think there's some festering. The knife had been in fruit, you say? I regret, we must cauterize."

"Then do it."

In Lan, though spring promised excitement, the long snow had already not been dull.

Raldnor of Ioli, slain by maddened patriot or paid assassin, had left Amlan in some confusion. The young Prince-King, Emel son of Suthamun, had heard of the event with obvious alarm. He shed tears in the presence of the soldiers, who thought it not unseemly. He was only a boy, and Raldnor had been a father to him. But the mourning went on, and Emel, having locked himself away, stayed locked away. The soldiers became restive.

During the first days following the assassination, a council was formed comprising the several captains attached to Raldnor's monopolies. Needless to say, squabbles had soon broken out. Before the month was done, there had been fighting in the streets between the cohorts of this and that commander. On the last day of the month one of the council was found dead in a wrecked wine-shop. A batch of days into the succeeding month, a few other captains met nemesis—one in a trough of sheep-swill, which provided inspiration for the army's poetic side.

There ensued an inevitable relay seizing of power. Two officers grabbed it, were murdered, two others were elected by cheering soldiery in the Palace Square. These held on for quite a while. The end came when a man rode into the city of Amlan from the south. He brought with him a thousand Karmians, some his own, others he had gathered up en route, and was pitched into a sudden siege when fellow Karmians slammed the gates in his face.

During the second night someone opened the gates, however, and the arrival arrived, with all his men. What had swung the balance was the uncertainty now rife in Amlan. The newcomer had once been a guard in the private army of Kesarh. He still seemed gilded by authority.

Biyh had been sent to Elyr with a small command, to reconnoiter and suborn, not long after he had returned with his King from Dorthar. Biyh had no ambition, or thought he had none. He was a dogsbody, a jack, would take on any job—guard, warrior, messenger. As Prince Rarmon himself had noted, Biyh had not gone up in the world.

But something in the turmoil of Lan, the indigenous revolts, the takeovers and plots and spontaneous slayings, had pushed him to a sort of precarious eminence. Rather to his own startlement,

Biyh had snatched his chance. Maybe seeing Rem's elevation had given him an appetite.

Getting Amlan, he took down the current leaders. Biyh meant only to imprison them, but the men were in a nasty mood and tore them to fragments in the Square.

Biyh began to tidy up the city, which was in a sorry state. He trod on no toes, distributing wine and beer and women liberally, producing the figurehead Emel—Biyh knew the worth of a figurehead—to help implant the notion of fair behavior and honor.

Biyh even visited the brother-sister Lannic King and Queen in the royal apartments. Pale under their darkness, they tolerated him. He was genuinely glad to see them still receiving food and comforts in their interior exile. Native Lan needed its figureheads, too, and Biyh had half feared he would find them lying on the woven carpets in a suicide pact.

One evening, Biyh also paid a longer than usual visit to his postulant King.

The boy had seemed doleful from the start, and frightened. Now, alone with him, Biyh beheld terror.

"It's been a bad time, this, my lord," said Biyh, who was never above platitudes, "but you must bear up. Recollect your father. The men love you. Karmiss will be yours." Biyh did not in fact believe this. He intended to make overtures to Kesarh when the weather broke, and hand everything back to him, Emel included, providing he, Biyh, gained by it.

Emel, who surely could not have guessed, began to cry.

Biyh patted the youngster's shoulder, and had a curious impression the boy was perfumed, if very faintly, with a woman's scent.

Remembering how Am Ioli was supposed to have concealed him, Biyh waxed inquisitive. On some pretext he next morning raided Emel's sleeping-room. Emel, who had lived with shrill panic since the day of Raldnor's death, was able to hide and evade only so much. Biyh let out a laugh. Something in the type of laugh encouraged Emel; he had heard it before, and that had been in bedchambers, too.

In a while Biyh said, "Don't worry, I'll keep your secret," and sat down on the bed. Half an hour afterwards, he was in it.

It so happened, Biyh's tastes ran to such dualities as Emel's. Also unlike Raldnor, Biyh was sexually well-mannered.

Emel found himself all at once cherished and petted. Here was one lover who did not disappear, one protector who did not loathe and carp, or mean to be rid of him. Safe at last?

* * *

When he had been nothing in the world's eyes, Kesarh had
ridden back from Tjis to the capital in a brazen chariot, a flare of
swords, a rain of flowers, and Istris handed her heart to him. A
King, he walked into Amlan.

The crossing had not been rough. Ulis Anet could not, he once
thought, have prayed hard enough—or the bane had stayed in the
knife. The three black shadows, though, had kept behind them.
The ships of the Lily docked, and the shadows anchored on the
horizon. It did not matter for the moment, might even prove
useful, this appearance of a Free Zakorian rear guard.

The troops were thick in the port. Events had been sorted six
days ago, after further information boarded Kesarh's ship: A spy
from along the coast who rowed well. The successive juntas now
had names, and the current ruler, Biyh, was once a Number
Nine, whose thousand men swelled the three and a half thousand
at Amlan. As the snow receded other areas had declared for
Biyh—or in error for Raldnor, not knowing him to be dead. The
puppet "King," said the spy, was Suthamun's son, or a crafty
double dug from somewhere.

As the oars of the boat brought him in to shore, Kesarh
estimated the armored phalanx screening the wharves was two
thousand men at least. They did not block the way in, but they
could close like jaws on whoever entered.

They were not sure, yet, if it could be him. If he could be
such a fool.

Then the boat grounded. He stood up and stepped over on to
the ice and shale, then straight up the great stair on to the quay.

Discipline had grown flabby, and a vibrant mutter began to
run at once. Most of them knew him by sight, considerable
numbers had spoken with him, or supposed they had, in Karmiss,
when the Lannic adventure was mounted.

Presently the sounds died out. They stared, metal and faces
and the metal faces of shields, hostile and ungiving. They were
out of love with him now, Am Ioli's falsehoods, and the riot and
the rift from homeland, had seen to that, and the blank cold
madnesses of the winter.

Kesarh stood, alone, in their midst. He had left the rest of his
men behind on the ships. They, too, had thought him insane, but
admired it. They knew his gambit. They said to each other, it
would be possible to walk after such a man into fire. As they sat
on the ships.

He was not wearing black, but the salamander scarlet, with the
lizard emblem in gold on breast and back—like a target. The
hair-fine coat of steel was worn under it, invisible. They only

saw he was unarmed. No sword, no dagger, not even the knives
that could be carried in sleeves or gauntlet-cuffs or the cuffs of
the high boots—they squinted after the tell-tale lines, and they
were never there.

He appeared very young, almost cheerful, with a light clear
color. He did not greet them. He only looked at them, into their
faces, steadily, one by one. Some of the faces turned grim, in
others the eyes flinched aside. But he was not offering them a
challenge. The regard was measured, finding them out, but never
too much.

Minutes dropped away, and nothing else happened. Finally,
two of Biyh's freshly appointed captains came forward and met
him.

They did not know, of course, what to say to him. They were
in declared arms against him, and here he was, empty-handed,
serene, kingly.

"My lord," one of them blurted, "what is it you want?"

"My destination," he said, "is the city."

"I can't answer for the men," said the other. "Your life's
teetering on two thousand sword-points. Why don't you go back
to your pretty ship? They'd probably let you."

Many heard this. The air was conductive, the acoustics rather
good. An uneasy jeering noise went round, and metal clacked on
metal. When it stopped, Kesarh spoke again. He spoke over the
captains' heads to the two-thousand-odd soldiers who hated him,
with a lover's hate, abused. His voice, the actor's voice trained
long ago, used always to effect, traveled to almost all of them.

"These men are Karmians, as I am. I don't fear my brothers,
gentlemen. Shall we get on?"

He started to walk then, and as he did so, the jaws began to
close on him. As they closed, he made spontaneous contact with
them. He had—and used—the magic thing, recall. He recollected names, personalities, officers and rank and file alike,
human beings he had met years before, exchanged one word
with. He blazed there in the raw colorless day, his scarlet like a
beacon, the salamander targets crying out to them where they
might strike. When they jostled him, he touched them. His hands
were steady, reassuring, gentling them like zeebas or horses.
When they pressed closer now, it was to touch in turn, no longer
rancor. Where they could not see him, they shinned up walls.

And now, the accusations came, because they felt they could
talk to him.

Already on the Amlan road, going toward the city, this huge
cloud of men—the port left nearly defenseless. *Kesarh*, they

said, or *King*, Shansarian fashion. It had none of the smack of insolence. It was the intimacy employed in religion.

Why? they said. Why withhold supplies? Why desert us here? Why the wedding with Free Zakoris?

He exonerated himself. He told them the game to be played, Lan the bulwark, Free Zakoris the stepping stone. Vis the stake.

His voice, reaching the perimeters, translated into the pockets where it did not reach of itself, stimulated them. His strength and his certainty, the easy confidence, each of them his counselor, consulted now, given reasons. And all the time he was in the midst of them. The guilty man did not come naked and fearless into the lions' pit. One who did not love them, moreover, could not trust them so.

There was a flat-topped rise by the road, and they urged him up on it.

He stood above the road and the metal cloud, talking to them, familiar, as if everyone of them knew him well. The sun blushed through and laid its patina on the hills, the ice, on him.

He told them some joke, and they laughed. And there was some banging of fists on shields.

He had not discounted them. They were not blamed or shamed or to be set on. It seemed there would be riches ahead, beside which Raldnor of Ioli's "bounty" would be dross. And he was too, the magician Raldnor had never been, and that no other was.

And then someone came running, and thrusting out of the crowd, bawled at him:

"Suthamun! Suthamun!"

"Yes," said Kesarh. "What of him?"

"His son," the man shouted hoarsely, "you murderer—"

"No," said Kesarh.

It was apparent then, the superstition, the sway of the pale races also wielding vast power.

Their heat had frozen suddenly in the sunlight, his two thousand brothers, Visian Karmians, mixes, the few score Shansarians, of whom this shouting man was one.

"I had thought," said Kesarh, "Emel son of Suthamun died of plague. Raldnor told me this. You yourselves believed Raldnor's lies. And so did I. Emel was his pawn. If it is Emel."

They yelled out, wanting to absolve for him their wrong of rebellion, to give it credentials: "Yes! *Emel! Emel!*"

Again he waited. When quiet came he gazed at them. It was as it had always been. His courtesy and his arrogance. They had been noticed, as was their right, by a god.

"I recollect Emel very well," he said. They were listening, bound. "The might of the goddess," Kesarh said. "She crushed Suthamun's dynasty, and left only Emel behind it. They say the goddess dreams the world. We're just the pictures in Her brain. If Emel lives, then the kingship is his, Karmiss is his, you, gentlemen, and I, all his." He looked at the Shansarian and said, in the Shansarian tongue of Suthamun's court, "As She wills it."

He walked most of the way to the city with them, and at midday they shared food with him on the road.

At some point a King's agent, concealed till then in the crowd, broke the careless ranks and returned to the port, so to the Lily ships: "Not won yet, but winning."

It was farcical, and diverted him. Somewhere else, in the core of heart or mind, it enraged him. That he had come again to this, this striving, this unavoidable tax paid the conquerors, the Chosen of the goddess. One of whom had casually seeded Kesarh himself. Unknown father. Only the always-weeping wretched woman wandering at Xai, that black-haired Karmian princess, abased and pining, like some pathetic bitch-dog. Hanging herself for Val Nardia to stumble into the cold feet. Their mother. Damn her. *She* had understood the sorcerous weight of the pale races. She had let it annihilate her. But he, Kesarh, had dragged the legend down. Only to have it rise again. The snake at Tjis. The snake which had been a sword.

The light fever was beginning, just a fraction, to blur the edges of his judgment. Not enough to be calamitous.

The doctor on the ship had proved incompetent. The hot iron had not been applied for long enough, and the infection reinfested the little cut in his left forearm. It would have to be done again.

When the moronic soldiers had fumbled against him on the road, finally lifting him and bearing him into the city, the whole arm had sung out, a low, dense note of pain. Kesarh dealt with that because he had to. But each man who clutched him he could have killed. In the city, on the steps above the Palace Square, where the brother and sister King and Queen had formerly given audience, he had gone through the entire theatrical once more. And taken them once more.

They seemed to be his, now, the four thousand, five thousand troops at Amlan.

It only remained to deal with Biyh. That should not be too

difficult, there had been an obscure message left at a village up the coast, Biyh's offering, all reverence and fidelity.

And then, to round off this bloody day, the inevitable acknowledgment—on the steps, elevation, and proximity to the stinking drunken rabble of soldiers—of the Prince-King Emel.

Somewhere in the war, Emel was again about to die. Obviously.

But it should not have been necessary. Should not have been here for him, this pitfall. Raldnor overreaching himself, Suthamun, damnable Ashara-Anackire—

"That may be of help, my lord."

The second physician—the other was laid up, a flogging—straightened from his task. The wound, now packed with medicine, seemed numbed, but not eased.

"Tonight," said Kesarh, "come back here and cauterize it. This time, efficiently."

"Don't worry, my lord. I saw what happened to your other attendant."

"You were meant to. What's this?"

"Something to cool the fever."

"And which will make me drowsy? Do you suppose I can afford to sleep here?" Kesarh pushed the cup aside and it fell to the floor. The arbitrary violence was unusual. As a general rule, Kesarh was fair to underlings. The wine merchants of Karmiss, who had rebuilt their trade on his patronage, adored him, praising his magnanimous charm and personal power. The very men outside, despised, would have fought Free Zakoris for him this minute. That had been part of the spell in the old days, too. Even those who were accorded punishment felt they had been singled out.

Rem . . . Why was he thinking of Rem-Rarmon Am Dorthar. Raldnor's son. Riding, somewhere, on some errand—Val Nardia's child. No, it was himself, riding to Ankabek which was no more. And the child . . . No, the child had been a nightmare. It had never happened, any of that.

The second physician, who had got in only an hour ago, with the rest of Kesarh's slight staff, bowed himself, unseen, out.

Biyh was the next visitor.

Kesarh had ordered himself by then.

They went through everything. The obeisances, the fawnings, the agreements. Without doubt, Biyh had been constant. He would be rewarded. A knife's length between his ribs before summer. But one need not explain that.

Knives. That brainless Xarabian mare. Had her knife been anointed?

Even from a battlefield no wound had ever festered. That flying splinter in the sea-fight off Karmiss, which should have put out his eye, deflecting, leaving a clean scar hardly visible.

Only the snake at Ujis had ever poisoned him, and that at his own discretion. The scar from that was clearly marked. It lay half an inch above the spot where Ulis Anet's knife had gone in.

Val Nardia, threatening him with just such a tiny knife, unable to use even her nails against him. She had found it simpler to harm herself.

"You did well, Biyh," he said. "I shan't overlook it. You've earned Lan's Guardianship, at least."

Biyh, missing he had been given what he already had, flowered into idiot grins.

"But Emel, my lord?"

"He imagines I may dispose of him, since Raldnor swore I attempted it, last time."

"Quite, my lord."

"Reassure Emel," said Kesarh. "He's my King. He'll leave me charge of the armies, I think. I'm a soldier. Let us all stick to the thing we're best at."

Biyh shifted. He had, after all, been one of the Nines. He had seen how Kesarh's mind could work. He knew some ten-year-old secrets, and knew that Kesarh knew that he did.

"My lord, there's something—" Biyh hesitated. He gnawed his lips. When Kesarh did not prompt, he said, "there's something Raldnor did, to safeguard Emel. Or rather, himself."

"Dressed the boy as a woman and taught him harlot's manners. So I gather."

"Well, my lord, actually rather more than that."

The black and merciless eyes, glazed with a strange opaque brightness—fever, they said an assassin had tried to stab him at Istris—pinned Biyh to the air so he writhed. Better come out with it, make a love-gift of it. Left to himself, Kesarh would learn sooner or later, one could not use it for bargaining, and look what he had done with the troops, spun them round like a wheel. He was as much the showman and the mage as ever—

"Raldnor brought in Ommos surgeons. They did what the Ommos have a talent for." Kesarh gratified him by blinking. "Yes, my lord. The Prince is no longer any sort of a man. Gelded. Not fit to be a king, not by Vis standards, let alone Shansarian. You wouldn't want to make a fuss here. They're that touchy. But the council in Istris—"

Kesarh started to drink wine. There was a silence. Kesarh eventually said, "And how do you know?"

Biyh shrugged. Honesty was the wisest course.

"I don't mind 'em like that. I've seen him stripped. I've had him." After another silence, Biyh, feeling more secure than he had for days, added, "You might let him live. Or you might not. But he can't harm anyone, poor little beggar."

Emel himself did not hear this culminating plea. He had heard the rest.

Having been penned in Amlan's palace so many months, he was privy to several of its more interesting crannies. He had sometimes, fascinated and repelled, played voyeur to Raldnor's sadistic bed-sports, utilizing an unfrequented overhead gallery with a loose tile or two. Kesarh, as the intermediary captains had done, installed his suite in Raldnor's apartments. It had not been difficult to employ the previous method.

From the moment Karmian ships had been sighted, Emel had felt the gray draught of death drizzling on his neck. Then Kesarh was in the city, and the soldiers cheered just as loudly as on the night Raldnor had produced his insurance among the torches. Emel considered bolting, but the palace was rushing with men. Kesarh entered the palace. Not only one apartment, he was in every shadowed place.

The act of going to eavesdrop on fate needed all Emel's courage. While he did it, even listening to Kesarh's earlier words, Emel had not deemed himself reprieved. To be told he would live and be a king always had intimations of a death-sentence. They had all, had they not, promised him that? But he had been praying, too, not to Ashara or any deity of name, but to some unformed god of the self, that Biyh would somehow gain a means to protect him. For Biyh, surely, was faithful. Then Biyh surrendered him uncaringly.

Emel returned to his bedchamber. He had picked up a flair for cruelty from Raldnor, and coming on a beetle on the door, pulled off its legs as he wept with fear. Hearing the steps approach along the corridor, preface to the executioner, he crushed out its life also under his heel, a counterpoint.

Another gaudy orange sunset lit the ceremony on the stairway, hitting the painted walls and tiers of the palace, the stout painted wooden pillars with their lotuses of indigo and henna, and capitals of flying bis. Kesarh had requested that the King and Queen be present, and they sat in their bone chairs with bone bracelets, behind him up the steps. She was lovely, and her brother-husband was sick, still. Kesarh had asked after his health, and the Queen had said, "It's nothing, lord King of Karmiss."

"Since I put men into Lan," said Kesarh, "he's been failing."

"Just so," she said. "He and I, we are Lan. Distress this earth, and we are stricken."

"Are you?" he said. "You yourself seem to bloom, madam."

"A painted complexion," she said. "Didn't they tell you, lord King, even Lans know something of deception."

He thought of Val Nardia again. Sister and wife.

Then he went out into the sunset, and the bone chairs came, and the other participants of the play. The soldiers crammed the Square and hung from the rooftops and trees to see. There would be Amlans, too, watching. Perhaps the reinstatement of blond rule, this sham, would seem bitterly humorous to Lan, also.

At each breath, the light throbbed. In an hour or so, there was the second cauterization to look forward to.

Emel was being escorted down the stair.

And the soldiers, catching sight of him, trained to it now, shouted and banged their shields.

The racket swarmed in Kesarh's skull, but he moved about to welcome the boy—who was not even that—the one mistake that had been made and which could not be rectified till Karmiss.

Emel gazed up, too frightened to avoid the hypnotic eyes of Kesarh. The hand that touched Emel's shoulder had lost none of its physical power. It had lifted him to horseback and into chariots, it had guided and led him. Once, in winter, when his own child's hands were frozen, Kesarh had returned them to life, chafing them in his own. Emel had worshipped Kesarh. Kesarh who wanted to murder him.

Kesarh seemed to peruse him now, stern, compassionate. Then he turned to the soldiers. He said to them, the words ringing across the square: "This is indeed Emel. My King's son, and my King."

And then, as they bellowed all over again, Kesarh knelt to him.

It was not like Raldnor, but solely like that other time, at Istris in the map chamber. The kneeling man. But the sunset had grown thicker, more like blood now on the shining black of the hair, the bloody garments.

Emel twisted to face the soldiers, and reckoning he was about to speak to them himself, a unique event, they hushed each other and abruptly all the cacophony was gone, leaving just a hollow of ominous red light.

Emel stared at them. They had cheered him, too, had always

cheered him. They liked him—it must be so. And there were
many of them. And Kesarh, his enemy, was only one.

The desperate solution came to Emel suddenly. He knew he
had mere seconds to implement it. He flung up his arms, and
screamed at them in his high girlish voice. "It's lies! He'll kill
me! Kesarh will kill me! Don't let him—please save me—help
me—"

Over and over, the same phrases spurted forth. The shrill
wailing penetrated, its anguish apparent even where language
was obscured. The front rows of Karmian soldiery reacted, a
murmur, sulky and unsure, questions and denials, passed backward.
It might have burnt itself out. While Emel's throat was not
strong, he could not have managed very much more.

But Kesarh had risen to his feet. Looking down at this screeching eunuch, his cold blood seemed to boil. "Be quiet," Kesarh
said. But Emel did not heed. He cowered away and began to
bawl, sobbing and flailing.

There was malice in it too. It was malice which had lent Emel
the bravado. To damage the ones who betrayed him, even as he
tried to escape them. And because of this, when Kesarh reached
out again to grasp him, hold him still, Emel rounded, snarling
through his hysteria. And Emel too reached out, beating and
clawing at Kesarh to keep him off.

Emel did not know about the tiny festering agony of the
wound. If he had known, instinctively, he might have tried to
avoid it.

But the attack—which from blow appeared vitiated, nothing—
came down repeatedly there, and exactly there. The pain exploded through sinews, into the pit of an arm, the breast and
throat, the vitals. And seeing Kesarh recoil, Emel lashed out
again and again.

The soldiers were in fact chuckling, some of them, not realizing quite what went on, finding the spectacle funny; the feeble
smitings of their boy King. Then Kesarh struck him.

Probably, they expected a slap. It was not a slap.

They were all fighters, and however sloppy they had become,
most of them that saw it saw too the blow was enough to break
Emel's neck. And that it did break it.

Like something falling to pieces, the boy collapsed and top-
pled all the way down the stair, and into the front rank of
soldiers at the bottom. Who leaned over him and tried him, and
then let go, muttering. It had a different timbre now, this noise,
and it spread rapidly.

The light was almost gone. Last dapplings of red still lit up the murderer on his self-chosen stage of steps.

He did not move or speak. It was not the pain or the fever or the rage which had changed him into stone. Perhaps irony had some part in it. He had used death so often and so adroitly in private. Yet he must have known, in the most public fashion possible he had just now written out his epitaph.

TWENTY-THREE

Dhaker, the Opal-Eye, directed his eternal wink through the night toward the shore, and said, "Something burns."

He was correct in this.

The three Zakorian galleys, letting out sail to a shoreward wind, circled nearer. Before too long, the distant flashing of flames became self-explanatory. Most of the port of Amlan was on fire.

Outriders of the navy of Free Zakoris, Dhaker's triad had kept the reavers' agility. They had a diplomatic reason for going in, which was that Kesr Am Karmiss, ally of King Yl, had patently joined battle with the rebel Karmians in Lan. But the long hot winter prowling Thaddra, and Dorthar's barren, guarded north, had put them in key for a fight. And doubtless there would be spoil, a city of it, with such drink and women as Karmiss had not consumed.

The boats swam to land, avoiding the Karmian anchorage, which seemed, however, deserted. When they got ashore, most of the battle in the port was over; only bodies, the odd looter, the fires, remained. The Amlans were gone, too. Off into the hills, likely. Hills and mountains were the soul of Lan.

Dhaker organized his men. A company stayed to scour the port, and keep faith with their own ships. The rest took off along the Amlan road.

Nearer and later, the glow over the city wall gave sign of some incendiary action also here. Their mission gradually altered focus.

Free Zakoris hated Kesarh, despite any treaty. He had the yellow man's blood, and besides had spent his youth and young manhood humiliating her. Now he might fall into Free Zakorian hands. Yl would be interested no doubt, to get such a prisoner, while Karmiss and the east would loosen on the tree.

It was the Shansarian troops who began the riot in Amlan. Their motive was unvarnished: Emel was theirs. When Kesarh was taken, albeit like a felon, into the palace, they had called council. The time of soldierly governance had gone to their heads, and they demanded the slayer of their rightful king be given back to them. Feeling scaled high. They cursed Kesarh. He was Vis, scum, a black jackal. This led to a personalization of insults all round. The Vis soldiery, who had also enjoyed the autonomy, not only of Lan, but in Kesarh's Visian Karmiss, took exception. Others came in on every side. There really was no discipline left in Amlan. Raldnor and his successors had eroded it, and Kesarh, who could have got it back, was disqualified. They sprang for each other's throats, howling. Vis against Shansar, mix against both, company against company. And while it went on, messengers and berserkers alike carried the story and the bloodbath to the port. The remainder of Kesarh's escort, hurrying off the convoy of Lily ships, were intercepted on the road.

One frantic contingent, beating a way through insane Shansars and roaring Istrians, through the fire-hung city and the streams of evacuating Lans, reached the palace doors—now the ultimate and single defended area—and thus the surviving Karmian command. This happened to be a bemused Biyh.

"Commander, three shiploads of Free Zakorians are coming."

"Hell and the pit," said Biyh.

He was not far out.

There were not even six hundred of them, the Zakorians, but they were eager, barbaric and in good order.

The port had had no defense. The gates of the city stood wide. Nor could any unity be brought to the maelstrom. Kesarh, of course, could have done it. But Kesarh, of course, had been conducted to the cellar. "My—lord," Biyh had said there, solemnly, between dismayed nerves and dumbfounded curiosity and a certain oblique pleasure. "For your own protection, I must leave you here. Bound, and guarded." Kesarh had grinned, or showed his teeth like a dog when afraid, one was not sure. One hastened away and landed in this mess.

Biyh hustled together the seventy men who were holding the entries of Amlan's palace. He had already made an effort to stir out the Lannic Army from the Salamander barracks. But most of these had made a run for it, or gone to aid their families in the pandemonium.

In the end, Dhaker Opal-Eye's force cut neat swaths to the door. Not seeking to engage battle, save where it was most tempting, many of the groups of fighters had overlooked them. The palace defenses retaliated bravely, but not for very long. They were dispatched against walls, on galleries, under columns. At length, Free Zakorians had the palace. They did not attempt to retain it. They looted but did not unleash fire, searching diligently. The King and Queen were gone, persuaded by the remnant of their own guard, who successfully gathered them away into Lan's night-smurred soul, under cover of chaos.

Dhaker's men did, nevertheless, get into a cellar over five gutted Karmians. They found Kesarh, manacled as they would have wished.

"Here is the one," said Opal-Eye, "who is not a king. Well," said Opal-Eye, "you're not a king now, Kesr Am Karmiss."

Not only shackled, but burning with fever, he was no difficulty to deal with. They hacked a way back to the road, to the port and to their ships, killing here, looting there.

Leaving embers on the skyline, their slaves rowed them north.

Dhaker himself cauterized the infected wound in his captive's arm. He heated the iron white-hot and kept it on the roasting flesh for as long as was needful, perhaps some seconds more. Dhaker did not want his trophy to die before they rejoined Yl's fleets, but also, Dhaker's father had been at Tjis.

The house, so agreeable and fruitlessly tranquil, was abruptly full of screaming.

Ulis Anet stood to face the doorway as one of the winged pairs of feet flew in.

"Madam—"

"What is it?"

She was told.

The King of Xarabiss' daughter turned and walked away into the garden. She ignored the turmoil. White pigeons, offended by the sudden din, dashed to the sky between chasms of rose-red wall.

The Lily ships were coming back from Lan. From Istris other ships were setting forth to bring the Karmian remnants out. The length of Lan, they said, men galloped, calling in the troops, summoning them from hills and crags, from the valleys and the villages. Every man of Karmiss must return. Lan would be abandoned, rent and used and left lying, for Free Zakoris to have if Free Zakoris willed it.

The Black Leopard would move toward Karmiss herself, very shortly. No longer an ally—the devourer. The treaties were all torn up.

Kesarh, regicide and madman—Free Zakoris had Kesarh.

She had dreamed of something, she could not even properly remember. A serpent was in it, and its teeth glittered like knives. She had wept in her sleep, and woken weeping. And now she knew. And wept once more.

She did not love him. She loved him. And he would die, and Karmiss would die, and she was to blame, so her dream had shown her, save she could not remember it, or why.

"Lady, you'll be cold. Here's your nice cloak, with the kalinx fur, he gave you."

"No," Ulis Anet murmured. But they lifted her from the grass, began to bear her away.

"Hush, lady. Istris isn't safe. Full of crazy soldiers and ships coming in. The Warden's to enforce curfew. And the baker said, black galleys, the Leopard, seen at sunset—"

A male voice. "We're going inland. Come on, lady. You're delaying us."

She was bewildered. She thought they would sell her as a slave.

"Kesarh," she said.

"Forget him, lady. He's sliced in segments, feeding fish."

"*Shush!* Let her alone."

The night closed her eyes. She slept in the arms of her maids.

Stars patterned the darkness.

They were in the hills of Karmiss.

She stared at the stars, and some philosophy or aberration filled her so she lifted her hands. In Elyr, star-gazers understood such fancies.

There was a small inn, and when the sun came up she was alone. Even the ankars and the ornaments they had brought for her had disappeared. The cloak of black and white furs had disbanded into live animals and slunk under the door.

The inn-keeper stood over her.

"Fine lady—fine *whore*. What'll you pay me with?"

He raped her. At any other time, such a terrible thing would have sickened her, driven her mad. But she was beyond it. All the while he abused her, her conscious mind was far away.

"You'll have to try harder than that," he said.

He told her she could sweep out hearths and carry water, and he would whip her for negligence. Had she been sold and never known it?

She got up from the bed and faced him.

"I am the King's mistress," she said.

"The *King*—we'll be ripped in shreds because of this king. Out! I'm sorry I soiled myself with you, you red-haired slut."

There was a road. It went to Ioli, where she had never been. People in flight from every city and town seemed to travel the road in either direction, moving on to it and off it at various subsidiary tracks. There were carts, wagons, lowing beasts, the clatter of pans tied together, and the elderly, too weak to go on, resignedly sitting to die on the verge.

Ulis Anet walked inside the moving entity the multiple evacuation had become. She did not know where she went. Was Ioli secure? Never. Where then? West, and off the island. To Dorthar, where the Storm Lord could protect them. Rot Kesarh. May the crows tear his liver! An old woman, of good family and well-dressed, dropped in the way of a wagon, which was halted with cursing and complaints. Ulis Anet lifted the old woman up, vaguely reminded of a grandmother in Xarar, where the hot spring heated the palace even during the snow. The old woman clung to her. Ulis Anet, having rescued her, could not make her let go. Ulis Anet said, "Kesarh. He was my lover." The woman spat on her. Catching sunlight, the spittle shone. A pebble struck her arm. Fickle—they had loved him, only three days before, when she had not.

Outside Ioli, she joined a makeshift camp, shared its fire, and back darkness came and stars.

They made about the fire ghastly buffoonery of how death loomed and they would all die. "And a Free Zakorian's standing there, with a bloody great sword. He says to me, Where shall I put this? And I just pray my mate here's got his bloody great mouth open." Or they sang songs: "No morning star to bring us from the night."

A man tried to lie over her.

"Kesarh," she said. "He—"

The man beat her, but not much.

She was a pariah. He would not soil himself.

*   *   *

There were ships standing off at such and such a location, bound for Dorthar. Somehow she was with a family who had given her food and were now taking her to the ships.

She imagined entering Dorthar and throwing herself, a suppliant, at the wheels of Raldanash's chariot as he rode by on the way to war.

"Why are you laughing?" the children asked her.

"Stop that. She's daft, poor bitch."

When they arrived at the shore, there were no ships. The family made off westward and deserted the lunatic, who was an ill omen.

She wandered awhile with the wandering light, then sat down on a stone.

The waves blew against the beach. But there was no peace. In the silence, she saw Kesarh and what the Free Zakorians would do to him. She had heard of the exploits of his valor, Tjis, the sea-fight off Karmiss a year ago. She was afraid she would see it in truth, the mental barrier giving way, letting his mind pour into hers, his torture and death, and she could do nothing.

She did not properly understand any of what had taken place, only its outcome. And sometimes she did not believe that either, though she knew it was so.

He had not died. Not yet. She would be aware of his death. Perhaps.

Not much before sunset, a storm cloud began to cross the water, miles off to the northeast. Ulis Anet left the stone and wandered into the surf, and stared at the blackness of the cloud until it melted away against the land. An hour after, another storm cloud, this one red, crept to the sky. At first she took it only as a vestige of sunfall. But it was the nightmare, black cloud, red—Zakorian ships, and fire.

She ran, inanely, the way the family had gone, westward, from the night.

In the blackness, she started back initially, thinking she had reached more arson. But then she perceived it was a group of torches. There was a shallow cove, with boats, rough-made, leaky things, groaning on to the waves one after another.

She came among the people there. They were few. Their lights caught her and someone said, "Look—ulis-hair. A good omen."

She had been an ill omen before.

"Where are you going?" she asked.

"The island."

She gazed at them. Karmiss was an island.

"The holy shrine," said another.

"The Leopard took it already. He won't bother to come back. It'll be safe there."

They were going over to Ankabek, in the shadow of the moonless night.

They let her go with them, for her lucky hair.

Vodon's men had cast Her into the sea from the rocks, Ashara-Anackire, the goddess of Ankabek. Down there She lay, dreaming, as she dreamed in Ibron above Koramvis. It was said She had once dreamed the world.

A sable shell on the sable sky, aureoled with stars, the island rose from the sea.

Have I come this way before, quick, and dead? the Xarabian thought. Val Nardia had done so.

Beyond the landing, the island went up, but the village had been gouged by the Leopard. They said not one living creature had survived. Only ghosts dwelled here now, a slain priestess and her folk, but who had ventured to see?

They entered the village and did what they could with it. Bits of walls provided wind-breaks. They stretched hide across and tented them in, and lit fires. A lizard was spotted, a gray jewel on a rock, life after all. Supper was cooked. Their normalcy was genuine and glad, but here, in the haven, there was to be always the scent of things omitted, the condition of the earth beyond; they did not mention Vis.

She could not eat, thinking of Kesarh. A woman patted her hand. "Ah, you've lost someone, I expect."

Ulis Anet looked beyond the earth, up into the stars, and then the stars drew her away, on to a stony path and through an uncanny wood. It was blackened, but here and there some branch or bough had survived, and put out resinous buds, sweetening the sweet air. It was an hour's walk.

The temple stood at the island's summit. The upright slot of the entrance was very high, the doors broken in and their machinery uprooted. There were old black markings on the walls. But, although the way had been breached below, up here the clue to ingress had not been come on. The circle of the inner Sanctuary was still shut.

Ulis Anet went to the stone and laid her forehead and the palms of her hands upon its coolness.

Val Nardia had hanged herself. *Is it for some such finality I too was brought to Ankabek?*

A night bird fluted in the cremated groves outside. Life in death.

But Kesarh, Kesarh—

Ulis Anet sank to her knees. She pressed her lips to the unpenetrated wall. A prayer of the Amanackire came to her, from somewhere in childhood, and she said the words aloud, not knowing why, or their significance, her tears warmer than the burned stone.

"Not what I lack, nor what I desire, but give me only what I am."

After a moment, the stone moved. Part of the wall fell slowly back before her. The wall was like a pipe, and the pressure points that sprung the slabs were set low down and could only be come at by kneeling. They responded to breaths of differing shapes, such as were formed phonetically. There were more than a hundred keys, all prayers, of which Ulis Anet's was merely one.

Beyond, the Sanctum was despoiled, as the pirates had left it, and without light. But she stepped into it. She was afraid, understanding the wall would close. Incarcerated, she could only then seek a way out through one of the inner doors Vodon's men had forced, and so through the labyrinth of under-passages—

She stood in the blackness now, smashed pottery or human bones under her feet, without even the statue of the goddess to comfort her.

And yet, the goddess might be conjured. She was there for all who cried out to Her—Not what I lack or desire. What I am.

No, it was not Val Nardia's phantom which hovered here.

It was the woman they had whispered of on the boat, Eraz, the priestess.

"Help me," Ulis Anet said to her, in the dark.

The help is in you. You must help yourself.

"Yes," said Ulis Anet. "The help is in me. I must help myself."

The message of Free Zakoris to Karmiss had been terse. We have your King. Will you ransom him? The Warden of Istris sent to learn the substance of this ransom. The ransom was Karmiss. It was a witticism. Kesarh had awarded the Leopard Prince Rarmon, the Storm Lord's brother. But the Leopard wanted Kesarh himself and now had him. Karmiss the Leopard would also have, given or taken. Already there were paw marks on the beaches.

As heat began to come into the days, the black thunder clouds poured down the seas of Vis.

In Dorthar's north, the ballistas started their dialogue with a hostile ocean. It was not much more than an exercise, there, something to divert that eye of Raldanash's kingdom and a portion of men and armaments. One night, a company of Dortharians swam out and fired four Zakorian ships. As the upper decks exploded, the Dortharians went on to hole the undersides and, breaking their chains, liberated most of the slaves. Gallant heroics these, worth a song. But forgotten when fifty Free Zakorian galleys sailed into the major estuary of the Okris river. For a fleet of any size, this was the road to Dorthar's hub, and the delta garrison was seven thousand strong. It held the river mouth against the onslaught, which now gave no sign of decreasing. As further black ships drifted to join their fellows, further battalions, mostly Xarabians and Dortharian-Vathcrians, were force-marched or skulled east to shore up the blockade.

Ommos. Ships clustered black against her coast. She had been breached at Karith, that enduringly weak spot, but the Dortharian troops stationed inland against this contingency had ambushed and beaten Yl's forces off and back into the sea.

Xarabiss reported skirmishes at Ilah's port. Her watchtowers farther north sent up crimson dragon-breath.

Eastward, Lan, trampled in the mud of passage, kept still, kept silent. None came to take, as yet, but the empty villages were portent enough. The smoke had settled, flowers opened on the hills, but men might have gone away to the moon.

Westward, all Vardian Zakoris was mobilized, and the little ally kingdoms, Iscah, Corhl and Ott. Alisaar's fleets, approximating one hundred and twenty-two ships, continued up and down her jagged edges. The Shansar fleet had sailed from Moiyah, thirty carved swans, snake-headed, going west.

It now seemed plain, Yl would bring the bulk of his navy west to south against Alisaar and Old Zakoris, then through the Inner Sea between Alisaar and Xarabiss to Ommos, already sorely harried, and so upward to the womb of Vis, Dorthar.

The Leopard did not conceal its plans. Now it would strike here, now there. It was everywhere at once. For more than twenty years it had been building ships and men to feed this summer.

A forest fire tore the jungles northwest of Vardish Zakoris. Three thousand men, with chariots, catapults and siege engines hauled by monsters of the swamps, palutorvuses—which some, never having seen them, feared—burst against Sorm's outposts under the dividing mountains. Free Zakoris stared at conquered Zakoris. Zakorian defenders defied their Vardian officers, slew them, and defected. Tattered, Sorm's force withdrew, leaving the borders in Yl's hands, fabricating a new border, afraid the Leopard would steal by them elsewhere.

The Leopard had entered northeastern Thaddra too, via her rivers. There were Free Zakorians in strategic Tumesh, now, under the tall peaks, the dragon's crest of Dorthar. On the pass above, the Dortharians readied themselves.

Once, the oceans beyond all land southwest and south had been mythologically discounted as the Sea of Aarl. As Raldnor Am Anackire had learned, there were marine volcanoes west and south of Alisaar, the seed of the myth. Other, less lethal, passages to the second continent had since become well known to traders.

The withering of the Aarl-bane had additionally opened sea roads around Alisaar into the Inner Sea; formerly, no ship would risk going farther south than Saardos.

It had also, of course, laid wide the way for Free Zakoris.

Coming south, hugging the western shores of Vis as it must, the great fleet would be more than a month in voyaging. There was no land-route possible. Thaddra melted there into a nameless morass of diseased swamp and jungle ancient as the world, unclaimed by any, offering nothing. Where this slab of hateful earth jutted down toward Alisaar, a high beacon had been inaugurated on a rocky promontory. Small unsigiled vessels paddled about the area, keeping the watches of half the countries adjacent.

The great fleet was already moving. The most current sighting estimated a hundred and sixty-five ships, packed with men as Free Zakoris was proficient at packing—maybe eighteen thousand fighting men.

Their slaves rowed not only chained, but blindfold, in case by some accident they might catch a glimpse of those they met, their own countrymen, and be seized with patriotism, or some fantasy of being saved. A handful of slaves had already mutinied. They were tortured on the decks, as the others, blindfold but not deaf, rowed on. Only when these warning voices could no longer scream, did corpses go into the sea. Huge lizard-creatures slid from the jungle coasts and hastened out to feast.

One sunrise, the foremost galleys sighted a tower of glass flying over the water, an iceberg, driven by eccentric currents and winds to slow dissolving under the dry western sun.

The Free Zakorians did not care for it, this cold clear thing. They said it had the torso and breasts of a woman.

*   *   *

The Dortharian fleet was anchored off Thos.

The Middle Lands had seldom fought by sea. Dorthar's strength had been chariots and men and mighty walls, since the time of Rarnammon. Even in the Lowland War she had thrust away the ships of the Sister Continent, and engaged in combat on land, until the land moved like the sea and ended the battle.

The shipwrights were Vathcrians, and the ships were Vathcrian in style, high-beaked and beautiful. Their white sails glistened, blazed with the rust and black Oragon of Dorthar, gold and black with the Serpent and Cloud, the white on amber on white of the goddess banners of the Dortharian Anackire. The Vathcrian flotilla had in turn put out the blue regalia of Ashkar, brave as if for celebration. The Tarabine flotilla, already colored for blood, reflected the sea into wine. But the fleet numbered less than a hundred vessels. No reinforcements had come from the homelands, no message. Though the Karmians' vaunting seemed done, it was too late. Alliances were blowing chaff. The Middle Lands stood alone as, since the snow, they had reckoned to stand.

When Raldanash rode into the port near sundown, Thos turned out to wave and exalt. Enough flowers were blooming that they could fling them to him and his men, the glitter of mail in dying sunlight. Next year there might be, after all, no more flowers, no more sun, for any of them.

In the garrison overlooking the harbor, the guardian, too aged to fight but with two sons down on the ships, bowed and stammered and went away, leaving the King and his commanders to their talk.

After dinner, that too dwindled. Most of them set off to bed with willing febrile Thosian women. Everywhere there was a glut of virgins to be had, girls anxious to lose their maidenheads to a hero or a friend. If Free Zakoris had them, they knew how it would be.

When the moon rose, Raldanash was alone, seated unsleeping in the guardian's bedroom which, hung with the gaudiest silks, was his for the night.

"My lord," Vencrek had said at Anackyra, "your place is here, in your capital. Not jaunting to meet Free Zakoris at the mouth of the Inner Sea—"

"Farther west," Raldanash had corrected absently.

"Wherever. Do you think Yl doesn't daydream of that? You *there*, and the Leopard breaking in here from Okris, or out of Ommos. Raldanash, we're holding Ommos by an inch of skin—it could happen any day."

"You will defend Dorthar," said Raldanash, "with distinction and common snese."

Vencrek used an explicit Vathcrian oath. "Dorthar without a heart. Kingless."

"The people of Dorthar expect me to go where I am going, to intercept the Leopard in its might, the greater force, at sea. Not idly to wait for them to reach us, a hundred and sixty ships."

"My lord, I've never known you to act in such a precipitate—"

"If Rarmon had been here—"

"If Rarmon had been here he would have snatched the crown and brought Yl galloping in to share it."

"No," said Raldanash, "you really shouldn't listen to Free Zakorian propaganda."

Vencrek said, moving into the tongue of Vathcri, "Why are you doing this?"

Raldanash, too, changed to the language of home. "I've told you."

"No, my lord, you haven't told me."

Raldanash had looked at him then, and Vencrek had suddenly pushed all the military paraphernalia aside, walked across the chamber and flung his arms round him, as if they had been boys again, in the valleys.

To be embraced with such frantic affection, love and anger, shook Raldanash, but he suffered it, was even momentarily comforted. When Vencrek let him go, Raldanash began quietly, "If it were not for your support and kindness—"

But Vencrek, striding back to the papers, said, "There will be twenty Amanackire priests on the King's galley, I hear." Raldanash said nothing. Vencrek said: "I wonder why?"

"To invoke Ashkar-Anackire."

Vencrek said, "My lord, I know some of the legends, too. The lines of energy that supposedly cross Vis. The line shot from the goddess temple above Koramvis—to Vathcri. I hazard you mean to meet the Leopard's ships on that line of Power, as near as your theologians and cartographers can judge it."

"Then, that's your hazard."

Vencrek turned, posed, had his suavity again. He said in Visian: "I see. Well, I'm probably all error. I know you leaned to the life of a sacerdote when a child, my lord, and still do. But you've never been sufficient idiot to throw Dorthar away for it."

They spoke of military deployments.

Only at the door did Vencrek say, very lightly, "Of course, you've left no heir. What's to become of us all if you go down?"

"Amrek left no heir," said Raldanash. "The goddess provided one."

Now, in Thos in the moon brightness, one recollected a workshop in the hills and the making of a crescent bow, and a ten-year-old Vencrek running through the waist-high grasses, yelling, waving the bow. And the terraces up to the temple, the cool enamel of live snakeskin, the shadows, and: "When you're King of all Vis, what'll I be?" "My Counselor." And Vencrek frowning, "But I want to fight, lead your armies." "The wars are over," Raldanash had said. They had agreed, that being the case, Counselor was best.

Later Sulvian glided across the moonlight, her white hair blowing, but it had merged with some imagery of his father's, some telepathic symbol lodged in his brain at birth. For Sulvian crumbled into gilded ashes and blew away along the night.

The elegant ships took wing with the morning.

They sailed southward, the crenellated shore always visible on the left hand: Steep-shelved Ommos, the plain-lands of Xarabiss, where watchtowers sent up flowers of blue smoke. There was a mild following wind.

After twenty-five days, the Storm Lord's fleet came into the glassy water between Xarabiss and the borderland of Alisaar and Old Zakoris. Here, a cordon of Xarabian and Dortharian-Vathcrian vessels had been stationed across the sea, between garrisoned watchtowers on either coast. The original plan had chosen a point farther south, where the sea channel was narrower. But Alisaar's withdrawal from alliance had made her unacceptable as the western end of this oceanic rope. Nor was the chain mighty. Twenty-three galleys maintained it, equipped with such war machinery as could be spared. The two garrisons were of similar bulk. It was a last-ditch measure. Success elsewhere and the element of surprise would favor it, but if most if Yl's force swept into the channel, the cordon had no hope, save to delay.

Beyond the northern edge of Alisaar, the sea spread wide again. Xarabiss melted away in a sunset cloud as they turned southwest toward the open waters of war.

It had taken the Thaddrian most of two days to clamber through the rubble and into the uplands beyond. Rising, winning through, these had touches of allegory. Gradually the plains city of Anackyra, its martial show, its multitude of soldiers, the apathetic fear of its citizens, vanished. Within the shambles of Koramvis there had been halts, to rest, to search about. There was no longer any sure way over the wide river, but he found a little raft, some native robber's, perhaps, and rowed himself unchallenged to the farther shore. That side there was the "Merchant's Road" a path for travelers coming from the mountains, a project begun and abandoned before it reached the southern bank, falling itself in disrepair.

When he broke out of the lawless damaged loveliness of the ruins, the hills opened like honeycomb on either side. A great bird flew up before his coming, then loomed above him on broad wings.

The sun was just going down and the evening was limpidly gathering all about, when he saw below him the dragon's eye, Lake Ibron, like a pearl.

They had not gone up to the temple, or where the temple had been before the quake threw down the hill. They sat almost indolently among huge grass-grown boulders.

He saw at first glance Lowlanders, a fair Xarabian, one Vardish man playing dice with another, and the forms of two small red Lannic sheep questing in the grass for clovers. Standing up against the sheet of soft light that was the sky, were Amanackire, like a snowy grove. They stared at him, gods disturbed. But the Thaddrian looked past them, and seeing what he had come to find, he went to her.

He did not obeise himself. She was a part of the goddess, to whom he knelt only in ritual, never in fact, for that was not the proper way.

She told him, without speech, that he should sit.

He sat before her.

The lake, the light, bloomed at her back. Composed and pure as an icon, her symmetry was exquisite. But what pleased him most was her complete approachability. And that in the midst of a totality which seemed to alter the very air. In just this way the most valid things were come to. The sky itself, the sea, the world, magnificent and charged with meaning—a child might gaze at them and read them like an open book. This was the verity of Power.

He was the only sheer Visian there. The idea that he had been invited began to make a strange sense. It was a balance. In a short while, he produced from his priest's robe a square of cloth, and opened it on the rock for her. Inside were pieces of a shattered amber ring. Sparks of the sun were startled in them. Even the Amanackire came from their eminence to see.

The Thaddrian, who had watched Raldnor and Astaris ride away into the forests of the north, was something of a psychic hound. This talent had enabled him to know Rarmon who was to be Rarnammon, and long after, to track Rarnammon's path to the spot in Koramvis where enemies had taken him. The ring, shattered, had been abandoned. The Thaddrian had gathered up the bits carefully. It was not that it was a labor Ashni had set him, more a labor he wished in some way to perform for her, and which had therefore been allotted. Even on the Plains, there were sometimes offerings of fruit, or carvings, left for the goddess. She understood it was sometimes difficult, in moments of great joy, not to give thanks in concrete terms; the giver's need, not the recipient's.

Ashni drew the shards of the ring into her palm.

A woman now in the Zor had worn this ring. Ashni had worn the ring. Rarnammon had worn it. Another, the son of Yannul, had held the ring, though it burned him. A link of flesh and resin, still bonded.

The pieces were all in place now, all but the pieces of the ring.

The last ray of sunlight coiled through them, like a serpent. And then, the ring was whole, melded together, intact.

He heard their breathing, the circle of them all around, the sighs attendant upon miracle. But the Thaddrian grinned. And she smiled at him.

"Yes, *you* know," he said to her inside his skull, without words. "I am the one says miracles need not be, for gods to be. And to this day I never saw any reason why Raldnor and Astaris shouldn't be living in some lost thatched village of Thaddra, among those who didn't know them. Ordinary, happy, obscure. I can speak the jargon of the priests—the transcension, the chariot of flame that takes the god into heaven. And to me, that's so simple, so mundane. Miracles are nothing—the stuff of life. The flower blossoming, the invisible emerging from the womb—a child, resin turned into amber—miracles, nothing but miracles. But there's the fact beyond the miracle. The stone under the silver lake. What we are and must become. *That's* the reason and the perfect truth, and the answer to all the questions and the cries. Isn't it, Ashni-who-is-Anackire?"

And the reply was given him, just as the ring glowed on her finger. And the sun bloomed still in her eyes, though the sun had gone down.

TWENTY-FOUR

A white tower on a dark blue sky.

The sweep of the scattered city below.

And then the jungle-forest, the distances of Thaddra.

The tower had once been bowl-topped, forerunner of the towers of Dorthar. But the masonry had come down. Into what remained, the neck of the tower, a room with half a ceiling and many long shutterless windows, Tuab Ey trod like a cat. And stopped, staring.

Rarnammon stood in the center of the floor, looking at him, apparently waiting for him.

"I said I wouldn't visit your new—abode," said Tuab Ey, "but here I am. Now, tell me what you've been doing all these days and nights. Incantations and summonings? A few of them say they've seen lights flying to the windows like birds."

Rarnammon shook his head, very slowly. Tuab Ey was uncertain whether this was denial or wondering contempt. The qualities of Rarnammon had intensified. He seemed less penetrable than any other object, and yet lucent, day pouring through the eyes—

"You *are* a magician," said Tuab Ey. "Admit it. I don't believe in magic, and will laugh. Then perhaps I can coax you forth, mighty lord. My dog-pack wants to go north or east, and find Free Zakorians to kill. Someone came, one of Jort's pigs, said the north rivers were running with dead."

"Tuab Ey," said Rarnammon, "go down to the foot of the tower. Guard it for me. Keep the others out."

"Why?"

"The magic you referred to is about to be woken up. Incantations, summonings . . . not quite that. But lightning striking this tower might be a little thing."

"Don't talk in conundrums if you want something done. All right. I'll keep the gate for you. The others'll be off, anyway, if anything happens. What *will* happen? Apart from lightning."

"I don't know. I told you that before. But you have Lowland blood somewhere. I think you're necessary to this balance." A

378

hint of friendly bathos: "I'm sorry if it's inconvenient. But go
down now, if you will, Tuab Ey."

Tuab Ey backed a step, collected himself and said, "You look
like a god, standing there. Did you realize? Am I supposed to
worship?"

Rarnammon walked toward him through the sunlight of the
windows. It appeared to cling and cover him, that light, so that
when he stretched out his hand and laid it without pressure on
Tuab Ey's arm, and the light seemed to stream into it and
through Tuab Ey, it was only as expected.

Rarnammon put out his other hand to steady him.

Tuab Ey said quietly through the dizziness, "—Power. What
do I do with it?"

"Keep the gate."

Tuab Ey went down the stair, leaning on the wall, light filling
him, to keep the gate.

The day was hot, hazy. There was nothing unusual about it.
Yet he knew it was—the last day.

Ever since he had come into the tower—the high place stipulated in all lore—he had begun to move mentally toward this
time. Even in his ignorance he had moved, as a child learns to
walk in ignorance of walking.

There had been dreams, hallucinations, voids, the sense of
dropping to earth from the stars, without impact.

Now there was the sense of crisis.

Rarnammon was not alone. Others gathered, as forces gathered.
The world seemed one endlessly indrawing breath.

As the day turned, Rarnammon became aware of the tower
shutting itself about him. The very glare and heat in the window-
places solidified, making a screen where there was none. The
haphazard noises of the ruin faded.

It was conceivable he might die. But then, he might have died
on a hundred occasions. In his years as a thief, in Kesarh's
service at Tjis, in Lan outriding the caravans, in Dorthar, in the
hands of Free Zakoris. Each moment of survival was a gift.
Since he had come back to himself here in this fallen city, his
physical persona had meant less. He had felt part of some
entirety, one bough of one great tree.

Rarnammon lay down on the floor, and the lights crossed
themselves in the air above him. A bird flew over the gap in the
ceiling on yellow gauffered wings.

It was the final expression of external matter. He closed his
eyes and went inward. The madness, the letting go of the fleshly

self, had taught him. As his half-brother Raldanash was,
Rarnammon also was now an adept.

His consciousness descended, entered another place, and so
stepped forth.

One vast eye, seeing without sight, and in the sightless seeing,
all other senses were bound, and yet further senses the flesh
could not employ.

He sensed, in this manner, Tuab Ey below him at the foot of
the tower, seated in the entrance. A shape—the man, Galud—
was there, bending over him, asking what went on, and Tuab Ey
was sending him off, and Galud obeyed, stumbling.

A coalescence of radiance and color was sinking to a river of
moistures and shade; sun and forest. Every insect and beast of
the forest gleamed and blinked. The lives in the city's arid bones
flickered like the wings of moths.

Under the city, through veils of stone and soil and rock, the
well ran deep, and glowed. It was already awake, communing
with itself. The tower delved it, like a vein into a heart.

Sightless, seeing, Rarnammon beheld the other glowing hearts
away and away from him, yet near as his own hands lying on the
floor forgotten.

He was not afraid. Only some fragment of him remembered
his father at this instant, Raldnor, who had borne all this alone.
And before Raldnor, Ashne'e, who had been the beginning, the
first spark struck against the darkness.

Then he made contact with the starry, fiery heart, perhaps
before he was quite ready. But unreadiness did not hinder him.
He was blown upward, scorched and spun, but knew the strength
of his sailing wings, to ride, and to pace, the whirlwind.

Galud, rushing in among his fellows, was caught by the
One-Eared and shaken.

"Look at the sky!" hissed Galud.

They went to look.

Though the sun was setting, the whole heaven was throbbing
with an extraordinary brilliance. It seemed as if they were about
to see its arteries, or as if portions might be ejected.

"What's that sound?" said Galud. They listened. The sound
was not in the city. It could not be heard.

They stood listening to this soundless sound, as all over the
ruins others had paused to listen.

In the colony of lepers to the west, faceless things crawled
into cavities to hide.

Miles off in the forests, the chorus of the birds was chopped to dumbness, lizards froze, still water bubbled, creepers uncoiled like snakes from the trees.

The sun had already sunk beyond the ruined city of the south. Dusk sprinkled the colonnades and terraces that had had their youth in the era of Ashnesea.

The market of the Lepasin seemed deserted. Only a small wind played about there, with scraps of paper and petals and dust.

All around, the houses were boarded in, curtained over, shuttered. No light showed.

In the high place of the dark palace, seven figures, so white they seemed without blood, stood with white blowing hair between the broken sticks of columns. They were the guards, the custom. Their pale eyes took the tint of twilight, turning blue and uncanny.

Inward, flowers that had been brought rustled on the ancient floor paintings, the chips of citrine and garnet. The wind moved like the sea through the palace.

Lur Raldnor lay inside the darkness, his black hair poured on the mosaic. The Lowlanders, his kindred, had trained him. He had come to learn and to understand so much, that in the end he was afraid he would be the weakness that must lessen the chain.

Now he was beyond such fear.

His body lay like a corpse. The Amanackire guarded him as if he were a dead king. They would let no one through. They themselves, binding their minds with his, fenced and toughened his psyche.

To his awareness as he soared above it, the lines of force created on the surface of the palace were clear as silver bands. Silver steam described the city. Drunk on prayers, it murmured, sang, without sound.

He was prepared to give his life. He had been prepared to give it in battle. This was battle. But such thoughts were done. The cistern under the city was yielding up its vitality in thrusting surges, like a heart.

The city was all silver now. Far off, it struck a golden shadow, Rarnammon. . . .

And to the east a shadow like molten bronze—

Medaci was the Lowlander who held the gate in the Zor.

She stood at the entry to the mansion in the black night. Seeing her take her position there, knowing from some arcane tradition or instinct of tradition, her hair raying on the wind and the folds of her cloak, she was supernatural; a creature of the firmament. Yannul saw her, turned and went with the others to the chosen area two or three streets away. He had remonstrated at the beginning. He must remain at hand. Very well, the power of the planet would course upward, yet still some animal might come by and harm her. She was beyond him by then, and did not listen, he thought. She had gone so swiftly, he felt she had died. It was his younger son who explained, leading Yannul aside. There would be no animals, no interruptions. Medaci did not even have to bear the unleashing of Power. Safca was elected for this. Safca would bear it. But Medaci was the guardian, some ingredient or symbol of the balance.

Yannul knew, as they all did, when the Power of the city began to stir. It was a terrible, wonderful, unspeakable thing.

He tried to blind and deafen himself with it.

He did not want Medaci to have been "chosen" even for this. Had she not already suffered enough through the psychic use of others? And he recollected the plain under Koramvis, the silent harp-string plucked over and over.

All along the opposite bank, over their river, the villages of the Zor would be watching, offering their own rituals to the esoteric night. The city gleamed, maybe, for those who could see it. Yannul did not want to see it. He was tormented. Finally he walked off from all of them, and from his own son, into the city's enormous shadow, and sitting down in shadow commenced to pray, as once long ago, only for life, except now it was Medaci's life.

The Lowland woman, the golden Amanackire who was Medaci, held the gate, the mansion on the hill. The high place. It had put out its temporal fires.

Safca, circling somewhere in the roof, (briefly amused, visualizing herself a pigeon), perceived the bronze light of the city's aura start to wash away the gloom.

How did I come to this? Safca inquired. *I am nothing.*

But she recalled the bracelet on her left wrist, and what it hid, what had been hidden since birth—the other bracelet, abhorrent, or maybe beautiful: A ring of fine pale metallic scales, incorporated in her dark skin. Her mother had not lived long in Olm. A Lanelyrian, she had still grown used to Dorthar and the luxury of the Koramvin court, which was extended to a favored slave. Freed, she had fled back to Elyr and Lan, when the Lowlanders came. She had caught Dortharian superstition, for an excellent reason, perhaps. Olm's guardian saw her, made her his concubine, lost interest. The child was born, premature, unimportant. On her deathbed, Safca's mother had tapped Safca's bracelet and the deformity they had concealed beneath. "From your father," she had said. That was the only time, and that was all. She never said who had had her in Koramvis, whose cherished slave she was, who had freed her to escape. Nor positively had she ever said she was with child already when she lay back for the guardian. Only dreams had guided Safca after. She was never sure.

But now she was strong, Her wings beat and bore her up, and as the gigantic flame began to rise, a paean of joy, a hymn, tore through her wordlessly. And she believed she might be what her mother had indicated, and that her destiny sprang from it. So it was, conception, birth, the second birth called death.

The fabric of stones and sky gave way. Medaci lay like a smooth cool bead within the inferno that lifted Safca upward.

But northwest, a white flower of fire steadied the ecstasy and madness.

Bronze and silver and gold, the weavings of the light wove them all to that whiteness, which was Koramvis and her hills and the eye of the sleeping lake.

It was, in this high place, the swarthy Thaddrian who held the gate, guardian, black feather in a balance of pallor. A priest, he was not quite unversed in metaphysical conduct, or the intangible. And he had his own talents. His terror was nothing, nor did he count it.

Below him, the fair men and women maintained their own equilibrium, facing up toward her where she was on the hill's crest, a tiny figure like a little doll.

But the Thaddrian, though facing away from her, knew the light came up through her, and presently, mundanely, he noted his own shadow cast before him on the earth, jet black from the dawn of whiteness on the crest of the hill.

In all its quarters and corners, the night lay, to the human eye, deep as water over every inch of Vis. The stars followed their courses. The moon went down. The hour before true dawn came quietly across the sea.

The ships like sleeping birds anchored, wing-folded, five miles off the tip of Alisaar. Her clockwork patrols, if they had noted them, had noted also their diplomatic distance, and let them alone. Alisaar might, besides, have other more pressing business.

The beacon on the edge of the western jungle wilderness had

been seen to blaze by those who took heed of it. Thirty-five galleys of Free Zakoris, emerging from nowhere like things born out of mud, had swung northwest, perhaps to harry Saardos, or to attempt the Corhlish and Iscaian beaches.

Report stated the greater fleet of the Leopard, which kept on toward the Inner Sea, had grown like a conjuring trick to one hundred and seventy-six ships. There had been bays along that chartless jungle coast, where uncountable vessels might shelter, and slip out to join the concourse, or carry its dealings elsewhere.

Word was, eastern Karmiss had been covered, as if by a swarm, bleeding and on fire, the smoke of Istris one more cautionary beacon.

The mountain Pass from Thaddra into Dorthar would be fluid with battle.

On the passes above Vardish Zakoris, where Yl's men now ran at will, the Dortharians would use the mechanics of avalanche to block the way. Even if the device had been betrayed, the Leopard would be in difficulties to prevent it. To swamp the Okris delta must be easier. The last message from that region had all the river inlets in arms, the reeds on fire, the stone towers holed by catapults. The wind, blowing to Anackyra, bore ashes and the cries of men, which could not be a fact, and was only a parable of despair.

In Xarabiss, the troops of Thann Xa'ath had retreated from the port of Lin Abissa, leaving the docks alight. A Xarabian detachment had pulled out of Moiyah and marched back to the border, to the Dragon Gate and Sar. There were similar desertions elsewhere, men forging homeward.

In the hour before dawn on the sea once called for Aarl, those who waked or watched on the King's ship, saw Raldanash go by, walking on the open deck. Here and there a low-voiced greeting was exchanged. His whiteness, clothing and hair, seemed nocturnally luminous, as was the sea itself in patches. At the rail above the prow, he spoke with the captain.

They stood awhile, gazing west.

At sunrise, the vessels would make on. Yl's great fleet, nearly twice their numbers, would sail to meet them. The area of meeting had been established by some Amanackire priest. It had a religious purpose.

The goddess would, naturally, be with them. The captain, leaving his King to his final living privacy, went away along the deck. A man of Marsak in Dorthar, the captain had never credited Anack, though he had wisely given her lip-service and offerings. Over the black water, he saw now the ghostly Ashkar banners of the Vathcrian galleys. And, moved by a sudden fury, the captain spat in the ocean, in case after all She might be real and he could show her how he rated Her paucity.

Raldanash son of Raldnor observed the sea, with its patches of fire that did not burn.

Soon, he would return to the foredeck cabin, and don the non-physical armor of his training. To linger here was just the humanity in him. His affairs otherwise were in order. But he had wished to bid farewell.

Already pulses, unheard, unseen, unfelt, rocked the world.

An hour, a little more, and it would come to pass. If there was not power or strength or faith enough, it would fail.

There would be, therefore, power and strength and faith enough.

The captain from Marsak, his nervous hatred and act of defiant wrath, these Raldanash had noted, as he could take note of all the welter of thought and will and wish about him. He was even aware of the creatures far below, the huge fish deeply meshed in the currents of the ocean, as they swam out their alien time, valid and unknowable. And he longed to go away with them, stripped of intellect and burden. But could not, would not.

My father, also, was alone like this, that night under Koramvis.

Raldanash sighed.

Those who watched him covertly saw only the handsome face, the royal bearing, a king who had the ichor of gods in his arteries. A mote of trust and perverse hope settled on his watchers. By his excellence, he seemed to prove to them a miracle was possible.

But Raldanash had clasped hands with life, and surrendered it.

When the man of the Amanackire came noiselessly to him, calling without words, Raldanash, Storm Lord and Dragon King, turned back along the deck to make ready.

The great fleet of Free Zakoris, veering eastward now with the tidal currents and winds of sunrise, did not know there was a line drawn across the sea.

They had made sacrifice to Rorn as the disc of the sun escaped his halls. The brief barking prayers were done, though still the bluish streamers of incense rose from every prow of those one hundred and seventy-six ships.

Yl himself rode this arm of his fleets. He straddled there, close to the Rorn god of the King Ship. Behind him was the mass of sail, ochre-colored, with the Black Leopard scrawled over it. The dawn was in the Zakorians' faces. They had gained indications that enemy shipping might come out to greet them. They expected Shansarian Alisaar, or Xarabiss, more than they looked for Dorthar and Dorthar's King.

As for the line of psychic force, it was invisible and apparently immaterial.

What they did come to see was a sudden turbulence in the glimmering water fifty oar-lengths away.

Yl's captain pointed. There was a parcel of shouts.

"Huge fishes, Lord Yl, leaping from the depths."

There were so many of these fish, they slowed to let them by.

When the arcing, snakelike forms and the sea-flushed spray had settled, a shadow came out of the sun.

The watch-horns sounded. The Zakorian galleys flung themselves to battle-stations before the devices of Dorthar had even been read.

Braziers roared. Fresh smokes curled up into the morning sky. The ballistic weapons were hauled and secured in position on their shrieking chains.

"They don't come on, my lord."

"Shy? We shall go to embrace them, then," Yl said. "Dorthar, and Ralnar's son, crushed in the fist."

Across the slight interval of water, oars idle, the Storm Lord's fleet stood waiting on his order. Which did not come.

"My lord—" said the captain from Marsak.

Raldanash was above him, by the rail. Somehow, a group of Amanackire had got between him and his officers.

All at once, the air was changed. It seemed to ignite, as if the sun had slipped from cloud, but the sky had been clear since dawn.

The captain did not speak again. He wet his lips and rubbed his temples, wondering if only he was effected. All about him, surreptitiously at first, the soldiers did similar things. It was like a sort of drunkenness when the stomach was not full. A rush of clarity that equally obscured. A folding away. A going outward—

The sea began to shiver.

Long waves, like those foretelling storm, raced and broke about the ships.

No wind blew. The sky was pristine.

The sea bucked and tumbled.

They had seen large fish, could it be they were rising again, under the very keels?

Men ran about. A scatter of orders were bawled. Then silence came back. Yet, there was a sound. It seemed rather to be in the skull than in the passages of the ears.

Above them, Raldanash, in the prow. Not moving. Doing nothing.

That white hair was like a flame. Flame ran along the edges of him, a man cut from parchment, burning.

Men cried out now.

A huge sheen enveloped the ship, reflected in the pounding pouring waves.

The foremost Free Zakorian galleys were approaching ramming speed when the sea raised itself and slewed against them.

As the first great runners hit them, oars flailed, breaking rhythm. Then the massive sweeps were shattering like twigs, and a terrified howling came from the rowers' decks below. On the floundering timbers all about, men crashed over in a rain. A catapult tilted slowly and fell into the water.

"In the name of Zarduk—" Yl, struggling to his feet, gripped his captain by the neck.

The man pointed wildly.

"Something—something in the sea!"

Between the careering, speed-smashed Zakorians and the silhouetted static ships of Dorthar, the water spouted upward, black and combing, sediment and spray and gusts like mist or steam, blotting out now the sight of each fleet from the other.

Something indeed was active there, some massive hulk or beast, thrusting up from the floor of the ocean—

Aarl, place of submarine volcanoes—the story flooded a thousand minds. They called to each other in horror, remembering—

And then in a spume and spurl the ocean was ripped apart.

Walls of water a hundred feet high or more burst into the air. Darkness threw itself over them. The sea would be next. It would crush them in its fist.

And yet, the sea did not fall back as it must, dashing them in pieces, swallowing them whole. The sea hung like a curtain there, glittering and quivering, and the sun began to soak through, and the sea dried in the sun, upright in the sky.

Raldanash had become the mirror, of bronze and silver and gold and white light. His brain separated from his body, then his consciousness.

He floated high in the air, a seabird, weightless, and beheld the ships below, pale and dark, like figures on the war-table at Anackyra. And the sea surged up between.

Flame from the north sheared through. He was aware of Rarmon, very near, as if he were at his shoulder in some fight, their shields locked. Yet Rarmon-Rarnammon was miles off. A communication passed between them, speechless and without format, understood instantly, then gone.

The two lesser fires were nearer. They entered and refocussed, swelling, ascending. From the east and the south. He knew the beings searing in the fire, male, female. They touched him, and each other, and the gold light of Rarnammon. The fourth light was beyond them all, so pale it had a core of blackness. Ashni. Sunrise. Morning Star.

Raldanash, or the awareness Raldanash had become, felt itself consumed in the conflagration, without pain or fear, peacefully. And as he died, the fifth ray of the star exploded outward, the psychic orgasmic energy of the spirit.

The filaments flared, from outer point to center and so to each outer point once more, and every filament as it centered and returned, centered and returned, spun off from itself the newborn intersecting threads. Over all Vis, the woof and weft of a colossal loom crackled and sparkled and gave birth.

The sea was in the sky.

Then a figure was there, girded by ocean, tall as the roof of heaven.

The Dortharians saw Anackire.

She towered, She soared. Her flesh was a white mountain, Her snake's tail a river of fire in spate. The eight arms stretched in the traditional modes. Her eyes were the sun twice over. She spoke to them, in their minds, wordless. She said: *It is ended*.

But the men of Free Zakoris did not see Anackire, the Lowlander-witch they abhorred. They saw Rorn, their own god, who was black, with sea-plants in His ebony hair and jewels in the palms of His hands. And with one of these gargantuan hands, as He leaned down all His length toward them from the ether, He pushed their ships firmly away, firmly but carefully, for He did, being theirs, care for them.

Rorn spoke in words. It was a voice of tempest, and His breath was salt. *You won your land,* Rorn said to them. *Be proud of your kingdom, carved from Thaddra, and be also content. The rest is not yours to take. It is I RORN who say this.*

They lay on their faces before Him.

Blue sea gems flashed in His teeth. Thunder encircled His head.

At last they looked, and saw only a white shade of his blackness, waning on the day. They had been moved back like game pieces many miles. The Dortharian fleet was not to be seen. The sky was overcast and troubled, the sea beneath littered with timbers, bits of ironware, and coals that had spilled and not yet gone out. There were, too, a host of broken swords, split cleanly in the midst of the blade.

They had not lost a single vessel, or one man.

Their slaves clamored below, an outcry, in which the names of many gods were mingled.

Yl kneeled trembling before the little Rorn god in the prow.

Above, the ochre sail had parted from the yard. The emblem of the Leopard of vengeance and war had been smeared into shapelessness as if by some immense hand.

The gods walked all Vis that day.

Ten miles from Saardos, Rorn appeared before thirty-five Free Zakorian ships, admonished them, and turned them. He kept one foot on the distant land as He breathed on their sails and blew them southward. The fleet of Alisaar encountered Him, too. When men, maddened by the sight, tried to immolate themselves in His honor, Rorn told them such death was not needful. The Shansarians in the fleet, however, declared they had witnessed Ashara of the fish's tail. The sun was caught in Her golden hair. Her breasts were lovely. She reminded them of the Homeland.

As, in the person of Ashkar, She reminded the Vardians, Tarabines and Vathcrians in Xarabiss, the Lowlands, and elsewhere.

Close to the port of Lin Abissa, She uncoiled from the road, and Her skin was honey, Her serpent's tail red copper, and Her hair was red as wine. But the Free Zakorians there saw Rorn, striding through the charcoaled ships, the smoke on His shoulders.

In Thaddra it was Zarduk, Who routed Yl's forces from the border forts of Vardian Zakoris. And Zarduk, too, on the mountain Pass above Tumesh, Who rose out of the stones. The sun was not in His eyes, it made His belly. Black, magnificent, His masculine form enclosed the whirling solar disc. His breath was incense and heat, a scorching dust wind.

The Dortharians on the Pass saw this: A dragon out of their mythological genesis. It drove down the sky; incendiary beams shot from its carapace and jaws. They expected both the enemy and themselves to be at once incinerated. But not a man was lost, here as elsehwere.

Zarduk was in the delta of the Okris.

The spoons of catapults snapped off against their buffers. The black ships shuddered. Zarduk's feet were braced in the river, which barely reached His knees, his fiery belly blinded them, or should have done. Anackire, or a creature much like Her, was positioned at His left side.

In Ommos, the god was duality, both feminine and male: Zarok-Anackire.

In Ylmeshd, Yl's city in Thaddra, a golden glow stained the anthill dwellings, emanating from the cave tample of the fire god, causing some panic.

It was said that priests, stealing in to see, found the topaz Eye from Ankabek, brighter than a lamp, had been transported of itself into one of the eye-places of the Zarduk. That a Zakorian deity should have, thereafter, half the gaze of a Lowlander, was so suitable to resultant legends of that day, it was later suggested Yl himself, not the gods, organized the matter on his return.

Ashara appeared to blasted Karmiss. She rose above Ioli like a daytime moon. In Istris, Rorn had seemed to shake the city, very gently, as if to shift crumbs from a mat.

Stray Leopard ships making for Lan came upon Him seated on the ocean. He said they must go back to Thaddra. They believed Him.

The versions were endless. All differed. Ten men in one place had each seen a vision no other saw. Stars fell, mountains moved, bells rang in the sea.

Yet the words, uttered to the ear, the brain, or the heart—they were substantially the same.

And the felled ballistas, the broken swords, lay thick as flowers where the dead should have lain.

The four fires, the burning-glass, joined like the amber ring, now letting go the light.

Each drew away, became an incandescent dot. The web of force grew dim. Went out.

The dulling of the vast effulgence revealed another, lesser effulgence, where, everywhere, there were shining the tiny faint lights, the miniature trusts and prayers of a world, the will of a multitude to persist—fuel for the vaster flame. And then these also were dimmed. All but one.

The shattered mirror, that had been the focusing will of Raldanash, embers now, retained to itself the palest after-images of linking fire, one of which led northwest to the man who was his kindred, and one northeast toward the aurora of Ashni. But the subsiding embers could not sustain these connections. The trails of fire vanished. Soon only one slender and translucent link remained, scarcely visible while the larger lights had blazed.

This final light did not yet fade.

Its nether point, located on that line of Power which ran from Koramvis to the Zor, was the place of the earliest sacrifice, Ankabek.

She felt his dying, embers to clinker, Raldanash who had been her husband, far away, miles of land and space and time.

She had come to her discovery along a steep and sightless mental tunnel, which she entered voluntarily when the door mechanisms closed her within the Sanctum. At the closing, she had lain down on the marvelous mosaic floor she could not see, and eventually, after some struggle, her ego and her name had gone from her.

Ulis Anet, Val Nardia, Astaris. She had been each of them and none.

She had trusted that Eraz would guide her, but she must guide herself, and so she did. She was so tired, it was not hard to choose this road, or follow it.

As if in a boat on a black winding river, she poled upstream, sleeping or awake she could not be sure, nor did it concern her.

Her mind filled itself slowly. The deep dreams, the conclusions, the solitudes. She herself came last of all, behind a train of fantasies. The inner she.

And so at length she opened the single eye of the spirit, and became one with the will of the world.

And when that will, having created its great sorcery, flowed away, she beheld Raldanash and how he died.

A mortal woman, she had detested him for his unintentional cruelty. Such pettiness was irrelevant now. Now, emerging from her own purgation, she knew his, reckoned up what he had given, asking no recompense. She herself had no special psychic endowment, but she, like all things, held the magic of the force of life. And all around were the stones of Ankabek of the goddess, invocation of Anackire.

Selfishly then, to redeem her own pain by knowing its littleness, she held out the lamp of Ankabek, slightest of fires.

And so she did learn pain's littleness. She learned in the surge of joy as this stranger, who was nothing to her and to whom she was nothing, yet heard her, yet answered, and reached out across the endless distances to receive the proffered light.

The ships of Dorthar circled in the vortex of sea and sea-wrapped wind.

Only the Amanackire had dared go to the Storm Lord and lift him. He was borne to the cabin.

Without comprehending, his men had seen he was the pivot of the miracle. Now, contending with the tempest, there was no leisure to dwell on it.

Some wept, but there was salt water on all their faces.

Raldanash lay on the royal couch as the ship jumped at the blows of the storm.

The Amanackire stood by. They did not mourn. Ruthless in their faith, and pitiless, certain all men lived forever. What was death? Having only just participated in the lesson, they had missed it. Physical life was also sacred, and to be saved.

Then they felt the telepathic stirring, turned to Raldanash, and saw his eyes open, the golden eyes in the dark face.

He had come back from somewhere he had already forgotten.

His body was weak and drained, listless, would scarcely obey him or acknowledge him. But the vitality in him was like a seed, which would become again the tree. His brain was already vital.

He did recollect the instant, in the very act of falling, that he had seen they had won.

The symbols were no more than that, gods were the emblem, as language was the expression of incorporeal thought. They had used only the power and strength and faith of mankind. It had been enough. The world was ended, and begun.

And I, too, live.

The men in the black galleys rocking above Lan, having seen nothing sensational, were bewildered.

There had been unseasonal storms that day, the winds casting from all directions. When night entered the world, a soundless calm drew in, as curiously unnatural as the turbulence before. In the heavy blackness the stars exhaled their glare. The moon came up from the hollow ocean. It was like some nightfall of history, aeons old.

The men in the two black galleys, hesitated uneasily and listened to the emptiness and stared out at the stars. The ships were the command of Dhaker Opal-Eye. The third of their number had gone down at Karith, when Dorthar sent Free Zakoris back into the water. Such orders as Dhaker received had then dispatched his crews to Karmiss. Dhaker had objected. His own ship carried a passenger of whose identity King Yl was informed. A Karmian of stature, relevant to Karmiss' present predicament. The Karmians might attempt to help—or at least to capture—this man. But Dhaker had no desire to reveal at large his prisoner's name. Evasive, he could get no purchase on the obstinacy of the Free Zakorian command then licking wounds off Ommos. So, his ships turned for Karmiss, and skirted her. Dhaker had reckoned to join the Leopard's forces at Okris delta.

Rough weather caught them less than fifty miles from their objective. They sought to ride it out, but were blown instead, disordered, into the east.

There were weird coronas in the storm. Fires came to perch along the masts and rails. Dhaker had beheld such wonders before. He kept his soldiers busy, and gave them wine and beer, and sent beer down to the slaves. In the evening, the squall had almost parted the two ships, but the abrupt leveling of the sea brought them together again.

Then came the mystery of darkness and open water.

A few hours after, there arose a wailing from the slaves. Someone had been possessed by bad dreams, now they were all catching it like plague. The steady hiss of the whips eventually doused this noise.

"They say Rorn walks over the ocean, a giant, with the moon in his hand."

"*I've* not seen him," said Dhaker. "Not even with my missing eye."

Suddenly, he was moved to visit his guest.

It was dark as night, but starless, in the lowest closed place of the ship. This underdeck, counterbalance to the tall stack of the vessel above, lay below the waterline, beneath the rowing positions. It might be utilized as cargo hold, or as dungeon. Dungeon now it was. The prisoner, naked but for hair and filth, sprawled there unmoving, till the Zakorian's lamp and feet found him out.

"Well, my lord," said Dhaker, "did you enjoy the storm?"

Kesarh, bloody and bruised on the rusty chains that, during the upheaval, had obviously slammed him over and again into the thick ribs of the ship, looked up at him. The black eyes still had cold heat in them. They should have been filmed over, if not blind. Dhaker's surgeon had pulled the lashes out, repeatedly. Yet, through the caked blood, the cold heat and the sight continued.

Dhaker liked this unquenchable quality. It would make Kesarh more difficult, therefore more interesting, to kill.

"Istris was in splinters, the last I heard," said Dhaker. "Does that make you sad?"

But Kesarh's emotions were well-chained up, you saw, like his body.

Dhaker kicked him, lightly, in the mouth. A side tooth had been broken earlier, and Dhaker had allowed them to cut the lobes from the prisoner's ears. These he had then sent to Yl as token, with the message of capture. That was sufficient for now.

Dhaker went up again, noting on his way that the rowers had stayed restless after their discipline.

The night was fine, and Dorthar comparatively near.

It was after midnight when the horns mooed.

Some twenty ships of Free Zakoris had appeared in their path, seeming to have been storm-thrown as they were, off course, and heading back northwestward.

Dhaker's pair of galleys rowed in among their brothers.

Not a man but was struck immediately by the silence, almost idleness of every neighboring deck.

Most of the sails were taken in, but here and there one hung from the yard, torn by the gales. The torches of Dhaker's ships picked out on these remnants a muddy smear no longer recognizable as the war Leopard.

Dhaker's galley came up with the flotilla's lead ship. Like all the rest, she was poorly lit. The men on her deck stood like pillars, or went about their work as if drugged.

"To Dorthar?" Dhaker shouted out, not bothering with intermediaries.

When the call was answered, Dhaker was amazed.

The Free Zakorians were not bound for Dorthar. The war was—*abandoned*. They went home to Yl's kingdom, in Thaddra.

"Are you mad?" Dhaker bellowed. He seized a rope and would have swung over, but their captain had come on deck now, and gestured him away.

"Not madness. The gods spoke to us."

"Gods—you mean some augury—"

"Rorn, and Zarduk. Their heads brushing the sun. I have seen it myself. He spoke to me, and his voice was intense. We're to live in Thaddra. We were told. The sword's broken."

"Crazy. This one is crazy." Dhaker looked at his men, who gazed in awe at the silent ships all about them, setting their inexorable course for Thaddra.

The barren dialogue was abrogated, and Dhaker's vessels drew away.

The black flotilla with its anonymous sails went drifting on, a phantom thing, dumb and demoniac as the night it vanished into.

In the world there were days and alternating periods of sunlessness, there were hours and minutes, scenes and the responses to scenes, and weather. Below, in the underdeck, there were none of these things. There was blackness, the shackles, stench, the taste of stench, or of blood, the dull noises of the ship. Being thrown against the ribbed kernel of the dungeon, that was military engagement or a storm. Daybreak was seldom, and only a lamp. The various tortures had served in the beginning as a means of telling time—the crescendo of pain, the pain's slow ebbing. But now pain was universal and constant and varying—the gnawing of the fractured tooth, the bite of the chains in the raw wounds they had made. It was no longer helpful.

One could think, of course, and frequently lose consciousness. Like a hibernating animal or a sick animal, Kesarh had this trick. Awake, he was never completely lucid, and knew it. All the same, he had not surrendered. He expected to outlast this misfortune, though he had neither fantasies of sudden rescue nor of an act of gods, in whom he did not believe. Nor, since he did not believe in a god within, did he presume himself capable of some feat of self-deliverance. His optimism, if such it could even be termed, had no roots therefore in fact.

His resistance was his will, stronger than all the rest of his many strengths.

He refused to finish here and in this way. Could not conceive of it.

That conversation which had taken place between the Leopard ships by night had not, obviously, been relayed below. Yet there was some insubstantial whiff of it to be sensed. Soon, if timelessly, other awarenesses swirled through the timbers. The slave-rowers picked them up, became fractious or terrified. The sharp screams of men under the less tolerable of the whips grew nearly ceaseless.

In a quintet of days—unseen, unknown: Above—Dhaker's vessels had had other meetings. Some of these were with Free Zakorians beating a way from Karmiss, as Rorn had instructed them. They babbled of prodigies and were gone. Later, a brace of Kumaean vessels appeared around a headland, for they were in sight of the Dortharian coast by now. Outnumbered, but wild for a fight, Dhaker's galleys had turned to attack, but the ships of Dorthar avoided and eluded them.

There was talk then of raiding the first village they came to, but probably all such would be evacuated, or defended.

Dhaker's men were bewildered and afraid. Tensions were not restricted to the slaves. There must be some release. Dhaker had begun to believe the insane tales other Zakorian vessels gifted him. If not their truth, at least its effect.

On the fifth day a herd of sea-ox came swimming on a great lacy wake, and the horns were blown and a furor started. His men had been moaning that Rorn arose out of the depths, before Dhaker roared them into stillness.

Something was needed. Up in the world of days and nights and time and weather, Dhaker decided.

When Kesarh was brought into the torch-lit cabin, Dhaker studied him with some pleasure.

His captive's body was painted by abrasions and the sores induced by chains, yet it had not wasted. After the perpetual dark below, the eyes were winced to slits, but the ice-flame of the black pupils stared through unabated. Kesarh had the royal atoms of Karmiss with the savage Shansar strain; and something more. He was not broken, not even twisted out of shape.

There was food and drink. Dhaker invited his prisoner to dine. Kesarh, without comment, did so. There was no look of desperation, and none of the distrustful questioning almost any other man would have let slip. *He supposes he will get through all this,* Dhaker thought. The notion astonished him. Kesarh's will was powerful even now, and Dhaker for a second half doubted. Was it possible Kesarh might somehow escape?

There was a vague sound outside, Dhaker's orders being carried out. He abruptly recovered his wits. Escape was not possible.

"You love me well," said Dhaker to Kesarh. "You've confidence I won't seek to poison you."

Kesarh had ended his meal, scrupulously.

"And cheat Yl?" he said.

"Oh, but Yl has lost interest in killings," said Dhaker. "I've heard the signals have failed to show. His ships foundered against Ralnach of Dorthar, then, and never reached the Inner Sea. That, or the gods sent him home with all the rest."

Kesarh did not react to these riddles. He said, clearly,

"Or else he remembers the treaty he made with me, and therefore with the might of Shansar-over-the-ocean."

"No, I don't think he remembers that, Lord Kesr. I don't think he remembers you at all. Vis has gone mad. In the land of madness, the sane must do as he reckons fit."

Kesarh's eyes had opened, striving with the murky light. Dhaker felt the extraordinary authority of them.

They sat in silence, neither prepared to ask the other to speak. Dhaker rose.

"The cushions, there. Take rest. Sleep."

At last Kesarh said to him, "You have something strenuous in mind for the morning."

"My father," said Dhaker, "died at Tjis. I knew him. He was

good to me. It's not sure we'll reach home port, the world having addled." The iron eyes never faltered. Dhaker nodded and went out. The door of the cabin was guarded, though he did not imagine Kesarh would attempt heroics. Even a quick death would not be attempted, for Kesarh did not credit he could die at all. He would sleep now, hoarding his endurance. In agony and hopelessness he would cling to life, assured it was his right, until the final drop squeezed through his fingers.

A while before dawn Dhaker Opal-Eye reentered the cabin and regarded the unconscious man, his strong physique, which was about to become its own worst foe. On the left forearm, the wound Dhaker had cauterized had healed curiously, leaving a scar resembling that of a serpent's bite.

"Take him now," Dhaker told his men. "Let him come to it as he wakes."

They did this, dragging Kesarh out into the nacreous vacancy that was ship and sea and sky. As the stars melted, they slung the chained man down, and hauling up his arms, hammered the spikes through his fetters to hold them in position. Then they raised the pole and secured it in a series of jolts, close to the king-sail. He was fully awake by then, and knew. It was an old method of execution, and very simple, common to all western lands, formerly a slave's sentence in Dorthar.

Suspended from the pole by his upraised arms, his heels had already found the narrow resting place, and gripped there, taking the weight of his body. It would be a struggle to do this, but he would struggle to do it. There was a similar rest under the buttocks that might also be put to use, awkwardly and with difficulty. Since the hanging man would not be able to breathe without recourse to these supports, he would constantly resort to them. Constantly slide from them, constantly regain them. The struggle would be never-ending.

Held by the wrists alone, the lungs cramped, the blood would not move. Asphyxiated, the condemned soon fainted; death could come inside a morning. But that was the swift way. This way was not swift. And Kesarh's will, his haughty demand to live, would prolong the combat beyond total exhaustion. Three-quarters a corpse, he would still be struggling, sliding, struggling, gasping and grasping, losing an inch, a moment at a time.

And he would be given water, and food while he could eat it. It might go on for days.

Now there was light, and dark. There was sunrise through the great sail. There was sunset at his back, his own hanging shadow flung before him along the deck. Men would not cross over it. It was bad luck.

Later, he did not notice this anymore.

Air came by straightening, pinioning the heels and calves or the lower back or the buttocks against the pole. In a dizzying rush, the arms loosened somewhat, the lungs were able to expand. One did this until the anguish of the position forced feet or spinal muscles to give way. Then the former agony re-commenced.

Shortly, all agonies were the same. To be lifted and to breathe in agony, or to let go and to sink in agony, stifling.

He drank the water and swallowed the gruel.

He glared into the sky.

The sea was very flat, the deck flirted like a dancer. Men moved about, or stood, watching him. They were ghosts. They had no meaning. Nor the sky nor the sea. Only pain meant anything. But the pain was life.

At the fourth sunrise, he had forgotten his own name.

He heard them talking below. A man with a mote of flame in his eye, touched Kesarh's feet, gently, like a caress.

"Kesr, do you live, still? The fourth day, Kesr Am Karmiss. I never knew any to last so long." And then, "He's bleeding from the mouth. Blood from the lungs."

Kesarh turned his head. The sky was crimson and light split the sail. Something came and tapped his face. It was a bowl, pushed up on a stick. Water. He turned to put his lips to the bowl.

"No," said a girl's voice, softly, against his ear, or in his brain. "Don't drink it. Kesarh, don't drink."

"Go away," he said. His tongue found the water. "Bitch."

"No," she said. "Don't drink."

The water had no taste and he did not want it, though his thirst raged. His body tried to cough. Lances ran through his ribs. Then her hands came and held him. Cool, fragrant, better than the water.

"Listen to me," she said. "Since we were children, whom did we have to trust save each other?"

"I must live, Val Nardia," he said. "Get back what they took from me. And if you want me to live, I can. For you. Poison, disease, the wound of any battle—nothing. I'll run through flood and fire and thunderbolt—Val Nardia," he said.

"I am here."

"I shall live," he repeated. A strand of her red hair moved against the red sky as she held him. It was Val Nardia, and no other. No alter image. His head was on her breast.

"Live then," she said. "Let go, and live."

Below, Dhaker stirred, fingering the opal eye. The man who held up the bowl said, "He doesn't take the water."

"He's dead," said Dhaker.

They gave him neither to Rorn nor to the fire-burial of the yellow races. They left him to rot on the pole, or for the seabirds to feast on. Long before they came to Thaddra, only bones remained of him, which might have been the bones of any man who had died.

BOOK FIVE—*Morning Star*

TWENTY-FIVE

High on a golden stone in the furnace of noon, the woman sat looking across the river. Behind her the black walls of a ruin went up. The sun of the hot months had burned her nearly as black, all but the silver bracelet on her left wrist—which, drawing close, you saw was not a bracelet, but a ring of bright scales native to her flesh.

Yannul, having come out of the ancient city of the Zor, stood under the boulder. The farther shore was occupied, as usual, with its normal uneventful business. For almost a month it had been so. Since that night, that sunrise, of Power, when the world had seemed to chime like a bell. Easy with supernatural things, the villages across the river had soon put magic aside, a commonplace.

"Safca," he said, after a while.

"Yes," she said, "I know. You're going home."

"The villa-farm at Amlan," he said. "Medaci thinks we should go back. She says our elder son will get there. We don't know where he is. But—safe, she says."

"Oh yes," said Safca. "Yes, your son is safe and well." Her voice was remote, and beautiful. He had never realized, in the beginning, she had a beautiful voice. Perhaps it was a legacy of royal blood. For she had that, too, did she not? "Yes," she said again, "I have that, too."

"I shall never," he said, "get used to having my mind read."

"I'm sorry. Your secret thoughts are secure enough. But some things burst out, barking like dogs. I still don't know, Yannul, if it's true."

"That you're Amrek's daughter? You aren't like him. But the mark on your wrist—"

"The curse of Anackire."

Yannul said, "Maybe it wasn't a curse. Only an emblem. It hasn't harmed you. Could Amrek have misunderstood?"

She looked down at him. Her eyes were black Vis eyes—the Storm Lord Amrek's eyes? She had altered a great deal. If she had the heritage of that line did not really matter anymore. She could reign here if she wanted. The Lans who had followed her would make her a queen, without being asked. But she was a priestess too, and possibly temporal rule meant nothing. Zastis fell late this year, and was almost due. The small camp in the ruined city was restive, eager, and you saw the same in the villages over the river. Even he, finding Medaci had not changed, returning from the inferno no winged avatar but a woman. . . . Silly as adolescent lovers, they had coupled in a wild orchard under the walls, and scolded each other after, grinning.

But Safca, walking with a dozen male eyes scorching on her, gave no indication. Up on her rock now like a lioness, she watched the sky or a man with equal complacence, and no haste at all.

And if she had caught that thought, she did not answer it.

"Will you stay here," he said eventually, "the city?"

She said: "All places are one." He perceived she reckoned this to be so. "But for others—the town we came by. Or Lan under the mountains. Since Lan is accessible again. The passes are open."

"I know it."

"But there were no messengers," she said, her innocent eyes far away. "How could you know this?"

"Telepathy rubs off."

Safca smiled. "I see your son," she said, "Lur Raldnor, riding from the Lowlands. You must be proud of such a son."

Something wrenched at Yannul. He said, "What else do you see?"

"Many things."

She would not tell him. Only what it was his right to be told. That night, that morning, were distant as the stars, but he tried, if reluctantly, to conjure them.

"Do you," he said, "frequently see Anackire?"

"We are all Anackire. Anackire is everything."

"Then, no record. It was a dream—the war, the breaking of the sword."

"In Elyr," she said, "the towers are watching for a star."

"They'll see one, too." He grinned again.

"No, not Zastis, Yannul. Not an evening star of desire. A morning star of peace."

Yannul glanced over the river.

"I remember," he said slowly, "Koramvis."

But the woman on the rock said, "The past is the past."

And then he too saw, her mind focusing for his, Lur Raldnor riding under the sun. There was a second black ruin behind him, the length of the Plains and the little land of Elyr between, but Lur Raldnor was singing, some antique song Yannul half recalled, so he found he also began to form the words of it, noiselessly.

"Yes, father," said Lur Raldnor. "I know you hear me." He laughed at the sky. This was something he had yet to get used to. Having formed part of a mental colossus, he still had not mastered the everyday techniques of mind speech. It was like starting to make love and looking through the velvet surface to the skeleton.

One could fathom why the Sister Continent, growing mercantile, had begun to suppress its telepathy.

There were Sister Continent ships at Moiyah now, and over in Shansarian Alisaar. Some made on for Vardian Zakoris, for Dorthar and for Karmiss. It seemed they had held assembly down there in the south, and decided to reserve judgment on the war in Vis. So the old alliances stood after all. Now they ventured in as warlike friends, to an area less tumultuous than expected. Although in Karmiss, Shansar's comradeship would be welcome enough. Istris had suffered. Word had it she was wrecked. The Warden had seized authority, of course. But Shansarian autocracy would be reestablished before the year turned, the Lily thoroughly eclipsed by the goddess with the tail of a fish. Ashyasmai would be Ashara, once more. As for the banner of the Salamander—it was burned, ironic fate for a fire-lizard. Kesarh's ending was not so efficiently tabulated.

Which reminded one of Rarmon. But then again, one knew about Rarmon, too, what had chanced, and what was to come. Destiny, like the metaphorical girl's flesh, translucent and to be looked through.

There had been no problem that way with the Xarabian girl, who was not naturally a telepath. She had wept when Lur Raldnor bade her farewell, and told him she would call her son by his name. But Lur Raldnor, though he had not disillusioned her, had foreseen she would not bear his son.

He went back to singing the song of the Lannic hills his father had taught him long ago. Magic had its place. There were other things. He knew he was young and the earth was beautiful. And that anyway he, and everything, lived forever. But he had known that since Medaci told him, when he was three years of age.

* * *

"And it's farewell on Thaddra, now, is it? To me, who risked his fine skin under that damned tower," said Tuab Ey in the wine-shop at Tumesh. "Dorthar. What can Dorther offer you? Soft living and the King's favor, and rich food and good liquor—what's that to the healthy life you could lead with us, eating raw orynx in the jungle in the rain."

"Come with me," said Rarnammon. "You earned whatever I can get you."

"Humble thanks. I'm a lord here. Among lords I'd be scum, and I know it."

Tuab Ey stirred the stew with his dagger. "As for the tower. Some god passed over us. I heard his wings. Now I credit gods. But I lived through it. Galud says the tower raged as if it was alight."

"Galud may be wise."

"Then there were the lepers, apparently all cured. Even Jort verified that."

"Jort may be—"

"Wise, too? Hmm. So you're some god's golem," said Tuab Ey. "Priest-king. Hero. Come and be human with me."

The man with the black hair and yellow Lowlander eyes looked at him, until Tuab Ey dropped his gaze, entertained to be bashful.

"Fare well and prosper in Thaddra," said Rarnammon eventually.

"And you in Dorthar, you bastard of a king's bastard."

Outside the sun seared on an old marketplace. Slaves were being sold under an awning. For a moment Rarnammon, in the shadow of the shop door, saw a red-haired woman in with the lot. But Astaris' hair had been dyed black, they said, when Bandar put her up for sale here.

Galud glared at him as he brought over the Zeeba. Rarnammon rode away through the town and up into the foothills, his mind crowded by different things. Somewhere Yannul's son was riding too, and somewhere that woman he had met in Olm sat on a rock. Safca, Amrek's daughter—the revelatory visions had failed him there, or else been masked by some stronger will.

The city of Rarnammon dwindled behind Rarnammon son of Raldnor, a drumbeat fading over the miles.

The drumbeat of Dorthar lay ahead.

Sometimes, he wished he did not hear it. At others it alerted him. The time of the miracle had gone by; one could not remain at such a pitch. And had he not once brooded in Lan that there was nothing for him, that he was not enough in himself to ask anything of existence. The visions, which had revealed so many things, had left him oddly nearsighted in other ways. It was foolish now to balk or to step aside. There had always been witchcraft in Dorthar.

Raldnor had fled his own legend. But that was Raldnor.

The blueness of the mountains poured down and the forests curled away. There was no trace of Free Zakoris, only a broken machinery of siege abandoned on a slope.

They were raising a mighty stonework seven days along the Pass, to mark the visitation of the dragon the Dortharian soldiery had seen. The sculpture was homegrown, crudely if earnestly done. That might account for its curious shape. It was not like a dragon, more an enormous turtle, jaws and fins extruded from the discoid carapace.

He did not question the soldiers about it. They in turn did not recognize him—he did not allow them to. When he was gone, only then, rumor moved among them. But they pointed out to each other that the man they took him for in retrospect had betrayed Dorthar to the Leopard, and would not dare to be coming back.

Rarnammon was still on the Pass when Zastis began. The Star slunk up behind the moon, and dippered the mountains with its soft red flame. He was alone, and trying to sleep out the dreams that came, tinged like the mountains by the Star; he recalled a story that Zastis had been a palace the gods made for themselves in the clouds, a love-palace, which caught fire. Being a thing of the immortals, it burned on, unquenchable. And rising at certain seasons, inspired men, now, with lust.

The dreams themselves were uncharactered. Awake, he dredged up memories. But these also seemed to have no true relevance. He had been through a greater whirlpool now than pain or pleasure or sex.

The sentry posts on the Pass, as it cut into Dorthar, were Zastis-lax. The miracle had disorganized them, too. Some had grown authoritarian, or they had turned religious.

Finally, he came down from the mountains, through the huge boulders that had collapsed into fresh attitudes after the great earthquake, and settled there to seeming permanence.

He was on the path above that lake they called Ibron, no company, he thought, but the floating birds, when a glowing whiteness was suddenly against the curve of the hillside before him.

A man had fallen here, from a racing chariot, to the lake.

Rarnammon beheld a spinning shape, and looked through it to the Amanackire who stood beyond.

There was an interim, then. They did not move or communicate. He did not try the mind speech with them, nor let them probe him, he was strong enough to prevent it now. Such things remained an intrusion to Rarnammon. At length he lost patience. He said aloud: "I'm not my father, as you understand. Tell me what you want, or get out of the way."

He disliked them, so cold, so pale. Unearthly impure purity. Not Lowlanders anymore, but something novel and quite alien. The white eyes met his and were lowered unwillingly. They did not care for him, either, or that he, not they, had wedded the psychic storm. They jealously wanted to be gods, gods in the ancient manner: Men who were paranormally superior to, and held sway therefore over, other men.

"Son of Raldnor," one of them said, "are you on the road to Anackyra?"

"Where else?" he said.

"Raldanash is ours," they said, for all of them seemed to speak as one now, some mental overlay not to be avoided. "Raldanash we accepted, though his skin is the dark man's skin."

"This is a warning of some sort?"

"Yes," they said.

"Explain it."

"You are not ours. Nor will we be yours."

"Then, I've heard you out. Where's Ashni?"

"She went away over the hills. Some are with her."

"But not you," he said. "That must rankle."

As he spurred the zeeba, they seemed to smoke into the flank of the hill. It might be a trick, but he did not think so. Maybe they had learned that art of projecting the image from elsewhere.

Riding on, he made sure no other recognized him en route to the city. He met no more Amanackire.

He used the random "Merchant's Road" through the ruins to the river. Some thief was operating a ferry and poled him across.

When he got in at one of Anackyra's white gateways, entering the heat and rush of the metropolis, it seemed as if a pane of clear glass enclosed him. It was not only the cloaking anonymity he kept about himself. He was removed.

The city, which had been reprieved from devastation, was everywhere discussing the wonders of gods and sorcery, and everywhere ignoring them. Trade and commerce flourished. Men argued and hassled in the dust. Two girls fought shrieking by a wine-shop. Incense and the rasp of gongs rose from the temples. Five of the sacred prostitutes, the Daughters of Anackire, crossed an avenue, guarded by temple soldiers. These women were bare-breasted, their nipples capped and rimmed by gilt, gold in the yellow veils of their skirts, their hair bleached, topaz in their ears and navels.

Rarnammon turned to look after them, dully amazed. Not only at the absurdity of the world.

Vencrek, Warden of Anackyra, said, "You're here, as he mentioned you would be. Your disguise must have been a nice one to get you through the streets."

"And Raldanash?" Rarnammon asked.

"He lies at Moiyah, with the fleet. There are Vathcrian ships there now, from the Homeland."

The Storm Palace was cool, and perfumed with shrubs and trees and the unguents of costly women. The languid gestures of Zastis, the scents of Zastis, breathed about them, everywhere.

"The council will be convened in the hour, my lord," said Vencrek. "You have that much time. The royal apartments were opened and made ready. As he ordered it."

"What is the council to be told?" Rarnammon said.

"What the city's to be told. That you were ordered to Zakoris-In-Thaddra on a secret mission, at the wish of the Storm Lord. That this mission was accomplished with honor, and should the war have proceeded to its logical ends, your valor would have placed you at Raldanash's side, his chief commander."

"Did you agree to this?"

"He's written to me," said Vencrek. "I have the letters and the proclamation here, the latter still under his unbroken seal. He reposes utter trust in you. I can't do otherwise."

"But you can," said Rarnammon, "do precisely otherwise."

"Yes, you would have got that from Kesarh, no doubt. Yl's pirates fed the fish with him, I gather."

Rarnammon did nothing, waited. After a time, Rarnammon said, "Do I assume Raldanash informed you of all his plan?"

"I take it he informed *you*, my lord."

"Yes."

"How?"

Rarnammon shrugged, deliberately. He said, "I thought that in Vathcri mind speech between brothers was not unusual."

Vencrek paled under his pale skin's tan. One could not ascertain why; it could be from many reactions.

"Yes, then," he said, "you and I both know that Raldanash

means to give up the crown of Dorthar. Means to abdicate and wander the backhills of Vathcri instead, as some starveling priest."

"If he can find solace that way," said Rarnammon, "why not? He never wanted this."

"While you, of course," Vancrek said, "always wanted it."

"Maybe. I won't deny I may have done. I am, after all, Raldnor's son. What was he? Priest and King. I'm the part of him that coveted glory in the gaze of men, perhaps. And Raldanash is the priest—meditation, and the hills of home. What do you want to do, Vencrek? Raldanash gives me his voice. If you can't stomach it, you must go."

"I'll stomach it," Vencrek said. "I don't want the backhills any more than you do. You'll see how well I'll stomach it. I can earn your favor, my lord." The blond head lifted, the Vathcrian smiled. "Let's see, my lord, if you can earn mine."

Later, when the council was done with, the shouting and dissension—had not Raldnor himself cast away this very kingship in the wake of victory?—the paid gossips were sent out to ply their trade through the city, just as in Istris all those short years ago. The people would be manipulated. The council would be manipulated. The customary bribes were negotiable here, as anywhere. Rarnammon who had been Rem knew the business, and dealt ably. He had besides Raldanash's decree to back him.

One considered Raldanash, picked up almost dead on the deck of that ship, lying dreaming the Dream of the goddess in the Lowland port of Moiyah. And the vessels of Vathcri evolving on sunset water, like an omen.

And Rarnammon wanted Dorthar. Yes, it was sure.

When the correct amount of days and nights were judged past, he rode through the city in procession and a gem-encrusted chariot. Standing in the Imperial Square on a dais beneath the giant statue of his namesake, he addressed the crowds, employing every gambit Kesarh had ever shown him, and won them, and heard them roar for him, the huge cry going up like birds. Kingship was more than triumph, more than a shout. But the King's blood that had come down to him, from Raldnor and Rehdon, remembered the sound a people make for their King, and welcomed it, as a right.

"The coronation's for the last quarter of Zastis. You must wed all his wives," said Vencrek. If there was a cutting edge in that, it was softly gloved. "Every king in Vis is obliged to send his representative or be present in person. Apparently, Yl himself will arrive. The kingdom of Zakoris-In-Thaddra is no longer building war-galleys. He's promising to give you slaves and palutorvus tusks."

"Is there any news of a man named Kathus, an Alisaarian?"

"Yl put his counselors to death on his return. He said they'd gone against the edict of the gods, advising him to unholy conflict. One man evaded the sentence. An Alisaarian."

(So, he was landless again, Kathaos the Fox, running, and too tired to run, Kathus-Kathaos, who despised all religion and disbelieved all gods, saddled with a continent run amok with piety. Once he had ridden for the only break of light in the sky. But the light was an illusion. Or else illusion was a reality he had not bargained on.)

"And Kesarh Am Karmiss feeds the fish," said Rarnammon quietly.

"Pirates," said Vencrek. "They unswore allegiance to Yl when he capitulated, did for Kesarh, and now roam the sea in packs again. The oceans north and east may need some cleaning up before the snow. We note, even the miracle," said Vencrek, "didn't conclude every battle, my lord."

There were no longer Amanackire about the court. They had gone away into the hills above Koramvis. Ashni was there, men said. But it did not seem to Rarnammon that she was. The glints of the psychic beacons had died down in his mind. He no longer kept unconscious track of Yannul's son, or Amrek's daughter in the Zor. Raldanash had retreated on an inner tide. Ashni, like some all-pervasive light, seemed to surround them, and yet was nowhere in particular.

"There was a priestess the Amanackire may have followed," Vencrek said, shadowing Rarnammon's thoughts in the endless way of telepaths. One grew accustomed to it. "There's also a priestess on Ankabek again."

"Yes," Rarnammon said, not listening. Music rippled somewhere. The trees beside the colonnade were sinuous with Zastis, when sex invaded everything. And there had seemed to be no time. . . .

"Astaris, according to some."

"Astaris no longer exists."

"Do you recall the Xarabian princess, Xa'ath's daughter?"

In Karmiss, it was the Festival of Masks. In the east, where Istris was rebuilding, lamps strung the scaffolding, and banners dripped from gutted houses. When Free Zakoris came, the volume of smoke had blown to smear Ioli, but there was only torch-smoke now. The beer and wine flowed as it had always done. And on this occasion of war, the wines had been spared. Next year would be a fine one for the vintage they called now *Salamander*. It seemed one wine merchant, at least, still loved him.

Karmiss had much to talk of, between the drinking and the kisses. The Warden had fled the island. There was a Shansarian regent from over-the-ocean. A King-Elect was found among the rubble of Suthamun's house. Something clever was managed. The boy had been got on a Karmian woman and had coppery skin to set off his fairness. Nor was he a eunuch.

There was a Storm Lord elect in Dorthar. His mother was a Vis-Karmian. Istris toasted him on the bell-ringing carts and by the fire-scorched harbour, choosing to forget, even if they knew, he had been also Kesarh's henchman. Gossip detailed a magnificent progress, by land and river, through Dorthar. Now the Dortharian ships lay off Tjis. The Shansarian regent had gone there and clasped hands with Rarnammon son of Raldnor. A pledge had been made to raise up Ankabek of the goddess, that the Leopard had destroyed.

That isle, they said, was held by specters. But there were specters at Istris and Ioli, too, for the festival—in fancy-dress and drunk.

The royal biremes rested a mile out from Ankabek. Their emblems were the goddess and the Dragon of Dorthar. As yet, the man who was to be Storm Lord, had not selected a personal device. From the landing of the island, they looked merely charming toys. Not that any came to see. Those who had chosen Ankabek as a refuge had long since received happier news and returned across the straits to mainland Karmiss. Only seabirds were left now. Wading in the ringed shallows, they took flight, when an oared boat ran out at them from the ocean.

Presently a pavilion went up on the beach of shale. A party of Vathcrians and Dortharians, laughing and sporting or theosophically serious, strode to investigate the twice-deserted village. One man climbed away from it. He passed into the fire-blackened groves above and was lost to sight.

They were not all finished, the trees of Ankabek. Here a twig, a branch, there a whole young sapling, was bladed with the ruby leaves of summer. And from some, the quick and the dead boughs, metal discs hung quivering and unsounding, smirched or bright, in the windless air.

The walk was of the same duration as it had always been. But coming out at the crown of the island, seeing the husk of the temple, memory itself pierced the side. Events had happened here. Now everything was gone, only the walls, the trees fighting back to bud and leaf, the scope of the sea and the sky beyond, indifferent and unassociable.

The Lowlanders burned their corpses for this very reason, to expunge each physical life, its worth already integrated by the soul, and only the soul persisting. It was hard on those who remained behind.

Rarnammon, he himself one that remained in the wake of death, saw between the phantom trees, another. He had not been assured he would discover her here. Raldanash's mind had hinted something, of her presence, the rekindling of his flagging strength through Ankabek and through the ingenuous medium of this woman.

She was seated on the ground, clad in one of the temple robes, dusty black as the burned trees. The blood-red hair matched with the sprays of new leaves. A strange picture.

He went closer, moving silently, not wanting to alarm her. He had recognized the stance as that of meditation. At ten yards' distance he paused. Her face was tilted slightly up into the sunlight, and her eyes were partly open. It was Ulis Anet, much as she had been. But then, too, it was Val Nardia. For a moment he missed the torc with the pearls Kesarh's sister had always worn at court. Before his impressions sorted themselves.

Her eyes widened abruptly, and he knew she saw him. Although maybe where he stood, there were other persons, less corporeal.

"Ulis Anet Am Xarabiss," he said carefully. "Do you remember me?"

"Rarnammon," she said. Because she rendered him the full name as now it was, it was obvious her awareness had been heightened. Obvious, in other less decided ways. She stared at him for some time before she said, "I'm no priestess, my lord. My being here is an accident. You'll find me rather odd. I've stayed alone some while. Atonement, self-examination. What do you want with me?"

"Perhaps nothing," he said.

She came gracefully to her feet, and the light sifted through her hair, between her fingers when she spread her hands.

"When I first looked and saw you," she said, "I saw Kesarh. The darkness—and then—Raldanash. Your eyes, do you understand? But you're like him. Like them both." She wept then, slowly and thoughtfully, as if without grief. He stood and watched her. In a space, she touched her palms to her cheeks and the tears and the weeping were gone. "Let me show you a marvel of the island," she said. She moved away toward the headland, and he went after her. Her beauty, which he had never properly seen before, flowed from her like her shadow between the stems of the trees.

West of the temple, the burned groves gave way to burned oaks, and the sea spread under them, a long stretch down. Among the grasses stood a small stone Anackire, rough layman's work. He wondered who had put it there.

Ulis Anet walked to the edge of the rock.

"It's curious," she said. "I never asked the spot and I might have been misled. But the sun's westering. This is the hour when it occurs."

"What is it?" he asked her gently. He did not think her without reason, but he was half afraid to go near her, that his arm or sleeve might brush against her, or his voice. As if she might disintegrate. Or as if some hurt would spring from proximity.

But, "There," she said, and pointed to the deep water below.

And suddenly something dazzled, a spear of amber light starting up from the sea.

They looked at it, each of them transfixed. And then the dazzle flickered out.

"They flung the statue down from these rocks," she said. "Anackire. Could it be some ornament, Her hair—or a jewel—"

"The Free Zakorians took Her eyes," he said, "but one of the Leopard ships went down. The current, maybe, brought it back—"

They gazed at the water, disbelieving now that it had ever revealed anything.

After a while, he offered her the food and wine he had brought.

They sat by the oaks above the sea to share this picnic. He recollected, he thought, Kesarh and Val Nardia sitting here. There was a timelessness and a lack of urgency, but under all, the anomalous sense of change, nervous and unanswerable.

Once, a golden snake spilled through the grass. The serpents of the goddess had survived, and now the island was theirs.

The man and woman spoke, ordinarily, of extraordinary matters.

Shadows extended in bars across the ocean, on the rocks. The west flushed; the east flushed as if in reflection, anticipating the Star.

"You don't mean to stay here," he said. "You hadn't made up your mind to be an acolyte or a hermitess?"

"I considered it. But you must advise me. You were one with the great web of Power. A god."

"No," he said.

"At least," she said, "for a night and a day. The hem of that fire passed over the island. I'm a witness. You were a god. You tell me then, my lord, where I should direct my steps, how I should spend my life. You know he died because of me."

"Kesarh died because of Kesarh."

"I put my guilt and terror aside. Ankabek taught me to do that. But not how to live out the rest. Ankabek says only: *Wait*."

"Come to Dorthar, then. She speaks more loudly and to greater purpose."

"Never to me."

The sun stepped upon the tide. The world swam in scarlet lights and shades. The Star crushed out a rose along the eastern horizon.

"Ulis," he said, "this conversation about gods—if this were some brothel in Istris I'd cringe with shame. I've had what I wanted, and it was never a woman. And now this is a ruin and a rock with burned trees on it. A damnable couch. And I want you."

Her face was wholly blank, and then the blankness dashed away in laughter.

"The Storm Lord apologizes to his handmaiden for an uncomfortable bed?"

"And for his lack of knowledge, which fails to team with his years."

"Zastis," she said. Her voice was very low. "It's Zastis. And every moment of it I was alone here, until now."

He found her mouth then, through the sinking of the sun. It was sweet and unknown country that the sunset made.

Somewhere in the hills above Koramvis, the Thaddrian watched the stars of dusk come out, and the Red Moon among them, and then the last Star of all, redder than the cookfire on the stones.

Zastis disturbed the Thaddrian, but he was used to it and to setting his body aside.

He had made the fire on the stones to add normalcy, but it did not. The lake was far off, the mountains loomed. This hilltop seemed bizarrely out of the world while being totally within the world. All around, the Amanackire, the tawny and the icy-pale, sat meditating, some through the formula of prayer.

The Thaddrian thought of the miracle they had wrought. Then stopped thinking of it. The mystery was over. He was homesick for his temple on the plain, the fat High Priest and his wine jars—and his surreptitious ladies, at this season. For the useful scrolls and cartographies, the rituals, so empty but so pretty. He was thirsty for mediocre things. He had forgotten, having grown irritable with it, his love for mankind.

"Soon," she said.

He glanced up and saw Ashni standing across the fire.

Her smile was so lovely, so redolent of everything that did no harm yet was limitless—sky, stars, light.

"You're going then, madam," he said. It was rhetorical, requiring no reply, getting none.

Gradually all their eyes, even those weird pallid eyes, were coming to her.

She told them, succinctly, with no words, that now she would leave them.

None of her Lowlanders objected. They bore it, pridefully, the Chosen Race, the Children of the Gods. He felt the loneliness creep down like wolves from the mountains. Did no other feel the loneliness, too?

She's only a girl, he thought stupidly. Fourteen, fifteen. Long, silken hair and lily skin. But her eyes found him again. She was not only a girl, at all. There had been that legend in Thaddra of a wolf child. Some mirror-image of prophecy. What could she be now?

But she was walking away, quite briskly, as she always walked—a swift and effortless glide, hair fluttering out like butterflies—something to be done. Up the hill. There was a rock there, about a hundred feet above. She went right the way to the rock, and climbed it in three steps. She seated herself on the rock, and he could see her there. They could all see her.

What would happen?

It was like a soft little rill, a child's giggle, or a stream's, in his brain. His personal creed had always denied that final metamorphosis. Raldnor and Astaris had ridden into the jungle on a wagon. Ashni, at some juncture of the night, would walk away among the hills, alone.

When he woke, near dawn, the rock on the hill was vacant, and the Thaddrian priest of the Dortharian Anackire comprehended that this was what she had done.

He was raking the ashes of the fire, looking for the sausage he had let be blackened there, when some strangeness made him lift his head again.

The sky was already expanding, a crystal smoked with gold in the east. Then a tiny silver sun with streaming hair was birthed out of the gold.

The Thaddrian jumped to his feet, clutching the cindery sausage in his hands, waving it at the Amanackire until they roused, some waking, some simply moving in, sleepless, across the hill.

There in the morning sky blazed the star.

In Elyr they would be whispering, murmuring in their solitary towers. They had foretold the star, the appearance, its passing away. For now, they would worship it, a sign of peace, the ray of hope.

In all Lan they would be seeing it, from their blue heights, from out of their close-wrapped valleys. The young man riding into Amlan with a ragged clatter, Yannul's son, would look across the roofs and see it and swear, knowing others of his kindred saw it too. And Safca, in the eye of a dark tower of the Zor, like any Elyrian, would spy the star and hold out her hand, childishly to view it on her finger's end. Raldanash, land-bereft on the sea that folded toward Vathcri, in the stern of a blue-sailed ship, would look, the outcry of the sailors lost on him. He would smile to see the star, so like a tear. All over Vis they saw it, woke and saw. On Ankabek, the man and woman, hero and heroine under the oak trees, beheld the star caught in the branches like one more disc of silver. Their bodies still locked, they turned back again to find light in each other.

The Thaddrian, having got up the hill, learned that the rock's far side was a minor precipice from which no one could have descended save by means of wings. He loosed the sausage down it, like an offering. Ashni had stolen by all of them, then, even the sleepless Amanackire, as they snored. She was gone to be a peasant in Thaddra, or to run with wolves.

He grinned at the sky, crying with joy.

"And yet," he said, "Ashni, you are also the Morning Star."

TANITH LEE

"Princess Royal of Heroic Fantasy and Goddess-Empress of the Hot Read."

—**Village Voice** (N.Y.C.)

☐ **THE BIRTHGRAVE** (#UE1776–$3.50)
☐ **VAZKOR, SON OF VAZKOR** (#UE1709–$2.50)
☐ **QUEST FOR THE WHITE WITCH** (#UJ1357–$1.95)
☐ **DON'T BITE THE SUN** (#UE1486–$1.75)
☐ **DRINKING SAPPHIRE WINE** (#UE1565–$1.75)
☐ **VOLKHAVAAR** (#UE1539–$1.75)
☐ **THE STORM LORD** (#UJ1361–$1.95)
☐ **NIGHT'S MASTER** (#UE1657–$2.25)
☐ **ELECTRIC FOREST** (#UE1482–$1.75)
☐ **SABELLA** (#UE1529–$1.75)
☐ **KILL THE DEAD** (#UE1562–$1.75)
☐ **DAY BY NIGHT** (#UE1576–$2.25)
☐ **THE SILVER METAL LOVER** (#UE1721–$2.75)
☐ **CYRION** (#UE1765–$2.95)
☐ **DEATH'S MASTER** (#UE1741–$2.95)
☐ **RED AS BLOOD** (#UE1790–$2.50)
☐ **SUNG IN SHADOW** (#UE1824–$2.50)

DAW☐**sf**
BOOKS

Have you discovered . . .

JO CLAYTON

"Aleytys is a heroine as tough as, and more
believable and engaging than the general run
of swords-and-sorcery barbarians."
—*Publishers Weekly*

The saga of Aleytys is recounted in these DAW books:

☐ DIADEM FROM THE STARS   (#UE1520—$2.25)
☐ LAMARCHOS   (#UE1627—$2.25)
☐ IRSUD   (#UE1640—$2.25)
☐ MAEVE   (#UE1760—$2.25)
☐ STAR HUNTERS   (#UE1871—$2.50)
☐ THE NOWHERE HUNT   (#UE1874—$2.50)
☐ GHOSTHUNT   (#UE1823—$2.50)